GREEKS
BEARING
GIFTS

Also by Philip Kerr

PHILIP KERR

A BERNIE GUNTHER THRILLER

GREEKS BEARING GIFTS

Quercus

First published in Great Britain in 2018 by

Quercus Editions Ltd
Carmelite House
50 Victoria Embankment
London EC4Y 0DZ

An Hachette UK company

A CIP catalogue record for this book is available
from the British Library

HB ISBN 978 1 78429 652 0
TPB ISBN 978 1 78429 653 7

10 9 8 7 6 5 4 3 2 1

Typeset by CC Book Production

Printed and bound in Great Britain by Clays Ltd, St Ives plc

This book is for Chris Anderson and Lisa Pickering,
to whom I am very grateful.

They have plundered the world, stripping naked the land in their hunger . . . they are driven by greed, if their enemy be rich; by ambition, if poor. . . . They ravage, they slaughter, they seize by false pretences, and all of this they hail as the construction of empire. And when in their wake nothing remains but a desert, they call that peace.

TACITUS, *The Agricola and the Germania*

PROLOGUE

January 1957

This would seem like the worst story ever told if it had not happened, all of it, every detail, exactly as I have described.

That's the thing about real life: it all looks so implausible right up until the moment when it starts to happen. I have my experience as a police detective and the events of my own personal history to confirm this observation. There's been nothing probable about my life. But I've a strong feeling that it's the same for everyone. The collection of stories that make us all who we are only looks exaggerated or fictitious until we find ourselves living on its stained and dog-eared pages.

The Greeks have a word for this, of course: 'mythology'. Mythology explains everything, from natural phenomena to what happens when you die and head downstairs, or when, unwisely, you steal a box of matches from Zeus. As it happens Greeks have a lot to do with this particular story. Perhaps with every story, when you stop to think about it. After all, it was a Greek called Homer who invented modern storytelling, in between losing his sight and probably not existing at all.

Like many stories this one is probably much improved by taking a drink or two. So go ahead. Be my guest. Have one on me. Certainly I like a drink but honestly, I'm not a hopeless case. Far from it. I sincerely hope that one night I will go for a drink and wake up as an amnesiac on a steamer that's headed for nowhere I've ever heard of.

That's the romantic in me, I guess. I've always liked to travel even when I was quite happy to stay at home. You might say that I just wanted to get away. From the authorities, most of all. Still do, if the truth be told, which it seldom is. Not in Germany. Not for me and quite a few others like me. For us the past is like the exterior wall in a prison yard: chances are, we'll never get over it. And of course we shouldn't be allowed to get over it, either, given who we were and everything we did.

But how is one ever to explain what happened? It was a question I used to see in the eyes of some of the American guests at the Grand Hotel in Cap Ferrat where, until recently, I was a concierge, when they realized I was German: How was it possible that your people could murder so many others? Well, it's like this: When you walk through a big fish market you appreciate just how alien and various life can be; it's hard to imagine how some of the fantastic, sinister, slippery-looking creatures you see laid out on the slab could even exist, and sometimes when I contemplate my fellow man, I have much the same feeling.

Myself, I'm a bit like an oyster. Years ago – in January 1933, to be exact – a piece of grit got into my shell and started to rub me up the wrong way. But if there is a pearl inside me I think it's probably a black one. Frankly, I did a few things during the war of which I feel less than proud. This is not unusual. That's what war's about. It makes all of us who take part in it feel like we're criminals and that we've done something bad. Apart from the real criminals, of course; no way has ever been invented to make them feel bad about anything. With one exception, perhaps: the hangman at Landsberg. When he's given the chance, he can provoke a crisis of conscience in almost anyone.

Officially, that's all behind us now. Our National Socialist revolution and the devastating war it brought about is over and the peace we have since enjoyed has, thanks to the Americans at least, been anything but Carthaginian. We stopped hanging people a long time ago and all but four of the several hundred war criminals who were caught and locked up for life in Landsberg have now been released. I do believe that this new Federal Republic of Germany could be a tremendous country when we've finished fixing it up. All of West Germany smells of fresh paint and every public building is in a state of major reconstruction. The eagles and swastikas are long gone but now even the traces of them are being erased, like Leon Trotsky from an old Communist Party photograph. In Munich's infamous Hofbräuhaus – there most of all, perhaps – they'd done their best to paint out the swastikas on the vaulted cream-coloured ceiling, although you could still make out where they'd been. But for these – the fingerprints of fascism – it would be easy to believe the Nazis had never even existed and that thirteen years of life under Adolf Hitler had been some dreadful Gothic nightmare.

If only the marks and traces of Nazism on the poisoned, bivalve soul of Bernie Gunther could have been erased with such facility. For these and other complicated reasons I won't go into now, the only time I'm truly myself these days is, of necessity, when I'm alone. The rest of the time, I'm obliged to be someone else.

So then. Hallo. God's greeting to you, as we say here in Bavaria. My name is Christof Ganz.

CHAPTER 1

There was a murderous wind raging through the streets of Munich when I went to work that night. It was one of those cold, dry Bavarian winds that blow up from the Alps with an edge like a new razor blade and make you wish you lived somewhere warmer, or owned a better overcoat, or at least had a job that didn't require you to hit the clock at six p.m. I'd pulled enough late shifts when I'd been a cop with the Murder Commission in Berlin so I should have been used to bluish fingers and cold feet, not to mention lack of sleep and the crappy pay. On such nights a busy city hospital is no place for a man to find himself doomed to work as a porter right through until dawn. He should be sitting by the fire in a cozy beer hall with a foaming mug of white beer in front of him, while his woman waits at home, a picture of connubial fidelity, weaving a shroud and plotting to sweeten his coffee with something a little more lethal than an extra spoonful of sugar.

Of course, when I say I was a night porter, it would have been more accurate to say that I was a mortuary attendant, but being a night porter sounds better when you're having a polite conversation. 'Mortuary attendant' makes a lot of people feel uncomfortable. The living ones, mostly. But when you've seen as many corpses as I have you tend not to bat an eyelid about being around death so much. You can handle any amount of it after four years in the Flanders slaughterhouse. Besides, it was a job and with jobs as scarce as they are these days you don't look a gift horse in the mouth, even the spavined nag that had been bought for me, sight unseen, outside the doors of the local glue factory by the old comrades in Paderborn; they got me the job in the hospital after they had given me a new identity and fifty marks. So until I could find myself something better, I was stuck with it and my customers were stuck with me. I certainly didn't hear any of them complaining about my bedside manner.

You'd think the dead could look after themselves but of course people die in hospital all the time and, when they do, they usually need a bit of help getting around. It seems the days of patient defenestration are over. It was my job to go and fetch the bodies off the wards and take them down to the house of death and there to wash them before leaving them out for collection by the undertakers. In winter we didn't worry about chilling the bodies or spraying the place for flies. We didn't have to; it was just a few degrees above freezing in the mortuary. Much of the time I worked alone and, after a month at the Schwabing Hospital, I suppose I was almost used to it – to the cold, to the smell, and to the feeling of being alone and yet not quite alone, if you know what I mean. Once or twice a corpse moved by itself – they do that sometimes, wind usually – which, I'll admit, was a little unnerving. But perhaps not surprising. I'd been alone for so long that I'd started talking to the radio. At least I assumed that's where the voices were coming from. In the country that produced Luther, Nietzsche, and Adolf Hitler, you can never be absolutely sure about these things.

On that particular night I had to go up to the emergency room and fetch a corpse that would have given Dante pause for thought. An unexploded bomb – it's estimated that there are tens of thousands of these buried all over Munich, which often makes reconstruction work hazardous – had gone off in nearby Moosach, killing at least one and injuring several others in a local beer hall that took the worst of the blast. I heard it go off just before I started my shift and it sounded like a standing ovation in Asgard. If the glass in the window in my room hadn't already been Scotch-taped against drafts it would certainly have shattered. So no real harm done. What's one more German killed by a bomb from an American flying fortress after all these years?

The dead man looked like he'd been given a front row seat in some reserved circle of hell where he'd been chewed up by a very angry Minotaur before being torn to pieces. His jiving days were over, given that his legs were hanging off at the knees and he was badly burned, too; his corpse gave off a lightly barbecued smell that was all the more horrifying because somehow it was also, vaguely and inexplicably, appetizing. Only his shoes remained undamaged; everything else – clothes, skin, hair – was a sight. I washed him carefully – his torso was a piñata of glass and metal splinters – and did my very best to fix him up a bit. I put his still shiny Salamanders in a shoe box, just in case someone from the deceased's family turned up to identify the poor devil. You can tell a lot from a pair of shoes but this couldn't have been a more hopeless task if he'd spent the last twelve days being dragged through the dust behind someone's favourite chariot. Most of his face resembled a half kilo of freshly chopped dog meat and sudden death looked like it had done the guy a favour, not that I'd ever have said as much. Mercy killing is still a sensitive subject on a long list of sensitive subjects in modern Germany.

It's small wonder there are so many ghosts in this town. Some people go their whole lives without ever seeing a ghost; me, I see them all the time. Ghosts I sort of recognize, too. Twelve years after the war it was like living in Frankenstein Castle and every time I looked around I seemed to see a pensive, plaintive face I half-remembered from before. Quite often these looked like old comrades, but just now and again they resembled my poor mother. I miss her a lot. Sometimes the other ghosts mistook me for a ghost, which was hardly surprising, either; it's only my name that's changed, not my face, more's the pity. Besides, my heart was playing up a bit, like a difficult child, except that it wasn't so young as that. Every so often it would jump around for the sheer hell of it, as if to show me that it could and what might happen to me if it ever decided to have a break from taking care of a tiresome Fritz like me.

After I got home at the end of my shift I was extra-careful to turn the gas off on my little two-ring cooker after I'd finished boiling water for the coffee I usually had with my early-morning schnapps. Gas is just as explosive as TNT, even the splutteringly thin stuff that comes squeaking out of German pipes. Outside my dingy yellow window was an eighty-foot-high heap of overgrown rubble, another legacy of the wartime bombing: seventy per cent of the buildings in Schwabing had been destroyed, which was good for me, as it made rooms there cheap to rent. Mine was in a building scheduled for demolition and had a long crack in the wall so wide you could have hidden an ancient desert city in there. But I liked the rubble heap. It served to remind me of what, until recently, my life had amounted to. I even liked the fact that there was a local guide who would take visitors to the summit of the heap, as part of his advertised Munich tour. There was a memorial cross on top and a nice view of the city. You had to admire the fellow's ingenuity. When I was a boy I used to climb to the top of Berlin's cathedral – all 264 steps – and walk around the dome's perimeter with only the pigeons for company; but it hadn't ever occurred to me to make a career out of it.

I never liked Munich all that much, with its fondness for traditional Tracht clothes and jolly brass bands, devout Roman Catholicism and the Nazis. Berlin suited me better and not just because it was my hometown. Munich was always a more compliant, governable, conservative place than the old Prussian capital. I got to know it best in the early years after the war, when my second wife, Kirsten, and I were trying to run an unfeasibly located hotel in a suburb of Munich called Dachau, now infamous for the concentration camp the Nazis had there; I didn't like it any better then, either. Kirsten died, which hardly helped, and soon after that I left, thinking never to return and well, here I am again, with no real plans for the future, at least none that I would ever talk about, just in case God's listening. I don't find he's nearly as merciful as a lot of Bavarians like to make out. Especially on a Sunday evening. And certainly not after Dachau. But I was here and trying to be optimistic even though there was absolutely no room for such a thing – not in my cramped lodgings – and doing my best to look on the bright side of life even though it felt as if this lay over the top of a very high barbed-wire fence.

For all that, I took a certain amount of satisfaction in doing what I did for a living; clearing up shit and washing corpses seemed like a suitable penance for what I'd done before. I was a cop, not a proper cop, but a useful stooge in the SD for the likes of Heydrich, Nebe, and Goebbels. It wasn't even a proper penance like the one undertaken by the old German king Henry IV, who famously walked on his knees to Canossa Castle to obtain the Pope's forgiveness, but perhaps it would do. Besides, like my heart, my knees are not what they once were. In small ways, like Germany itself, I was trying to inch my way back to moral respectability. After all, it can hardly be denied that little by little can take you a long way, even when you're on your knees.

In truth, that process was working out for Germany a little better than it was working out for me, and all thanks to the Old Man. This was what we called Konrad Adenauer, on account of how he was seventy-three when he became West Germany's first postwar chancellor. He was still in power at eighty-one, leading the Christian Democrats and, unless you were a radical Jewish group like Irgun, who'd tried to assassinate the Old Man on more than one occasion, it had to be admitted he'd made a pretty good job of it, too. Already people were talking about 'the Miracle on the Rhine' and they weren't referring to Saint Alban of Mainz. Thanks to a combination of the Marshall Plan, low inflation, rapid industrial growth, and plain hard work, Germany was now doing better economically than England. This didn't surprise me that much; the Tommies always were too bolshy for their own good. After winning two world wars they made the mistake of thinking the world owed them a living. Perhaps the real miracle was how the rest of the world seemed to have forgiven Germany for starting a war that had cost the lives of forty million people – this in spite of the Old Man having denounced the whole denazification process and bringing in an amnesty law for our war criminals, all of which certainly explained why there was a lingering and general suspicion that many old Nazis were now back in government. The Old Man had a useful explanation for that, too: he said you needed to make sure you had a good supply of clean water available before you threw out your dirty water.

As someone who washed dead Germans for a living, I couldn't disagree with this.

Of course, I had more dirty water in my bucket than most and above all else I was appreciating my newfound obscurity. Like Garbo in *Grand Hotel*, I just wanted to be alone and loved the idea of being anonymous more than I liked the short beard I'd grown to help make this work. The beard was yellowish grey, vaguely metallic; it made me look wiser than I am. Our lives are shaped by the choices we make, of course, and more noticeably by the choices that were wrong. But the idea that I had been forgotten by the cops, not to mention the world's major security and intelligence agencies, was pleasing, to say the least. My life looked good on paper; indeed it was the only place it looked as if it had been well spent, which, speaking as someone who'd been a cop for many years, was in itself suspicious. And so, to facilitate my life as Christof Ganz, in my spare time I would often go back over the bare facts of his life and invent some of the things he'd done and achieved. Places I'd been, jobs I'd had, and, most important of all, my wartime service on behalf of the Third Reich. In much the same way that everyone else had done in the new Germany. Yes, we've all had to become very creative with our résumés. Including, it seemed, many members of the Christian Democrats.

I took another drink with my breakfast, just to help me sleep, of course, and went to bed, where I dreamed of happier times, although that might just as easily have been a prayer to the god of the black cloud, dwelling in the skies. Since prayers are never answered it's hard to tell the difference.

CHAPTER 2

When I went into work the following evening the Moosach bomb victim was still there, laid out on the slab like a vulture's abandoned banquet. Someone had tied a name tag to his toe which, given the fact that his leg was no longer attached to his body, seemed imprudent to say the least. His name was Johann Bernbach, and he was just twenty-five years old. By now I knew a little more about the bomb from what was in the *Süddeutsche Zeitung*. A five-hundred-pounder had exploded on a building site next door to a beer hall in Dachauerstrasse, less than fifty metres from the municipal gasworks. The gasometer contained over seven million cubic feet of gas, so the feeling expressed in the newspaper was that the city had had a lucky escape with just two people killed and six injured and I said as much to Bernbach when I saw him.

'I hope you had a few beers tucked away when you got your ticket punched, friend. Enough to take the edge off the shrapnel. Look here, it won't matter much to you now, but your unexpected death is not being treated with quite the reverence it warrants. To put it bluntly, Johann, it seems everyone's glad it's only you who's burnt toast. There was a gasometer near where that giant marrow went off. It was full of gas, too. More than enough to keep my little department in this hospital busy for weeks. Kind of fitting you should end up here, given it was an Ami bomb that killed you. Until last year this was the American hospital. Anyway, I've done my best for you. Pulled most of that glass out of your corpse. Tidied up your legs a bit. Now it's up to the undertaker.'

'Do you always talk to your customers like this?'

I turned around to see Herr Schumacher, one of the hospital managers, standing in the doorway. He was an Austrian, from Braunau am Inn, a small town on the German border, and although he wasn't a doctor, he wore a white coat anyway, probably to make himself look more important.

'Why not? They seldom answer back. Besides, I have to talk to someone other than myself. I'd go mad otherwise.'

'My God. Oh, Jesus. I had no idea he looked as bad as this.'

'Don't say that. You'll hurt his feelings.'

'It's just that there's a man upstairs on Ward Ten who's pre-pared to formally identify this poor wretch before he's discharged this evening. He's one of the other people who were caught up in yesterday's bomb blast – he's now a patient in this hospital. The man's in a wheelchair but there's nothing wrong with his eyes. I was hoping you could wheel him down here and help take care of it. But now that I've seen the corpse – well, I'm not so sure he wouldn't faint. Jesus Christ, I know I almost did.'

'If he's in a wheelchair maybe that won't matter so much.

Afterwards I can always wheel him somewhere to recover. Like another hospital, perhaps.' I lit a cigarette and steered the smoke back out through my grateful nostrils. 'Or at least somewhere they have clean laundry, anyway.'

'You know you really shouldn't smoke in here.'

'I know. And I've had complaints about it. But the fact is I'm smoking for sound medical reasons.'

'Name one.'

'The smell.'

'Oh. That. Yes, I do see your point.' Schumacher took one from the packet I waved under his nose and let me light him. 'Don't you usually cover them up with something? Like a sheet?'

'We weren't expecting visitors. But while the laundry guys are on strike all the clean sheets are for the living. That's what I've been told, anyway.'

'Okay. But isn't there anything you can do about his face?'

'What would you suggest? An iron mask? But that's not going to help with the formal identification process. I doubt this poor Fritz's mother would recognize him. Let's certainly hope she doesn't have to try. But given his more obvious similarity to nothing you can put into words that don't take the name of the Lord in vain the way you just did, I think we're probably into the more hermetic realm of other distinguishing marks, don't you agree?'

'Does he have any?'

'He has one. There's a tattoo on his forearm.'

'Well, that should help.'

'Maybe. Maybe not. It's a number.'

'Who gets themselves tattooed with a number?'

'Jews did, in the concentration camps. For identification.'

'They did that?'

'No, actually we did that. Us Germans. The countrymen of Beethoven and Goethe. It was like a lottery ticket but not a lucky one. This fellow must have been in Auschwitz when he was a kid.'

'Where's that?'

Schumacher was the kind of stupid Austrian who preferred to believe that his country was the first free nation that had fallen victim to the Nazis and hence was not responsible for what had happened, but it was a harder argument to make on behalf of Braunau am Inn, which was rather more famous as the birthplace of Adolf Hitler and quite possibly why Schumacher had left in the first place. I couldn't blame him for that. But I wasn't disposed to argue with anything else he believed. He was my boss after all.

'Poland, I think. But it doesn't matter. Not now.'

'Well, look, see what you can do about his face, Herr Ganz. And then go and fetch the witness, would you?'

When Schumacher had gone, I searched around for a clean towel and in a cupboard I found one the Amis must have left behind. It was a *Mickey Mouse Club* towel, which was less than ideal but it looked a lot better than the man on the slab. So I laid it gently over his head and went upstairs to collect the patient.

He was dressed and expecting me and while I'd been expecting him I wasn't expecting the two cops who were with him, although I should have been because he'd agreed to help identify a dead body, and that's what cops do when they're not directing traffic or stealing watches. The smaller of the cops was in uniform and the other was dressed like a civilian; what was worse, I vaguely recognized the big Fritz in plainclothes and, I suppose, he vaguely recognized me, which was unfortunate as I'd hoped to avoid the Munich cops until my beard was a better length, but it was too late for that now. So I grunted a general-purpose good evening, which was a couple of consonants short of being sullen, took hold of the chair, and wheeled the patient toward the elevator with the two cops in tow. I didn't worry about them minding my manners as I was just a night porter after all, and they didn't have to like me, they just had to follow me down to the mortuary. It wasn't a good wheelchair since it had a definite bias to the left but that was hardly surprising, given the size of the injured man. Of greater surprise, perhaps, was the fact that the chair managed to roll at all. The patient was a fattish man in his late thirties, and his beer belly sat on his lap like a bag containing all his worldly goods. I knew it was a beer belly because I was working on getting one myself, just as soon as I had a pay rise. Besides, his clothes stank of beer, as if he'd had a two-litre stein of Pschorr in his lap when the bomb went off.

'How well did you know the deceased, Herr Dorpmüller?' asked the detective as he tailed us along the corridor.

'Well enough,' said the man in the wheelchair. 'For the last three years he was my pianist at the Apollo. That's the cabaret theatre I run in the Munich Hotel, just up the road from the beer house. Johann could play anything. Jazz or classical. To some extent my wife and I were all the family he had, given what had already happened to him. It's too bad that it should be Johann who was killed like this, of all people. I mean after what he'd gone through in the camps as a boy. What he survived.'

'Do you remember anything at all?'

'Not really. We were just about to leave to open the cabaret for the evening when it happened. Do you know exactly what happened yet? With the bomb, I mean.'

'It looks as if one of the men working on the building site next door to the beer hall where you were drinking must have struck the bomb with a pickax. Only we've yet to find anything of him left to ask about that. Probably never will, either. My guess is that the local smokers will be inhaling his atoms for the next few days. You're a lucky man. A metre nearer the door and you'd have been killed for sure.'

As I wheeled the man along I couldn't help but agree with the detective. I was looking down at two burned ears that looked like the petals on a poinsettia, and there was a long length of stitching on the man's neck that put me in mind of the Trans-Siberian Railway. His arm was in plaster and there were tiny cuts all over him. Clearly Herr Dorpmüller had enjoyed the narrowest of escapes.

We took the elevator down to the basement where, outside the mortuary door, I lit another Eckstein and like Orson Welles narrated a few sombre words of warning before taking them inside to see the main feature. If I cared about their stomachs that was only because I was the one who was probably going to have to mop the contents of their stomachs off the floor.

'All right, gentlemen. We're here. But before we go in I feel

I ought to tell you that the deceased isn't looking his best. For one thing, we're a little short of clean laundry in this hospital. So there's no sheet over his body. For another, his legs are no longer attached to his body, which is quite badly burned. I've done all I can to tidy him up a bit but the fact is you aren't going to be able to identify the man in here in the normal way, which is to say, from his face. He doesn't have a face. Not anymore. From the look of it his face was shredded by flying glass, so it bears no more relation to the photograph in his passport than a plate of red cabbage would. Which is why there's a towel covering his head.'

'Now you tell me,' said the detective.

I smiled patiently. 'There are other ways of identifying a man, I think. Distinguishing marks. Old scars. I even heard of something they've got now called fingerprints.'

'Johann had a tattoo on his forearm,' said the man in the wheelchair. 'A six-figure identification number from the camp he was in. Birkenau, I think. He only showed it to me a couple of times but I'm more or less sure the first three numbers were one four zero. And he'd just bought a pair of new shoes from Salamander.'

While he inspected the tattoo I found the shoes and let him inspect them, too. Meanwhile I stood beside the uniformed cop and nodded when he asked if he could smoke.

'It's the smell,' he confessed. 'Formaldehyde, is it?'

I nodded again.

'Always sets me off.'

'So is it him?' asked the detective.

'Looks like,' said Dorpmüller.

'You're sure?'

'Well, as sure as I can be without looking at his face, I suppose.'

The detective looked at the Mickey Mouse towel covering the dead man's head and then, accusingly, at me.

'How bad is it really?' he asked. 'His face.'

'Bad,' I said. 'Makes the Wolf Man look like the Fritz next door.'

'You're exaggerating. Surely.'

'No, not even a little. But you can feel free to ignore my advice any time you like. Nobody else listens to me down here, so why should you?'

'Goddamn it,' he snarled, 'how do they expect me to positively ID a body without a face?'

'It's a problem all right,' I said. 'There's nothing like a mortuary to remind you of the frailty of human flesh.'

For some reason the detective seemed to hold me accountable for this inconvenience, as if I was trying to frustrate his inquiry.

'What the hell's the matter with you people in here, anyway? Couldn't you have found something else to cover his face? Not to mention the rest of him? I've heard of naked culture in this country but this is ridiculous.'

I shrugged an answer, which didn't seem to satisfy him but that wasn't my problem. I never minded disappointing cops that much. Not even when I was a cop.

'This stupid towel is disrespectful,' insisted the detective. 'And what's worse is you know it is.'

'It was the American hospital,' I said by way of an explanation. 'And the towel was all I had.'

'Mickey Mouse. I've a good mind to report you, fellow.'

'You're right,' I said. 'It is disrespectful. I'm sorry.'

I snatched the towel away from the dead man's head and threw it in the bin, hoping to make the detective shut up. It almost worked, too, except that all three men groaned or whistled at once and suddenly it sounded like the South Pole in there. The cop in uniform turned on his heel to face the wall and his plainclothes colleague put a big hand over his bigger mouth. Only the injured Fritz in the wheelchair stayed looking, with horrified fascination, the way a rabbit stares at a snake that is about to kill it, and perhaps recognizing for the first time the micrometre-thin narrowness of his own escape.

'That's what a bomb does,' I said. 'They can erect all the monuments and statues they want. But it's sights like this poor fellow that are the real memorials to the futility and waste of war.'

'I'll call an undertaker,' whispered the man in the wheelchair, almost as if, until that very moment, he hadn't quite believed that Johann Bernbach was actually dead. 'As soon as I get home.' And then he added: 'Do you know any undertakers?'

'I was hoping you might ask me that.' I handed him a business card. 'If you tell Herr Urban that Christof Ganz sent you he'll give you his special discount.'

It wasn't much of a discount, but it was enough to cover the small tip I'd receive from Herr Urban if he got the business. I figured the only way I was ever going to get out of that mortuary was by looking out for my own future.

CHAPTER 3

It was ten o'clock that night when Adolf Urban, the local undertaker, showed up to take Johann Bernbach away to his new and
more permanent home. Urban rarely said very much but on this
occasion – moved by the sight of the dead man's face, some new
business, and perhaps a few drinks he'd enjoyed before coming to
the Schwabing Hospital – he was gabby, at least for an undertaker.

'Thanks for the tip,' he said, and handed me a couple of marks.

'I don't know that it was such a good one, maybe. You've got
your work cut out with this one.'

'No. It will be a closed casket, I should think. Be wasting my
time trying to make this fellow look like Cary Grant. But your
face interests me more, Herr Ganz.'

I almost winced, and hoped I hadn't been recognized. From
previous conversations I knew Urban had cremated some of the
less important Nazis the Amis had hanged at Landsberg in 1949.
Not that any of them were telling tales but in my experience
you can't be too careful when it comes to a past you're trying
to shake off like a bad cold.

'The fact is I'm short of a pallbearer. I was thinking – you being here on nights 'n'all – you could come and make a bit of extra cash working for me during the day. Come on. What else are you going to do in the daytime? Sleep? There's no money in that. Besides, you've got the face for it, I think, Herr Ganz. Mine's a business that requires a poker face and yours looks like it was grown under the felt on a card table. Doesn't give anything away. Same as your mouth. Man in my business needs to know when to keep his trap shut. Which is nearly always, *always*.'

His own face was a lopsided, almost obscene thing, like a piece of melted plastic, with a permanently wet nose that resembled a very red and stubby cock and balls, and eyes that were almost as dead as his clients.

'I'll take that as a compliment.'

'It is in Germany.'

'But while my face might fit your requirements, I don't have the wardrobe for it. No, not even a tie.'

'That's not a problem. I can kit you out, suit, coat, tie, just as long as you like black. You might have to get rid of that wispy beard. Makes you look a bit like Dürer. On second thought, keep it. Without it you'll be too pale. That's no good in a mourner. You don't want to look like someone who'll come back after dark and feast on one of the bodies. We get a lot of that in Germany. So. What do you say?'

I said yes. He was right, of course; quite apart from being almost nocturnal I needed the cash and there was no money to be made staying in bed all day. Not with my figure. So a week or two later found me wearing a black tailcoat and tie, with a shiny top hat on my head, and an expression on my lightly trimmed face that was supposed to convey sobriety and gravitas. The sobriety was debatable: the early morning schnapps was a habit I was finding hard to control. Fortunately for me it was the same expression I used for dumb insolence and scepticism and all the other winning qualities that I possess, so it didn't require me to be Lionel Barrymore to pull it off. Not that I put much store by my qualities; any man is just made up of some deportment and behaviour that have met with the silent approval of a very small number of women.

It was snowing heavily when I climbed out of a car in the Ostfriedhof Cemetery as one of four men employed to carry Bernbach's casket into the crematorium where, Urban said, the Amis had secretly cremated the twelve top Nazis they'd hanged at Nuremberg in 1946. Less well known was the fact that the ashes of my second wife, Kirsten, were also to be found in Ostfriedhof. When it was all over and Urban came to give me my pay and my tip I said nothing about this, largely out of shame that I hadn't visited the place in the cemetery wall where the urn with her remains was to be found – not once since her death. But now I was there I intended to remedy that. Suddenly I felt properly uxorious.

'I thought the dead man was a Jew,' I said to Urban as we watched the mourners file out of the neo-Gothic Holy Cross Church where we'd just committed his body to the flames. These included most of the people from the Apollo cabaret, as well as the big irritable detective I'd recognized in the mortuary at the hospital.

'Not practising.'

'Does that make a difference? If you're a Jew?'

'I wouldn't know. But these days it's not so easy finding someone to conduct an ikey funeral in this town. Last time I did one the family had to send to Augsburg for a rabbi. Also there's the fact that Jews prefer to be buried, not cremated. And with the ground this hard that makes things doubly difficult. Not to mention that there's still a lot of unexploded ordnance in the old Jewish cemetery over at Pfersee. There's no telling what's buried in that ground, especially under all this snow. So I persuaded his friends, who have very generously paid for everything, that for the purposes of this funeral, the deceased should be buried as a Christian. After all, it'd be a shame to have anyone else blown up by an old American bomb, don't you think?' He shrugged. 'Besides, what does it matter what happens to you when you're dead?'

'There speaks the undertaker.'

'It's a business, not a vocation.'

'I'm sure I don't care what becomes of me.'

Urban looked around. 'Besides, there are plenty of Jews in Ostfriedhof already. Many of the prisoners from Dachau were cremated and their ashes scattered here.'

'Along with those top Nazis you mentioned?'

'Along with those top Nazis.' He shrugged. 'I'm sure we can trust the Lord to sort out who's who.' He handed me an envelope. 'Can I count on you tomorrow? Same time. Same place.'

'If I'm alive, I wouldn't miss it.'

'You will be. I'm sure of it. When you've been in the trade as long as I have, you get a feeling for that kind of thing. You might not think it but you've got a few years left in you, my friend.'

'You should run a clinic in Switzerland. There are people who'd pay handsomely for a positive diagnosis like that.' I lit a cigarette and looked up at the sky. 'I kind of like this place. One day I might move here permanently.'

'I'm sure of it.'

'Need me anymore?'

'No. You're through for today. Go home, get into your casket, and get some sleep.'

'I will. But first I have to go and see someone. Dracula once had a bride, you know.'

With my envelope in my pocket I walked away and, after a great deal of searching – some of it inside my own soul – I found Kirsten's stoic remains. I stood there for a while, apologized profusely for not having visited before – not to mention a host of other things – and generally took a walk to the far end of memory's rickety and probably unreliable pier. I'd have stayed out there longer but BELOVED WIFE OF BERNHARD GUNTHER was chiselled on the stone panel in front of the urn, and out of the corner of my eye, I saw the big detective from the hospital heading my way. By now I'd remembered his name, but I was still hoping to prevent him from discovering mine. So I took off at an angle, lingered in front of another memorial tablet in a pathetic attempt to throw him off the scent, and then headed toward the main gate, only he was hiding in ambush for me behind the tomb of Grand Duke Ludwig Wilhelm of Bavaria. It was large enough, just about. The big cop was even bigger than I remembered.

'Hey, you. I want to talk to you.'

'Well, as you can see, I'm in mourning.'

'Nonsense. You were one of the pallbearers, that's all. I asked about you. At the hospital.'

'That was kind. But I'm making a good recovery now, thank you.'

'They said your name was Ganz.'

'That's right.'

'Only it's not. My wife's maiden name is Ganz. And I'd have remembered that the first time we met. A long time ago. Before Hitler came to power, I think. Before you grew that beard.'

I was tempted to make a remark about his wife's maidenhood and thought better of it; it's not just conscience that makes cowards of us all but false names and secret histories. 'Maybe your memory is better than mine, Herr – ?'

'It's not. Not yet, anyway. On account of how I haven't yet remembered your real name. But I'm more or less sure you were a cop back then.'

'Me a cop? That's a laugh.'

'Yeah. I remember thinking that, too, because you were a Jew-loving Berlin cop looking for this detective I used to know at the local Praesidium. My old boss.'

'What was his name? Charlie Chan?'

'No. Paul Herzefelde. He was murdered. But as I recall, we had to lock you up for the night because you nobly thought we weren't doing enough to find out who killed him.'

He was right, of course. Every word of it. I never forget a face and especially a face like his, which was made for denouncing heretics and burning books, probably both at the same time, one on top of the other. Laugh lines as hard and lacking laughs as a wire coat hanger were etched on either side of a nose that looked like the thorn on a halberd. Above the hooked nose were the small, expressionless blue eyes of a giant moray eel. The jaw was unfeasibly wide and the complexion vaguely purplish, although that might have been the cold, while the man's height and build and white hairs were those of a retired heavyweight boxer. I felt that at any moment he might feel me out with his jab or plant his big right fist deep in what still remained of the solar part of my plexus. I remembered his name was Schramma and he'd been a criminal secretary at the Munich Police Praesidium and while I didn't remember much more about him I did remember the night I'd spent in the cells.

'That's what was funny, see? Nobody liked Paul Herzefelde. And not just because he was a Jew the way you thought. People thought he was a crook. On the take. You could have seen that just looking at his clothes. It was strongly suspected that one of Munich's biggest fraudsters – a fellow named Kohl – had bribed him to look the other way. People thought it was Nazis that killed Herzefelde but it probably wasn't. My guess is that, not satisfied with the bribe, Herzefelde tried to squeeze Kohl for more and he didn't like it.'

'I think you're mistaking me for someone else. I've never met anyone by that name. And I was never a policeman in Berlin. I hate cops.' I thought about the résumé I'd been writing for myself and chided myself for neglecting the Weimar Republic years. 'I *did* work in Berlin for a while. But I was a doorman at the Adlon Hotel. So maybe that's where you saw me. Herr—?'

'Schramma, Criminal Secretary Schramma. Look, friend, it doesn't bother me if you've got yourself a new Fritz Schmidt. Lots of people have these days and for all kinds of smart reasons. Believe me, a cop who lives in this town needs two simultaneous telephone directories just to know who the hell he's talking to. But if you *were* looking for a job, then maybe I can help you. For old times' sake.'

'I don't think you really mean to help me, do you? My impression is that you're trying to shake me down in the hope that something might fall from my pockets. But I'm a man with two jobs, which means I'm broke, see? That should be obvious. And any apples left on my branches are probably half-eaten or rotten by now.'

Schramma grinned sheepishly. 'Knowledge is power, right? I don't know who said that but I bet it was a German.'

I didn't contradict him. Nor did he see the irony in his last remark.

'Look, what the hell do you care who I am? I'm so down on my luck I have casinos offering me a job to come and jinx their high rollers. I tell you again, I'm nobody, you big ape. You're wasting your time. There are blackboard monitors in school classrooms who are more important than me.'

'Maybe. Maybe not. But I can promise you this. As soon as I figure out who you really are, Ganz, you're mine. Like you, I have to do one or two other jobs just to make ends meet. Security work. Private investigations. Most of the work is tedious and time-consuming but sometimes it's also dangerous. Which means I can use an ex-copper like you in all sorts of ways I'm quite sure you can easily imagine.'

I could see that was true. I wasn't sure what he had in mind but I'd intimidated enough lowlifes as a policeman in Berlin myself to know that none of this was likely to be to my own advantage.

'And don't even think of disappearing. If you do that I'll just have to name Christof Ganz as a suspect in some old case that nobody gives a crap about. You know I can make you fit all kinds of descriptions. Probably done that shit yourself.'

I flicked my cigarette butt at the smooth green ass of the angel who was looking out for the soul of the Grand Duke and gave an exasperated sigh, which sounded a lot less exasperated than I was actually feeling.

'Go ahead and do your worst, copper. But I'm leaving now. I'm late for an appointment with my favourite barman.'

It was all a bluff, of course. I might have been possessed of a poker face but I had nothing in my hand.

CHAPTER 4

I'd finished work at the hospital. I went to the washroom beside the mortuary to clean up but while I was there I examined my face without much enthusiasm. What I had against it was its air of disappointment and its lived-in look, the shifty red eyes and furtive expression, as if it was always expecting the tap on the shoulder that might usher its shy owner to a car and then a prison cell for the next ten years.

I went out the main entrance and walked between two concrete pillars with snakes wrapped around outsized censers on the top; they were much too high up to ask what they were doing there, but I was dimly aware that the ancient Greeks had regarded snakes as sacred, their venom as remedial, and maybe their skin-shedding as symbolic of rebirth and renewal, which as an idea certainly worked for me. It might have been early morning but there were still one or two real snakes around and one of them was sitting in a newish BMW in front of the hospital. As I came out the hospital door, he leaned across the passenger seat and, with a cigar still in his face, shouted through the open passenger window.

'Gunther. Bernhard Gunther. As I live and breathe. I was just visiting an old friend in the hospital, and now you turn up. How are you, Gunther? How many years has it been since we saw each other last? Twenty? Twenty-five? I thought you were dead.'

I stopped on the sidewalk and looked inside, debating my choices and discovering what was obvious, which was that I really didn't have any. Schramma was shouting so that other passersby could hear him and make me feel all the more uncomfortable. He was smiling gleefully while he did it, too, like a man who'd come to collect on a bet he'd won and I'd lost. If I'd had a gun I would probably have shot him or maybe myself. I used to be afraid of dying but now, on the whole, I find I'm looking forward to it, to getting far away from Bernie Gunther and everything to do with him, from his tangled history and uneasy way of thinking, from his inability to adjust to this modern world; but most of all I'm looking forward to getting away from all the people who knew him, or who claim to have known him, like Criminal Secretary Schramma. I've tried being someone else several times but who I am always comes back to kick me in the teeth.

'I told you I'd find out who you are. Hey, come on. Don't be such a sore loser. You don't know it yet, but I'm here to do you a favour, Gunther. Seriously. You'll thank me for what I'm going to tell you. So hurry up and get in the car before someone realizes that you're not who you say you are. Besides, it's too cold to sit here with the window open. I'm freezing my plums off.'

I ducked into the car, closed the door, and wound up the window without saying a word. Almost immediately I wished I'd left the window alone; Schramma's cigar smelled like a bonfire in a plague pit.

'You want to know how I found out who you are?'

'Go ahead and amaze me.'

'The Munich Police Praesidium came through the war pretty much unscathed. The records, too. Like I said, I knew we met sometime before Hitler. And that meant it was before Heydrich, too. Heydrich was chief of police in Munich for a while and changed the filing system. He was very efficient, as you probably know. All that cross-referencing he did still comes in handy sometimes. So it was relatively simple to find the name of a detective from the famous Alex, in Berlin, who was our guest for the night after assaulting our desk sergeant.'

'As I recall the incident, he hit me first.'

'I'm quite sure of it. I remember that sergeant. A right bastard, he was. It was 1932. Twenty-five years. How about that? My God. How time flies, eh?'

'Not at this present moment.'

'Like I said before, it doesn't bother me what you did during the war. The Old Man says it's all ancient history now, even in the GDR. But every so often the commies still feel obliged to make an example of someone, just so as they can distinguish their own tyranny from the fascist one that went before. Could be they want you. Could be they might have you, too. Old Nazis are about the only kind of criminals the West is disposed to send back across the border these days.'

'It's nothing like that,' I said. 'I'm not a war criminal. I didn't kill anyone.'

'Oh, sure. Christof Ganz is just the name you write poetry under. Your nom de plume, as it were. I get that. I like to move under the radar a bit myself, sometimes. For a cop, I mean. Then there's Interpol. I haven't checked with them yet, but I wouldn't mind betting they have a file on you. Of course, I can't look at that one without putting a flag up. Once I've asked, they'll want to know why I want to know and maybe they'll try to take it a stage further. So from here on in it's your call, Gunther. Only you'd better make sure it's the right one, for your sake.'

'You've made your point, Schramma. You've found some leverage and you have my cooperation. But get to the part where you want to do me a favour, will you? I'm tired and I want to go home. I've spent all night ferrying corpses and if I stay here any longer I'm liable to search your big ugly mouth for a coin.'

He didn't get it. Not that I cared. Mostly I'm talking for myself these days. And wit only sounds like wit when there's someone around to appreciate it. Most of the time people like Schramma just talked too much. In Germany there was too much talk, too much opinion, too much conversation and none of it very good. Television and the wireless were just noise. To be effective, words have to be distilled as if they've arrived in your balloon via a retort and a cool receiver.

'Have you heard of a local politician called Max Merten? Originally from Berlin, but lives in Munich now.'

'Vaguely. When I was at the Alex there was a Max Merten

who was a young district court counsel from the Ministry of Justice.'

'Must be the same Fritz. Done very nicely for himself, too. Nice house in Nymphenburg. Smart office on Kardinal-Faulhaber-strasse. He's one of the co-founders of the All-German People's Party – the GVP, which is closely associated with the socialist SED. The other founder is Gustav Heinemann, who used to be a prominent member of the CDU and the interior minister until he fell out with the Old Man. But money's tight for politics right now. Funds for new parties are thin on the ground. I mean, who wants to be rid of our miracle-working Konrad Adenauer – apart from Heinemann, of course, and some oversensitive Jews?

'So a few weeks ago Max Merten hired me, privately, to check out the bona fides of a potential new Party donor – General Hein-rich Heinkel, who's offered to fund the GVP. But Merten has a not unreasonable suspicion that Heinkel is still a Nazi. And he doesn't want the GVP taking any tainted money. Anyway it turns out that Merten was right, although not in the way he suspected. Heinkel's ten thousand is actually coming from the GDR. You see, Merten's business partner is a prominent German politician by the name of Walter Hallstein, who's the Old Man's foreign minister in all but name, and the fellow who's been conducting our negotiations to set up this new European Economic Commu-nity. The GDR hates the idea of the EEC – and more particularly the European Defence Community, of which West Germany will be an important member – and has planned an elaborate under-cover operation to discredit the GVP and Merten in the hope that some of the mud they throw will eventually stick to Professor

Hallstein. Now, you might ask why an old Nazi is fronting money for the GDR. Well, Heinkel's eldest son managed to get himself arrested in Leipzig, where he is currently languishing in a jail cell as a guarantor of his father's cooperation. If he does exactly what he's told, the young man will be released. That's his deal.

'A few nights from now Heinkel is going to pay over the money in cash to Merten at the general's house in Bogenhausen. There's a room in Heinkel's house that has been suitably decorated with swastikas and other evidence of the general's continuing Nazism. While Merten is there the police will turn up to arrest Heinkel for various offences, including selling Nazi memorabilia. And in order to save his skin Heinkel will tell the police that the money was actually meant as a bribe for Professor Hallstein.'

'And you found out all this how?' I asked.

'I'm a cop, Gunther. That's what cops do. We find out stuff we're not supposed to know about. Some days I do the crossword in twenty minutes. Others I dig up shit on people like you and Heinkel.'

'So why are you telling me all this, and not Max Merten?'

Schramma puffed his cigar silently and as his curious blue eyes narrowed I began to guess the whole dirty scheme, which is a bad habit of mine: I've always been possessed of a sneaking and uncomfortable feeling that underneath any evidence to the contrary I'm a really bad man – which makes me better able to second-guess other bad men. Maybe it's the edge you need to be a good cop.

'Because you've told Max Merten that General Heinkel is on the level, haven't you? That's it, isn't it? The cops aren't going to come at all for the simple reason you're planning to snatch the GDR's money for yourself. You're going to turn up an hour or two before Max Merten and rob this general.'

'Something like that. And you're going to help me, Gunther. After all, it's quite possible that Heinkel may have company. A man who robs alone is a man who gets caught.'

'There's only one thing worse than a crook and it's a crooked cop.'

'You're the one with the false identity, Gunther, not me. In my book that says you're dirty. So spare me any lectures about honesty. If I have to I'll take care of the job myself. Of course, that will mean you'll be in jail or, at the very least, on the run. But I'd much prefer it if you were there, backing me up.'

'I'm beginning to understand a little more about what happened to Paul Herzefelde back in 1932,' I said. 'It was you who was squeezing that fraudster, wasn't it? Kohl, was it? Did Herzefelde guess as much? Yes, that would fit. It was you who killed him. And you who let the Nazis take the blame because he was a Jew. That was smart. I've misjudged you, Schramma. You must be awfully good at pretending to be a good cop to get away with it for so many years.'

'Really, it's not so difficult these days. The police are like everyone else in Germany. A little short on manpower after the war. They can't afford to be so fussy about who they have back on the force. Now you, you really are a smart fellow, the way you figured all that out in just a few minutes.'

'If I was that smart I wouldn't be sitting in this car talking to a bastard like you, Schramma.'

'You're selling yourself short, Gunther. It's not every day you solve a murder that's twenty-five years old. Believe it or not, I like that about you. And it's another reason I want you along for the ride. You don't think like a normal person. If you've survived this long as someone else, I figure you can see things coming. Situations developing. I can use experience like that. Now, and in the future. There's no one left in Munich I can really trust; most of my younger Ettstrasse colleagues are too honest for their own good, and more importantly, for mine.'

'I'm glad to hear that. I'd hate to think we lost a war just to keep scum like you in uniform.'

'Keep using your mouth if that helps. But I figure some money will shut you up. I'll make it worth your while, Gunther. I'll give you ten per cent. That's a thousand marks. Don't tell me you couldn't use a thousand marks. Fate looks like it's been dogging your footsteps for a long time now with a length of lead pipe in its hand.'

As if to make the point there was now an automatic pistol in his own big hand and it was jammed up against my liver, which I figured I could ill afford to lose in spite of the damage it had already sustained after years of heavy drinking.

'Just don't get too clever with me, Gunther,' he said, and nodded at the hospital's front door. 'Or it'll be your corpse that's short of a face in that stinking mortuary.'

CHAPTER 5

A pewter-coloured sky compressed the cold, even landscape; for a Bavarian town Munich is as flat as a mattress and just as comfortable, and there's no part of Munich more comfortable than Bogenhausen, on the east bank of the Isar River. General Heinkel's house was a white three-storey villa with louvred green shutters, about thirty windows, and a vaguely fairy-tale stillness. You could hear the river in the drains and, in the little church that was opposite where Schramma had parked the BMW, the sound of an organist practicing a Bach cantata that might have been *O lovely day, o hoped-for time,* only that wasn't how I regarded it. A green picket fence sloped gently down to an untidy line of deciduous trees that bordered the Isar. On the other side of the empty cobbled street was a small military hospital for soldiers whom the war had left maimed or horribly disfigured. I knew this because while we were sitting in the car we watched in uncomfortable silence as a group of maybe ten or fifteen of them trooped out of the gate to take their afternoon constitutional around Bogenhausen. One man glanced in our window as he passed by although, in truth, it was hard to believe that this had been his intention as a large part of his face was pointed in completely the opposite direction. The man behind him seemed to be wearing a pair of thick goggles or spectacles made of pink flesh that were the result, perhaps, of some plastic surgery that was intended to remedy extensive facial burns. A third man with one eye and one leg and one arm and two crutches appeared to be in charge, and I thought of Pieter Bruegel's famous painting *The Blind Leading the Blind* and shuddered as I considered my own comparatively good fortune. It's true what Homer says that sometimes it's the dead who are the mighty lucky ones.

'Jesus Christ,' exclaimed Schramma, relighting his cigar. 'Will you look at that goddamn hink? And I thought you were ugly, Gunther.' He took out a silver hip flask and bit off a large piece of the contents.

'Show a little respect,' I said.

'For what? That little hit parade? Better those limping hinks than me, that's what I say.'

'In this particular case I'm forced to agree with you. They *are* better than you, Schramma. And always will be.' I shook my head. His company was beginning to become tiresome. 'What are we waiting for anyway? You still haven't said.'

'We're waiting for the money to turn up, that's what. As soon as it does we're in business, but not until. So stop flapping your tongue and take a bite of this.'

He handed me the flask, on which were engraved the words

Thank You, Christian Schramma, for being our Wedding Witness, 25.11.1947. Pieter and Johanna. I almost laughed at the idea of a snake like Schramma being the best man at anyone's wedding; then again, it wasn't just the German police who were short of good men, it was everyone these days. Pieter and Johanna included. I took a swig from the flask; it was cheap schnapps but nonetheless welcome. Alcohol is the best accomplice for almost any crime you care to mention.

'I'm just saying,' he said. 'It's a bit of a shock, that's all. To see men like that walking around the streets, scaring the horses. They should wave a red flag or something, like they used to do when a train was coming.'

'The sea always looks nice until the tide goes out,' I said, 'and then you see all the ugly things it hides. Germany's a bit like that, I think. I mean, we've got more of that kind of thing than most. It's to be expected and we shouldn't be surprised when we find what's really there. That's all *I'm* saying.'

'Me, I'm more of a Darwinist, I guess. I tend to believe in a Germany in which only the strong will survive.'

'That's a new idea.'

'Oh, I don't mean politically. Politics are finished in this country. I mean survival not just of the fittest, but of the best, too. The best people to make the best cars and the best washing machines and the best vacuum cleaners. It seems so obvious that I wonder why Hitler didn't think of it himself. Germany, the manufacturing powerhouse and the economic master of Europe. And with that, a new realism. Sure, human values will have importance but for a long while yet the cold numbers will have to take precedence if we're going to be back on top where we belong.'

I took a second swig and handed back the flask. 'Is this the speech you gave at the wedding or at Bretton Woods?'

'Fuck you, Gunther.' Schramma took a swig from the flask and swished it around like a mouthwash. He needed it with the cigar he was smoking. 'As soon as I get enough money from this whole deal I'm going to buy myself a share of the economic miracle. I'm going to go into business for myself.'

'And this little caper is what? Pro bono publico?'

'I mean I'm going to become a manufacturer. I'm going to buy myself this nice little factory I know that makes cutlery.'

'What do you know about manufacturing?'

'Nothing. But I know how to use a knife and fork.'

'Now that is a surprise.'

'Seriously, though. This is what's going to give Germany an advantage over England, for example. That bottom line on the balance sheet. The Tommies mistakenly believe that their victory has earned them the right to those human values first. That's why they created their welfare state but history will prove they can't afford it. You see if I'm wrong.'

There was more of this; maybe Schramma saw himself as the new Paul Samuelson, not that it mattered because after a few minutes I stopped listening. That's probably good advice with all economists. After a few more minutes a man wearing a Gannex coat and a Karakul hat came up the slope from the river end and went through the gate of the white house.

'Here we go,' said Schramma.

He'd already given me a scarf with which to cover my face but now he took out a Walther PPK, worked the slide, thumbed the hammer down to make it safe, and handed it to me, but then held on to the pistol for a moment so that he could deliver a short lecture.

'Just so you know, I have to pay someone out of my share, and this person knows who you are.'

'Oh? Who's that?'

'All you need to know is that if you double-cross me then you'll be double-crossing him, too. So don't go getting any bright ideas, Gunther. I want you watching my back, not putting a hole in it. Clear?'

'Clear.' But of course it wasn't, not by a long chalk. I knew there was now a round in the chamber – it was impossible to work the slide on an automatic without putting some brass in there – but I had no idea if that round was live or blank. The way I saw things it was taking a risk, him giving me a loaded gun, so why would he? What was to stop me from robbing him of the ten thousand when he'd finished robbing the general?

I figured a blank would serve his purpose just as well as a live round; no one was going to argue with a pistol, and if I had to shoot, my making a loud noise would be almost as effective as putting a bullet in someone; safer for him that way, too. Of course, I might have worked the slide myself and dropped the round into the palm of my hand and found out one way or the other but, in a strange way, it suited us both for me to act as if the gun was loaded, even if it wasn't. Naturally it had crossed my mind that the real purpose of his asking me along was not to watch his back but to see if he could really trust me or even to be the fall guy. I figured I had a better chance of coming through it all unscathed if I actively allowed Schramma to believe that I believed I was properly heeled.

He let the gun go and I thrust it quickly into my coat pocket.

We got out of the car and I followed him through the picket gate. We walked around to the side of the house and the back door. The organist had started playing another cantata, which the rooks and crows seemed to enjoy more than I did, the way they were joining in on the chorus. By now there were a few lights on in the house but only on the second floor.

Schramma stopped by a wheelbarrow that was leaning against the wall and glanced in the window through the back door, which wasn't locked. A few moments later we were in the house. There was a strong smell of apples and cinnamon in the air as if someone had been baking strudel but it didn't make me feel hungry. In fact, I felt a little sick; I couldn't help but notice that the grip on the .38 in Schramma's hand was Dekka-taped as if he planned on leaving it at the scene, which didn't augur well for anyone, me least of all. You don't plan to leave a gun behind unless you've used it. So I was feeling scared about what I'd let myself in for. But what choice did I have? Christof Ganz was just getting started in life and it wasn't like there were any other new identities available to me. Not even in Germany. For the moment, at least, my foot was well and truly caught between the serrated steel jaws of Schramma's mantrap.

Schramma balanced his half-chewed cigar on the side of the kitchen table, pulled the scarf over his nose and mouth, outlaw-style, and then nodded at me to do the same. We walked quietly along a dimly lit corridor toward a room with voices at the front of the house.

CHAPTER 6

Inside the room everything looked straightforward enough: a short man with a Kaiser Wilhelm waxed moustache and wearing a green leather waistcoat, the general was standing in the dining room, opposite a man in a Gannex coat who was younger than I'd supposed, with one of those little blond beards beloved of aspirant Leninists. The money, all ten thousand of it, lay on the red-checked tablecloth under the eyes of a Northern Renaissance portrait of a young woman with a folded vellum letter in her hand. If it was good news her expression wasn't giving anything away. Then again, she was losing the hair on her crown, so she didn't have much to be cheerful about.

'Who the hell are you?' spluttered the general. 'What's the meaning of this?'

'The gun and the mask ought to be a bit of a clue, General,' said Schramma. 'I mean to steal this money. But if you do exactly what you're told you won't get hurt.' He stood to one side and jerked the gun at the door. 'Downstairs. Now.'

The general walked to the door but the other man stayed put as if Schramma hadn't been speaking to him.

'You too,' added Schramma.

The man in the Gannex coat frowned as if this was somehow a surprise to him. 'Me?'

Schramma put the gun against the man's head and lifted the edge of the Karakul hat so that it now sat on the back of his blond-haired head like a skullcap. Quickly he frisked him for a gun and not finding one said, 'What do you want, a memo? Yes, you too.'

The man in the hat gave Schramma an angry, bitter sort of look, almost as if they knew each other, and perhaps he would have said more but for the gun in the cop's hand. It's never a good idea to be brave around a .38. People have been shot for less. I expect the general knew that. And like me perhaps he'd noticed that the butt of the gun was taped, and the trigger, too, probably. So he bit his lip, wisely I thought, and walked ahead of us, with me bringing up the rear like some dumb postilion who looked like he was just along for the ride.

I followed the three men down the creaking wooden stairs. At the end of a long stone-flagged corridor was a big grey metal door with two lock handles. Underneath a spy hole was the word PANZERLIT. It was an old bomb shelter.

'Open it,' Schramma told the general.

'What are you going to do?' asked the general, turning the handle. He opened the door and switched on the light to reveal a largish wine cellar. A rich smell of mildewed bottles and damp filled the air. I didn't know much about wine, but I estimated there must have been almost a thousand bottles in there. It was the best-equipped bomb shelter I'd ever seen.

'I'm going to lock you in here so you can't call the police,' said Schramma. He jerked the pistol again. 'Get inside. Both of you.'

'You won't get away with this,' said the man in the hat. He snatched it off his head and held it between his hands like he was about to pray.

'No?'

'No. You're making a big mistake. You know who this money belongs to? To the foreign intelligence division of the East German Ministry for State Security, that's who.'

'Shut up and get in the cellar,' said Schramma.

'The MfS will come after you. You know that, don't you? This money is only going to buy you a lot of sleepless nights.'

'That's all right. I don't sleep much anyway.'

The two men walked into the wine cellar and turned to face Schramma as he followed them a short way inside. Then he put his forefinger in one ear and what with the tape on the butt of the gun I knew for certain that he was going to kill them both. Instinctively I took a step back as he took one forward – so that he didn't miss his target, I guess – and, the next moment, he shot the general and then he'd shot the man in the hat as well, both of them at close enough range to do some fatal damage. In the earsplitting second's gap between the two gunshots I decided I might very well be his third victim and, stepping quickly back again, I slammed the steel door behind me and jammed it shut with a large axe handle that someone had left lying on the floor.

I snatched the mask from my face and took a deep breath of the combusted air. My ears were whistling from the gunshots and it was a second or two before I even heard Schramma hammering on the door and shouting. Through the peephole I could see one of his bright eyes fixed on me like a piece of blue topaz. Meanwhile I managed to jam the other handle with half a brick. The aroma of strudel in the house was gone; now it was just gunpowder and death I could smell.

'What the hell do you think you're doing, Gunther?' he shouted quietly. 'Let me out of here.'

'I don't think so,' I said.

'Don't be an idiot. We don't have time for this. We need to get out of here in case someone reported hearing those shots.'

'I'm glad you mentioned that.' I dropped the magazine from the Walther and inspected the ammunition quickly. Blanks. Like I'd thought. 'Why did you kill them? You didn't need to do that.'

'Why take the risk of them identifying us? That's the way I look at it.'

'Oh, I get that. Only the way I figure it, you were going to shoot me, too. Why not? Right now I'm more expendable than a stick of celery.'

'What makes you say that?'

'Well, for one thing, you're a corrupt cop who knows how to dress up a murder scene. And for another, this gun you gave me is loaded with blanks.'

'Sure. I wanted to see if I could trust you. Look, listen to me. Let me tell you about these two Fritzes I just shot. The one with the hat was Stasi. The other was a Nazi war criminal. Got away with it for years. No one's going to weep about these two. They both had it coming.'

'I've pulled the trigger a couple of times on some people who had it coming. At least, that's what I told myself at the time. Now I realize that all of us have got it coming. Me, probably. You, especially.'

'Forget that. They're dead now. Look, maybe ten per cent of the take wasn't fair of me. I get that. So how about half? I'll give you half the money. Only don't leave me in here. What do you say, Gunther?'

'I say no deal.'

'I'll even give you a job in my new cutlery business.'

'You've got nothing I want, Schramma.'

The blue eye in the spy hole narrowed and then disappeared. 'If you look through the spy hole you can see me unload my revolver before you open the door. How about that?'

'I doubt that would work, either. My guess is there's a third gun in your coat pocket. The one you were going to use on me and then leave behind in that Stasi man's hand.'

The eye returned to the spy hole.

'Think about it, Gunther. You can't call the cops. Because who do you think they're going to believe? Me, a local cop with thirty years' service? Or you, a man who's living under a false name? Right now we can both walk out of this place like we were never here.'

'You make a good point. And of course I'm not going to call the cops. Who said anything about me calling the cops?'

'So what are you going to do? You can't just leave me here.'

'Sure I can. Someone will turn up. Maybe.'

'The general lives alone.'

'Then I'd say you'd better hope there's a corkscrew in there. All that wine. Be a shame to waste it. Might be a while before someone shows up and lets you out.'

'And you.' The single blue eye narrowed again. 'You'd better hope I never get out of here,' he yelled. 'Because if I do I'm going to kill you, Gunther.'

My ears were still ringing like an alarm bell; an alarm bell that was warning me that the longer I stayed there the more likely I was to be in serious trouble; not that my leaving there would be the end of it either. I had the traces of a plan half-formed in my head but it went against all my instincts.

'This is a bad idea, I know. But it was you who backed me into this corner. Besides, we both know that you were going to kill me anyway. That's why you had the grip on that gun taped. So you could leave it behind and make it look like I was shot while trying to rob these two. I figure I've bought myself some breathing space for now. With ten thousand marks I can get a long way from Munich. By the time someone finds you in there I'm going to be far away from this city. Maybe out of the country. You just worry what happens if the cops do show up and find you with a murder weapon and two bodies. Even the Munich cops aren't so dumb they can't figure this one out. What we have here is a locked-room mystery where the only mystery is how you were dumb enough to get yourself caught in the first place.'

'Don't you believe it, Gunther. In spite of any evidence to the contrary I'm good at my job. They'll listen to me.'

'Mister, you're good. Very persuasive. I bet you could sell a butcher a steak. But I'll take that risk. That just happens to be what I'm good at.'

CHAPTER 7

I tucked the gun under my waistband, ran upstairs, filled my pockets with the money, and stepped, cautiously, outside the white house. No one was around and, according to my ears, the organist was still playing Bach as if nothing had happened. Maybe that's why people like his stuff. I didn't return to the car. It wasn't mine. Instead I walked down the slope through the trees and then up the street onto Max-Joseph Bridge to cross the Isar, pausing in the centre to stare down at the turbulent, coffee-coloured waters in an effort to clear my head of some of what had just taken place. There's nothing like the sound and sight of a river in spate to help flush the human spirit of what ails it, and if that doesn't work you can always drown yourself. When I was sure no one was around on the bridge I dropped the Walther into the river and then walked west, as far as the English Garden. I wasn't sure why it was called that. To me there seemed nothing particularly English about it – unless it was the number of snotty-looking people riding tall horses or walking big dogs; then again, it might have been the presence of a huge

Chinese pagoda. I'm told no English garden is complete without one. There was a beer garden next to the pagoda, where I had a quick one to steady my nerves; it was getting close to the time when I was supposed to report at the Schwabing Hospital for work, but with ten thousand marks in my coat pocket and a couple of bodies in my wake I figured I had more urgent things to do if I wanted to stay out of jail. So I went to a small taxi rank and asked the driver to take me to Kardinal-Faulhaberstrasse in the centre of the city. Once there, I walked up and down a while, inspecting names on the shiny brass plaques on the doorways until, next to a bank, I found the one I was looking for – the one Schramma had thoughtfully informed me about: *Dr Max Merten, Attorney at Law*. Trusting a lawyer didn't seem like much of a plan and it went against all my instincts – some of the worst war criminals I'd ever met had been lawyers and judges – but I could see little alternative. Besides, this was a lawyer with a special interest in my case.

There was a cage elevator but it wasn't working so I climbed up a wide marble staircase to the third floor, where I stopped for a minute to catch my breath before going in; I needed to look and, more importantly, sound calm – even if I wasn't – before telling a lawyer I hadn't seen since before the war that we were both of us connected with a double murder. A woman I presumed was Merten's secretary was getting ready to go home, and catching sight of me, she winced a little as if she knew I was going to delay her. Her bright yellow hair had probably been styled by a whole hive of bees and seemed to act as a crucial counterweight to her chest, which seemed both remarkable and appetizing at the same time. You can call me cynical but I had an idea that maybe her typing and shorthand skills weren't the main reasons why she'd been hired.

'Can I help you?'

'I'd like to see Dr Merten.'

'I'm afraid he's about to go home for the night.'

'I'm sure he'll want to see me. I'm an old friend.'

I wasn't wearing my best clothes so I could see her wondering about that.

'If I could have your name?'

I was reluctant to use my real name and I didn't think there was any point in giving my new one; it wouldn't have meant anything to Merten; nor did I want to mention Schramma's name, for the simple reason that he was now a murderer. Even the most loyal of secretaries can find that kind of thing a little too much.

'Just say I'm from the Alex, in Berlin. He'll know what that is.'

'The Alex?'

'Since you ask, it was the Police Praesidium. Like the one you have here in Munich. But bigger and better. Or at least it was until Karl Marx came to town. I used to be a policeman, which is how we know each other.'

Slightly reassured now that she knew I had once been a policeman, Merten's secretary went to find her boss. She stepped into a back office, leaving me with the expensive view out of the corner window. Merten's offices were opposite the Greek Orthodox church on Salvatorstrasse. Built of red bricks in the Gothic style, the church looked oddly out of step with everything else in that otherwise uniformly Baroque street. I was still looking at it when the secretary came back and informed me that her boss would see me now. She showed me into his office and then closed the door behind us, as Max Merten came around his desk to greet me.

'My God, I never expected to see you again. Bernie Gunther. How long has it been? Fifteen years?'

'At least.'

'But not a cop, I think. Not anymore. No, you don't look like a cop. Not with that beard.'

'It's been a while since I carried a badge.'

'Have a seat, Bernie. Have a cigarette. Have a drink. Would you like a drink?' He checked his watch. 'Yes, I think it's time.' He went over to a big Biedermeier sideboard and lifted up a decanter the size of a streetlamp. 'Schnapps? It's that or nothing, I'm afraid. It's the only thing I drink. That and anything alcoholic.'

'Schnapps.'

He was much bigger than I remembered, in almost every way: taller, louder, broader, fatter; his silver-haired head was huge and looked as if it belonged on a stone lion. Only his hands were small. He didn't look younger than me, but he was, by at least a decade. He wore a good-quality thick tweed suit, ideal for a Munich winter, and while this didn't fit him well – the waist of his trousers was positioned just below his breast, like a life belt – he was in more urgent need of a dentist than a good tailor; one of his front teeth was gold but the rest weren't so good, perhaps a result of the large number of cigarettes he smoked. The office was pungent with the smell of Egyptian cigarettes. I smoke a lot myself, but Max Merten could have smoked for West Germany. His cigarettes arrived between his thick pink lips from a packet of Finas on his desk, one after the other, in an almost unbroken thin white line, one passing on a tiny flame to the next, like the baton in a never-ending relay race. He handed me a glass and then ushered us both to some comfortable armchairs beside the window, where he drew the heavy curtains and sat down opposite me.

'So what have you been doing with yourself?'

'Trying to stay out of trouble.'

'And not succeeding if I know you.'

'That's why I'm here, Max. I need a lawyer. It's just possible we both do.'

'Oh dear. That sounds ominous.'

'You hired a cop to do some freelance work for you. Christian Schramma.'

'That's right.'

'You wanted him to check out the bona fides of a potential donor for this political party you've started. The CVP.'

'GVP. That's right. General Heinkel. I wanted to find out where his campaign money was coming from.'

'Well, Schramma hired me. Not so much hired, perhaps. I didn't have much choice in the matter.'

'To check out the money?'

'I thought so, but as things turned out he wanted me to help him steal it. I didn't have much choice in the matter, either. I'm living here in Munich under a false name. For the obvious reasons.'

'The war.'

'Exactly.'

'So what precisely has happened? You're not a thief.'

I told him everything that had taken place inside the general's house. And then placed the money on his desk, all ten thousand marks of it.

'Then General Heinkel is dead.'

I nodded.

'But who's the other man that's been murdered?'

'I don't know his name. But I think he worked for the East German foreign intelligence service. The MfS.'

'What's the DDR have to do with this?'

'You were going to go to the general's house tomorrow morning, to collect the money for the GVP, right?'

'Yes.'

'The MfS planned to have the local police turn up to arrest the general who, in order to clear himself, was then going to allege that the money was a bribe for you and your friend Professor Hallstein.'

'Why would the general do such a thing?'

'Because, according to Schramma, the Stasi have his son in a Leipzig prison cell. My guess is that the fellow from the MfS was in this with Schramma. But that Schramma double-crossed him.'

'I see. This is all very disturbing.'

'For me, too.'

'I had no idea that Christian Schramma was such a dangerous man.'

'Cops have guns. And they mix with all kinds of bad people. That makes them dangerous.'

'And Schramma is still there? Locked in the general's wine cellar with the two bodies?'

'That's right.' I sipped some of the schnapps and helped myself to a cigarette. 'Given that it was you who hired him in the first place, I thought you might have an idea about what to do next. But for the fact that I'm living under a false name, and your friend's a cop who's put a lot of years into the job, I'd have called the police myself and left them to it. I was hoping you might do it instead of me.'

'You did the right thing coming to me, Bernie. I mean from what you've said, it looks like an open-and-shut case: two bodies and the killer and the murder weapon all in one locked room. But experience tells me that even cases that look open-and-shut have a habit of not closing properly, from an evidentiary point of view. And then there's the Munich police, of course. If Schramma's corrupt, then there's every chance that there are others who are also corrupt. That they'll pretend to believe his story and just let him go. No, this needs very careful thought about who to call, and when. It may be that I shall have to inform the Bavarian State Ministry of Justice.'

'That's up to you, of course. But whoever you tell, please bear in mind that if it should come to my needing a lawyer, I can't afford to pay you. I'm hoping my coming here and putting you in the picture about everything that's happened would be enough for you to take me on as your client for free.'

'Oh, surely. And I do appreciate it. Very much. After all, you could easily have disappeared with the money and I'd have been none the wiser about any of this.'

'I'm glad you see it that way, Max.'

'By the way, what do you expect me to do with all this cash?'

'That's up to you. No one but me knows you have it.'

'How much is here, anyway?'

'Ten thousand.'

'I suppose I'll have to give it to the police.'

I took a long drag on the cigarette and narrowed my eyes against my smoke. If it made me look cagey and thoughtful that was always my intention.

'I get the feeling you have a few ideas of your own about what should happen to the money,' said Merten.

'If you give it to the police you'll have to say where you got it. Or who gave it to you. The first looks awkward for you. The second looks just as bad for me. My advice would be to use it for the GVP after all. Like you always intended. It's not like you can hand it back to the DDR.'

'But if I do keep the money for the GVP, then that begs the question about what to do about Christian Schramma. We can't just leave him there. Can we? With those men dead and Schramma locked in the cellar it's quite possible the police may never arrive at the general's house tomorrow expecting to make an arrest. Without Schramma or someone else to tell them, he could be there for a while. The general was a bit of a recluse. I'm not sure he even had a housekeeper.'

'I have an idea about Schramma, too.'

'Let's hear it.'

'You hired him. You can get rid of him. No, I don't mean like that.'

'Then how?'

'We go back there and talk him into keeping his mouth shut.'

'Now?'

'Now.'

'You're right, of course. There's no sense in putting this off and hoping it will go away. The devil's favourite piece of furniture is the long bench. And you really think we should let him go?'

'That's about the size of it.'

'But he's killed two people in cold blood.'

'Informing the police won't bring them back. And will only cause us both trouble. Once he's in the police station there's no telling what he'll say. To men who are his friends. They won't want to believe us.'

'True. All the same, I don't like it. He's still got a gun, you said?'

'Mmm-hmm.'

'Suppose when we let him out of the cellar he shoots us? Or brings us both back here, takes the money for himself, like he intended, and then kills us both?'

'I think I know a way of preventing him from doing that.'

'How?'

'Got a camera?'

'Yes.'

'All right. This is what I think we should do.'

CHAPTER 8

We drove east in Merten's Mercedes, along Maximilianstrasse, and crossed the Isar on Maximilian's Bridge, before turning left and north up Möhlstrasse. Merten hadn't been to the dead general's home before so I was giving him directions. It was snowing again and in the car's headlights the flakes resembled the bubbles in a glass of weiss beer.

'I'm very grateful for this,' admitted Merten.

'Don't mention it, Max.'

'Look, I don't care what you did in the war. Really, it's none of my business. But I am supposed to be an officer of the Bavarian court. So it might be best if at least I knew something about your present predicament. If I am going to be your lawyer you should tell me if you are wanted for anything in particular. Beyond the obvious.'

'What's obvious?'

'I mean your past service, with the SD.'

'There's nothing really. I know how it looks – me having a false name – but my conscience is clear.' I wasn't sure about that; but, for the moment at least, I didn't feel inclined to tell him my whole life story. 'The fact is, I'm an escaped Russian POW. I killed a man at a camp in the DDR while making my escape. A German. If they caught me they'd chop off my head. But more probably the Stasi would prefer to just have me quietly murdered.' This was true at least.

'That's all right then. For a moment I thought – well, you can guess what I was thinking. There were always lots of stories that were told around the Alex about the famous Bernie Gunther. That Himmler kicked you once. That you worked for the likes of Goebbels and Göring, but that you mostly worked for General Heydrich.'

'Reluctantly.'

'Was that even possible?'

'It was if Heydrich decided it was.'

'I guess so. The last I heard of you, they'd sent you to Russia as a member of a police battalion, working for that other murderer, Arthur Nebe, with Task Group B.'

'That's right. Only I didn't murder anyone.'

'Oh sure, sure, but how many did he kill? Fifty thousand?'

'Something like that.'

'Hard to believe that two or three years later he was part of the Stauffenberg Plot to kill Hitler.'

'Actually, I find it harder to believe that he murdered fifty thousand people,' I said. 'But he did. Nebe was full of contradictions. Mainly he was a cynical opportunist. In the early '30s a die-hard Nazi; by '38, part of an early plot to get rid of Hitler; after the miraculous fall of France, a committed Nazi prepared to do anything to advance himself, including mass murder; and by '44, when he saw the way the wind was blowing, part of Stauffenberg's incompetent plot. If he was a character in a book you wouldn't believe him even possible.'

'No, I suppose not. Anyway, there but for the grace of God. If it hadn't been for your good advice I might be in the same position as you, Bernie.'

'Why do you say so?'

'What I mean is, it was you who talked me out of joining the Party and the SS. Remember? Just before the war I was an ambitious junior lawyer in the Ministry of Justice and keen to advance my career. At that time joining the SS and the Nazi Party was the quickest way to make that happen. Instead I stayed put at the ministry, thankfully. If you hadn't put me off the idea, Bernie, I'd probably have ended up in the SD and in charge of some SS special action group in the Baltic States charged with killing Jewish women and kids – like so many other lawyers I knew – and now *I'd* be a wanted man, like you, or worse: I could have met the same fate as those other men who went to jail, or were hanged in Landsberg.' He shook his head and frowned. 'I often wonder how I'd have handled that particular dilemma. You know – mass murder. What I would have done. If I could have done – *that*. I prefer to believe I would have refused to carry out those orders but if I'm really honest I don't know the answer. I think my desire to stay alive would have persuaded me to do what I was told, like every other lawyer. Because there's something about my own profession that horrifies me sometimes. It seems to me that lawyers can justify almost anything to themselves as long as it's legal. But you can make anything legal when you put a gun to parliament's head. Even mass murder.'

'Turn right up ahead and then keep the river on your left.'

'Okay.'

'So what kind of war *did* you have, Max?'

'Thankfully uneventful. I got drafted into the Luftwaffe when the war started and served for a while in an anti-aircraft battery in Bremen and then in Stettin. That was very quiet. Too quiet, really. I mean I was just plain bored. And so in 1942 I went to the War Board and volunteered for the army. Went through officer training, made captain, and got myself a nice quiet posting somewhere warm and sunny. Matter of fact, I had quite a good time, all things considered.'

'Turn left on Neuberghauserstrasse and then pull up. It's only a short walk but we'd best make sure that the cops aren't there before we go inside. And don't forget the camera.'

He lit a new cigarette with the butt of the previous one and threw that away. 'Good idea.'

He parked the Mercedes up the street from the white house and then we stood beside the car for several minutes before I was satisfied the murders were, as yet, undiscovered.

'I'll go in first, alone,' I said. 'Just in case. Give it a couple of minutes. I'll go up to the second floor, switch a light on and off to let you know it's all right before you follow. There's no sense in us both getting arrested. But if I do get pulled, then make sure you come to the Praesidium as soon as you can. I've spent the night in there before and I didn't like it.'

'Thanks, Bernie. I appreciate it.'

I walked toward the white house, past the church, and through the picket gate. The back door was still unlocked, and a few minutes later Max Merten and I were standing in the kitchen. Schramma's cigar was still balanced on the edge of the kitchen table where he'd left it.

'What's that noise?' he asked. 'Can you hear it?'

'I imagine it's Christian Schramma shouting for help.'

We went downstairs where I found his blue eye staring out of the peephole, like before.

'Let me out of here,' he yelled through the steel door.

I went to the spy hole and peered back at him. He hammered the door as if he wished it had been my face and then took several steps back. It was clear he'd found a corkscrew; there were at least two bottles open that hadn't been open before.

'I'm prepared to let you out,' I yelled back. 'But on three conditions.'

'What are they?'

'First that you write out a full confession in your notebook. I know you have one because I saw it in your coat pocket when you produced that .38. I can read what you write through the spy hole. The second is that I see you take the tape off the handle of that revolver and empty every chamber. I figure you have four rounds left. You can drop each one of them into a bottle of wine. When it's nicely covered with your fingerprints you can put the gun on the table where I can see it.'

'And the third condition?'

'This is going to take a bit more time. I want to see you drink the contents of several bottles. Only when I'm satisfied you're completely drunk and incapable will I open this door. If this all happens to my satisfaction, Dr Merten and I will wheelbarrow you back to your car and drive it to the English Garden, where we'll leave you for the night to sleep it off.'

'What happens then?'

'The deal is this: we'll forget you had anything to do with these murders if you forget about me. And about the money. The money is going to the GVP after all. I'll go back to my shitty job at the hospital mortuary and you can go back to yours, keeping law and order in this beautiful city. So long as you keep your big mouth shut about everything, no one is ever going to know that you killed these men. But if a cop in a silly hat so much as tells me off for whistling in the street, then I will conclude that all bets are off and the police are going to find that gun with your fingerprints and your confession.'

I didn't mention the camera. I wanted the existence of photographs of Schramma pictured beside two bodies to be an extra source of friendly persuasion, should I ever need one.

'Fuck you, Gunther. You too, Merten. Fuck you both. I figure someone is bound to turn up here before very long, and then let me out; and when they do—'

'No one's coming. The general lived alone like you said.'

'Someone will come. *The cops will come*. Tomorrow. That's right. They'll come because I told them to come, to arrest the general and Merten. Like I told you before.'

'No. I think that's what those two men you murdered believed was going to happen. But no. I think you hoped their bodies would lie there, undiscovered, for as long as possible. Enough time for you to distance yourself nicely, anyway.'

'You can believe what you like. But I can tell you, they'll be here tomorrow. And when they get here I'll tell them you framed me. Sure, it looks awkward for me. But who do you think they'll believe? Me, a cop with twenty-five years on my badge. Or you? A man with a false name.'

'Fair enough. You make a good point. Only think about it. I could have left you here to starve to death, but I didn't. I came back for you. However, I can see you're not inclined to be reasonable. So I won't be back again. I can't take that risk. And this time I'll be sure to switch off all the lights and lock up behind me. Bogenhausen is a very private area. People keep themselves to themselves. Could be months before they find you. Starvation is a rotten way to die. But maybe if you drink enough of that wine, you won't notice the pain quite so much. I hope so, for your sake. There's a small cemetery next door. Strikes me that buried alive in this cellar you're already as good as there.'

I switched off the basement light, which also controlled the light inside the wine cellar, and I pushed Max Merten toward the stairs, as if we really were leaving.

'All right, all right,' shouted Schramma. 'You win, Gunther. I'll do it your way, you bastard.'

I switched the light on and walked back to the spy hole ready to invigilate the whole laborious process of ensuring I had something closely resembling a future.

CHAPTER 9

It went to plan, almost. Even with four bottles of good Spät-
burgunder inside of him, Schramma still managed to find a
gun in his pocket to try to shoot me – it was the one he'd been
planning to use on me all along, after I'd shot the two dead
men with the .38 – and I was obliged to render him completely
unconscious with a quick uppercut. After we'd taken his photograph with the dead men, we dragged him upstairs and out
into the garden, where we loaded him onto the wheelbarrow
and transported him back to his car. It was dark and snowing
heavily and no one saw us. In Bogenhausen we could probably
have carried him out of the house in the middle of a summer's
day and no one would have noticed.

With Merten following I drove the BMW across the bridge to
the English Garden and abandoned it and Schramma in a quiet
spot close to the Monopteros, which is a sort of hilltop Greek
temple to Apollo, one of the more popular gods in Munich. He
is after all the god of prophecy, and the Bavarians like a bit of
that. Hitler certainly thought so.

'Suppose he freezes to death,' said Merten.

'I doubt that'll happen.'

'I wouldn't like to have any man's death on my conscience.'

'Don't worry about it. He'll be fine. When I was pounding the beat in Berlin I came across many a drunk who'd survived a colder night than Schramma'll have in that BMW. Besides, this is my idea, not yours. So even if he does die, you needn't blame yourself. I can live with it after what he had in mind for me.'

'I need a drink.'

'Me too.'

'Somewhere jolly, I think. Those two dead men are stuck on my retinas. Come on. I'm buying.'

Merten drove us south to the Hofbräuhaus on Platzl, a three-floor beer hall that dates back to the sixteenth century and where Hitler once made an important speech in the upstairs hall, only no one mentions that now. These days people are more appreciative of a small brass band. We took a corner table with a window ledge as wide as a coffin lid and ordered beers that were as tall as umbrella stands. I tried to keep count of the lawyer's smokes, not from bland curiosity but out of a desire to feel better about my own habit; sitting beside Merten I felt better than I've felt in a long time. I even managed to convince myself I was in the peak of health. The man smoked like the Ruhr Valley. For a while we just drank and smoked and spoke not at all but gradually the music and the beer got to us and eventually I said, 'Speaking as a Berliner, there's a lot that's wrong with Munich but it certainly doesn't include the beer. Nowhere on earth has beer like this. Not even Asgard. At one time or another I must have sampled every beer in this place. Not much of a hobby, I know, but it beats collecting stamps. Tastes better, too.'

'Do you ever miss Berlin, Bernie?'

'Sure. But right now Berlin's Amelia Earhart, isn't it? Marooned on an island in the middle of a vast and hostile sea of red. So there's no point in wishing we were with her.'

'Yes, but there's something about Munich that's not as good as Berlin. Only I'm not sure what that is.'

'If Berlin is Amelia Earhart, then Munich is Charles Lindbergh: rich, private, vain, and with a very questionable history.'

Merten smiled into a beer that was the colour of a good night already enjoyed and soon to be flushed away. 'I owe you,' he said.

'You said that. And you needn't say it again. Just keep buying me beers.'

'No, but really I'd like to help you, Bernie. For old times' sake. You said you're a mortuary attendant at the Schwabing Hospital?'

'Did I?'

'A man of your special skills is wasted doing that.'

'To what skills are you referring, Max? Covering up a murder scene? Knocking a man out? Managing not to get shot?'

'Being a cop, of course. Something you did for a great many years.'

'That must be why I'm on such a generous police pension now.'

'I happen to know of a job that's going, here in Munich. You might be very good at it.'

'I have a job I'm very good at. Looking after the dead. So far I've had no complaints. They don't mind me and I don't mind them.'

'I mean a regular job. A job with a few prospects.'

'All of a sudden everyone's offering me work. Listen, Max, cops are not good people. All of our best qualities get poured into the job and life gets the dregs. Don't ever mistake me for a decent guy. Nobody else does.'

'Look, just listen to me, will you?'

'All right. I'm listening.'

'A respectable job.'

'Ah. That lets me out then. I've not been respectable for a great many years. Probably never will be again.'

'I'm talking about a job in insurance.'

'Insurance. That's when people pay money for peace of mind. I wouldn't mind some of that myself. Only I doubt I could afford the premium.'

'Munich RE is the largest firm in Germany. A friend of mine, Philipp Dietrich, is head of their claims adjustment department. It so happens he's looking for a new claims investigator. An adjuster. And it strikes me you'd be very good at that.'

'It's true I know plenty about risks – I've been taking them all my life – but I know nothing about insurance, except that I don't have any.'

'"Claims adjuster" is just a polite way of describing someone who's paid to find out if people are lying. Correct me if I'm wrong, but isn't that what you used to do at the Alex? You were a seeker after the truth, were you not? You were good at it, too, if memory serves.'

'Best leave those memories alone. If you don't mind. They belonged to a man with a different name.'

'The splash around the Alex was that for a while you were the best detective in the Murder Commission. An expert.'

'I certainly saw a lot of murders. But take my advice, if you're looking for truth, don't ask an expert on anything. What you'll get is an opinion, which is something very different. Besides, cops and detectives aren't experts, Max, they're gamblers. They deal in probabilities, just like that French fellow Pascal. This guy is probably guilty and this guy is probably innocent, and then we leave it to you lawyers. The only people who will always say they're telling you the truth are priests and witnesses in court, which gives you a pretty good idea of what truth is worth.'

'Working for MRE has more of a future than working in a mortuary, I'd have thought.'

'I'm not so sure about that, Max. We're all going to end up there sooner or later.'

'I'm serious. Look, give me a few days to speak to Dietrich about you. And let me stake you to a new suit. Yes, why not? For an interview. It's the least I can do after what you've done for me. Tell me that you'll consider this. And give me an answer in the morning. But don't leave it any longer than that. Like the saying goes, the morning has gold in its mouth.'

'All right, all right. Just as long as you stop being so damned grateful to me. Kindness might seem like the golden chain that holds society together but it breaks me up. I can't take it. Not anymore. I know just where I am when people are cruel or indifferent. That never disappoints. But for Christ's sake don't be kind to me. Not without a parachute.'

CHAPTER 10

A short walk from the English Garden, Munich RE was headquartered on Königinstrasse, close by the German Automobile
Club, in an ochre-coloured four-storey building of some antiquity that was the size and shape of a small university, with an
Ionic colonnade and lots of trompe l'oeil stucco. The rusticated
wooden doors and tall iron railings looked like an insurance
man's dream with all security risks covered: a Gypsy parliament couldn't have broken into the place. One of the two
wings at either side of a paved courtyard was being renovated
and several gardeners were sweeping the snow away from
the main door, probably in case anyone slipped on it and fell
and made a claim. Most of the cars parked out front were
new Mercedes-Benzes or BMWs, without so much as a scratch
on any of them. Clearly there were some very careful drivers
in that part of Munich, unlike the rest of the city, and all of
them insured. If you'd told me the building was the police
headquarters or the central criminal court or an archbishop's
palace I'd have believed you; and from the ritzy look of the

place I concluded that it had been a while since they'd paid out on a suspect policy.

I went along to the side entrance on Thiemstrasse. Above another robust-looking door was the stone head of a woman badly scarred by flying shrapnel, like many others in Munich. Inside the door was a reception area where tradesmen were welcome and that was almost true; it was staffed by two women who were just as stone-faced as the one outside. Behind them were two fire extinguishers, a bucket of sand, a fire hose, and a substantial fire alarm. Just being in that building felt as if it was going to add at least a year to my life.

Herr Dietrich came down and fetched me up to his second-floor office himself, which was decent of him. He was tall and substantially overweight and like everyone else in there – me included, thanks to Max Merten – he wore a granite-grey suit that, I soon learned, reflected his attitude to insurance claimants. He had very large ears and walked in a neat, girlish way, with his wrists pointed at the ground as if balancing on a tightrope or – and more likely – as if he'd been told to walk and not run in case his grey bulk caused an accident. In his modern office overlooking the extensive back gardens, he offered me a seat and then served me his entire worldview along with a cup of good coffee and a glass of water on a little steel tray.

'Insurance is all about statistics,' he said. 'And in this department, those statistics are, more often than not, little more than crime figures, on account of how a great many customers are crooks. Not that Herr Alzheimer likes me to come right out and say as much. Herr Alzheimer is the chairman of Munich RE and diplomatic, to say the least. It's bad business to mention all the crooks we insure. But my job is to call a spade a spade even when most people will argue that it's a heart or a diamond. They don't seem to realize that by putting in a false insurance claim they're committing a serious fraud. But that's what it is. And it happens every day. If I told you half of the outrageous lies that some of the most respectable citizens expect us to believe you'd say I was exaggerating.'

'No, not even if I thought so. You see, as it happens, I'm a bit of a cynic myself, Herr Dietrich.'

'Cynicism is a very respectable school of philosophy. For the ancient Greeks there wasn't anything shameful about saying you were a cynic. In my humble opinion there's nothing wrong with a good dose of cynicism, Herr Ganz, and you'll soon find out that Diogenes is the patron saint of the claims adjustment business. As long as my department continues to think that way then this remains a profitable company. But please don't think we're hard-hearted. We're not. We're actually performing a valuable public service. That's the way I look at it. By not paying out on fraudulent claims we keep premiums low for honest customers. But right now I'm short of good men with keen noses for dishonesty. I need a claims adjuster who can think the same way as I do.'

'I'm sure you've noticed my prominent ears, Herr Ganz,' said Dietrich. 'My nickname around this office is Dumbo. You know, like the little elephant in the Walt Disney cartoon? Most people think my ears are funny. And this is all right with me because, like that little elephant, these big ears are my fortune. They're why I'm running this department. Now I certainly can't fly, but I do have the advice of Timothy Q Mouse, who whispers things that only these big ears can hear. Ideas that go straight into my subconscious mind. You see, Timothy says when he thinks there's something wrong with a particular claim. Dr Merten tells me you were once a very good detective. In what is now East Berlin. Which is why you can't provide a written reference.'

'That's about the size of it, Herr Dietrich.'

'So it's fortunate that Dr Merten is prepared to vouch for you personally. In my opinion that makes you a very good risk. A very good risk indeed.'

'I'm grateful for his confidence in me.'

'Did you enjoy police work?'

'Most of the time.'

'Tell me about the part you didn't enjoy.'

'The hours. The money.'

'Not enough?'

'Not nearly enough for the hours. But I knew it would be like that when I started so I was prepared to live with that. For most of the time. Expecting a wife to live with all that was something else.'

'Would you call yourself a trusting sort of man, Herr Ganz?'

'Well, now, here's the thing about trust. There's nothing to it. Trusting people is simply a matter of ignoring your best instincts and all your experience and suspending disbelief. The fact is, the only way you can ever be sure if you can rely on someone or not is to go ahead and rely on them. But that doesn't always work out so well. People usually behave like people and let you down and that's that. Of course, if you know they're going to let you down then you won't be disappointed.'

He grinned and made a noise deep in his large belly I assumed was something like approval.

'Tell me, Herr Ganz, are you fit?'

'Sure,' I lied. 'Just don't ask me to dance around a streetlight with an umbrella.'

'Dangerous things,' he said. 'Every year almost a hundred people in West Germany are seriously injured as a result of someone who was careless with an umbrella.'

Suddenly I had a glimpse into the hazardous world he inhabited, in which everything a human being did came with its own inherent risk. It was like having a conversation with an atomic scientist: nothing was too small to be significant. 'Is that a fact?'

'No, it's a statistic,' he said. 'There's a difference. You can't always put a price on a fact. So. I have another question. Just how cynical are you, Herr Ganz?'

'I have twenty-five years' experience of living in a tub on the streets of Berlin. Is that what you mean?'

He smiled. 'Not quite. What I mean is, give me an example of *how* you think.'

'About what, for instance?'

'I don't know. Tell me something about politics. Modern Germany. The government. Anything at all.'

'You know it could just be that I'm a bit *too* cynical for your tastes, Herr Dietrich. With my mouth I could be talking myself out of a job here.'

'You can talk quite freely. It's *how* you think I'm interested in, not *what* you think.'

'All right. Try this on, sir. We live in a new era of international amnesia. Who we were and what we did? None of that matters now that we're on the side of truth, justice, and the American way of life. The only thing that's important in Germany today is that the Americans have a canary in the European mine so that they'll have enough time to get out if the Russians decide to come across the border. And we're it. Tweet, tweet.'

'You don't think the Amis will defend us?'

'After what we did? Would you?'

Herr Dietrich chuckled. 'You're the man for me, Herr Ganz. I like the way you think. Scepticism, yes. This is essential in the claims-adjustment bureau. Don't believe what you've been told to believe. Expect the unexpected. That's our motto. I pride myself on being an excellent judge of human nature. And it's my opinion that you're my sort of man, sir. When can you start work?'

'What's wrong with February first?'

'All right then. Now you're talking. But first I have to ask Herr Alzheimer to approve your appointment. He's the chairman of the board but he takes a special interest in my department, so he'll want to meet you himself. Is that agreeable to you, Herr Ganz? Are you prepared to endure a moment of scrutiny in Alois Alzheimer's office?'

I was on my best behaviour so I said it would be an honour and Dietrich must have believed me because he picked up the telephone and made a call. A few minutes later we were walking upstairs into a more rarefied atmosphere. Certainly the grey carpets were thicker. There was a lot of wood panelling on the walls, too, which, while nice, struck me as a potential fire hazard. I might even have pointed out the lack of a safety net in the stairwell; someone could easily have fallen over the banister from the fourth-floor landing, especially if someone hit him first, or waved a gun around. Calculating risks was already second nature to me.

According to Max Merten, Munich RE had insured all of the Nazi concentration camps against fire, theft, and other risks. They'd also been in business with the SS. I certainly wasn't about to look for any moral high ground where that was concerned. Besides, I actually believed what I'd told Dietrich about international amnesia. Nobody was losing any sleep about what Germany did in the war. Nobody but me, perhaps.

The chairman's office was an eyrie fit for some giant bird of prey and the small thin man who occupied the premises was no less keen-eyed than any mythical hawk or eagle. Alzheimer was a smooth, rich-looking Bavarian with a tailor-made grey suit, a light tan, dark hair, darker eyebrows, and a face as shrewd as an actuary's life table. If Josef Goebbels had stayed alive he might have looked like Alois Alzheimer. While Dietrich went about the task of recommending me, the chairman gave me an appraising sort of look as if he were calculating how long I had to live and what the premium on my policy ought to be. But even Pollyanna could have seen that I was a risk too far. In spite of that, the chairman of Munich RE approved my appointment. I was now a claims adjuster making twenty-five deutschmarks a week, plus bonuses. It wasn't a fortune but it paid a lot better than the mortuary; like my mother used to say, it's good to make ends meet but sometimes it's nice to have enough to tie a bow. And I owed it all to Max Merten. I walked out of the building feeling almost happy with myself. Insurance seemed no less obscure than what I'd been doing at the hospital and therefore every bit as appealing. More so, perhaps. Even the word 'insurance' seemed to underwrite a desirable element of safety. It was hard to imagine a disgruntled claimant putting a gun to my ear while he argued the finer points of the small print in his policy.

I was wrong about that.

CHAPTER 11

'Do you know where the Glyptothek is, Christof?'

'I know where it is,' I told Dietrich. 'I'm not sure what it is.'

'It's Munich's oldest public museum and the only one in the world solely dedicated to ancient sculpture. There was a break-in last night and I'd like you to go and see what's been stolen. Which is another way of me telling you to find out if they're going to make a claim. If they are – check them out for contributory negligence, that kind of thing. Something that might affect a payout. Did someone leave a door unlocked or a window open? You know.'

'I know.'

And I did. Before joining Berlin's Murder Commission I'd attended enough burglaries to feel confident and even quite nostalgic about investigating this for Munich RE.

It was about a thirty-minute walk southwest to the museum on the north side of Königsplatz; the Glyptothek had been badly damaged in 1943–44 and restoration was now almost complete but there was still scaffolding on the side of the west wing and

I wondered if this was where the break-in had occurred. Behind a portico of Ionic columns with two wings adorned with niches were the exhibition rooms deriving their light from a central court and, in a way, the place reminded me of the offices of Munich RE, which said a lot more about the insurance business than it did about the plastic arts, at least in Germany. The marble group on the pediment featured a one-armed Athena ordering around a bunch of workers who couldn't have looked more indifferent to her protection, which made me think they were already members of a trade union – and very probably English, since none of them seemed to be doing much. Outside the entrance was a police car; inside were a lot of Greek and Roman marble sculptures, most of them too big to steal or already too badly damaged to notice if they'd been damaged, so to speak. A uniformed cop asked me who I was and I gave him one of my new business cards, which seemed to satisfy him. They certainly satisfied me; it was several years since I'd had a business card and this one was as stiff as a starched wing collar.

The cop told me the break-in had taken place on the floor above and, noting an alarm bell as big as a dinner gong and a ladder under the stairs, I followed the sound of voices as I climbed to a suite of offices on the second floor of the west wing. A detective was inspecting a cracked window that looked as if it had been forced open, while another was listening to a man with glasses and a chin beard, whom I took to be someone from the museum.

'It's very odd,' said the man from the museum, 'but as far as I can see almost nothing was taken. Just a few very small pieces, I think. When I think of all the treasures they could have stolen, or vandalized, my blood runs cold. The Rondanini Medusa or the Barberini Faun, for example. Not that it would be easy to move such a thing as our treasured Faun. It weighs several hundred kilograms.'

'Was anything damaged?' asked the detective.

'Only the desk in my office. Someone forced it open and had a good rake around in the drawers.'

'Probably kids,' said the detective, 'looking for some easy cash.'

It was about now that they both noticed me and I stepped forward with my business card and introduced myself. The detective was an inspector called Seehofer and the Fritz from the museum was Dr Schmidt, the deputy assistant director.

'It looks as if you've had a wasted journey, Herr Ganz,' said Seehofer. 'It seems that nothing has been recently damaged or taken.'

I wasn't convinced about that. 'Is that where they got in? These kids.'

'Yes, it looks as if they climbed up the scaffolding.'

I walked over to the window. 'Mind if I take a look?' I asked the detective inspector.

'Be my guest.'

I put my head out the window. There were fresh-looking footprints on some planks stacked nearby. They might have been a builder's footprints but I'd already seen a similar footprint on the carpet by the office door. A big fellow by the look of it and not kids at all, I thought. But I didn't contradict the detective inspector. I decided it was best to keep on the right side of him for now.

'Do you get many visitors in this museum?' I asked Dr Schmidt.

'It's February,' he said. 'Things are always a bit quiet in February.'

'What about the alarm?' I asked. 'Why didn't it go off?'

'What alarm?' asked Seehofer. 'There's an alarm?'

'I don't know,' said Dr Schmidt, as if he'd only just thought of it, and clearly he hadn't mentioned it to the detective inspector, who looked slightly irritated to discover the existence of such a thing now.

'If you could show me where the bell is, sir?' said Seehofer, a little too late to fill any insurance investigator's heart with confidence.

We went back downstairs, crossed the hall, and looked up at the bell that was mounted on the wall about a metre above our heads. From where we were standing it wasn't going to reveal very much and after a while I felt obliged to move things along a bit and fetched the ladder from under the stairs.

'I should be doing that, you know,' said Seehofer as I mounted the ladder, which, now that I was working for an insurance company, felt a bit less than safe on the polished marble floor.

I nodded and came back down without a word, happy not to take the risk. I wasn't about to get paid my twenty-five marks a week if I fell off a ladder.

Seehofer went up the ladder, looked down precariously several times, and finally managed to reach eye level with the bell, where his powers as a detective really started to kick in. 'That explains it,' he said. 'There's a piece of folded card between the bell and the clapper.'

'Then don't for Christ's sake pull it out,' I said.

'What's that?' he asked, and pulled it out. The bell began to ring, very loudly, almost causing Seehofer to fall off the ladder. Losing his nerve for the height he was at, he came quickly down again.

'Can you turn it off, sir?' I shouted at Dr Schmidt.

'I'm not sure I know how,' he admitted.

'Who does?'

'The security guard.'

'Where's he?'

'Er, I fired him when I discovered the break-in. I imagine he's gone home.'

Since none of us could now hear ourselves think, let alone speak, I felt obliged to take the piece of card from Seehofer's nervous fingers, go back up the ladder myself, and replace it between clapper and bell, but not before unfolding it to reveal that it was actually an empty packet of Lucky Strike cigarettes.

I came back down and said, 'Why is this ladder here?'

'It was up all day yesterday,' said Schmidt. 'One of the builders was using it to replace the lightbulbs in the ceiling fixtures.'

'So it might have been left unattended for some length of time.'

'Yes.'

'Then my guess is that whoever broke in here last night came into the museum as a visitor yesterday and, seeing an opportunity, went up the ladder and disabled the alarm with that empty cigarette packet.'

Seehofer murmured, 'Lucky Strike. But not for some,' which hardly endeared him to Dr Schmidt, whose sense of humour was understandably absent that morning.

'It looks very opportunistic,' I said. 'Like our man saw his chance to disable the alarm on the spur of the moment and used the first object that came to hand.'

'Which makes it all the more surprising that nothing was stolen,' said Schmidt. 'I mean, this was planned. I can't see kids going to that amount of trouble. Or with that amount of fore-sight. Can you?'

'Could I see inside those desk drawers?' I asked him. 'If you don't mind, sir.'

'Certainly, but there's nothing to see. Just some museum stationery and some guidebooks. Perhaps a few very small artefacts that were kept in a desk drawer. I'm not sure exactly. It's not my desk. It's the assistant director's.'

'Maybe we could ask him what's missing, if anything.'

'I'm afraid not. He's been ill for some time now. In fact, I doubt he'll be coming back at all.'

'I see.'

We went back across the hall, which was when we caught a glimpse of a large marble statue in a Pantheon of a room by itself, and if this caught our eye it was not because it had been damaged but because of what it was: a life-sized statue of a Roman faun or Greek satyr, legs akimbo – one of them at a right angle to the rock he was seated upon – who looked like he was suffering after a late night in the Hofbräuhaus. The indecorous statue was extremely well rendered and left nothing to the imagination.

'Christ,' said Seehofer. 'For a moment I thought he was the real thing. It's very – very realistic, isn't it?'

'That's the Barberini Faun I was telling you about,' said Schmidt. 'Greek. Possibly restored by Bernini after being badly damaged during an attack by the Goths almost a thousand years earlier.'

'It seems that history is always repeating itself,' I said, momentarily picturing those previous Germans in some desperate fight to the death.

Back in the office I took a look inside the desk. 'Anything stolen from in here?' I asked. 'A cash box, perhaps.'

'No, not so much as a ticket roll.'

'Then why do you keep it locked?'

'Habit. Sometimes I leave my own valuables in there. A gold pen. A nice cigarette lighter. My wallet. But not on this occasion. Not when I go home. Really. It's most extraordinary. Everything looks just fine.'

I might have agreed with that but for something I'd seen on the desk that didn't look as if it belonged anywhere except in an ashtray. It was a half-chewed cigar projecting at a right angle from the edge of the desk like the leg of the Barberini Faun.

CHAPTER 12

What should I have done? Told Detective Inspector Seehofer that a cop I knew who'd murdered two people had broken into Munich's oldest museum and stolen – nothing? A cop he would probably know, too? So I said – nothing. A lot of the time nothing is the best thing to say. Especially in a new job when you're still trying to make an impression. An acquaintance with murderers and crooked policemen doesn't inspire the confidence of any insurance company. All the same I did wonder what Detective Schramma had been up to. Of course, it might have been someone else who was the true culprit. But deep in my gut I knew it was he who'd broken into the Glyptothek, just as I'd known with absolute certainty that the Barberini Faun was a man. If I'd been a detective myself and not a claims adjuster I might have taken the cigar butt for analysis and possibly matched it to the one found in the dead general's house in Bogenhausen: the cops had found those bodies now and, according to the newspapers, they weren't saying very much, which was the same thing as saying they hadn't a clue who was responsible. Which suited me fine. The last thing I wanted was to see Schramma any time soon. Whatever he was up to now wasn't any of my business. And helping the cops wasn't part of my new job description.

In truth, however, the job was very boring and seemed to involve a lot of staring out the window. Most days I did a lot of that. Frankly I couldn't have felt more bored at Munich RE if I'd spent a couple of hours trying to guess the speed of the grass growing in the office back garden.

A week or two passed in this way. A pile of claims files started to accumulate on my desk. I was supposed to read these, looking out for anything suspicious, before passing them on to Dietrich with recommendations. Car fires that might have been arson, burst water pipes that had been deliberately sabotaged – we got a lot of those in the early spring – family heirlooms lost or damaged on purpose, bogus personal injuries, fraudulent loss-of-earnings claims. But there was nothing that raised so much as an eyebrow, really. After Dietrich's explanation of his opinion of some of our clients, I felt disappointed to say the least. I prayed I might find something suspicious just to alleviate the boredom. And then Ares, the Greek god of war, violence, bloodshed, and the insurance industry, answered my prayer with a juicy life claim.

Now this was how life insurance worked: an insurance company and the policy holder made a simple contract where, in exchange for an annual premium, the insurer promised to pay a designated beneficiary a sum of money upon the death or serious injury of the insured person. But after many years with Kripo in Berlin, the whole idea of one person profiting from another person's death just looked suspicious to me. It was ignorant of me, really – life insurance was one of the most profitable parts of Munich RE's business – but old habits die hard. I guess it's true what they say: detectives are simple people who persist in asking obvious or even stupid questions, but I figured that was what I was being paid for and, like I say, I was very bored. Besides, a substantial amount of money was involved.

The facts were that a thirty-nine-year-old man had fallen to his death under the train to Rosenheim at Holzkirchen Station. He'd had a three-star policy with MRE since July of the previous year for which he'd been paying four marks a month: death, personal injury, and loss of earnings. The widow's name was Ursula Dorpmüller, aged thirty-one, and she was our claimant; she lived in Nymphenburg, at Loristrasse number 11, top flat. The husband was Theo Dorpmüller; he'd owned a cabaret bar on Dachauerstrasse and the police said he'd fallen off the railway platform because he was drunk. In other words, they were perfectly satisfied that his death had been accidental; then again, they weren't facing a large insurance claim. There was a receipt in the dead man's coat pocket for a five-deutschmark dinner for two at the Walterspiel, which ruled out suicide in my mind. You don't normally eat and drink so well when you're planning to kill yourself. Frankly, that was the only real reason the cops thought he was drunk in the first place: on the bill were two bottles of champagne and a bottle of the best burgundy. Maybe he was drunk, I don't know, but if the policy paid out, Ursula Dorpmüller was set to make twenty thousand deutschmarks, which would have made her the original merry widow. Twenty thousand buys an awful lot of handkerchiefs and a whole ocean of deepest sympathy. Ursula worked as an air hostess for Trans World Airlines on Briennerstrasse and made an excellent salary. Before that she'd been a nurse. She was away in America, visiting her sick mother, when her husband, Theo, was killed. She played the church organ every Sunday at St. Benno's just up the street from her apartment and was on the committee of the Magnolia Ball – a charity event arranged by the German-American Women's Club. She also did a lot of work with another charity, which helped East German and Hungarian refugees, and she sounded like a thoroughly decent woman. I might never have raised her case with Dietrich if I hadn't remembered that I'd heard the name Dorpmüller before and recently, too; it took me several nagging days to remember from where. Finally it came to me. And when it did I went straight to see Dietrich.

'Timothy Q Mouse and I need to have a word in Dumbo's ears,' I said.

'What about?'

'The Dorpmüller claim,' I said. 'I don't like it.'

'She seems like a decent enough woman.'

'Yes, she does, doesn't she? And that's precisely what I don't like about her. She's a saint. She's Hildegard of Bingen, that's who she is, and let me tell you, saints don't normally collect twenty thousand deutschmarks free of income tax.'

'I take it you've got something more substantial for saying this than your gut feeling.'

'Before I got this job I was working at Schwabing Hospital, as you know.'

'I figured that's where you got your concern for your fellow man.'

'While I was there they brought in some people who had been seriously injured after an unexploded bomb went off.'

'I read about that. Not one of ours, fortunately. The policy, I mean. Not the bomb.'

'Actually, you're wrong about that. One of the injured was the Fritz who went under the train. Theo Dorpmüller.'

'Was he now? Badly injured?'

I pictured the man in the wheelchair I'd taken to the mortuary with Schramma, to identify Johann Bernbach.

'Not badly. A few burns. But certainly enough to have a week off work.'

'My ears just started to flap. And Timothy says, "Hello".'

'My point is this: he didn't make a claim for loss of earnings. The man has a three-star policy for death and personal injury and he didn't claim a penny. Why?'

'Timothy says, "Hello again," and, "Are you sure it was the same Fritz?"'

'I'm sure. I'm also sure that it means just one thing.'

'That he didn't know he had a three-star policy with Munich RE. He couldn't have done. Because if he'd known about it he would certainly have claimed for loss of earnings.'

'Exactly.'

'Good work, Christof.'

'I think you and Timothy need to check out Ursula Dorpmüller.'

'Not going to happen. Just look at this desk. That's the trouble with this business: too much paper. I'm chained to this office like that fellow with the liver and the eagle. I just don't have the time to check her out. But you, Diogenes, you could take her on. You've just made this case in my eyes, and now you need to run with it.'

'All right. But how should I handle it?'

'Like this. Make the woman believe we're going to pay off on the policy without any problem. That you're satisfied with her claim but that you just want to check out a few petty details. Get her to sign a few useless bits of paper. You need a copy of her passport. Her driving licence if she has one. Her birth certificate. Her marriage certificate. Keep stringing her along. Any moment now the cheque will be raised by our accounts department and the minute it is, you say you'll hand it to her in person. Really, it's just a formality. The twenty thousand is as good as in the bank. If it's taking so long it's because it's such a large amount. Be as nice to her as if she was your mother, assuming you had one. Butter her up like a Christmas goose. Make love to her if you have to. But in private I want you to treat her like she's Irma Grese. And see what's in Irma's kit bag.'

Irma Grese had been an SS guard hanged for war crimes by the British in 1945; by all accounts she'd been known as the 'beautiful blonde beast' of Belsen.

'I get the picture. It's an ugly one but I can see exactly how to play it. Good cop, bad cop, Jekyll and Hyde.'

'Maybe. But Timothy Q Mouse likes that Fritz in Shakespeare better. The one who plays Othello for an idiot.'

'Iago.'

'Yes, him. On her side, but not on her side. You gain her confidence and hope you can trip her up.'

'All right.' I frowned. 'If that's how you want it. You're the boss.'

'What's the matter? You don't look convinced by my strategy.'

'No, it's not that. I was just thinking.'

'About what?'

'For one thing, we're talking about premeditated murder here. And a conspiracy. Someone must have pushed Dorpmüller off that station platform. My guess is the person he had dinner with. A friend. A good friend, given the cost of dinner.'

'According to the police report, it was late at night, dark, with just Dorpmüller on that platform.'

'So someone already thinks they got away with it.'

'The widow?'

'The widow has an iron-clad alibi. She was in America when her husband was killed.'

'Yes, that's right. Which means she must have had an accomplice. A co-conspirator.'

'Exactly.'

'I can tell there's a lot more on your very dirty mind, Christof.'

'Look, Herr Dietrich, I've been here at Munich RE for five minutes. So I don't want to step on anyone's toes.'

'That's all right, they're probably insured.'

'Not against this kind of thing. No one is insured against the escape of something dangerous from another man's mouth.'

'Spit it out, whatever it is. You've done pretty well so far.'

'All right. How well do you know the salesman who sold Dorpmüller the policy?'

Dietrich flicked open the file and consulted the names on the insurance certificate.

'Friedrich Jauch,' he said. 'I've known him since he came here about two years ago. Smart fellow. Good-looking, too. Used to be an auctioneer at Karl & Faber before he joined MRE. As a matter of fact he applied for your job.'

'As a claims adjuster?'

'That's right. Only he's too smart for the sales department to let him go. Makes them too much money. So the top floor made me turn him down.'

'When was this?'

'A month or two ago.'

'Then long after he sold Dorpmüller his policy?'

'Yes, I suppose so.'

'Interesting.'

'You think he might be involved?'

'If Dorpmüller didn't know he had the policy, then who signed those application forms? That's what I'd like to know. I'm thinking it was Frau Dorpmüller. Maybe with the connivance of Friedrich Jauch.'

'And maybe more than that.'

'Could be. Could be someone pushed Dorpmüller off that railway platform. Could be that someone was Friedrich Jauch. Could be that's why he applied for a job in claims. Just so that he could scupper a possible investigation by this department. Think about that for a moment. It's a nice sweet scheme, investigating a claim on a policy that he'd sold himself.'

'You have got a dirty mind, haven't you. Now I come to think about it I was a little surprised he applied for the job in the first place. It's not just MRE who make money from Friedrich Jauch's salesmanship. It's him, too. What with commission, becoming a claims adjuster would have meant a substantial pay cut.'

'Did you ask him about that?'

'Yes. He said he was getting a little tired of shaking hands and smiling all day. That he'd been thinking a job in claims might suit him better.'

'How did he take it when you turned him down?'

'Just fine. They sweetened his deal as a salesman. Gave him a company car and another per centage point on his commission. He could hardly turn up his nose at that.'

'Not without it drawing attention to himself.'

'Of course, there is another possibility. It could be that Dorpmüller just didn't get around to claiming for his time off work. That he was too busy.'

'You don't believe that. And nor does Timothy Q Mouse.'

'But I *want* to believe it,' said Dietrich. 'There's a subtle difference. Friedrich Jauch is almost a friend of mine.'

'Look, it's not like Dorpmüller's premium would have gone up if he'd claimed. He was covered for that, too.'

'You noticed that, as well? You learn fast, Christof.'

'I've learned not to make allegations like this without evidence. And the evidence is all written in that file you're holding.

I've read it, cover to cover. And I'm still walking away with something bad on my shoe.'

'So what would you suggest?'

'It's the widow who'll be expecting the Irma Grese treatment. After all, she's the one in line for the big payday. Not Friedrich Jauch. So why don't I tail him for a couple of days? See what I come up with. If they are in this together he'll be keeping his head low for now. If they had any sense they'll have made an agreement not to contact each other until after the cheque is paid over. So all the trust is on his side. Especially after she has the money. Which means that maybe we can flush him out like a rabbit.' Even as I was talking to Dietrich I felt I was sharpening my blunted forensic skills like a razor's edge on a leather strop. 'Yes. That might work. Here's what I'd like you to consider.'

'I'm listening.'

'I'd like you to speak to the accounts department and have them raise a certified cheque for twenty thousand deutschmarks, payable to Ursula Dorpmüller.'

'After all you said? You disappoint me.'

'But here's the thing. Get them to date the check a week ago. And to let you have a photostat.'

'What are you planning?'

'To test the age-old theory that there's no honour among thieves and even less among murderers.'

CHAPTER 13

It probably took a German to invent the idea of an archduke. A German duke, that is, not satisfied with being an ordinary duke. It was much the same, I supposed, with German insurance men: According to Friedrich Jauch's job title he was the Chief Senior Sales Executive in Charge of New Business Development. As if to match his long title, he was very tall and straight and thin; in his pale grey suit and light green tie he most resembled an aspen tree. I suppose he was in his mid-thirties, although his boyishly styled fair hair and lisping, high-pitched voice made him appear even younger. Young enough and stupid enough to see murder as an easy solution to a common problem: money and the lack of it. We'd met a couple of times before but this time I engineered it so that I seemed to meet him accidentally, on the broad marble staircase leading down to the magnificent main hall in MRE, just a couple of days after I'd first shared my suspicions about him with Dietrich. He was on his way out somewhere, wearing a hunter-green loden coat and a hat with half a badger attached to the crown.

'Good afternoon, how are you?' I said brightly.

'Well, thanks. How are you settling in here at MRE? How's Dumbo?'

'Is he always so grumpy?'

'Always.'

'I think he believes he's all that stands between this company and financial ruin. By the way, maybe you'd like to know, we paid off on the Dorpmüller life claim.'

'You did? Right. Good. At least I think it's good. It was a lot of money, as I recall.'

'That's right. It is. I looked into all the facts but we couldn't see anything suspicious about it. Much to Dietrich's irritation. As you can probably imagine. He hates paying up on a claim of that size. Anyway, I delivered the cheque myself. As a matter of fact I have a photostat here in this file. Perhaps you'd like to see it. If it was payable to me I'd probably have it framed.'

I opened the file under my arm and showed him the copy of a cheque for twenty thousand deutschmarks made payable to Ursula Dorpmüller, hoping he would notice the date.

'Look at that,' I said. 'Twenty thousand deutschmarks. What I couldn't do with money like that.'

'It's a lot of money, all right.'

'I didn't want to trust it to the postal service, given how much it was. So I delivered it to the widow personally. Took it round to her apartment in Nymphenburg, just a few days ago. I'm still finding my feet a little around here and I'm still not exactly sure how the bureaucracy of insurance works, but anyway, I thought you'd like to know.' I closed the file and offered him my friendliest smile, as if he were one of my best friends at MRE.

'Right, right. Thanks a lot. I'm glad you did.'

'That's a very nice-looking woman, you know. Frau Dorpmüller, I mean.'

'I suppose she is.'

'I certainly thought so. Sometimes I wonder if good-looking women know the effect they have on men. Mostly I try not thinking about them at all. For my sake and theirs. The women close to me have not had the best of luck, one way or another. Leaving the female of the species alone has, for me, come to seem like a kind of valour.'

'Is that so? You surprise me. Perhaps you're more dangerous than you look.'

'I hope so.'

His smile was as thin as his parchment skin. Aspens are suited to colder climates and the wood is famously hard to burn but as I chatted Friedrich Jauch's pale neck started to turn bright red, as if his whole body were slowly catching fire. Clearly our conversation was having the effect I'd hoped for. Any doubts about his guilt were now gone. In my time as a cop in Berlin I'd interrogated some of the great Grand Master Liars, and Friedrich Jauch wasn't one of those. His guilt and greed for a share of the settlement made him more transparent to me than some bloodless deep-ocean fish. The fact was I'd only just returned from handing over the cheque to Ursula Dorpmüller at her apartment in Nymphenburg, but I wanted Jauch to suspect she might have double-crossed him and was holding out on whatever deal they'd previously made. Even if they'd agreed not to meet for a while he would probably insist on a meeting now, as a result of what I was telling him – had to, and he'd certainly assume she was lying when she told him that she'd only just received the cheque. As soon as that seed of doubt took root in his mind I was betting their conspiracy would start to unravel like the wool of a cheap sweater.

'Well, thanks for letting me know, Christof. I appreciate it. But I can't stand here chatting. I'd better get on. Clients to meet. Sales to make.'

'Nice talking to you,' I said, and carried on up the stairs to where I'd left my coat lying on a hand-carved fauteuil. I grabbed it, went back down to the hall, watched him turn right out of the colonnade onto Königinstrasse, and then followed.

It had been a while since I'd tailed a suspect, and I was looking forward to repeating the experience. Frankly the chase made me feel young again, like I was a junior detective back at the Alex when the commissars used to train us like bloodhounds. It was the best training in the world, as a matter of fact. I once followed a man for three days without him knowing I was there, and he didn't even have a letter M chalked on the back of his coat. Ideally I would have had a partner to follow Jauch effectively but then he was by now probably too much preoccupied with doubt and suspicions concerning his co-conspirator to be looking out for a tail. Besides, I had done this a thousand times, whereas for him this was probably his first time being followed by a trained detective. If I was right it would probably be the last time he was followed, too.

I shadowed him to the corner of Galeriestrasse, where he stepped into a telephone box and made a call. A few minutes later he came out, crossed onto Ludwigstrasse, and took a cab from the taxi rank. First rule if you think you're being tailed: never take a cab from the taxi rank unless it's the only one free. Here there were three, which meant it was easy for me to jump in another and follow him to wherever he was going. A few minutes later, in the south part of central Munich, his cab stopped and he got out on Sendlinger Tor Platz. But I stayed in my cab for a moment and watched. This area, extending from the Marienplatz beyond Rindermarkt, had been almost entirely destroyed during the war and was being rebuilt on new and uniformly modern lines; recent demolitions had laid bare the Löwenturm, one of the towers of the old town wall, and clear views were to be had across several empty spaces. It was easy to keep Jauch in sight. He couldn't have made it easier for me wearing a hat like that. It was a Gamsbart, a Tyrolean hat with a beard that was supposed to make the wearer look like a character. He might as well have been carrying a Nazi flag. After a few moments he ducked into a cinema and I followed.

At the ticket desk I smiled at the toucan-faced cashier behind the glass and said, 'That fellow who came in with the stupid hat – the Gamsbart. Where's he sitting? I want to make sure I'm not behind him.'

'Stalls,' she said.

I smiled again. 'Give me a seat in the front dress circle, will you? Just in case he keeps it on.'

'Film's just about to start,' she said, handing me my ticket before going back to her nails and her copy of *Film Revue*.

I went in and found my seat a few minutes before the lights went down, just in time to spot Friedrich Jauch, alone in the middle of the stalls, almost immediately beneath the front row of the dress circle where I'd positioned myself, not close enough to hear anything of what he might say, but close enough to notice if anyone sat anywhere near him. He put the hat on the seat next to him where it sat, quite noticeably, like a much-loved pet. I sat forward and, leaning my chin on the red velvet parapet, I found I was able to flick my eyes between the screen – the film was *Bhowani Junction* – and Friedrich Jauch without even moving my head. The cinema was more or less empty; a film about the British Empire was hardly a popular subject in Germany. I lit a cigarette and settled down to wait for the other show I'd come for.

I'd always enjoyed going to the cinema, even when Dr Goebbels was pretending to be Louis B Mayer. Being part of a cinema audience felt like something attractively infernal to me. There was the darkness and the smoke, of course; there was the grandiose architecture, the gold curtains and the cheap marble and the red velvet; there was the paradox of being anonymous among a group of people; and there was the drama taking place on the big screen, like watching the gods struggle and screw up badly. It was as if real life had been suspended or abruptly curtailed in some antechamber of purgatory. There was all of that and the fact that I'd always wanted to die in a cinema, for the simple reason that a movie would give me something better to think about than the actual business of breathing my last. Ava Gardner looking down on me with those emerald eyes of hers, not to mention the sight of her ample chest in a slightly too-tight British army shirt, was much better than some muttering po-faced priest every time.

It was only now I realized that it was Ava who Ursula Dorpmüller had reminded me of. Meeting her at the apartment in Nymphenburg it had been all too easy to imagine poor Friedrich Jauch falling in with this seductive siren's plans; the wonder was how she'd ended up being married to a slob like Theo Dorpmüller in the first place. Maybe she'd married the poor bastard because it's easier getting generous amounts of life insurance when you're still in your thirties. I felt sorry for him. I even felt sorry for Friedrich Jauch. I hoped he'd enjoyed her body because where he was probably going they didn't allow conjugal visits. West Germany might not have had the death penalty like France and Great Britain but from my own experience I knew that Landsberg Prison was no holiday camp.

After a while I tore my greedy eyes away from Ava's chest and noticed that the seat immediately behind Jauch was now occupied by a figure wearing a fur coat and a lilac head scarf. The two lovers were pretending not to talk but then Jauch turned around and took her hand, which clinched it in my eyes. These two couldn't have looked more guilty if they'd been Ava Gardner and Frank Sinatra. Now all I had to do was get to a telephone and call Dumbo Dietrich.

I went through the fire exit and ran downstairs and outside. If the cops were quick they could pick them both up, one after the other, when they left the movie theatre like two strangers in the night. It was true that most of the evidence against them was circumstantial, but an experienced detective would easily break them down under interrogation; the only question was which of them would crack first. I had my own theory about that. Jauch had carried out the murder, so he had the most to lose – and she would rat him out. She wouldn't be able to help it. That's just what women do.

On the west side of Sendlinger Tor Platz, in front of the Nussbaum Gardens, was the Matthäuskirche, a soulless Protestant church built in 1953 with a high red-brick square tower that looked like somewhere to train firemen or, more likely, kill them. If he'd been looking, God must have thought German architects had lost all sense of reason. Nearby was a row of phone booths with more character than the church, and from one of these I called Dumbo. There were a couple of East German refugees begging in front of the church and I tossed a couple of coins their way when I came out of the phone booth. It wasn't looking at refugees that upset me; it didn't. It was them looking back that bothered me: one German staring at another and seeming to say, *Why me and not you?* The worst thing was how so many of the younger ones still managed to look like the blond, blue-eyed master race.

I hurried back to the cinema, where I bought another ticket, this time for the stalls. I breathed a sigh of relief. The lovers were seated together now where I'd left them, quite unaware of the disaster that was about to turn their world upside down.

Ava fixed her big green eyes on me and shook her head as if

to say, *How could you betray them, you rotten bastard? They couldn't help it. That life insurance money was the only way they could make their love work.*

Or some such crap. But then Ava was trouble. Anyone could see that. That was probably the reason I loved her. And it was just as well for us both that I'd promised myself to leave Ava alone.

CHAPTER 14

Time passed, slowly, and then one freezing day near the middle of March, I got the summons to go upstairs for an audience with Mr Alois Alzheimer himself – the kind of summons for which a bottle of oxygen might almost have been required, such was the rarefied atmosphere that existed on the fourth floor. When I got there Dietrich was already seated in a brown leather Biedermeier bergère and, for a moment, until I saw the bottle of Canadian Club in Alzheimer's hand, I thought I was in some sort of trouble. That comes naturally to anyone who has as much to hide as I do.

'And here he is,' said Alzheimer, pouring me a large one in a crystal glass the size of a small goldfish bowl. 'The man who saved us twenty thousand deutschmarks.'

Everything in the office was of the finest quality. There was so much oak panelling on the walls it was like being a Cuban cigar in a humidor, while the grey carpet under my feet felt like a mattress protector. In the stone fireplace a log the size of a trench mortar was smoking quietly. Next to a little Meissen desk set and an impressive photograph of Alzheimer with Konrad Adenauer in a silver frame was an RCA Victor clock radio, and among the many leather-bound volumes on the bookshelf were a Slim Jim portable TV and an Argus slide projector; outside the door, Alzheimer's secretary's fingers were busy on an IBM electric typewriter that sounded like a light machine gun. Clearly he was a man who had very simple tastes, for whom the best was probably quite good enough.

I glanced over at Dietrich, who was already nursing a glass. 'They finally admitted it?'

'We just heard from the police. They both put their hands up to everything.'

'Took longer than I thought,' I said, raising my glass to the news. 'In my day we'd have had a confession within forty-eight hours. And I'm not talking about any strong-arm stuff, either. You keep someone awake for twenty-four hours with a Kaiser lamp in their face and pretty soon they'll forget even the most well-rehearsed story.'

'These days criminals have rights, unfortunately,' said Alzheimer.

'And don't forget, Frau Dorpmüller suffered a heart attack,' said Dietrich. 'The police weren't allowed to question her until she was out of the hospital.'

I pulled a face and laughed.

'You think she was putting it on?' asked Alzheimer.

'There are plenty of ways to feign a heart attack,' I said. 'Especially when you're an experienced nurse like she was. I think she was stalling for time until she'd got her story straight. Or until she found an opportunity to escape. Probably both. I'm surprised the cops still have her in custody.'

'That's right,' said Dietrich. 'She was a nurse, wasn't she?'

'As a matter of interest,' said Alzheimer, 'how would you pull something like that off? I mean it sounds like something we ought to be aware of in our industry, don't you think, Philipp?'

For a moment I hesitated to tell them the full story; it wasn't one of my proudest moments as a Berlin detective, but then there weren't many of us who'd lived through the war who didn't have something to hide. According to Max Merten, Alois Alzheimer and MRE's previous chairman, Kurt Schmitt, had been close friends of Hermann Göring and were both taken into custody by the Americans after the war; it was generally held that Schmitt had even been in the SS, so it really didn't seem the moment to be coy about my own record. I swallowed the whiskey and prepared to open the ancient Gunther family crypt just a crack.

'I was once obliged to arrest a doctor for being a Quaker,' I said. 'This would have been 1939, probably. He was a pacifist, you see. We had him in custody and then he had his heart attack, so-called. Very convincing he was, too. We were completely fooled and took him to hospital, where they confirmed our diagnosis. But he'd faked it. Mostly it's down to your breathing. You breathe fast deep breaths through the mouth, not the nose, and you hyperventilate and poison yourself with too much CO_2. Chances are you'll faint, like he did. When you come to, you pretend to mix up your words, complain of a pain in the arm and the throat, but crucially not the chest, and maybe affect the paralysis of an eyelid, or even your tongue. Once he was in hospital, a doctor friend got hold of some adrenaline and used it to keep up the deception. At least until the doctor's wife, who'd decided she didn't like him or the Quakers anymore, showed us a paper he'd written on the subject of feigning a heart attack in order to avoid military service, which he'd been handing out to students at Humboldt University, in Berlin. Luckily for him we weren't yet at war, which meant he narrowly escaped the death penalty, for which I admit I was relieved. As it was he got two years in prison. I wasn't a Nazi myself but I fought in the trenches during the first lot and so I've always strongly disagreed with pacifism. When it comes to war I tend to think in terms of "my country, right or wrong".'

Ignoring this mention of the Nazis – nobody ever mentioned the Nazis unless it was absolutely unavoidable, especially in Munich – Alzheimer said, 'Your candour is very much appreciated. And may I say, admired. I had no idea that such a thing was even possible. Did you, Philipp?'

Dietrich smiled. 'No, but I'm not surprised, sir. You know what a cynic I am. Still, people never cease to surprise me. The things they'll do to make a quick mark. I was, however, surprised about Friedrich Jauch. The man came to my home on more than one occasion. I must say I feel very let down by him.'

'So do we all, Philipp, so do we all. His had been a most promising career. They'll certainly miss him in sales.'

'To think I even offered him a job in claims. I thought I was a good judge of character.'

'But you are,' insisted Alzheimer. 'It was you who found Herr Ganz, was it not?'

'I suppose so.'

'Which is in itself a subject for congratulation, given that Herr Ganz here has taken to the insurance business with such obvious alacrity. One door closes and another opens. It's most opportune. You must certainly write something for the company magazine on this fake heart attack business. Don't you think so, Philipp?'

'Absolutely he must, sir.'

'I'm asking myself if there is anything else we might learn from him. What do you say, Herr Ganz? Can you teach two old dogs like Dietrich and me something new?'

I swallowed more of the whiskey, let Alzheimer refill my glass, and lit one of his cigarettes.

'I wouldn't presume to teach you your business, sir.'

'Presume away,' he said. 'No one learns without making mistakes.'

'You might care to consider having all new life policies witnessed by a third party. Ursula Dorpmüller was paying her husband's policy in cash, which was how he knew nothing about it, so you might also consider the use of direct debits in the future. To avoid the possibility of fraud.'

'Those are both good ideas,' said Alzheimer. 'I'm beginning to wonder why we didn't think to employ an ex-detective in the claims department before now. Are you a religious man, Herr Ganz?'

'Not really, no.'

'Good. Because that enables me to speak freely. As a businessman it always seems to me that every company needs its own Jesus. Not necessarily the man in charge but another man who gets things done, who works miracles, if you like. I'm beginning to think that you could be such a man, Herr Ganz. Wouldn't you say so, Philipp?'

'I would, sir.'

'I was just doing my job.'

But Alzheimer was not to be denied his opportunity to talk and to be generous. 'We should find some way of rewarding his vigilance, Philipp. But for him this company should be poorer to the tune of twenty thousand deutschmarks. Not to mention the fact that we would still be employing a murderer in sales.'

'I agree, sir. Perhaps a raise in pay.'

'By all means a raise in pay. Let's say another five marks a week. And since Friedrich Jauch is no longer employed by us, let us also reward Herr Ganz by giving him the man's company car. Plus expenses. How does that sound, Herr Ganz? I take it you can drive.'

'Yes, I can drive. And thank you. A car would be very welcome. Especially in this weather.'

We all looked at the window and at the snow that was once more blowing through the grey air outside; through the glass it looked like interference on a poorly tuned television set. But the thought of not having to walk or catch a tram to work again filled me and my shoe leather with joy.

'And tell me, do you speak any other languages?'

'Russian, French – fluently – English, and a bit of Spanish.'

'You don't speak Greek, I suppose.'

'No.'

'Pity. Because I do believe a working holiday in Greece might also be in order. As a reward of sorts, for work very well done. It will be an opportunity for you to stay in a nice hotel and in a more agreeable climate. Perhaps even to enjoy yourself for a couple of days. We were thinking you might perform a routine investigative service for MRE at the same time. You may or may not know that one of our more important business sectors is in marine insurance. However, Walther Neff – our leading average adjuster – has been taken ill. Like I say, it's a routine matter, more or less. A German vessel, the *Doris*, was lost off the coast of Greece after catching fire. We have a local man, Achilles Garlopis, who knows about ships and who will do most of the actual donkeywork, of course. And Dietrich will tell you what else has to be done, in detail. But we do urgently need someone to go down there to check out a few things – such as if the owner has appointed his own general average adjuster, if we're looking at an actual total loss or a constructive total loss – to ensure that everything proceeds smoothly and according to our own guidelines – and to authorize any expenditure, of course, pending a final settlement. Someone trustworthy. *Someone German.*'

'Sir, the one thing I know about ships is that it only takes a small leak to sink a large one. After the *Titanic* and the *Gustloff*, I'm amazed that anyone will insure them at all.'

'That's why the marine insurance business makes so much money. The larger the risk, the bigger the premium. Besides, it's not ships that are giving us any cause for concern here, Herr Ganz, it's the Greeks themselves. The plain fact of the matter is that when it comes to matters involving money – our money – the Greeks are not to be relied upon. These goat bangers are probably the most profligate race in Europe. With them, lying and dishonesty are ingrained habits. When Odysseus finally returns to Ithaca, so accustomed is he to lying that he lies to his own wife, Penelope, he lies to his elderly father, he even lies to the goddess Athena. And she herself is no less glibly tongued. They simply can't help it. The possibilities for fraud are endless. But with a man with a keen eye such as yourself, MRE stands a good chance of adjusting this claim to our satisfaction.'

He refilled my glass with Canadian Club, only this time not as much, as if he'd already judiciously calculated my limit, which was more than I'd ever done myself; still, I thought it was nice to know he was looking out for my welfare. But later on, to celebrate my promotion, I bought a whole bottle of the stuff to celebrate and found out exactly why this whiskey was called Canadian Club.

'These are interesting times,' said Alzheimer, sitting on the edge of his desk in a way that made me think I was expected to listen. 'MRE is expanding into Europe thanks to this new treaty Adenauer and Hallstein are about to sign in Rome in a few weeks' time. It will result in the progressive reduction of customs duties throughout a new economic trading area comprising Belgium, Luxembourg, the Netherlands, West Germany, and France – so I think your French will be useful. Of course, the French think they are to become the dominant force in Europe but, as time will prove, their ridiculous attempts to maintain their ragged colonies in Algeria and Indochina will be a great disadvantage to them economically. This will leave modern Germany very much in the driving seat. Again. And all of this done without an army this time. Just some new European laws. Which will be a nice change, don't you think? And very much cheaper for all concerned.'

I could raise my glass to that, just about. I supposed the treaty of wherever it was could be seen as a declaration of good intentions: Germany would try its best to be nice to everyone and, in the interests of making money, everyone else would try their best to forget what Germany had done during the war. Bureaucracy and trade were to be my country's new method of conquering Europe, and lawyers and civil servants were to be its foot soldiers. But if Konrad Adenauer was anything to go by, it was really a coup d'état by a group of politicians who did not believe in democracy, and we were being guided toward a Soviet system of Europe without anyone understanding what was planned. Hitler could certainly have taken a lesson from the Old Man. It was not the men with guns who were going to rule the world but businessmen like Alois Alzheimer and Philipp Dietrich with their slide rules and actuarial tables, and thick books full of obscure new laws in three different languages.

Of course, what Alzheimer had said about the Greeks was unforgivable; I suppose his only excuse was – as I was about to discover for myself – that it was also true.

CHAPTER 15

From Frankfurt I flew on a DC-6B to Hellenikon Airport in Athens. Including a refuelling stop it was a nine-and-a-half-hour journey. It wasn't hot in Athens, not in March, but it was a lot warmer than Munich. I was met inside the airport building by a fat man carrying a sign for MUNICH RE. He had a drooping moustache and was wearing a well-rendered bow tie that might have looked smart but for the fact that it was green and, even worse, matched his tweed suit – and, very slightly, his teeth – and the overall impression, apart from the one that the suit had been made by a trainee taxidermist, was of a jovial Irishman in some sentimental John Ford film. It was an impression enhanced by the enamel shamrock in his lapel which, he later explained, was due to a lifelong enthusiasm for a local football team called Panathinaikos.

'Did you have a good flight, sir?' asked Achilles Garlopis, MRE's man in Athens.

'We didn't crash, if that's what you mean. After nine hours on a plane I feel like Amy Johnson.'

'It's not a civilized way to travel,' he said, taking my bag politely. 'Nor a natural one. Ships and trains – these are kinder to human beings, gentler. You won't find a Greek who disagrees with you, Herr Ganz. After all it was a Greek, Icarus, who first dared to conquer the skies and look what happened to him.'

Garlopis managed to make Icarus sound like one of the Wright brothers but there was nothing wrong with his German; it was near perfect.

'The gods dislike aviators as they dislike all blasphemy. Myself, I never disrespect the gods. I am a very pagan sort of man, sir.' He chuckled. 'I would sacrifice chickens if the priests did not object to it. For a religion based on bloodshed, Christianity is most peculiar in its attitude to animal sacrifice.'

'It doesn't keep me awake at night,' I admitted, hardly taking him seriously, yet. 'Not much does.'

'How is Mr Neff, sir? He had a heart attack, did he not?'

'You know Mr Neff?'

'Yes. He's been here on several occasions. We're old friends, Walther and I.'

'I believe he's recuperating. But for a while back there he wasn't so good.'

Garlopis crossed himself in the Greek Orthodox way and then kissed his thumb. 'I shall pray for him. Send him my regards the next time you see him.'

He walked me out of the airport to his car, a powder-blue Oldsmobile with an accent stripe and whitewall tyres. He noted my surprise at seeing the big American car as he placed my bag in the bedroom-sized boot.

'It's not my car, sir. I borrowed it from my cousin Poulios who works at Lefteris Makrinos car hire, on Tziraion Street. He will give you a very good rate on any automobile you like. Including this one.'

'I'd prefer something a little less noticeable. Like a Sherman tank, perhaps.'

'Of course, sir. I perfectly understand. But this was all he could spare me today while my own car is in the workshop. Rest assured, your hotel is much more discreet. The Mega, on Constitution Square. Not as good as the Grande Bretagne, but not nearly as expensive. Many of the rooms, including yours, have their own baths and showers. I have another cousin who works there who has made sure you have the best room and the best rate. You'll be living on velvet. It's also very convenient for the post office on Nikis Street, from where you may send telegrams to head office at ten drachmas a word, at all hours and on all days of the week. For anything else, you may contact me at my office on Stadiou Street, number 50, next to the Orpheus Cinema.'

Garlopis handed me a business card and eased his bulk behind the white steering wheel of the Oldsmobile while I lit a cigarette and climbed in beside him, settling onto the matching white leather upholstery. On the blue dashboard was a little silver-framed icon and a small plaster statuette of an owl.

'What's with the towels on the backseat?'

'Habit, I'm afraid. It gets very hot in the summer, sir. And I do sweat a lot. So it protects the leather.'

He started the engine and smiled. 'The new Rocket engine. Alert, eager, power when you need it, thrifty economy when you want it. I must confess to an absurd and rather boyish enthusiasm for this car. Ever since I was young I have loved all things American. What a country that must be to make such cars. Driving this I find it all too easy to imagine myself on a space rocket to the moon.'

'You wouldn't like the food,' I said, observing his girth. 'There isn't any.'

Garlopis put the car in gear and we moved off smoothly. After a while he pressed a switch to operate the car's electric windows.

'Electric windows. Isn't it wonderful? You look at a car like this and you think of America and the future. When Americans talk about the American dream it's not a dream about the past. That's the difference between the American dream and a British one, or a French one, or a Greek one. Ours is a dream that's always about the past; and theirs is a dream that's always about the future. A better tomorrow. Not only that but I sincerely believe they're prepared to guarantee that future for us all, by force of arms. Without NATO we'd all be playing balalaikas.'

'Yes, that's probably true.'

'I can assure you there are lots of American cars in Athens, sir. They're not quite as noticeable as you think.'

'All the same I'd still like you to change it.'

'Certainly, sir.'

Garlopis was silent for a moment while he played with the electric windows some more. But after a while he changed the subject.

'Since you mentioned food,' he said, over the noise of the Rocket engine, 'the best restaurant in all of Athens is Floca's, on Venizelos Street, where they will give you a very good price if you say you are a friend of mine. You should expect to pay a maximum of twenty-five drachmas for a good lunch.'

'Another cousin of yours?'

'My brother, sir. A most talented man in the kitchen, if unlucky in life. He has a gorgon of a wife who would terrify the Colossus of Rhodes. But do not mistake Floca's for Adam's restaurant, which is next door. That is not a good restaurant. It pains me to say so because I have a cousin who works there also and the stories he tells me would make your hair curl with horror.'

Smiling, I pushed my elbow out of the open window and tried to relax a little after the flight, although this was difficult, given the Greek's erratic driving. I hoped we wouldn't have need of the icon's protection.

'You speak excellent German, Herr Garlopis.'

'My father was German, sir. From Berlin. Garlopis is my mother's maiden name. My father came to Greece as the foreign correspondent for a German newspaper, married my mother, and stayed, at least for a while. His name was Göring, which we changed during the war for obvious reasons. My mother had eight aunts and uncles and all of those cousins of mine are on her side. You are from Germany, yes?'

'Yes. From Berlin, originally.'

'And do you travel very much, Herr Ganz?'

I thought of my recent trips to Italy, Argentina, Cuba, and the South of France, to say nothing of the eighteen months I'd spent in a Soviet POW camp, and then shook my head. 'Hardly ever.'

'I'm not a well-travelled man, myself. I've been to head office a couple of times. And once I went to Salzburg. But there was something about Salzburg I didn't like.'

'Oh? What was that?'

'Austrians, mainly. A cold, disagreeable people, I thought. Hitler was an Austrian, was he not?'

'We keep mentioning that in Germany, in the hope people will remember. Austrians most all, of course. But they don't seem to.'

'I wonder why,' said Garlopis in the voice of one who didn't wonder at all. 'If I may make a polite enquiry, sir? What other languages do you speak besides German?'

I told him. 'Why?'

'You'll forgive me for saying so, sir, but finding yourself alone and in need of help it would be best in all circumstances if you were to speak English, sir. Or even French. It's not that Germans are disliked, sir. Or that the English are popular. Far from it. It's just that so soon after the war there are some who are jealous of West Germany's economic miracle, sir. Who feel that our own economy has performed, shall we say, less than miraculously, sir. Indeed, that it has stagnated. Myself, I believe that Germany's success is good for all of Europe, including Greece, no matter how unjust it might seem to those of us who suffered so horribly under the thoughtless brutality of the Nazis. Only a strong Germany can help to guarantee that Europe doesn't become communist, as Greece almost did after the war. But please speak English whenever possible, sir. And exercise a degree of caution before admitting your true origins. To say you are Swiss would always be better than to say you are just German. After the terrible civil war we fought, Athens is not without hazards, sir, even for a Greek.'

'So I see.' I touched the large blue eye that was hanging on the end of the chain attached to the car key. 'That's for the evil eye, isn't it?'

'It is indeed, sir. I don't think one can be too careful in the insurance business, do you? I'm a great believer in minimizing all manner of risk.'

'And the owl?'

He looked sheepish. 'The goddess Athena is often accompanied by an owl, which traditionally symbolizes knowledge and wisdom. You can't have too much of that, can you? I have a silver coin in my pocket, a tetradrachm, that also depicts an owl, for good luck.'

'How about the icon?'

'Saint George, sir. Been looking after me and, for that matter, this country, since I was born.'

I flicked my cigarette away. 'So tell me about this ship that was lost. The *Doris*. I guess they weren't so well prepared for disaster as you seem to be, Mr Garlopis.'

'To business. I like that. If I may say so, this is commendably German of you. Forgive me for talking so much. That is very Greek of me. From my mother's side.'

'Don't apologize. I like to talk myself. That's from my human side. But right now I just want to talk about the ship. After all, it's the only reason I'm here.'

'As I think you know, the ship is German and so is the owner. The insured value was thirty-five thousand deutschmarks, which is two hundred and fifty thousand drachmas. Siegfried Witzel is a German diving expert who makes underwater films. One of these, *The Philosopher's Seal*, was about Mediterranean monk seals, first described by Aristotle, and for some reason it won a prize at the Cannes Film Festival. Don't ask me why. All I know about monk seals is that they're very rare. The *Doris* sank on an expedition looking for ancient Greek artefacts: statues, pottery, that kind of thing. Which are much less rare, at least in Greece. The ship was en route from Piraeus – the main port of Athens – to the island of Hydra when it caught fire off the coast of Dokos, which is another island near there. The small crew abandoned ship and made for the mainland in the life raft. The Hellenic Coast Guard in Piraeus is now investigating the loss, as is the Mercantile Marine Ministry here in Athens, but being Greek both of these bodies are slow and bureaucratic, not to say sclerotic. And to be quite frank with you, sir, their enthusiasm for investigating the loss of any German ship is unfortunately small. Which is perhaps not surprising, given that in the war Greece lost a total of 429 ships, most of them sunk by the Germans. But even at the best of times – and speaking of it as a purely investigative body – the Hellenic Coast Guard is slow; it's still looking into the loss of the *Lycia*, a British ship that ran aground off Katakolon last February, and also of the *Irene*, a Greek coaster that foundered southeast of Crete last September.'

'So we're on our own, investigatively speaking.'

'That's about the size of it, unfortunately.'

'Tell me about this fellow Witzel.'

'I think it's possible the gods sank his ship because they were angry with him, but I doubt they could have been more angry than he has been with me. In short, he is a man with a most violent temper. Rude, disagreeable, and impatient. He makes Achilles seem like a model of good grace.'

'Why do you say so?'

'I've tried to explain to him that nothing was going to happen until someone arrived from head office to adjust his claim against MRE but he's not much disposed to listen to me, a mere Greek. Since then I've been threatened with violence on more than one occasion.'

'By Witzel?'

'By Witzel. He's very tough, very fit, you see. As you might expect from someone who is a professional diver. He doesn't seem to suffer fools gladly, and Greek fools like me, not at all. Frankly, I'm glad you're here so you can deal with him. One German with another. Poseidon himself would find this man frightening. Not least because he carries a gun.'

'Oh?'

'And a switchblade.'

'Interesting. What kind of gun?'

'An automatic pistol. In a leather shoulder holster. Many Greeks do carry weapons, of course. Because of the Nazis. And before them, the Ottoman Turks. On Crete, it's quite common for men to carry handguns. But then Cretans are a law to themselves.'

'But Witzel is a German, you said. Not Greek.'

'Although not as noticeably as you, sir. He speaks our language fluently. As you might expect of someone who was living here before the war.'

'In my own experience carrying a gun tends to calm a man

down. You can't afford to lose your temper more than once when you have a Bismarck in your pocket. The police don't like it.'

'Well, I thought I should mention it.'

'I'm glad you did. I'll certainly remember that if I try to adjust his claim. What else can you tell me about him?'

'It's true that the man has lost his home as well as his livelihood, since he also claims to have been living on the ship. So this might account for his behaviour. However, I have also found him inclined to be evasive as well as angry. For example: in my opinion he has failed to supply an adequate explanation for how the fire on board the *Doris* might have occurred. I say *might have* occurred since I only ever asked him to speculate on what *could* have happened, which did not seem unreasonable, given the size of his claim. After all, one has to write something down on the loss report. Also, about the company that chartered the *Doris* to look for antiquities, he has been less than forthcoming.'

'Is it possible that they were looking for these antiquities illegally?'

'On the contrary. All of the permissions were obtained at the highest level. And I do mean the highest. The exploration licence was signed by Mr Karamanlis, no less.'

Konstantinos Karamanlis was the Greek prime minister.

'Mr Witzel seems to think that this trumps the need for all explanations. As if Karamanlis were Zeus himself.'

'Do you think his claim might be fraudulent? That he might have scuttled his own ship to get the money?'

'That's not for me to say, sir. I'm not a loss adjuster. Just a loss adjuster's humble agent.'

'Perhaps, but when he sent me down here, Alois Alzheimer, MRE's chairman, described you as our local shipping expert.' This was a lie, of course. But a little flattery couldn't do any harm.

'He did? Mr Alzheimer said that?'

'Yes.'

'That is most gratifying, sir. To think that a man like Mr Alzheimer knows a man like me even exists. Yes, that is most gratifying.'

'I'm new at this game, Mr Garlopis. I'm afraid I know nothing about ships. And even less about Greece. I'm here to cover for Mr Neff. So your own opinions about what happened to the *Doris* are more important than you might think. You tell me to authorize payment and I'll recommend we authorize payment. But if you tell me the case has only got one shoe we'll take a walk around and look for the other. Thirty-five thousand is a lot of money. Take it from me, people have killed for a lot less.'

'It's kind of you to say so, Mr Ganz. And I appreciate your honesty, sir.' Mr Garlopis chuckled. 'There are logical explanations for almost everything, of course. I accept that. But for several years I was a merchant seaman myself and I can tell you that the men who go to sea, especially here in Greece, hold many irrational beliefs, to put it mildly. Our own explanations for everything that happens here in Greece might not meet with much sympathy among our masters in Munich.'

'Try me.'

'You'll only laugh, sir, and think me a very credulous fool.'

'No, not even if I thought so.'

Garlopis talked some more and I shortly formed the impression he was one of the most superstitious men I'd ever encountered, but no less likeable for that. To my surprise he believed supernatural beings continued to inhabit the country's mountains, ancient ruins, and forests. The sea was no different, for he also believed in the Nereids – sea nymphs that did the will of Poseidon – and seemed more than willing to attribute all manner of disasters to their interference. This struck me as unusual in an insurance agent and I wondered how Mr Alzheimer would react if I sent him a telegram explaining that the *Doris* had been sunk by a sea nymph.

'Sometimes,' said Garlopis, 'that's as good an explanation as any. The waters around these islands are strange and treacherous. It's not every ship that disappears that can be properly accounted for. You'll forgive me, sir, if I suggest that it's a fault of you Germans to believe that absolutely everything has a logical explanation.'

'Sure, only it was the Greeks who invented logic, wasn't it?'

'Ah yes, sir, but if you'll forgive me again, it's you Germans who have taken logic to its most extreme. Dr Goebbels, for example, when he made a speech advocating the waging of total war – in 1943, was it not?

'Yes, I know, you'll tell me he was just echoing von Clausewitz. Nevertheless, it can be argued that it was this mentality that condemned Germany to a futile squandering of life on an unprecedented scale when the reality is – you should have surrendered.'

I certainly couldn't argue with that. For a superstitious man, Achilles Garlopis was also an educated one.

'In this case, however,' added Garlopis, 'I'm sure we'll find a better explanation for what happened to the *Doris*, one that will suit Mr Alzheimer and Mr Dietrich.'

'Let's hope so. Because I think the only monster Mr Alzheimer believes in is probably Mrs Alzheimer.'

'You've met her?'

'I saw a picture of her on his desk. And I think she was probably frozen for millions of years before he found her.'

Garlopis smiled. 'I've taken the liberty of asking Mr Witzel to come to the office at ten o'clock tomorrow. You can question him then and form your own conclusions. I'll come by the hotel at nine and walk you there. Will you require an early-morning call, sir?'

'I don't need an early-morning call, Mr Garlopis. I've got my bladder.'

CHAPTER 16

The Mega Hotel was in Constitution Square, named after the constitution the first Greek king, Otto, had been obliged to grant to the
leaders of a popular uprising in 1843. It was situated opposite the
Old Royal Palace, which now housed the Greek parliament, and the
Grande Bretagne Hotel, which was a lot nicer than the one I was
in. I took a walk around the tree-lined square after Garlopis had
left me, to stretch my legs, see a bit of Athens, and get a lungful
of the local carbon monoxide. The eastern side of the square was
higher than the western and was dominated by a set of marble
steps that led up to the parliament, as if you might have to make
some kind of effort getting to democracy. In front of this lemon-
coloured building a couple of soldiers called evzones were making
fools of themselves to the delight of a group of American tourists,
only they called it changing the guard. Dressed like Pierrots, they
made a very big thing out of not doing very much, regular as
clockwork. I guess it was no more ridiculous than anything you
could have seen performed by soldiers of the National People's
Army outside the New Guardhouse on Unter den Linden in what

was now East Berlin, but somehow like a lot of things in Greece, it was. Call me a xenophobe but there seemed to be something inherently comic about two very tall men each wearing a fez, a white kilt, and red leather clogs with black pompoms marking time and waving their legs in the air with an almost tantalizing uncertainty; indeed, it was almost as if these two were trying to send up the whole ceremony, which only seemed to make it all the more amusingly photogenic.

I bought some Luckys, a map, and a copy of *The Athens News* – the only English-language newspaper (there wasn't a German one) – and took these back to the bar at the Mega to have a drink and a smoke and to acquaint myself with what was happening in the ancient Greek capital. A lawyer in Glyfada had been murdered. There had been a spate of burglaries in Amaroussion. Some Greek cops from police headquarters had been arrested for taking bribes. The Hellenic Police Internal Affairs Division reported that ninety-six per cent of the population believed the Greek police were corrupt. And a German called Arthur Meissner was about to go on trial accused of war crimes. Apart from the relentlessly cheerful Greek music on some speakers above the bar, I felt quite at home.

Even more than I might have expected.

'How do you like those smokes?' said a voice speaking German.

'They're all right. I've been smoking them for so long I hardly notice, except when I have to smoke something else.'

'So you'd smoke something else if you liked them better?'

'There are a lot of things I might do if I liked them better,' I said. 'I just don't know what they are yet.'

The man at the opposite end of the bar was German, or perhaps Austrian, and in his mid-to-late forties. He was slim with
a thin hooked nose, a short moustache and a chin beard, a
high forehead, eyes with a strong hint of oyster, and, as far as I
could tell, he wasn't very tall. He was wearing a Shetland sport
jacket and whipcord trousers. His Adam's apple was the most
pronounced I'd ever seen and shifted around above his plaid-
gingham shirt collar like a ping pong ball in a shooting gallery.
His voice was a quiet nasal baritone with a lot of patience on the
edge. It sounded like the low growl of a house-trained leopard.

'I'm reading an English newspaper and spoke English to the
barman. So how did you mark me out as a German?'

'You're not a Tommy and you're not American, that much
is obvious from when you spoke. And the only way you'd be
smoking Luckys would be if you were a German living in the
American zone. Munich, probably. Frankfurt, maybe. The label
on the inside of your jacket says Hugo Boss, so I guess they've
finally been denazified. Good thing, too. That poor Fritz was just
a tailor. Trying to make a living and stay alive. You might as well
try to denazify the doormen at the Adlon.'

'You should have been a cop.'

He smiled. 'Not really. I was just kidding. As a matter of fact
I saw you checking in a while ago. Heard you speaking German
to the other fellow. The one with the flashy American car. And
but for the war I would have been a lot of things. Hungarian,
probably. I guess I'm lucky to be Austrian, otherwise I'd be
living under the damn communists and scratching my ass with
a hammer and a sickle. The name is Georg Fischer. I'm in the

tobacco business. And at the risk of sounding like a lousy commercial, here, friend, try one of these.'

He pushed a packet of cigarettes along the marble-topped bar.

'They're Greek, or Turkish, depending on how you look at these things.'

'Karelia. Sounds like they should come from the Baltic.'

'Fortunately they don't smoke that way. If there's one thing I hate, it's Russian smokes.' He blinked his lashless eyes slowly; they looked like smaller versions of his almost hairless skull.

'That's for sure.'

'Karelia is the oldest and largest tobacco company in Greece. Based in Kalamata, down south. But the tobacco comes from the Black Sea coast. Sokhoum. The leaves are almost like those in a cigar. Sweet on the tongue and cool on the throat.'

I lit one, liked it, and nodded my genuine appreciation. 'Life's full of surprises. The name's Christof Ganz. And thanks.'

'No, thank *you*. It's certainly nice to speak a bit of German again, Herr Ganz. Sometimes that's not such a good idea in this town. Not that you can blame the Greeks very much after the hell we inflicted on this damn country during the war. Hard to credit now. But I'm told that during the first year of the Nazi occupation there were children's bodies lying on the sidewalk in front of this hotel. Can you imagine it?'

'I'm trying not to. I try not to think about the war now if I can possibly avoid it. Besides, we've paid for it since, don't you think? Or at least half of us have paid. The eastern half. I think they're going to be paying for it for the rest of their lives.'

'Could be you're right.' He was staring straight ahead of him at a bar that contained so many bottles it looked like a cathedral organ. 'I get a bit homesick sometimes.'

'Sounds like you've been here a while.'

'My friend, I've been here so long I've started smashing the crockery when I'm in a good mood.'

'And when you're in a bad mood?'

'Who can be in a bad mood in a country like this? Maybe the Greeks are feckless. But in summer this is the best country in the world. And the women are very nice, too. Even the lookers.'

I pushed the pack back along the bar.

'Keep the pack,' he said. 'I've a suitcase full of them in my room.'

'You said you're Austrian?'

'From a village called Rohrbrunn, near the Styrian border in what used to be Hungary, so we used to call it Nádkút. But I lived in Berlin for a year or two. Before the war. So. What line of business are you in, Herr Ganz?'

'Insurance.'

'Selling it? Or paying it out?'

'Neither, I hope. I'm a claims adjuster. Buy you a drink?'

Fischer nodded at the barman. 'Calvert on the rocks.'

I ordered another gimlet.

'Insurance is a nice respectable German business,' said Fischer. 'We all need a business like that, where you can take a pause and draw breath, especially after everything that happened.'

He didn't say what but then he was Austrian so he didn't have to say it; I knew what he meant. Any German would have known.

'It's only when there's a pause that you can hear yourself think.'

'Nothing much ever happens in the insurance business. I like that. It's the only way you can get a handle on life.'

'I know exactly what you mean. Tobacco's a bit like that, too. Steady. Unspectacular. Unchanging. Harmless. Guilt-free. I mean, people are always going to smoke, right? My company is about to start exporting these cigarettes to Germany.'

'You just made a customer.'

'At least we are just as soon as the Greeks sign up for this new European Economic Community.'

'Any other tips? Besides not speaking German in Greece?'

He toasted me with the whiskey he'd ordered.

'Just one. Don't drink the tap water. They'll tell you it's safe. That it's made by the Americans. And it is – made by the Amis. Ulen & Monks; they own the Marathon Dam. But I'd stick to bottled if I were you. Unless you want to lose weight and fast.'

I toasted him back. He handed me his business card.

'Sounds like good advice.'

'If you get into trouble or you need my help, then call this number. We Germans have to stick together, right? What does the proverb say? Caught together, hanged together.'

CHAPTER 17

'What's the movie they're showing across the street?'

Garlopis came to the open window of his office on Stadiou and glanced down at the poster on the front of the Orpheus Cinema. He had fetched me from my hotel more than an hour earlier and now we were awaiting the arrival of Siegfried Witzel, our insurance claimant. He was late.

'*The Ogre of Athens*,' he said. 'Do you like going to the cinema, Herr Ganz?'

'Yes.'

'It's quite a popular film here in Greece. At least it is now. It's about a quiet little man who is mistaken for a murderer called Drakos. Enjoying this mistake, he rules over the underworld until the other crooks start to see their error.'

It sounded a lot like Hitler, but I shook my head. 'Not my kind of film. I prefer Westerns.'

'Yes, there's something about a Western that's pleasantly time-less.' He glanced at his wristwatch. 'Which would seem to be a concept with which Mr Witzel is also familiar. Where is he, I wonder?'

Outside the cinema a priest wearing a black surplice was cleaning his scooter; the whole city was plagued with them, like thousands of noisy, brightly coloured insects. I watched him polishing the red clamshell body of the scooter and winced as its distant relation came buzzing along the street, while out of the corner of my eye I could see Mr Garlopis feeling my struggle with the din of Athens and politely waiting to see if he should intervene on my behalf. When finally he did and closed the window, I almost breathed a sigh of relief.

'Athens is very loud after Munich,' I said.

'Yes,' he said. 'The gods are the friend of silence. Which is why they chose to live on mountaintops. And why rich men who wish to emulate them buy houses on hills, I suppose.'

On the walls were a large map of Greece and several photographs of the past and present Panathinaikos football team, and through the open door could be heard the sound of a secretary's fingers tickling the keys on a big typewriter.

'How long have you been working for MRE, Herr Garlopis?'

'Five or six years. During the war I was an interpreter and then after that I worked for my cousin's debt-collection agency. But that work is not without hazard. Bad debt is always a very sensitive subject.' He looked at his watch again and tutted loudly. 'Where is that man?'

'Does Herr Witzel have far to come?' I asked.

'I really don't know. He's been most evasive about his present address. He told me that since the boat was also his home he's been sleeping on the floors of various friends in the city. Although with his temper the idea that Herr Witzel has any friends at all seems wholly improbable. Would you like some Greek coffee, Herr Ganz?'

'No thanks. If I drink any more coffee I'll fly out this window. Has he got a lawyer?'

'He didn't mention one.'

'We'll need some sort of an address if we're going to pay out thirty-five thousand deutschmarks. His girlfriend's floor, Athens, won't satisfy our accounts department.'

'That's what I've been telling him, sir.'

'May I see the file on the ship?'

I came back to the desk and Garlopis handed me the details on the *Doris*. While I glanced over the contents, he summarized the vessel's specifications:

'The *Doris* was a two-masted schooner, thirty metres long, with a beam of eight and a half metres, and a maximum draft of 3.8 metres. She had a single six-hundred-horsepower diesel engine with a cruising speed of twelve knots. Built in 1929 as the *Carasso*, with five cabins, she was all wood in her construction, which probably explains why the fire took hold so fiercely.'

There was a single colour picture of a ship at sea with about eight sails; to someone like me who knew nothing about ships, it looked handsome enough, I suppose, and according to the file had been the subject of a recent refit. From what was written down I couldn't have said if the ship was seaworthy, but on a sea as smooth and blue as the one in the photograph she certainly looked that way.

'There's also a list of things kept on board that were lost that he's claiming for,' added Garlopis. 'Diving equipment, cameras, furniture, personal effects. More than twenty thousand drachmas' worth of stuff. Fortunately for him, he seems to have been quite scrupulous in keeping us up-to-date with receipts.'

A few minutes later we heard footsteps on the wooden stairs outside the office door and Garlopis nodded at me.

'That must be him now. Remember what I said, sir. About not provoking him. He's probably armed.'

A tall, bearded man, with wavy hair as thick and yellow as a field of corn on a windy day and eyes as blue as Thor's, opened the door and bowed stiffly. He had a round, tanned face, a bee-stung lower lip, and on his forehead above a slightly broken nose was an angry knot of muscles. He reminded me strongly of a painting I'd once seen by Dürer of an unidentified burgher: authoritarian, distrustful, severe – Witzel's was a very German face. He wore a blouse-type jacket made of pale leather with wool knit sleeves and collar, wheat denim jeans, brown polo boots, and a brown suede cap. On his wrist was a Rolex Submariner with a black rubberized wristband, and between his heavily stained fingers was a menthol cigarette. He smelled strongly of Sportsman aftershave, which made a pleasant change from the whiff of Garlopis's body odour that stuck to the Greek's familiar green suit like the smell of naphthalene.

'Herr Witzel, how nice to see you again,' said Garlopis. 'This is Herr Ganz, from head office in Munich. Herr Ganz, this is Herr Witzel.'

We shook hands in wary silence, like two chess players about to do battle. His hand was strong but quickly rotated over mine so that his palm was facing down and mine up, as if he meant to show that he intended to have the upper hand during our meeting. That was all right by me; this was only a conversation about insurance after all.

'Please, gentlemen, sit down,' said Garlopis.

Witzel sat down in front of the desk, crossed his legs nonchalantly, and tossed a packet of Spud and some keys onto an Imray nautical chart of Greece and the Peloponnese, which was when I noticed that in one of his ears was a little hearing aid about the size of a mint. And I wondered about the keys; for a man who claimed to be sleeping on a friend's floor, there were several on the key ring besides the evil-eye fob that everyone in Greece but me seemed to possess and a little brass ship's wheel.

'In order to process your claim, Herr Witzel, I'm going to need some more details about your business and what happened to your ship. I know this is a matter of great urgency to you, but please try to be patient. I have many questions. At the end of our conversation I hope to be able to issue you with – at the very least – a provisional check, to cover your immediate expenses.'

'I'm glad to hear it.' As he spoke Witzel stared daggers in the direction of poor Garlopis, as if reproaching him for not doing the same earlier on.

'You're a diver, aren't you?' I said.

'That's right.'

'How did you get into that business?'

'During the war I was in the German navy. With the Division Brandenburg, better known as the ocean warriors. Before that

I trained with the Italian Decima Flottiglia MAS, who were the leaders in the field of underwater combat.' He tapped the ear with the hearing aid. 'That's how I damaged this ear. A mine went off when I was in the water. After the war I bought the *Doris*, and stayed on down here, making underwater films, which was always my passion.'

'Under the circumstances that seems like a brave decision. For a German, I mean.'

'Not really. I did nothing during the war to feel ashamed of.'

Clearly the concept of collective guilt didn't feature in Witzel's way of thinking.

'Besides, I speak fluent Greek and Italian, and I've always gone out of my way to show the Greeks that I was certainly no Nazi.'

I nodded attentively but I wondered exactly how you went about doing something like that.

'As a result I always lived on the ship without any problems. Except for the usual ones, when you're a filmmaker: a lack of money. All filmmaking is expensive. Underwater, especially so.'

'What was the purpose of this specific voyage? I'm not yet clear about that.'

'It was a private charter. I'd found a few small marble and bronze artefacts on a previous dive in some waters off the island of Dokos – on what looked to be possibly the wreck of an old Greek trireme – and, thinking I might make some money out of this discovery, I contacted the Archaeological Museum in Piraeus with a view to fitting out an expedition to look for more. Not my usual kind of thing but I needed the money. Like I said, filmmaking is expensive. Anyway, they told me that at present, financing is tight for that kind of thing – it's not like Greece has a shortage of archaic bronzes and marbles, but they suggested that if I could find a German museum willing to put up the money, they would organize all of the necessary permissions in return for half of what we found. So I did exactly that. Professor Buchholz is a leading German Hellenist, and an old friend of a friend – someone I knew when I was at university in Berlin. Simple as that, really. Or at least it seemed it was until my ship sank.'

'You're a Berliner?'

'Yes. From Wedding.'

'Me too. What did you study?'

'Law, at Humboldt. To please my father, of course. It's a very German story. But he died halfway through my studies and I switched to zoology.'

'Like Humboldt.'

'Exactly.'

Witzel stubbed out his cigarette and then hung another on his lower lip like a clothes-peg. Meanwhile I unfolded the chart, turned it toward him, and came around the desk to look over his shoulder.

'Perhaps you could show me on the map where the *Doris* sank.'

'Surely.' Witzel leaned over the map and moved his forefinger down the Greek coast, about thirty or forty miles south of Piraeus, as the crow flies. While he leaned over the map I had an excellent view of what looked like an automatic in a leather shoulder holster under his left arm. Quite why a man who was diving for archaic Greek bronzes felt the need to carry a gun was anyone's guess.

'It was just about here when we discovered the fire,' he said. 'Latitude 37.30 north, longitude 23.40 east, off the eastern Peloponnese coast. It was late at night and dark, and so we put out an SOS; and while we fought the fire we tried to reach the mainland, but it quickly became clear that we would have to take to the life raft. The *Doris* is made entirely of wood, you see. She sank here in about two hundred and fifty metres of water. Too deep to dive for, unfortunately, otherwise I'd hire some equipment and go down to get some personal effects that are still on board.

'In the life raft, we put in at Ermioni. Myself, two crew, and Professor Buchholz. Then we contacted the local coast guard and told them not to bother looking for the *Doris* as it was already gone.'

I folded up the map again. 'Now, about the fire. Any idea of the cause?'

'The oil in the engine caught fire. No doubt about it. The engine was an American two-stroke diesel – a Winton, recently overhauled in the shop, and normally very reliable. But the Adrianos shipyard in Piraeus I used to take her to went bust and I had to get someone else in Salamis to do the most recent overhaul. My guess is that they cut a few corners to save money, that they used a cheap, low-viscosity oil instead of a more expensive, high-viscosity one, which was what you need for an engine like that. And the oil simply couldn't deal with the high temperatures. Typical Greeks. You have to watch them like a hawk or they'll rip you off. Of course, knowing that is one thing; proving it is something else. You'd be surprised at how quickly these bastards will close ranks when a non-Greek starts alleging incompetence.

Especially a German. I don't mind telling you, we've a lot to live down in this country.'

'I suppose so. This shipyard you used. What's the name of it?'

'A shipyard in Megara. Megara Shipyards, I think they're called.'

'And the artefacts you found. Where are they now?'

'They were on the ship. The *Doris* was my home. I kept everything of value there. Diving equipment, cameras, you name it.'

'I notice that you didn't put a value on the artefacts. In fact, they're the only thing you didn't put on the list of things for which you intend to make a claim.'

'No, I didn't.'

'All the same, they must have been quite valuable if they inspired an expedition to return to this old shipwreck.'

'I suppose so. But it hardly matters now, does it? I mean I don't have the paperwork to prove I ever had them. Or even what they were.'

'Oh, I don't think that would be a problem,' I said helpfully. 'Surely this Professor Buchholz could provide a value, couldn't he? After all, he must have seen the pieces when you were looking to get the expedition financed. To whet his appetite. We can ask him. I'll need to speak to him anyway, just in case he decides to make a claim against you, for whatever reason.'

'Why would he do that?'

'Oh, I don't know. But rest assured, you're covered for that, too.'

'He won't be making a claim.'

'You seem very sure of that, sir. May I ask why?'

'He just won't be. Take my word for it.'

'Did he have an insurance policy of his own?'

'I don't know. But if he had, it's nothing to do with me.'

'You might think that. But if he claims against his insurance then they might easily make a claim against Munich RE. I wouldn't be doing my job if I didn't try to speak with him. Just to make sure of what you say. Where can I get in touch with him?'

'I don't really know.'

'You must have had his address – when he first came to Greece.'

'I believe he was staying at the Acropolis Palace, here in Athens.'

'Well, perhaps he's there now.'

'Perhaps. But I think he may already have gone back to Germany.'

'No matter. I can contact him there just as easily. I'm going back to Germany myself just as soon as I've settled your claim.'

'So you are going to settle it, then?' he sneered. 'Instead of just asking a lot of damn-fool questions.'

'I'm surprised to hear you say that, given the sum of money involved.'

'Look, about the artefacts, let's forget about them, shall we? I don't want to claim for those. Not least because I don't want the museum in Piraeus chasing me for half their value. You can understand that, can't you?'

'I can understand. But it doesn't change anything. They might not chase you for half the value. But they might feel differently about chasing your insurance company.'

Until now I'd seen little sign in Siegfried Witzel of the ill temper Garlopis had mentioned, but this was about to change. Witzel was already grimacing and shaking his head irritably, which made Garlopis look nervous.

'Look, what is all this shit? I expect the runaround from him.' Witzel jerked his head at Garlopis. 'He's a damned Greek. But not from a fellow German. I've told you all I know.'

'You might think so. But it's also my job to find out the things you don't know. To put the umlauts over everything. You're an educated man, you understand that, surely.'

'Don't patronize me, Herr Ganz.'

'It could even be that with your cooperation I find enough evidence to sue the shipyard in Megara for negligence.'

'I don't want to sue anyone. Look, friend, I have to live here. Imagine how things would be if I started suing these people. We Germans have a bad enough name already.'

'Yes, I take your point. But I'm just doing my job. Looking after my employer's interests. As well as yours.'

'I've been a good customer. I've paid my premiums, regular as clockwork. And I've never made a claim before. You must be aware of *that*. The trouble with pen pushers like you, Herr Ganz, is that you think you can push people around just as easily as that Pelikan in your hand.'

'I don't push people around. Not even when I want to. But if I did, I'd think it better to be pushed around with a pen instead of with a gun like the one under your arm.'

Witzel smiled sheepishly. 'Oh. That.'

'Yes. That. Frankly, it makes me wonder a bit about you. The Bismarck, I mean. Not many of our claimants carry guns, Herr Witzel.'

'I've a licence for it, I can assure you.' He shook his head. 'When you're in seaports late at night as often as I am, you might carry a gun or a knife in the same way that another man might carry a pen. Fishermen play rough. And not just them. Eight years after a civil war just as bitter as the one fought in Spain, it's wise to go carefully on a strange island or in a big city. Fifty thousand people were killed in this country.'

'I'll buy that.'

'I'm not selling it. That's just a fact. Take it or leave it.'

'What I would like to take is your present address. Or the name and address of your lawyer, if you have one. And please, the address for Professor Buchholz.'

'I can't give you my own address right now. I'm staying with friends, which means I'm almost never in the same place twice. Until I get some damn money out of you people, I can't afford a hotel.'

'In which case you should appoint a lawyer to look after your interests. So that we can get in touch with you.'

'Very well. If you think it's necessary.'

'And Professor Buchholz? Where can I find him?'

Witzel looked vague. 'Somewhere in Munich. My address book with all his contact details was on the *Doris*, I'm afraid.'

'No matter. If he is a leading Hellenist like you say, he should be easy enough to get in touch with.'

I opened my briefcase and took out the certified cheque for

twenty-two thousand five hundred drachmas payable to Siegfried Witzel that I'd had drawn up before leaving Munich.

'What's this?' he asked.

'Pending any adjustment of your claim this is an interim payment on account to help tide you over. You can afford a hotel now.'

'About time.'

'I'll need to see some identification in order to give you this.'

'Of course,' he said, and handed me his passport, which was how I learned his age: he was forty-three, but looked a little older.

The sight of the cheque seemed to soften him a little and he even tried smiling, for once. 'Look, Herr Ganz,' he said, 'as one German to another, I'm asking you to forget about the artefacts that were lost on the *Doris*. I give you my word that no one is going to make a claim for them. Least of all me or the professor. People don't always behave at their best when a ship is sinking. I'll admit that neither I nor the professor conducted ourselves with any great credit and the fact is that he and I exchanged some pretty strong words before we parted, in Poros. I'm not the most even-tempered man, as you may have noticed. You see, when the time came to abandon ship I told everyone to bring something important to the life raft. I asked the professor to bring some water, a flashlight, and the Very pistol. Which he neglected to do. I was angry about that and even angrier when I found some of the artefacts in the professor's pockets when we were on the life raft. I don't suppose I would have minded about that quite so much if he'd also remembered the flare pistol and the water. It was dark when we abandoned the *Doris*. I had no way of knowing how long we were going to be in the boat, so the Very pistol and the flashlight might have helped with our rescue. Anyway, I was rough with him; I slapped him about a bit and accused him of stealing. A struggle ensued and the artefacts were lost over the side. He's hardly likely to treat any questions about me kindly now. In fact, the chances are he'll put the phone down the minute he hears my name. So save yourself the trouble of asking him.'

'Well, thank you for your very commendable honesty.'

'I'll find a lawyer and be in touch,' he said.

'There's a good one on the floor below,' said Garlopis. 'Herr Trikoupis. I can vouch for him.'

Witzel smiled thinly. He put the check in his back pocket, picked up his cigarettes and his keys, and went out of the office.

CHAPTER 18

'Commendable honesty?' Mr Garlopis chuckled quietly. 'I must confess to a certain amount of incredulity when I heard you say that, sir. And I don't mean to tell you your business. But please don't tell me you believe that man's story?'

'No, of course I don't believe his story,' I said, grabbing my coat. 'What you've said about him from the beginning seems perfectly accurate. I've seen foxes who were less evasive than Herr Witzel.'

'I'm very relieved to hear you say that, sir. It was all I could do not to laugh out loud when he was trying to persuade you not to contact Professor Buchholz. There's much more to this than meets the eye. I fear even a cyclops could see the flaws in his story. And did you notice the way he didn't contradict you when you talked about suing the shipyard in Megara after he'd already said it was in Salamis? I take it that was deliberate. If so it was a masterstroke, sir. I take my hat off to you. And the way you brought up the gun. I should never have dared even mention it. No, the man's story has more holes in it than the present government's political manifesto.'

I went onto the landing outside the office door and, peering over the wrought-iron banister, I watched Witzel go down the stairs.

'That's why I'm going to follow him. In my experience it's sometimes the quickest way to see how much of what a man has told you is on the level.' I was thinking of the way I'd followed Friedrich Jauch in Munich, and how that had worked well for me; perhaps following Witzel would prove equally productive. 'At the very least I'd like find out where he's living right now, and with whom. That might tell us something on its own.'

'But forgive me, sir, you don't know the city. Supposing you get lost?'

'That's the thing about tailing a guy. It's impossible to get lost. After all, he's bound to lead me somewhere and even if I don't know where that is, I can probably find it again.'

'Seriously, sir. I have to say, this doesn't sound like a good idea at all. I can't imagine Herr Neff ever doing such a thing as following one of our insurance claimants. Suppose Witzel sees you? Have you forgotten that he's armed?'

'I'll be all right.' I smiled. Part of me – the part that was still a detective – was already looking forward to what I had in mind. I'd enjoyed following Jauch, almost childishly so.

'Then would you like me to drive you, sir? I'm parked just around the corner and entirely at your disposal.'

'In that car of your cousin's? I might as well try to follow him with a couple of motorcycle outriders. No, I want you to stay here and try to arrange for us to meet with someone from the Archaeological Museum this afternoon. And see what else you can find out about that boat of his. You said it was called the *Carasso* before it was the *Doris*? So why'd he change the name? And when did that happen? Presumably the Mercantile Marine Ministry in Piraeus must have some information on that kind of thing.'

'New owner. New name. That's usually how it works, sir. It's not everyone who believes a new name brings bad luck to a ship. Although in this case it would seem that it has. Poseidon's ledger of the deep and all that.' He shook his head sheepishly. 'Pure superstition, of course. But sometimes it has to be admitted that these old customs are not without their foundations.'

'All the same. I'm curious.'

'Of course, sir. I'll get right on it. I've a cousin in the ministry who owes me a favour. An impossible and very conceited man but he might be able to help. In fact, I'll insist on it. If it wasn't for me he'd still be the janitor at the American Farm School in Thessaloniki.'

I heard the front door open and close and I went downstairs and out onto the street in time to see Witzel walking southeast down Stadiou toward Constitution Square, in the same direction as the roaring Athenian traffic. I was already looking for a taxi and, not seeing one, was wondering if I'd made the right decision in dispensing with Garlopis and the blue Oldsmobile, which was parked right in front of a florist's on Santaroza and immediately behind a pistachio-green Simca that Witzel had stopped beside. I told myself to remind Garlopis to get rid of the American car. As Witzel opened the Simca's door I quickly crossed the road and, speaking English, offered the young priest polishing the scooter outside the cinema a hundred drachmas if he would follow the Simca with me on the back. There was a banknote already vertical in my hand and he took it without a word, lifted the scooter off its stand, started the engine, and nodded over his shoulder for me to get on board. A minute later we were in the midst of the choking Athenian traffic and in heart-stopping pursuit of the Simca as it headed west along Mitropoleos.

'You American?' asked the priest, whose name was Demetrius.

'Swiss,' I yelled. 'Like the cheese.'

'Why are you following this man?'

'He stole some money from some friends of mine. I want to find out where he lives so I can fetch the cops.'

'Attica cops? They're as bad as the thieves. You'd be better off going to church and asking God to get it back for you.'

'Let's hope it doesn't come to that. I hear he often asks a saviour's fee. Like your immortal soul.'

Blasphemy is never a good idea when you're riding on the back of a scooter in Athens. I braced myself and closed my eyes for a second as we came perilously close to the wheels of an ice truck. Then I felt a strong jolt as the smallish wheels of the scooter hit a pothole and, out of fear that we would bounce off the road, I grabbed on to the priest's black cassock, which smelled strongly of incense and cigarettes in marked contrast to the stinky blue smoke that filled the streets, but the scooter stayed upright and about thirty metres right behind the Simca. Now that I was riding pillion I realized a scooter was perfect for following someone in Athens, if not for my nerves; the city traffic was so chaotic and undisciplined that I might never have kept up with Witzel in a yellow cab. Demetrius made light work of the pursuit and even found time to point out a building on our left.

'That's the old Metropolitan Cathedral of Athens where I work. Come in sometime and say hello to me and to Saint Philothei, whose reliquary is in there. She was beaten to death by Turkish Muslims for giving shelter to four women who'd escaped from a harem.'

'A lot of guys take that kind of thing much too personally these days. Especially when they've had a drink or two. At least I always think so. But please, keep your eyes on the road. We can do the sightseeing later. Better still, you can hear my confession now, while I'm riding pillion. That way we can kill two birds with one stone.'

The Simca turned abruptly south in the general direction of the Acropolis and we followed. Witzel was as angry a driver as he was an insurance claimant; a couple of times he extended all the fingers on his hand at other motorists, which, Demetrius assured me, was an obscene gesture called the *moutza*. The young priest didn't tell me what it meant; he didn't have to: in any language, an obscene gesture isn't usually meant to be an invitation to a waltz.

Witzel went left in front of some ancient ruins and we did the same, heading up the hill along a narrowing street with the Acropolis and whatever was on top of it now firmly in sight. Then, in front of a café, Witzel stopped the Simca, got out, and walked up the hill toward the Acropolis. For a moment I didn't appreciate that he had actually parked the car because this was

Greek parking and a thousand kilometres from the way people parked their cars in Germany, which was neatly and legally and with a certain amount of consideration for other people.

Without being instructed to do so Demetrius hung back a little, keeping the two-stroke engine running, and I more or less hid behind him to prevent Witzel from seeing me. This was easy; the priest was as tall as a Doric column and just as wide. He made the red scooter he was seated on look like a cocktail cherry.

I climbed off the back of the scooter and tried to steady my trembling legs; they say you learn something every day but all I'd learned so far was that I liked riding scooters even less than I liked being on the back of a wild mustang. Demetrius stroked his beard and promised to wait for as long as it took to smoke the cigarette I'd given him, so I gave him another for the back of his ear and, when I was sure Witzel was almost out of sight, I followed him on foot.

It was a quiet neighbourhood of empty tourist cafés, winding narrow streets, and neat little white stucco houses – the sort of old town neighbourhood you imagine probably exists only on a Greek island and not jumbled around the base of the Acropolis. Bouzouki music spilled out of windows like electronic signals sent by some frantic space traveller. Up ahead, a few intrepid Japanese tourists who had braved the Athenian morning cold were shopping for souvenirs. Like almost everyone else in Europe, Witzel paid the Japanese no attention. They were fortunate that way; fortunate that their own war crimes had been committed against the Chinese, the British, and the Australians in faraway places like Nanking and Burma. They could tour the historical sites of Greece without fear of assault, unlike myself. And maybe they just didn't give a damn the way we Germans did.

Witzel stopped for a moment to light one of his revolting menthol cigarettes, which gave me enough time to gain a little ground on him and, from the doorway of a shop selling cheap plaster models of the Parthenon, I watched him carefully to see where he would end up. A few moments later he paused in front of a dilapidated three-storey house with an almost opaque carriage lamp and shabby brown louvred shutters, produced his keys, and unlocked the narrow double-height door. A Greek flag was visible in a window on the uppermost floor and, behind a wrought-iron gate, an evil eye had been painted over an old wound in a gnarled tree trunk that was scratching itself against the wall like a mangy dog. I took a good look at the house, noted the address, which was helpfully recorded on a street sign behind the carriage lamp, and then decided to go back to the priest and his scooter. I might have stayed a bit longer but the house had a very private, closed-up look that made me think I wouldn't learn anything by just standing outside and keeping a watch on the place. I wanted to return to number 11 Pritaniou and surprise Siegfried Witzel later on, when maybe I'd gathered a little more information about the *Doris* and the diving expedition from the Mercantile Marine Ministry and the Archaeological Museum in Piraeus. Enough at least to contradict whatever cock-and-bull story he'd cooked up to make sure his insurance claim was settled. I was looking forward to that. But halfway down the gently sloping street, I was obliged to stop for a moment outside the Scholarhio café.

It's one of life's miracles that – most of the time – you don't notice your heartbeat. To that extent it's like being on a ship; when the sea is rough you can't help but pay attention to it. My heart had put in a couple of extra beats, like a virtuoso jazz drummer, just for the hell of it, perhaps, and then stopped for an unnerving fraction of a second, or so it seemed, which left me reaching to lean upon the whitewashed wall of the café – as if the ship's deck had shifted ominously under my feet – before it kicked in again, so strongly that I almost went down on one knee and which I now considered doing anyway because this always seems to be the best position to adopt when uttering a prayer. Somehow I stayed silent, even inside my own skull, for fear that I might hear God laugh at my mortal cowardice. I felt a pain in my back, as though from some infernal turn of the screw, and it began expanding through my trembling torso. Beads of sweat studded my face and chest like scales on a crocodile and my breathing quickened. I thought of Walther Neff and the heart attack that had put him in the hospital and me in his place representing MRE in Athens, and I almost smiled as I considered the irony of me dying in Greece, doing his job, while he recuperated safely at home in Germany. But straightaway I knew what needed to be done: I lurched into the café, ordered a large brandy, and lit a cigarette but not before snapping off the filter to smoke it plain and get my breath. The old remedies are usually best. Throughout both wars it was a strong cigarette and a tot of something warm that kept the nerves in check, especially when the shells were falling around you like rocks at a Muslim stoning. Once the nerves were sorted, the bullets wouldn't touch you; and if they did, you hardly cared.

'Are you all right?' asked Demetrius, when I returned to the red scooter. A handsome man, he looked like a house-trained Rasputin, at least before Yusupov invited him to dinner at his palace. 'You look a little pale, even for a Swiss.'

'I'm fine,' I said, a little breathlessly. 'Apart from having just had a near-fatal heart attack, I feel as well as I always do. But you might hear my confession now: I'm not really sure scooters agree with me. So thanks all the same, Demetrius, but I'll take a taxi back. Or I might even walk. If I'm going to die in Athens I'd prefer it to happen while I'm not actually in fear for my life.'

CHAPTER 19

Telesilla, the not unattractive red-haired woman whom Achilles Garlopis employed as a secretary, had narrow green eyes that were made narrower by the thickness of her eyebrows, the breadth of her nose, and, perhaps, the knowledge that I was a German. She knew who I was but still regarded me with what felt very like suspicion, which probably explained her obvious hesitancy in permitting me to await the return of Garlopis to his office. She told me he'd gone to the ministry in Piraeus, offered me a coffee that I declined out of respect for my delinquent heart, closed a filing cabinet that Garlopis had left open, and then went back to an adjoining office to sit at a typewriter beneath a large photograph of King Paul dressed in a British army uniform and wearing more stars on his chest than a Russian grand admiral, leaving me to take her employer's chair, where I was faced by a phalanx of photographs on the desk that showed a younger Garlopis with his large wife and even larger children. It was a very uxorious display and a little at odds with a recent copy of *Playboy* I found under the blotter. I leafed through it idly, ignoring some probably worthy articles on jazz, Mexico, and women in business in favour of Miss January, a voluptuous redhead called June Blair who managed to promise a great deal while showing very little of what had made her the Playmate of the Month. You could probably have seen more on any German beach, even in winter, and this made me think that it took a certain kind of genius to persuade men to pay for a magazine like this: the American kind, probably. After a while I closed my eyes. I was feeling tired after my walk back from the Acropolis and I may even have slept a little. In my experience there's nothing quite like an office chair to make a man feel that he needs to take a nap. Especially when Miss January's shapely image is still imprinted on the insides of his eyelids.

A bit later on I heard the slow footsteps of a big man coming upstairs and, opening my eyes, I concluded that Garlopis had finally returned.

'How did you get on, sir?' he asked breathlessly. 'Did you find out where he's been living?'

I stood up, left him to his own captain's chair, and went and sat facing the desk on a chair where I imagined Telesilla taking dictation under the lubricious eyes of Garlopis and, now that I considered the matter further, it occurred to me that she was not unlike the flame-haired playmate in the centrefold underneath the blotter. Maybe that was the reason Garlopis had bought the magazine in the first place. Either that or Telesilla had only been in the job since January.

'Pritaniou, number eleven, in the old town at the base of the

Acropolis. I couldn't tell if he's living alone there or not. But at least now we know where to find him. And you? Did you see your cousin at the Mercantile Marine Ministry?'

'I did.' Garlopis adjusted his bow tie and allowed himself a smile. 'And the news is – well, interesting to say the least, in that it provides us with a possible motive for a case of arson. I only say possible, sir. That's for you to decide, of course. But people have long memories in this country. With the many centuries of history we have, we need long memories.'

He found a cigarette, rattled a box of matches, lit up, and removed a piece of paper from his pocket. 'As we know, the *Doris* was formerly registered as the *Carasso*. I discovered that the previous owner was a Jewish merchant in Salonika, which, as you know, is now our second city, Thessaloniki. The Jewish merchant's name was Saul Allatini and he bought and sold coffee. Before the war, Thessaloniki was home to a large number of Jews. Possibly as many as there existed anywhere in Europe outside of Poland. Sephardic Jews mostly, from Spain; but also a great many who had fled from Muslim persecution in the Ottoman Empire. But unlike most countries, Greece, I'm proud to say, gave its Jews full citizenship, and they thrived. As a result of all this, perhaps the majority of people in Thessaloniki – at least sixty thousand – were Jews.

'Anyway, I don't want to embarrass you, sir, with a lachrymose tale of Jewish suffering in Greece – you being a German n'all – so, to cut a long story short, most of the Jews in Thessaloniki were deported to Auschwitz in 1943 and gassed to death. Meanwhile their property was subject to confiscation and resale by the collaborationist Hellenic government of Ioannis Rallis. Which is how the unfortunate Mr Allatini's three vessels – two of them merchantmen, and one his own private yacht, the *Carasso* – were sold to Greeks and to Germans at bargain-basement prices. Or rather to one particular German. The *Carasso* was bought by Siegfried Witzel for a pittance and he renamed it the *Doris*, and sailed it to Piraeus, where it remained after the war.' Garlopis paused and puffed at his cigarette for a moment. 'Those Jews who survived the camps – less than two thousand, it would seem – returned to Thessaloniki and found their homes and property in the possession of Greek Christians who had bought them in good faith from the Germans. And any attempts at Jewish property restitution quickly failed when a British-backed right-wing anti-communist IPE government came to power in Athens. None of these men had much time for the Jews, and of course Greece collapsed into civil war soon afterwards. A civil war that lasted three years. Since when there has been little appetite to open up these scars and say who owns what. Certainly the ministry has no record of anyone from the Allatini family as having petitioned it for the return of the *Doris*. At least none that my cousin was able to find.

'In defence of my country I should also mention that this regrettable situation is complicated by the fact that many of the properties bought by Jews long before the war had themselves been owned by Muslims previous to the so-called diaspora that followed the Greco-Turkish war of 1919–1922. Many Muslims were obliged to sell up at knockdown prices and emigrate to Turkey, while many Turks, including thousands of Jews, were obliged to leave their Turkish homes and go to Thessaloniki. So you see that nothing in this part of the world is simple. No, not even the status of the marble friezes taken from the Parthenon by the Turks, and sold to the British Lord Elgin for seventy thousand British pounds during the Greek war of independence that was fought against the Ottoman Empire. My own opinion, for what it's worth, is that Greece should set an example to the British and restore as much previously owned Jewish property as possible, regardless of the cost. But until that happens, this situation causes a great deal of bitterness among those few Jews who continue to live in Greece.'

'Enough for someone to set a ship on fire, perhaps?'

'It's certainly possible, yes,' admitted Garlopis. 'But here your guess is as good as mine.'

'It might explain why Herr Witzel feels the need to carry a gun. It may be that he's been threatened before.'

Garlopis nodded and stubbed out his cigarette in a Hellas pottery ashtray. 'In this particular context it's also worth mentioning that because of the civil war, the *Doris* was never insured against acts of terrorism. If it could be proved that the ship had been attacked for political reasons by Jewish activists, then this would certainly fall under the umbrella of war risk exclusions which, according to the terms of the policy, are considered fundamentally uninsurable.'

'And it would certainly be in Witzel's interest to allege that the engine caught fire because of a shipyard's negligence.'

'Exactly, sir.'

'What does the coast guard have to say about the incident?

Is there any way of proving that the ship really did sink out at sea where he said it did?'

'I'm afraid not, sir.'

'It's a pity we can't speak to this Professor Buchholz, in order to corroborate Witzel's story.'

'With that in mind, sir, after I'd been to the ministry, on Kolokotronis Street, I went just around the corner, to the Archaeological Museum and set up an appointment later on this week for us to go and see the assistant director, Dr Lyacos. At three o'clock, to be precise.' Garlopis looked at his watch. 'But while we're in Piraeus we should certainly make time to go to Vassilenas.'

'What's that?'

'The best restaurant in Piraeus, sir.'

'By the way, I don't suppose you have a cousin in the Attica police; I made a note of the licence plate on the car Witzel was driving.'

'No, sir. I'm afraid not.'

We went outside and walked to the Olds, where a beggar woman had taken up position, no doubt in the mistaken belief that the owner was a rich American. I knew quite a bit about being on the streets myself so I gave the woman twenty lepta and got into the car. But even the small change, which was made of aluminium, had holes in it.

'By the way,' I said, 'I told you to get rid of this car, didn't I? It's hard to move around quietly in this thing. And it's a magnet for beggars.'

'You're so right, of course,' he said as we drove away. 'And I will. Just as soon as my cousin is back in the office.'

'When will that be?'

'He took a couple of days off, sir. So perhaps the day after tomorrow. By the way, sir. If I could ask you not to give money to the beggars. It only encourages them. They're Hungarians, mostly, sir. Refugees from last year's terrible and abortive uprising. There's plenty of work for them in Greece – picking cotton – but they won't take it if people keep on giving them money, sir. It's bad for them and it's bad for us. In my opinion they're too proud for their own good.'

'It's only excessive pride that the gods punish, isn't it? Hubris? Which leads to nemesis?'

'Yes, indeed, that's quite true. And you do well to remind me of that, sir. But for my own hubris I might still be married – to Mrs Nemesis.'

'If you don't mind me asking, what went wrong?'

'In a word, Telesilla. She's what went wrong. She's what always goes wrong for a man such as myself. My head was turned, sir. The wrong way, too. Nothing actually happened between her and me, you understand. But I imagined it might and, unfortunately, in a moment of sheer delusion, I led my poor wife to believe that I was enamoured of Telesilla. Telesilla herself was entirely blameless and remains happily married. And she's a very good secretary. Which is why I couldn't bring myself to dismiss her. I mean, it would seem rather pointless now that Mrs Garlopis is no longer au courant.' Garlopis smiled sadly. 'And for you, sir? Is there a Frau Ganz?'

'No. That particular chapter of my life has now closed – forever, I think. Especially now that I'm working in insurance.

You wouldn't know it to look at me but I've had an interesting life. That's one of the reasons I like this insurance business. It feels like a nice quiet pew at the back of an empty church.'

CHAPTER 20

A few days later, after a very good lunch indeed, we went to the Archaeological Museum in Piraeus. Built by Themistocles at the beginning of the fifth century BC, the town was home to almost half a million people. It was the centre of Greek coastal shipping and the industrial heartland of Greece, with spinning factories, flour mills, distilleries, breweries, soap factories, and chemical manure plants. It certainly smelled that way. About a twenty-minute drive from Athens, the town had no important ancient monument thanks to the Spartans, who'd destroyed the original fortifications, and the Romans, who'd destroyed much else besides. That's the most comforting thing about history: you find out that it's not always the Germans who are to blame. Next to the museum was a virtual builder's yard of assorted archaic marble torsos that almost made me think I was back in the mortuary at the Schwabing Hospital. But inside the two-storey building there were many fine treasures, including a bronze statue of Athena that was as tall as a giraffe; she had one hand held out in supplication, as if she was begging for some small change, and, but for the rakishly worn hoplite's helmet, she reminded me of the Hungarian woman I'd tipped earlier on.

We found Dr Stavros Lyacos, the assistant director of the museum, in the basement, next to the laboratories for the maintenance of clay, metal, and stone objects. His office had a large marble eye on the wall and, lying on the desk, was a Greek fertility goddess rather more attractive than the morbidly obese German fertility goddess found at Willendorf. Even Dr Lyacos was more attractive than her. He was tall and thin with a small tight mouth, sharp heavy-lidded eyes, and half-moon glasses on the bridge of a pointy Pinocchio nose that helped to make his face look more fastidious than comically mendacious. He wore a generously cut double-breasted grey flannel suit with lapels as wide as a pair of scimitars, and a blue-striped bow tie. The red carnation in his buttonhole made him look as if he were going to a wedding and since he clearly wasn't, it made me think he was a man in possession of a large mirror and for whom the marble eye mounted on the wall was something of a personal statement. Smoking a cherrywood pipe, Dr Lyacos listened politely and smiled without any great warmth while I introduced myself and explained my mission, and then he went to fetch a file from a cabinet that stood between a headless marble lion and the torso of a young man who was missing most of his genitals and – not that it would have mattered in those tragic circumstances – both of his hands. Lyacos had no German nor very much English and, later on, Garlopis told me that he spoke a Greek that was full of ancient words, which was always the sign of an educated man.

He said that he'd met with both Siegfried Witzel and Professor Buchholz, that both men spoke fluent Greek, and that their permissions were gold-plated, in evidence for which he returned from the filing cabinet with a variety of official paperwork. These showed that the Germans' expedition had the blessing of no less a figure than the Greek interior minister, Dimitrios Makris, in the form of a handwritten letter on parliamentary notepaper, as well as all the proper consents and approvals from the Ministry of Public Works on Karageorgi Servias Street. There were also several forms stamped by the Naval Ministry on Paparigopoulou Street and the Greek coast guard in Piraeus. It seemed that Professor Buchholz had been most charming and even presented Dr Lyacos with a signed copy of his book on Hellenistic art, which he might have read had it not been in German. When I asked if he still had a copy of the book, Dr Lyacos said he had, removed it from a drawer in his desk, and laid it in front of me. The book, published by C. H. Beck and lavishly illustrated, was called *Hellenism: The Rise and Fall of a Civilization* and, as Lyacos had told me, was indeed signed by Professor Philipp Buchholz and inscribed in German and Greek: *To Stavros Lyacos, in gratitude for his generous help and assistance*. Lyacos proceeded to explain that the arrangement between the two museums had been that anything found by the expedition would be shared, with the museum in Piraeus having first pick and the museum in Munich having the remainder.

'Tell me, doctor, is it usual for all these permissions to be granted so quickly?' I asked, noting the close proximity of the dates on the official paperwork. 'All of this seems to have happened with a rapidity that, if you'll both forgive me for saying so, seems a little remarkable even in Greece.'

Not usual at all, was the doctor's answer; then again, the Ministry of the Interior had crabs in its pockets when it came to funding archaeology in modern Greece, which meant that it was stingy; this was the first Greek–German cooperation in the field of archaeology since 1876, when the Greek Archaeological Society had worked with Heinrich Schliemann at the royal graves site in Mycenae, so perhaps there was a hope that this might prove to be just as successful as that. It was, after all, Schliemann who'd discovered the famous golden mask of Agamemnon, now in the National Archaeological Museum of Athens. The two Germans had been very respectful and accommodating, Lyacos concluded.

I looked at Garlopis and shook my head. 'I can't see anything wrong here, can you? Everything sounds very proper.'

Garlopis shrugged and then translated what I'd just said for Dr Lyacos.

'Well, not everything, perhaps,' said Garlopis, interpreting what Lyacos now said. 'But after all, he says, this is Greece, so how could it be?'

'Like what, for instance?'

Lyacos puffed his pipe, looked uncomfortable for a moment, and then started to speak.

'He doesn't wish to say anything against a man as distinguished in the field of Hellenism as Professor Buchholz,' explained Garlopis. 'Even so, the small artefacts found on the wreck site by Herr Witzel had been identified by the professor as late Helladic when in the opinion of Dr Lyacos they were actually much earlier. Late Bronze Age, probably. But it's not uncommon for experts on antiquity to disagree about such things, so he doesn't think it's important.'

'Nevertheless,' I said, 'he sounds like he was a bit surprised by that.'

'He was, I think. Especially as there are some very similar late Bronze Age artefacts in the professor's book that are correctly identified.'

Lyacos turned the illustrated pages to reveal a photograph of a bronze tripod, a golden ring, and a little statue of a snake goddess.

'These,' said Lyacos.

I nodded and then closed the book.

'How do you go about getting the permission of someone like Mr Makris to look for this kind of stuff, anyway?'

Garlopis spoke to Lyacos for a second and then answered that he wouldn't know.

'Is he sure about that?'

The two Greeks spoke for almost a minute, during which time they laughed several times, and then Garlopis said, 'He says he believes that the minister of the interior, Takos Makris, has always done what Konstantinos Karamanlis tells him to do. And I have to say I agree with him there. Mr Makris is married to the niece of Mr Karamanlis, Doxoula, so it's certain that the two men are very close. After a man like Mr Makris gave his permission it's certain that everyone else in the government must have sat up and paid attention.'

Idly, I opened the book on Hellenism again – C. H. Beck was one of Germany's most prestigious publishing houses – and glanced over what had been written about Professor Buchholz in the author's biography on the flyleaf.

And it was then I noticed what I'd been too dumb to notice before: that Professor Buchholz was the assistant director at the Glyptothek Museum, in Munich.

It was certainly a coincidence that my first job as a claims adjuster working for MRE had been to investigate a break-in at the Glyptothek, but a remarkable one? There had been a time when I had strongly believed that a good detective was merely a man who collected coincidences – a perfectly respectable activity since Pascal and Jung – with the aim of connecting one or two of them until they looked like something more meaningful and concurrent. Of course, it's no great surprise that over a long period of time, as fortune takes its course, many coincidences should occur. But here the question was this: Did the several weeks that had elapsed since the break-in at the Glyptothek count as a long period of time and therefore enough to discount coincidence?

Or, to put this in a less mathematically naïve way, could I smell a rat?

CHAPTER 21

'Given our maritime history, we Greeks are much more likely to talk about smelling fish than rats,' said Garlopis, when we'd left the museum.

'Rats, fish, what's the difference? They both smell the same way when they're not where they're supposed to be.'

'But to answer your earlier question,' he continued, 'I don't happen to believe in simple coincidences very much. I have the whole of Greek tragedy there to back me up on this. What you Germans call coincidence Greeks like Sophocles tend to ascribe to the *Moirai* – the Three Fates. Divine weavers of a tapestry dictating the destiny of men.'

'It's always the females that seal a man's fate. That's certainly been my own experience.'

We were walking back to the car which, as before, had attracted a couple of expectant beggars and, as before, I handed out a few hollow coins. If the gods were watching I hoped they would see this act of kindness and reward my charity – that a muse, or whatever Garlopis might have called it, would provide some divine inspiration as to the connection, if any, between the Glyptothek in Munich and the Glyptothek in Piraeus. Stranger things had happened in Greece, surely.

'I expect you're right,' I said. 'About the coincidence. But it's giving me an itch that I guess I'll have to keep on scratching for a while. Either way I've already decided – more or less – to delay settling Herr Witzel's claim. There's too much here that doesn't bear scrutiny. At least, that's what I'm going to tell Dumbo at head office, so later on today I'll need to send a telegram. Not that I'm planning to tell Siegfried Witzel any of this. At least I don't think so – not yet. And not without a bulletproof vest.'

'I'm very relieved to hear it, sir. Myself, I want to be as far away as possible from that man when he hears any bad news.'

'Having said all that, Mr Garlopis, I do want to see his reaction when we surprise him at that address in Pritaniou. Which is where we're going now. If you're game, that is. Who knows? Perhaps we'll get lucky and find the professor there, locked in the bedroom. And he can tell us what really happened to the *Doris*. Seriously, though, I've an idea that our just being there will provoke Witzel to say something out of turn or make a mistake.'

Achilles Garlopis bit his knuckle, crossed himself, and grimaced. 'That's what I'm afraid of, sir. Look here, now that you know his address, couldn't you write to him and tell him that you're delaying settlement? The man's obviously dangerous.'

'What can I tell you? You might be right. You can wait outside in the car, if you like. I'll handle it. In which case maybe I'll tell him after all. It wouldn't exactly be the first time I've been the bearer of bad news.'

'If you don't mind me asking, aren't you scared?'

'Since the Ivans got the bomb? All the time. But of Witzel, no. Besides, disappointing people is what I'm good at. I've had a lifetime of practice.'

We drove back into Athens and to the old town at the base of the Acropolis. The green Simca was there but I told Garlopis to find another street and park. He drove down a few streets and pulled up on the sidewalk behind an empty police car and opposite what he said was the old Roman marketplace, although if he'd told me it was the Parthenon, I wouldn't have known any different. Of late I'd been neglecting my studies of late Bronze Age Hellenism.

'Why don't you stay here and watch the car?' I told Garlopis. 'Maybe some Hungarian beggars will turn up and you can shoo them away before I get back.'

'And suppose you don't come back?'

I pointed at the empty police car. 'You could tell the cops.'

'And if they leave before you return? What then? I should feel obliged to go and look for you, *on my own*. No, sir, I think it's better that I accompany you now. Then I'll know for sure that you're all right, or that you're not, and I won't be presented with a difficult decision like that. At least this way there's some safety in numbers.'

'Suppose he shoots both of us,' I said as we left the car behind.

'Please don't joke about such matters. I'll be quite honest with you, Herr Ganz, and I'm only a little bit ashamed to admit it, but I am a coward, sir. All my life I've had to live down my given name: Achilles. For that reason I prefer to be called Garlopis, or Mr Garlopis. But not Achilles. I am not nor ever could be a hero. Bravery is admirable but it belongs only to the brave and it often seems to me that the cemeteries are full of such brave men and not many cowards. Especially in Greece, where heroes are often as troublesome and combative as the gods themselves. It's my opinion that heroes often come to what the English call "a sticky end". Theirs is a most creative language. It paints a picture, does it not? A sticky end?'

'I've seen a few of those in my time. In German and in English.'

Garlopis talked all the way up the hill and onto the corner of Pritaniou, and he even talked while we watched the house at number 11 for a cautious ten minutes from behind the corner of a little church. The street was empty, as if the rocky outcrop supporting the citadel above had been a volcano that was about to erupt. The Greek was nervous, of course, and why not? It was me who was at fault. I was the one taking risks that were beginning to feel almost unnecessary. Garlopis was acting in the way one would always have expected an insurance agent to act: with extreme caution, and wisely reluctant to leave the safety of his desk and his captain's chair and the care of his voluptuous flame-haired secretary. But me – I suppose you could just say that old habits die hard. It was fun behaving like a cop again, to feel the sidewalk underneath my Salamanders as I watched a suspect's house. I wasn't worried about Witzel's gun. When you've been around guns all your life they don't seem quite so intimidating. Then again, that's probably one reason why, sometimes, people get shot.

We approached the shabby, double-height door. There was no

bell and no knocker and I was just about to bang on the woodwork when I noticed that the wrought-iron gate immediately
next to it wasn't locked, though it had been on my earlier visit.
I pushed it open to reveal a narrow flight of stone steps that led
underneath the bough of the evil-eye olive tree and up the side
of the house and, thinking that this might afford us with the
chance to spy on Witzel before we announced our presence, I
went through the gate, tugging a reluctant Garlopis behind me. I
might have left him but for the fact that he was easily the largest
thing in the street. Anyone opening one of the upper-floor shutters and glancing down would have noticed him immediately. In
his baggy green suit he might have been mistaken for Poseidon
clothed in seaweed, but to anyone else he looked suspiciously
like a man playing lookout for a burglar.

At the top of the steps we found a whitewashed wall with a
wooden door that felt as if it was locked. Hauling myself up to
check what was on the other side I saw a small courtyard with
a door that was only bolted, a sleeping cat, a dry fountain, and
several cracked terracotta pots that were home to some even
drier plants. If the place was occupied it was by someone who
cared very little about it. A rusted motorcycle lay in a state of
disassembly underneath a vine on which the grapes had almost
fossilized. I climbed over the wall, dusted myself down, and then
unbolted the gate to admit Garlopis. By now he was the same
colour as his suit. Meanwhile the cat stood up, stretched a bit,
and then left.

Ignoring what looked like the kitchen door I led the way down
a couple of wooden steps to a pair of French windows that were

so dusty they were almost opaque. One of the windows was ajar and, mindful of Witzel's gun, I slowly pushed it all the way open before stepping inside the house. Under the stairs was a large plastic bag full of sponges. The radio was on, but low so that it was just a murmur. The place smelled of cigarettes and ouzo, Sportsman aftershave, and something more acrid and combustible perhaps, and there was a heavily stained Louis XV–style caned sofa with half the seat stuffing hanging down on the floor like a bull's pizzle. An Imray sea chart lay open on a Formica-topped table next to a bottle of Tsantali, a packet of Spuds, and the cashier's cheque I'd handed him back at the office. On one wall was a collection of cheap plaster masks of the kind you could have bought in any local souvenir shop and which featured a variety of grotesque grey and green rictus faces that might have had something to do with Greek tragedy. But what they certainly had in common was their close resemblance to the man lying on the floor whose face was distinguished by its empty eye sockets and gaping mouth, not to mention a very definite look of abbreviated pain. Abbreviated by his death, that is. It was Siegfried Witzel and he'd been shot twice. I knew that because each shot had gone through an eyeball.

Garlopis covered his mouth and turned quickly away. '*Gam- iméno kólasi*,' he exclaimed. '*O ftochós.*'

'If you're going to throw up, do it outside,' I said.

'Why would someone do that?'

'I don't think it was his cologne. Although it is quite pungent. But I expect they had their reasons.'

The first bullet looked like it had come clean out of the back of Witzel's skull and hit a framed photograph of a racehorse; the spent bullet had cracked the glass and stained it ever so slightly with blood and brain matter. I bent down beside the body to take a closer look. The second bullet had been fired at closer range when the man was already lying on the floor; you could tell that from the amount of blood and gelatinous aqueous humour that had erupted out of Witzel's eye socket. From what I saw that second shot had been gratuitous and an act of pure sadism, designed, perhaps, to inflict an extra level of punishment and humiliation. Because if Siegfried Witzel had a next of kin it would be hard for them to stomach the sight of him like this. A closed coffin, then. No last kisses for Siegfried. Not without him wearing a pair of dark glasses.

Pressing my finger into the blood on the moth-eaten Persian carpet and then into the dead man's mouth, I said, 'The blood's dry but the body's not yet cold. I'd say he's been dead for no more than a couple of hours.' I opened his jacket; the holster was still there but the gun was gone and when I lifted his heavy, muscular arm to check for any sign of rigor and lividity I saw that the Rolex Submariner was still on his wrist. 'I think we can discount the possibility that this was a robbery. He's still wearing his diver's watch. By the look of things the killer's long gone. It appears as if you might have been right about the Jews after all, Garlopis. That maybe this was a revenge killing. I don't know, but that's not my problem. The local cops can try to figure out a motive. Which means we'd better make ourselves scarce. It would certainly make a nice tidy parcel if the cops could blame the murder of one German on another.'

I was talking to myself. Garlopis had returned to the backyard and was already smoking a cigarette to steady his nerves.

I wiped my fingers on the dead man's jeans and instinctively checked his pockets. All of them. As a beat cop in Berlin it was common practice to supplement your meagre wages with some of what you found in a murder victim's billfold and it was only after I made detective that I stopped doing it, but old habits die hard, and anyway, Witzel's pockets were empty of everything except the keys for the Simca and what looked like the front door. Besides, this time I was only looking for information, but if he'd possessed a wallet I couldn't see it. I stood up and took another look around; on the floor I found a spent brass case for an automatic: it was rimless, tapered, probably from a 9-mill automatic, and I'd seen a thousand of them before. I dropped it back onto the floor and went over to the table. The map open on the table was a different chart from the larger-scale one we'd spread out back in Garlopis's office. This one was for the Saronic and Argolic Gulfs, and had been marked up with ink, which wasn't all there was on it. There was blood on the chart, too, and it didn't look like it was spatter from the head shots; this was one large globular spot that looked as if it had dripped onto the waterproof paper while someone had been leaning over it.

I called out to Garlopis. 'There's one good thing about this, I suppose,' I said. 'It means we can relax. My job's over. With all due respect to your country, I can go and see the Parthenon now and then return home to Munich. Even if I was inclined to settle his claim there's no one here to pay. It's not our fault if Siegfried Witzel wouldn't give us the name of his next of kin, or a lawyer. Dumbo will be delighted, of course. Not to mention Mr Alzheimer. There's nothing those guys like better than adjusting a loss to zero. This will probably make their weekend.'

Garlopis didn't answer. I looked out the French window and saw him standing stiffly in the garden with his arms by his sides, like a statue; he seemed shocked and bewildered, as if he was more upset about Witzel's death than I would ever have imagined. But perhaps it was just the sight of a dead body, after all. I didn't blame him for that. Even in the land of Oedipus and Jocasta it's not everyone who can tolerate the sight of a man without eyes.

'What's your problem?' I asked, hoping to help restore him to his previous good humour. 'You never liked the guy anyway. At least now you don't have to worry about him shooting *you*. This is one loss that nobody can adjust. So we're done. You can go back to ogling that secretary of yours. And why not? She's very nice. I might ogle her myself for a couple of minutes if you've no objection.'

I lit a cigarette and moved closer to the French windows but froze when I saw an arm with a revolver pointed squarely at the Greek's head. I turned around to see if I could locate Witzel's own gun before deciding what to do but stopped and put myself in aspic jelly when I saw that there was a loaded Smith & Wesson pointed at me, too. I knew the gun was loaded because I was staring right down the barrel, as if the first shot might have gone through my own eye. I let the cigarette drop from my mouth. The last thing I wanted the man with the gun to think was that I didn't take him or it very seriously. And just in case

I'd forgotten, there was a body on the floor to remind me of just what a large-calibre revolver can do at close range. At the same time I wasn't at all sure if I was relieved or alarmed to see that it was a uniformed police officer holding it.

CHAPTER 22

After we'd been searched, the cops sat us on the disembowelled couch. There were three of them and it looked like they'd heard us coming over the back wall and had hidden in the kitchen until they were ready to make their move. Garlopis was already talking too much, in Greek, so I told him to shut up, in German, at least until we knew if the police were disposed to treat us as suspects or not. That's in the Bible so it must be true: Be sensible and keep your mouth shut: Proverbs 10:19. The officer in charge was a tall man whose dark, high-cheekboned face was part boxer, part Mafia don, and part Mexican revolutionary with more than a hint of Stanley Kowalski – at least until he found a pair of thick-framed, lightly tinted glasses and put them on, at which point he stopped looking dim-witted and thuggish and started to look thoughtful and smart.

'Find anything interesting?' The Greek's German wasn't nearly as good as that of Garlopis, but it wasn't bad either because it's not the end of the world when you don't use the best grammar. He had our wallets in his hands and so he already knew our names.

'Just the guy on the floor. And you, of course.'

'Where are you staying, Herr Ganz?'

'Me, I'm at the Mega. In Constitution Square.'

'You should have stayed at the Grande Bretagne. But I suppose either one of them would be convenient for the old Gestapo building in Merlin Street.'

I grinned, trying to enjoy his joke. 'His cousin works at the Mega,' I said, looking at Garlopis. 'So I guess that's just my bad luck.'

'So what are you two doing here?'

'If I told you we were selling insurance you'd probably think I was being sarcastic and I can't say as I would blame you very much. But that's not so far from the truth. I'm a claims adjuster. The dead man is a German called Siegfried Witzel. He owned a boat called the *Doris* that was insured with my company for almost a quarter of a million drachmas. I have a business card in my wallet that will help to establish those credentials. You can telegraph my office in Munich and they'll vouch for me and for Herr Garlopis. Witzel's boat caught fire and sank, he made a claim, and we came here today to tell him I thought there was something fishy about it.'

'Do you always climb over the back wall to sell insurance?'

'I do when I've become aware that the insured party carries a gun. Frankly, I wanted to see what kind of company he was keeping before I said hello again. Especially as I was now the bearer of bad news. In view of what's happened here I would say that my caution was well founded, wouldn't you?'

'You speak any Greek?'

'No.'

Garlopis started talking in Greek again. The Greeks have a word for it. So the saying goes. In fact, they usually had several words for it, too many in fact, and Achilles Garlopis was no exception. The man could talk without stopping for hours, the way a Belgian could ride a bicycle. So I told him to shut up, again.

'Why do you tell him to shut up?'

'The usual reason. Because he talks too much.'

'It's every citizen's duty to help the police. Perhaps he's just trying to be helpful.'

'Yes,' said Garlopis. 'I am.'

'I can see how that might help you,' I told the police officer. 'But I think you're smart enough to see how that might not help us. You're a busy man and you've got a murder to solve. And right now, in the absence of anyone else, you think we might be good for that.'

'I think it would be smart if you were to tell us everything you know about this man.'

'Oh, sure. Look, I know what to say. I just don't know if I should say it. That's just smart getting wise.'

The officer lit a cigarette and blew some of the smoke my way, which I didn't like.

'Do you speak English?' he said. 'My English is better than my German.'

'You're doing all right so far,' I said in English. 'What, were you a cop during the war?'

'Right now, I'm the one asking the questions, okay?'

'Sure. Anything you say, Captain.'

'Lieutenant. So why were you going to turn down his claim?'

'There were too many inconsistencies in his story. There was that and the gun he was carrying.'

'We didn't find a gun. Not yet.'

'Maybe not. But he's not wearing a shoulder holster because his wallet was so heavy. I think he was scared of someone, and it wasn't Munich RE.'

'Like who maybe?'

'That's obvious. Like the man who killed him, I expect.'

'Funny guy.'

'With all due respect, "like who" is your job, not mine. But Garlopis here tells me the boat – the *Doris* – was confiscated by the Nazis from some Jews during the war and sold to Witzel. Maybe those Jews or their relations decided if they couldn't get their property back legally, then they would just get even. Sometimes getting even is the best kind of compensation there is. But motive isn't something I usually bother with in my line of work. If there's evidence of fraud I turn down the claim and take the verbal battering. It's as simple as that. Generally speaking, I don't have to look too hard for a reason. On the whole people much prefer their insurance company losing money to doing it themselves. My job is to try to prevent that from happening. Which is why I was about to say no to Mr Witzel's claim. But at this present moment I wouldn't say no to a cigarette.'

The lieutenant thought about it for a moment and then had one of his men uncuff us, and I got my Karelias back. There's nothing as bad as the craving you get for a cigarette because they've been taken away by someone in authority. Someone who smokes. I expect the Greek cop knew that. And the greater the privation that precedes their return, the better the first one tastes. The liberty cigarette. Even Garlopis agreed with this empirical observation; I could tell by the way he hoovered down his first drag. Okay, we weren't out of the forest yet, but things were starting to relax, a little. Or at least as much as that's even possible when there's a dead body lying eyeless on the rug and someone has a gun on you.

'Would you mind telling your men to put their guns away? I had a good wine with my lunch and I wouldn't want to spill any of it on this floor. We're not armed and you know who we are, so we're not about to try to escape.'

The German-speaking policeman said something and the other two policemen holstered their weapons.

'Thank you.'

'Tell me more about his insurance claim.'

'If his boat was attacked and sunk for political reasons by Jewish activists, then this would certainly fall under the umbrella of war risk exclusions which, according to the terms of the policy, are considered fundamentally uninsurable. I think maybe he was trying to prevent us from finding that out.'

'And you'll have lots of paperwork back at the office to substantiate this story.'

'Not just there. If you look on the table you'll find a certified cashier's cheque from my company that was a small interim payment for his loss.'

The lieutenant stepped carefully over Witzel's body, went to the table, and looked down at the cheque without touching it.

'I thought you said you weren't going to pay up.'

'On the main claim? No. I think you'll agree there's a hell of a difference between the amount printed on that cheque and a quarter of a million drachmas.'

'You know what I also think?' said the cop, turning back to look at me. 'I think you've been around dead bodies before, Mr Ganz.'

'After the war we just lived through, that wouldn't be so unusual.'

'No, this was different. I was watching you both from the stairs. And listening to some things you said. Garlopis here, he behaved like a normal person. Saw the body, felt a bit queasy, and went outside to get some fresh air. But you – you were different. From what I could understand of what you said, you were looking at the body the way I do. Like a man with no eyes didn't bother you that much. And as if you expected this crime scene to yield some answers. The way you knew about the speed with which blood dries. That kind of behaviour tells me something.'

'And what does it tell you?'

'For a moment back there I thought you might be one of the answers. Now I think that maybe you are or were some kind of a cop.'

'I told you. I'm a claims adjuster for an insurance company. Which is a kind of a cop, I suppose. One that gets to go home at five o'clock, perhaps.'

'You must think I'm stupid, Mr Ganz. And you're a long way

from home. Who the hell do you think you're dealing with? I've done this job for twenty years. I can smell a cop the way an elephant can smell water. So don't make me have to hit you to get some straight answers. If I hit you, I can promise you'll write me a thank-you letter afterward. In Greek.'

'I've been hit before.'

'I can believe that. But let me tell you, I've slapped enough punks in my life to know the ones who'll hit back from the ones who'll learn to appreciate it. Metaphorically speaking, of course. Because the fact is, I don't need to hit you. We both know I can hold you for as long as I want. I can throw you both in jail or I can take away your passport. This is Greece, not the General Assembly of the United Nations.'

'All right. I used to be a cop. So what? With all the men killed during the war a lot of German companies can't afford to be fussy about the kind of people they take on these days. It seems to me that they'll employ just about anyone who can get the job done. Even if that means giving a job to some retired dumb cop like me.'

'Now that I don't believe. That you were ever a dumb cop.'

'I'm alive I guess.'

'What kind of a cop were you?'

'The honest kind. Most of the time.'

'What does that mean?'

'Like I said, Lieutenant, I stayed alive. That should tell you something.'

'Something else tells me that you know a little bit about murder.'

'All Germans know about murder. As a Greek you should know that.'

'True, but since there's a dead German on the floor I now have the crazy idea that a German ex-cop like you could help me solve this case. Is that unreasonable?'

'Why would I want to do that?'

'Because by not helping me, you'd be in my way. We've got laws against obstructing the police.'

'Name one.'

'Come on, Mr Ganz. You're at the scene of a murder. There's blood on your fingers and your prints are on that spent round of ammunition you were handling earlier. You didn't even come in through the front door. Until I find someone better than you, you're all I've got. You even knew the dead man. You're a German, like him. Your card was in the victim's wallet. So I might even be disposed to call each of you a suspect. How does that word sound?'

'Except that you were here first.'

'Haven't you heard of the murderer who returns to the scene of the crime?'

'Sure. I've heard of Father Christmas, too, but I've never actually seen him myself.'

'You don't think it happens?'

'I think it helps a lot of writers get themselves out of a tight spot. But I'd have to be pretty dumb to come back here if I killed this man.'

'A lot of criminals are stupid.'

'That's right. They are. But I never counted on that when I

was a cop. Not only that but it looks bad when cops don't catch those criminals. Bad for the reputation of cops everywhere.'

'All right. Let's work on the assumption that this killer isn't stupid. Why do you think he shot your man in the eyes? Why would someone do something like that?'

'How should I know?'

'Humour me, please. I have my own theory on this but I'd still like to hear what even an ex-detective has to say about it.' He flicked the cigarette he was smoking out the French windows. 'I am right, aren't I? That you were once a detective?'

'Yes. All right, I was. A long time ago.'

'Where and doing what?'

'I was a Murder Commission detective in Berlin for the best part of ten years.'

'And you held what kind of rank?'

'I was a police commissar. That's like a captain, I suppose.'

'So you were the man in charge of a murder investigation?'

'You might think that, yes. But back in Germany there was really only one man in charge all that time. And his name was Adolf Hitler.'

'Good. Now we're getting somewhere. So tell me, Commissar Ganz, why do you think Mr Witzel was shot in the eyes?'

'Your guess is as good as mine. My own guess is it was a revenge thing, maybe. That the killer is probably a sadist who enjoys not just killing people but humiliating them, too.'

'I agree. About the sadism, I mean. I have another question. Was Witzel by any chance a German Jew?'

'No,' I said. 'I'm quite certain he wasn't.'

'May I ask how you know?'

'He'd told us he was in the German navy during the war. It's highly unlikely he could have served if he'd been Jewish.'

'I see. Look, Herr Commissar, I think maybe we can help each other out here. My name is Lieutenant Leventis and I'll guarantee to keep you both out of jail if you hand over your passport and agree to help me. In a purely advisory role, of course.'

'Of course.'

'Two heads are better than one. Especially a head as grey as yours, Commissar.'

'Don't think my grey hairs make that head wise, Lieutenant. They just make me old. And tired. That's why I'm in insurance.'

'If you say so. But make no mistake, Commissar, Greece was never a country for young men. Not like Germany. It's old heads that have always mattered here.'

'All right. I'll do it.' I glanced at Garlopis. 'But didn't Cerberus have three heads?'

Garlopis pulled a face and then straightened his bow tie. 'You don't expect me to help, I hope. Really, sir, I don't think I can. Especially now, with a dead body lying at my feet. I think I told you before that I'm a coward, sir. I may have misled you there. I'm an abject coward. I'm the kind of man who gives cowards a bad name. I joined the insurance business because the debt-collection business was too hazardous. People kept on threatening to hit me, sir. But that now seems to be a very small thing, given the condition of poor Herr Witzel. And by the way, Cerberus was killed. By Hercules.'

'Only in some versions. And I can hardly help the lieutenant without your invaluable assistance, Garlopis.'

'That's right,' said the lieutenant. 'Your German is fluent, I think. And certainly more fluent than my English. So you're in. It's that or a drive to the Haidari Barracks, where at least one of you will feel very much at home. During the war it was the local concentration camp run by the SS and the Gestapo. We will leave you there on remand, while I look for evidence to prosecute you for Witzel's murder.'

Garlopis chuckled nervously. 'But there isn't any.'

'True. Which means it could take a while to look for it. Perhaps several months. We still use Block Fifteen at Haidari for keeping lefty prisoners in isolation.'

'He's right,' I said. 'Better helping him on the outside than being inside.'

Garlopis winced. 'It's Scylla and Charybdis,' he said. 'Choosing between two evils. Which, if you'll forgive me, is no choice at all.'

'Good, then that's settled,' said Lieutenant Leventis. 'So. If you'll both come with me, there are some pictures at police headquarters I'd like the commissar to take a look at.'

CHAPTER 23

On the way to police headquarters we made a detour. The Athens Gendarmerie was located on Mesogeion Avenue in a pleasantly large park. Surrounded with trees and grass, it was a three-storey, cream-coloured building with a red pantile roof and a series of arched windows and doors that were painted, patriotically, blue and white to match the flags that hung limply on either side of the main door. Lieutenant Leventis parked his car beside a row of squat palm trees that resembled a display of giant pineapples and went inside for a moment, he said, to hand over the spent brass we'd found at the murder scene to his ballistics people. Since I was handcuffed to Garlopis in the back seat I don't suppose he was too worried about either one of us running away; besides, Garlopis didn't look like much of a runner.

'What is this place?' I asked after a few moments.

'This is the police Gendarmerie, which has connections to the Greek army. Leventis belongs to the City Police, which is something different. They cooperate, of course. At least, that's the rumour. In Athens, the City Police are headquartered at the

Megaron Pappoudof, immediately opposite the Grande Bretagne Hotel, on the corner of Kifisias Street and Panepistimiou. Which is where we're headed next, I think.' He looked at his watch. 'I hope this isn't going to take long. I'm worried about the car. My cousin will be less than pleased if something happens to it.'

'I wouldn't worry about the car. Worry about us.'

'But why? The lieutenant said we'd be all right so long as we cooperate with him. By which he means you, of course. I don't think there's very much help that I can provide.'

'You're helping me to help him and that's enough. I don't want there to be any misunderstandings with him.'

'Well, now I'm worried that you're worried. May I ask why you're worried?'

'Because cops will say anything to ensure someone cooperates with them, especially when there's a murder to solve. Take it from me, you can't trust cops any more than you can trust their clients. Even now he might be booking us a nice quiet cell in this Haidari Barracks he mentioned.'

'There are no nice cells in Haidari. It's still the most notorious prison in all of Greece. Many heroes of the Greek resistance were tortured and killed there. And many Jews, of course. Although for them it was more of a transit camp to somewhere even more unpleasant. From Thessaloniki to Auschwitz.'

'That's a comforting thought. Look, I hope I'm wrong. What kind of man is this lieutenant, anyway?'

'Leventis? He struck me as quite a fair man, actually. A bit better than the average police lieutenant, perhaps, so I'm not absolutely sure if he's the type who can be bribed or not. But I've yet to see him write anything down, so he could still release both of us without having to explain why. For the right consideration.'

'I like the way you said "both of us". It gives me confidence in our professional association. How do you bribe a cop in Greece anyway?'

'The best way is with money, sir.'

'Is that a fact? You sound like you've done that kind of thing before.'

'Yes, but not for anything important, you understand. Traffic violations, mostly. And once on behalf of a cousin of mine who was accused of stealing a lady's handbag. But this is something different. At least it feels that way. Have you got much money?'

'That depends on the cop, doesn't it? I don't know how it works in Greece but generally speaking we don't bribe cops in West Germany because Germans can't hide behind a sense of humour if it goes wrong.'

'The Greek police do not have a sense of humour, either. If they had, they would not have become policemen in the first place. But they do like money. Everyone in Greece likes money. It was the Greeks who invented the use of money, so old habits die hard. Especially for the Attica police.'

Lieutenant Leventis appeared in the doorway of the Gendarmerie and walked back toward the car. Garlopis watched him with narrowed eyes.

'Against this man being bribed is the fact that he shaved this morning. And for another, he's wearing a clean shirt. The car we're sitting in is a Ford Popular, which is the cheapest car in

Europe. Also the watch on his wrist is just a cheap Russian model and he smokes Santé, which is a ladies' brand of cigarette. No man in Greece smokes these unless he's trying to save money.'

'Maybe he likes the lady on the packet.'

'No, sir. If you'll forgive me, this is a man living within his means. Besides, he walks too quickly for a man who'd take money. Like he has a purpose. I tend to think that corruption moves much more slowly in a country like this.'

'You should have been a cop yourself, Garlopis.'

'Not me, sir. As well as a coward I have always had very bad feet. You can't become a policeman if you have bad feet. Standing around and doing nothing all day is very hard on the feet.'

The lieutenant got back into the front seat and we drove into the centre of Athens; we made quick progress, too. As a way of getting around Athens I'd certainly recommend being driven by a policeman, even in a Ford Popular.

The Megaron Pappoudof faced the north side of the Greek parliament and the northeastern corner of Constitution Square and was set back from the main road, behind a tall wrought-iron railing. Overlooked by the St Isidore Church on the highest rock in Athens, which dominates the city like a Christian riposte to the Acropolis, the four- or five-storey building with its central pillared pediment was the Athenian equivalent of Munich's Police Praesidium, or the old Alex in Berlin. Leventis parked the car around the corner, uncuffed us, and then led the way through the main gate and up the marble steps to the entrance. Inside was almost a relief from the noise and smell of buses taking Greeks home from work and we were immediately faced with a colour portrait of

King Paul, who was holding a pair of white gloves, just in case he was obliged to shake anyone's hand or take a bribe. We climbed to the third floor.

Police headquarters are the same the world over: impersonal, worn, malodorous, busy – and already I felt very much at home. In spite of this, I would happily have turned around and walked over to my hotel for a bath and a drink, even if it wasn't as good as the Grande Bretagne. The notice board in the corridor outside the lieutenant's office was all in Greek but I knew exactly what it said because they'd had the same noticeboard at the Alex twenty years ago. Crime's more or less the same in any language. Garlopis and I sat down in front of a cheap wooden desk under the watchful eye of another cop who was leaning against the green-painted wall smoking a cigarette, and waited while Leventis fetched some files from a battered steel cabinet. It was a large office with green linoleum, a high ceiling with a stationary fan, a glass door, a water cooler, and another portrait of the king wearing a monocle, which really did make me feel at home. Somehow, and no matter where it hails from, royalty always manages to look a bit German. I expect it's something to do with the Prussian grenadier's ramrod they all shove up their arses before they have their portraits done.

'Do you like Greece, Herr Ganz?' said Leventis as he riffled through his case files.

'It seems very nice to me.'

'Our women?'

'Those I've seen seem very nice, too.'

'How about our wine?' he murmured.

'I like it. At least I do when I manage to get over the taste of the stuff. It tastes more like tree sap than actual wine. Still, the effect seems to be much the same and after the first bottle you hardly notice the difference.'

Garlopis smiled. 'That's very good,' he said. 'Most amusing.'

I didn't think Leventis was really listening, but I carried on anyway: 'They say the Romans used to make wine in the same way. That would certainly explain the decline and fall of the Roman Empire.'

He didn't answer and, after a while, I said, 'You know why we were at the house in Pritaniou. Why were you there, Lieutenant?'

'This morning one of the neighbours reported hearing the sound of an argument, followed by two shots. A patrol car found the body and then summoned me. The witness, who was cleaning the Glebe Holy Sepulchre Church opposite number 11, claims she saw two men leaving the house just before midday but couldn't describe them in any useful way.'

'Any idea yet who owns that house?'

'The neighbour thinks that Witzel might have been living there without the owner's knowledge. Squatting. It may even be that the owner has died. We're investigating.'

Leventis came back to his desk and sat down, smiling, but this time there was no cruelty in his smile, which made a nice change; only he wasn't yet through with threatening us.

'All of what I'm about to tell you now is confidential,' he said. 'I should hate to read about any of this in a newspaper. If I did I should certainly assume that one of you was responsible and have you both sent to Haidari Barracks. My captain – Captain Kokkinos, would insist on it.'

'We won't breathe a word of what you tell us, Lieutenant. Will we, Herr Ganz? You have our word. And let me just add that we're very happy to cooperate with you and Captain Kokkinos in any way you see fit.'

Leventis ignored him as he would probably have ignored a mosquito, or the relentless sound of Greek traffic.

'If,' persisted Garlopis, 'earlier on I gave you the impression that I was less than happy to help I should like to correct that now. We'll do anything we can to make sure that this murderer is caught, and soon. Anything. Including, might I add, paying a small fine or compensation for the illegal entry we made at the house in Pritaniou. In cash, of course. And whatever amount you think is appropriate. You yourself might give it to the owner when eventually he is found.'

'That won't be necessary,' said Leventis. He knew perfectly well what was being suggested but, generously, he chose to ignore that, too. 'Now then, to business. About a week ago, a lawyer was found murdered. In the suburb of Glyfada. His name was Dr Samuel Frizis.'

'I think maybe I read about that in *The Athens News*,' I said.

'Yes,' said Leventis. 'But the paper didn't publish any specific details. We've been keeping those back deliberately. You see, Dr Frizis was shot through both eyes, just like your friend Siegfried Witzel.'

'I wish you'd stop calling him our friend. Neither of us liked him, did we, Garlopis?'

'Indeed no. He was a most disagreeable fellow. Very bad-tempered. We were both afraid he might shoot one of us. Ironic when you think about it. Given what happened. But life's like that sometimes, isn't it?'

Leventis handed me a sheaf of colour photographs from the file. They showed a man lying dead on a plush-looking couch. There were several autopsy shots, which made for unpleasant viewing. All the blood in his head had drained away from his blackened eyes onto one shoulder of his tweed suit, while the other shoulder was quite unspoiled. On the marble table in front of the sofa was a little bronze statue of the goddess Diana holding a spear. It almost looked as if she might have inflicted the damage to the dead lawyer's eyes. Cruelly, I offered one of the photographs to Garlopis, who shook his head and then looked away uncomfortably.

'The killer used a rimless, tapered, 9-mill round just like the one that you found on the floor at the house in Pritaniou Street. My guess is that the ballistics people back at the Gendarmerie will find they were fired from the same gun. Most likely a Luger pistol, they tell me. We've been through Frizis's client list and appointment book and found nothing of any interest. So this new murder is a break for us, since it's very likely these two murders are connected. Although I really don't have any idea how.

'Back at the house in the old town you suggested that Witzel was possibly killed by Jews, in revenge for the confiscation of their property by the Nazis. But I must tell you that I think it's unlikely that Dr Frizis was murdered by Jews, not least because he himself was a Jew. And until Witzel was killed we had even

considered the possibility that Dr Frizis might have been murdered *because* he was a Jew. I am sorry to tell you that this is
becoming quite an anti-Semitic country. Anyway, Siegfried Witzel's murder also puts paid to that particular theory.'

'What kind of a lawyer was he anyway?' I asked.

'He must have been a good one if he could afford to live in
Glyfada,' said Garlopis. 'That's the most expensive part of town.
Everyone in Athens aspires to living in Glyfada.'

'He may have been a good lawyer,' said Leventis, 'but he wasn't
particularly honest.'

'You won't hear me arguing that one down,' I said. 'No good
lawyer is particularly honest, in my experience. But dispensing
with a lawyer is usually more straightforward. Withholding payment will do the job most effectively.'

Leventis took off his glasses and raised a finger. 'Fortunately,
I have another theory. It's about who killed him, if not why he
was killed. It's a little bit far-fetched, perhaps, but, well, see
what you think, Commissar. But first I need to tell you a story.'

CHAPTER 24

'I'm not a Jew but I was born in Salonika and lived there as a boy and had many Jewish school friends until I was thirteen years old, when my father got a job with the Commercial Credit Bank here in Athens. To some extent, I've always regarded Salonika as my real home. Whenever I go back, it's almost as if I once had another life, that I've been two people: that I had a Salonikan childhood and an Athenian manhood, and the two seem entirely without connection. Now, whenever I'm back there, I can't help thinking that life isn't just about working out who we are and what makes us tick, it's also about understanding why we aren't where we ever expected to be. That things might have been very different. It's the best antidote to nostalgia I know.'

I nodded silently. This was the Greek lieutenant's story but, in this particular respect at least, it was mine as well, and for a fleeting second I felt a strong, almost metaphysical connection with this man I hardly knew.

He looked distant for a moment – as if his mind was back in Salonika – and rubbed his jaw thoughtfully. The hair on his head was dark and shiny, with just a hint of silver, and, in the light from the tall office window, it resembled the skin of a mackerel. I guessed he was about forty-five. His speaking voice, which sounded like dark honey, relied a great deal on his hairy hands, as if he'd been trying to negotiate the price of a rug. The tunic of his uniform was tailored and it was a while before I perceived the size of the shoulders it was concealing. They were strong shoulders and probably capable of delivering great violence – a true copper's shoulders.

'As a boy I wanted to play basketball for Aris Thessaloniki – to be like my hero, Faidon Matthaiou. Not to become a policeman in Athens.'

'A great player,' agreed Garlopis. 'The patriarch of Greek basketball.'

'But here I am. A long way from home.'

'I know what you mean, Lieutenant,' I said, hoping to push us all back onto the path of his story.

'Salonika was established by Alexander the Great's brother-in-law, Ptolemy of Aloros, to be the main port for Macedonia; it's also been of central importance to Greece, Serbia, Bulgaria, even the Austro-Hungarian Empire. But most lastingly, for five centuries it was the Ottoman Turks who controlled the city and gave it a near autonomous status that allowed the Jews to become its most dominant group, with the result that, at the turn of the century, of the hundred and twenty thousand people who lived in Salonika, between sixty and eighty thousand were Jews. This was perhaps one of the largest numbers of European Jews to be found outside Poland; certainly it was the oldest community of Jews in Europe. And it's not an exaggeration to say that Salonika was the Jerusalem of the Balkans, perhaps even the Mother of Israel, since so many who once lived there are now in Palestine.

'I won't detain you, Commissar, by trying to explain how, over the many centuries, so many Jews in the diaspora, fleeing one persecution after another, ended up in Salonika; nor will I take up your time to explain what happened between the two wars and how Salonika became Thessaloniki and Greek, but in this most ancient city where change was a way of life, everything changed when the German army arrived and, I'm sorry to say, that change became a way of death. The alacrity with which the Nazis began to take action against Salonika's Jews was astonishing even to the Greeks who, thanks to the Turks, know a bit about persecution, but for the Jews it was devastating. The Nuremberg Laws were immediately implemented. Prominent Jewish citizens, including some friends of my own father, were arrested, Jewish property was subject to confiscation, a ghetto was built, and all Jews were subjected to violent abuse and sometimes summary execution. But of course much worse was to come.

'Following a series of military disasters for the Axis powers, Hitler reorganized his Balkan front and, as part of this process, it was decided to "pacify" Salonika and its hinterland. *Pacify*: you Germans have always had a peculiar talent for euphemism. Like "resettlement". The Jews of Salonika soon found out that these words meant something very different in the mouth of a German. A decision was made at the highest level that the

Jews of Salonika should be removed and deported to Riga and Minsk, for eventual resettlement in the Polish death camps. The city's Jewish community now came under the direct control of the SS and the SD in the person of an officer called Adolf Eichmann. He and several other SD and German army officers set themselves up in some style in a confiscated Jewish villa on Velissariou Street. The villa had a cellar they used as a torture chamber. There, wealthier Jews were interrogated as to where they'd hidden their wealth. Among these was a banker by the name of Jaco Kapantzi in whom the local SD took a special interest since he was also one of the richest men in Salonika. It infuriated these sadists that Kapantzi steadfastly refused to reveal where he'd hidden his money, so they decided to have him transferred by train to Block 15 at the Haidari Barracks in Athens. There, a notorious SS torturer by the name of Paul Radomski could go to work on Kapantzi night and day.

'But something must have happened on the Athens train to infuriate the SD and, in front of several other rail passengers, Kapantzi, still wearing his pyjamas and dressing gown, was shot. Perhaps he tried to escape, perhaps he said something, I'm not entirely sure what, but I think perhaps Kapantzi had probably realized that his best chance to escape further torture was to provoke the SD captain in whose custody he was travelling from Salonika into killing him. With his gun in his hand and the body still bleeding on the floor the SD officer asked the other passengers if anyone had seen anything and of course nobody had. The officer got off the train at the next stop and returned to Salonika. When the train eventually arrived in Athens, the man's dead body was still lying on the floor of the carriage, and there it became the responsibility of the Attica City Police.

'Obviously a murder had been committed and I was one of the investigating officers. Of course, we all knew it was the German SD who'd killed the man and for this reason there was no chance that we'd be able to do anything about it. We might as well have tried to arrest Hitler himself.

'But we still had to go through the motions and I managed to track down one of the other passengers. Eventually, I persuaded him to make a witness statement that I agreed to keep off the file until after the war and I quietly made it my business to find out more about the young SD captain who'd murdered Jaco Kapantzi in case one day I was in a position to bring him to justice.

'Perhaps this will sound strange to you now, Commissar. "Why bother?" I hear you say. After all, what's the fate of one man when more than sixty thousand Greek Jews died at Auschwitz and Treblinka? Well, to paraphrase Stalin – and believe me, there's a lot of that in Greece – it's the difference between a tragedy and a statistic, perhaps. And the point is this: Jaco Kapantzi was my case, my responsibility, and I've come to believe that in life it's best to live for a purpose greater than oneself. And before you suggest there's something in this for me, a promotion, perhaps, there isn't. Even if no one ever knows that I have done this I would do it because I want to do something for Greece and I believe this is good for my country.'

It had been a while since I'd had any thoughts like that myself, but I found I could still appreciate finding them in the heart of another man even if it was a cop who was threatening to put me in jail.

'And if all that wasn't enough, my father had worked for Jaco Kapantzi before moving to Athens. Indeed, it had been Mr Kapantzi who'd generously helped my father get his new job and even loaned him his moving expenses. So you might also say I took his death personally.'

Leventis lit a cigarette; his voice had lowered now as if he was drawing on something deep in himself, and I saw that it wouldn't be a good idea to make an enemy of this man.

'There's no statute of limitations when it comes to murder in Greece. And the killing of Jaco Kapantzi remains open to this day. I'll never know the names of the men who participated in the murders of my fellow countrymen in Auschwitz and Treblinka and besides, those crimes happened hundreds of miles north of here. But I do know the name of the individual SD captain who murdered Jaco Kapantzi on a Greek train. His name was Alois Brunner. Another German officer, an army captain, witnessed what happened, but I don't suppose we'll ever know who he was, only that my witness reports that he expressed some amused astonishment at Brunner's behaviour and advised that they should both leave the train. It's said that all detectives have a case that gives them a lifetime of sleepless nights. I'm sure you had yours, Commissar. Alois Brunner is mine.

'Not much is known about him. What I do know has taken me the best part of ten years to find out. Brunner was just thirty-one years old when he murdered Jaco Kapantzi on that train. Born in Austria he was an early recruit to the Nazi Party and having joined the SD in 1938, he was assigned to the Central Office for Jewish Emigration in Vienna, where he became Eichmann's close collaborator in the murder of thousands of Jews. After his time in Salonika, Brunner was named commander of the Drancy internment camp near Paris. This was in June 1943.

'I don't know how much you know about this kind of thing, Commissar – more than you'll ever admit, I expect, if the rest of your countrymen are anything to go by – but Drancy was the place where more than sixty-seven thousand French Jews were first confined and then deported to the extermination camps for resettlement. Seven years ago I took a short vacation in Paris and managed to find someone who'd been in Drancy – a German-Jewish woman who'd been hiding from the Nazis in the South of France until she was arrested. Her name was Charlotte Bernheim and somehow she survived Drancy and Auschwitz before returning to France. She remembered Brunner very well: short, poorly built, skinny – hardly your master-race type. She told me he seemed to have a physical detestation of Jews because once she saw a prisoner touch him accidentally and Brunner pulled out his pistol and shot him dead. Through both his eyes. And it was this particular detail that caught my attention because Jaco Kapantzi was also shot through the eyes.

'You begin to see my interest in the murders of Dr Frizis and Siegfried Witzel. Of course, Frizis didn't prick my curiosity until we found Witzel's body and began to see the German connection, and then of course you mentioned how Witzel's boat had been confiscated from a Salonikan Jew, which intrigues me even more. That and the killer's modus operandi, of course. It begins to look like a sort of homicidal signature. The idea that Brunner may even be back in Greece is of course enormously important to me. I'd love to catch this man and see him face the death penalty. Yes, we still execute our murderers, unlike you West Germans who seem to have discovered a new squeamishness about killing criminals. I'd give anything to see this man meet the end he deserves. These days we shoot murderers, but we used to send them to the guillotine. For a man like Brunner I'd start a petition to bring the guillotine back.

'But to continue with the story. In September 1944, Brunner was transferred from Drancy to the Sered Concentration Camp in Czechoslovakia, where he was tasked with the deportation of all the camp's remaining Jews – some thirteen thousand people – before the camp was finally liberated by the Red Army in March 1945. I've not found anyone alive from Sered who remembers Brunner. You Germans did your work too well there. After the war, Brunner disappeared. For a while it was even thought he was dead, executed by the Allies in Vienna in May 1946. But this was a different Brunner. It was Anton Brunner, who conveniently also worked for Eichmann in Vienna, who was executed. And my friends in the National Intelligence Service of Greece tell me that they strongly suspect that the American CIA and the German Federal Intelligence Service – the BND – may have deliberately helped to muddy the waters around Anton Brunner's end to protect Alois Brunner's postwar work for Germany's own intelligence services. Yes, that's right, it's not just German insurance companies that employ old Nazis.'

'I was never a Nazi,' I said.

'No, of course not,' said Leventis. But it was clear he didn't believe me. 'What's more certain is that Brunner is still alive and that he has good connections in the current German government. According to my sources in the Greek NIS, it's strongly believed that Brunner is presently working undercover for the German BND. Meanwhile a French court tried Brunner for war crimes in absentia in 1954 and sentenced him to death. And he's one of the most wanted war criminals in the world.'

Lieutenant Leventis opened another file and took out a black-and-white photograph, which he now handed to me. 'A friend of mine in the Greek NIS managed to obtain this from his opposite number in the French intelligence services, one of the only known photographs of Alois Brunner, taken in France sometime during the summer of 1944.'

I was looking at a man by a wooden fence in a field, wearing a belted leather trench coat, with a hat and gloves in his left hand and, as far as I could see, without even a badge in his lapel that might have helped to identify the man as a Nazi Party official. It was a good leather coat; I'd once owned one very like it myself before it had been stolen by a Russian POW guard. The man in the grainy picture didn't look like a mass murderer, but then nobody ever does. I'd met enough murderers in my time to know that they nearly always look like everyone else. They're not monsters and they're not diabolical, they're just the people who live next door and say hello on the stairs. This man was slim, with a high forehead, a narrow nose, neat dark hair, and an almost benign expression on his face; it was the kind of picture he might have sent to his girlfriend or wife, supposing he ever had one. On the back of the picture there was a description of the photograph, written in French: *A photograph believed to be of Alois Brunner, born 8th April 1912, taken August 1944, property of the Direction Centrale des Renseignements Généraux.*

'Alois Brunner would now be almost forty-five years old,' said Leventis. 'Which is the same age as me. Perhaps that's another reason why I take a special interest in him.'

Lieutenant Leventis continued talking for a while longer but I was hardly listening now; I kept looking at the thin man in the black-and-white photograph. Immediately I knew for sure that I'd met the man before, but it hadn't been during the war and he hadn't been calling himself Alois Brunner. I was quite certain of this. In fact, I still had the man's business card in my pocket. The man in the photograph was the same Austro-Hungarian cigarette salesman who had struck up a conversation with me in the bar at the Mega Hotel.

CHAPTER 25

There was a police radio on somewhere or maybe I was just hearing a few garbled, half-heard, barely understood words through the white noise that was my own thoughts. In the lieutenant's office, men and a few women came and went like the crew on a ship, handing him reports, which mostly he ignored. Eventually he got up and closed the frosted-glass door. With his glasses off Leventis looked a bit punchy; but with them on, his eyes missed nothing. He had seen my own eyes linger on Brunner's photograph for a little too long, perhaps. The man I'd met in my hotel bar was a war criminal. And not just any war criminal but one of the most wanted war criminals in Europe. It was sometimes a shock to realize that I wasn't the only German with a past. But I hardly wanted to confess to having met the man until I knew what he'd been after. Especially as he'd been a colleague of Adolf Eichmann. I'd met Eichmann once or twice myself, and I hardly wanted to admit this either. Not to some Greek cop I hardly knew. I liked Leventis. But I didn't trust him.

'You recognize him, Commissar?'

'No.'

'You looked like you know him, maybe.'

'I was taking a good look at him, that's all, just in case I did. I'm an ex-cop, remember? So old habits die hard. I was stationed in Paris for a while during the war and I was thinking it was at least possible that I'd met your man, Brunner. But our dates don't match. By June 1943 I'm afraid I was back in Germany. Besides, people look different when they're not in uniform. Behave differently, too. This fellow looks like he's on vacation.'

'You could help me to find him.'

'I already said I would, if I could.'

'Yes, but maybe you were just saying that to get your passport back and save yourself a trip to jail. The fact as I see it, Commissar, is that you have a moral duty to help me.'

'How's that?'

'Because you need to play your part in restoring your country's reputation. In the weeks and months after Germany invaded Greece this city was systematically starved by the Germans. Tens of thousands died. There were bodies of children lying dead in front of this very police headquarters and nothing any of us could do about it. And yet here we are, more than ten years after the end of the war and Germany has yet to pay a penny in reparations to the Greek government for what happened. But it's not just about money, is it? Germany's got plenty of that now, thanks to your so-called economic miracle. No, I believe collective guilt can be reduced more meaningfully by individual action. In this case, yours. At least, that's the way I look at it. This would be a more worthwhile kind of atonement than a mere bank transfer, Commissar, for what you Nazis did to Greece.'

'For years I succeeded in not being a Nazi,' I said. 'It was difficult, sometimes dangerous – especially in the police. You've no idea. But now that I'm here I discover I was a Nazi all along. Next time I come to your office I'll wear an SS uniform and a monocle, carry a riding whip, and sing the Horst Wessel song.'

'That might help. In any Greek tragedy death is always dressed in black. But seriously, Commissar, for most Greeks there is no difference between a German and a Nazi. The very idea of a good German is still strange to us. And perhaps it always will be.'

'So maybe a Greek killed Siegfried Witzel, after all. Maybe he was killed *because* he was a German. Maybe we've all got it coming.'

'You won't find anyone in Greece arguing against an opinion like that. But I'm thinking that as a German you might have some insights with this case that I couldn't possibly have. Let's not forget that two men have been murdered in Athens. And one of them was your insured claimant.'

We were talking but only half of me was listening to what Leventis was saying; the larger part of my mind was still trying to work out exactly why Alois Brunner had struck up a conversation at the bar of the Mega Hotel. Was it possible that Brunner had made me his stooge to help him find Siegfried Witzel so he could murder him? It would certainly explain why Witzel had been carrying a gun and why he'd been so reluctant to tell us his address: he was afraid. Still stalling for time I said, 'I'll help you, Lieutenant, okay?'

Even as I spoke my fingers were holding the same business card in my pocket that Brunner had given me himself. Georg Fischer: That was what he was calling himself now. What would happen if I called the number on the card? Was the number even real? And who'd told Brunner that I was at the Mega Hotel? That I might lead him to Witzel? Not Garlopis, although in that stupid blue Olds he'd have been easy to tail to and from the airport. Perhaps someone back in Germany had told Brunner I was on the way to Athens. Someone from Munich RE. Maybe Alzheimer himself. After all, Alzheimer knew Konrad Adenauer – there was that photograph of the two men on his desk. And if Alzheimer knew the Old Man, then perhaps he also knew someone in the German BND. But it was almost as if Brunner had been expecting me.

'But since you mentioned moral duty, Lieutenant, I feel obliged to say that it cuts two ways. If I am going to help you, I'll need some kind of written assurance that you'll keep your word and let us go. But supposing this *was* nothing to do with Brunner or supposing he's already left Greece, what then? I'd hate to find that you were more interested in your clear-up rate than in our innocence.'

'All right. That's fair enough.' Leventis leaned across his desk and pointed a forefinger as thick as a rifle barrel straight at my head. 'But first I need you to ante up, to show me that you're in the game. And then we'll talk about immunity from prosecution.'

'Like a suggestion from one detective to another, perhaps?'

'That might work.'

'I'm trying to think of something.'

'Then let me help you. There's a German interpreter who's currently on trial in Athens for war crimes.'

'Arthur Meissner. I read about that in the paper. Yes. Maybe he knows something that might help. Maybe he knew Brunner.'

'As a matter of fact, he did. He knew all of the Nazis who controlled Greece – Eichmann, Wisliceny, Felmy, Lanz, Student. But under Greek law I'm forbidden from trying to interrogate him now that he's on trial. Or to offer him any kind of a deal.'

'He might speak to me. Because I'm not a Greek.'

'I had the same thought.'

'Where is he now?'

'In Averoff Prison.'

'Look, you'll forgive me for saying so, Lieutenant, but a man who was merely a Greek interpreter doesn't sound like the worst war criminal I ever heard of. My own boss in the Berlin Criminal Police, General Arthur Nebe, was a very career-minded man who commanded a killing unit that massacred more than forty-five thousand people. That's what I call a war criminal.'

'To be perfectly honest with you, Commissar, Meissner's merely a man who was unwise enough to cooperate a little too enthusiastically with the occupation authorities. More of a collaborator than a war criminal. But it's a subtle difference in Greece. Too subtle for most people, given the fact that there are no German war criminals who've ever been tried for their crimes here in Greece. That's right. None at all. A few were tried for so-called hostage crimes committed in southeast Europe, but those trials were only in Germany. And most of those convicted were released years ago, pardoned at the instigation of the Americans and the

British, who established the Greek federal republic as a bulwark against the Soviet Union at the beginning of the Cold War. Among these men was Wilhelm Speidel, the military governor of Greece from 1943, the man responsible for numerous directives authorizing mass murders, including the massacre in Kalavryta. He was released from the Landsberg Prison in 1951. He was originally sentenced to a twenty-year prison term.'

'That's truly shocking,' said Garlopis. 'Isn't it, Herr Ganz?'

'So you'll forgive me for saying so, Commissar, but the trial of Arthur Meissner is as near as we've ever got to any kind of a war crimes trial here in Greece. Maybe now you understand why I was talking about your moral duty to help me find Brunner.'

'I can certainly see why you would put it in those terms, Lieutenant,' said Garlopis. 'And may I say that as a Greek who loves his country I will do all I can to assist Herr Ganz in any way he sees fit.'

Resisting the obvious temptation again to tell Garlopis to shut up, I put a cigarette in my mouth – it was the last one from the packet Alois Brunner himself had given me – and lit up, which gave me enough time to consider my situation in a little more detail. I wanted nothing to do with what Leventis was suggesting; keeping far away from any of my old comrades was a top priority for Bernhard Gunther. And I had no more time for moral duty than I had for taking early retirement. But I needed to string Leventis along; to make him think I was helping him without getting myself too involved. After all, like Brunner, I was also living under a false name, with a false passport to go with that.

'Well, what exactly did he do?' I asked. 'This Meissner fellow.'

'It's certain that he helped himself to the property of Greeks and Greek Jews. Some of the other charges – rape and murder – look rather more difficult to prove.'

'Is a deal possible? Would you at least be prepared to speak up in court on his behalf if he was to provide some information leading to the capture of Alois Brunner?'

'I'd have to speak to the state prosecutor. But maybe.'

'I'll need more than that if I do speak to Meissner. Even if he can't deliver information on Brunner it's possible he might give up someone else just as important. Come on, Lieutenant. This man needs some life insurance.'

'I will say this: if we were to catch a whale like Brunner, it would certainly take all the attention off a sprat like Meissner. And if he helped us to do it, I wouldn't be surprised if we let him go.'

'So let me speak to Meissner in private, at the prison. Just the two of us. It may be that I can persuade him to talk.'

Leventis looked at his watch. 'If we're quick we can just catch Papakyriakopoulos. That's the name of Meissner's lawyer. Every Friday evening, after a week in court, he always goes for a drink at an old bar called Brettos, which is about a ten-minute walk from here. I doubt he'll speak to me, but he might unload something to you.'

CHAPTER 26

Brettos was in a district of touristy Athenian backstreets called Plaka, and from the outside unremarkable; inside, the whole back wall was a virtual skyscraper of brightly lit liquor bottles and, given its proximity to the Acropolis, it felt like the world's most ancient bar. It was easy to imagine Aristotle and Archimedes drinking ice-cold martinis there in search of the final, clear simplicity of an alcoholic aphorism after a hard day of philosophical debate.

Seated on a high stool at a marble counter beneath a brandy barrel, Arthur Meissner's lawyer, Dr Papakyriakopoulos, was a shrewd-looking man in his thirties, with a neat moustache, dark marsupial eyes, and a profile like an urgent signpost. Lieutenant Leventis made the introductions and then discreetly withdrew, leaving me and Garlopis to order a round and to make the case for a meeting with Arthur Meissner at the court where he was being tried or at Averoff Prison, where he was being held on remand. Leventis said he'd wait for us at the café across the narrow street. The Greek lawyer listened politely while I quickly outlined my mission. Sipping a drink that looked and smelled more medicinal than alcoholic, he lit a small cigar and then, patiently, explained his client's situation, in perfect English:

'My client is of no importance in the scheme of things,' he said. 'This is the whole basis of his defence. That he was nobody.'

'Is that nobody like Odysseus was nobody? To trick the cyclops? Or nobody in a more existential sense? In other words, was he a cunning nobody or a modest, indefinite nobody?'

'You're a German, Herr Ganz? Which were you?'

Dr Papakyriakopoulos was Greek but he was still the kind of lawyer I disliked most: the slippery kind. As slippery as an otter with a live fish in its paws.

'That's a good question. The former, I'd say. It certainly took a lot of cunning for me to stay alive while the Nazis were in power. And just as much afterward.'

'In Arthur Meissner's case he was the sort of existential nobody that you describe, Herr Ganz. If you ever met my client you would see a simple man incapable of stratagem. You would meet a man who took no decisions, did not offer counsel, committed no crimes, was never a member of a right-wing organization, was not an anti-Semite, and had little or no knowledge of anything other than what was said to him in German and which he was obliged to simultaneously translate into Greek, nothing of which he remembers now. I imagine Mr Garlopis here would tell you that with simultaneous translation it's often impossible to keep any memory of the translations you made just a few minutes ago.'

'Oh, that's very true, sir,' said Garlopis. 'Unless one keeps notes, of course. I myself often kept notes to assist with simultaneous translations. But I always threw those away afterwards. The handwriting is all but illegible even to me sometimes, such is the speed with which one is obliged to write.'

'There you are,' said Dr Papakyriakopoulos. 'Straight from the horse's mouth, so to speak. I could have used you in court the other day, Mr Garlopis. As an expert witness. The fact is that for most of the occupation period when my client was employed by the Nazis he had no real acquaintance with the men for whom he was translating other than the fact that they wore Nazi uniforms and had the power of life and death over all Greek citizens, including him, of course. In short, he is a scapegoat for the failings of the Greek nation then and now. For Arthur Meissner to admit that he knew this German whom Lieutenant Leventis is looking for might prejudice his defence. He was just obeying orders and hoping to stay alive, and any evidence of his criminality has, so far, turned out to be little more than circumstantial or, worse still, worthless hearsay. Nevertheless, he is a loyal Greek citizen, and I will put it to him tomorrow that you are willing to help him. It may be that he agrees to meet you, and it may be that he does not. But might I ask, what is your interest here?'

'The lieutenant seems to think that as a German I have a moral duty to assist the police with their inquiry. I'm not so sure about that, to be honest. I work for an insurance company but before the war I was a policeman. I came to Greece to adjust an insurance claim made by a German policy holder called Siegfried Witzel. Witzel was found murdered earlier today in circumstances that lead Leventis to suppose that his death may be connected with a murder that took place during the war, and also with the recent murder of an Athenian lawyer.'

'Dr Samuel Frizis.'

'Yes. Did you know him?'

'Quite well.'

'If I assist Leventis with his murder investigation – if I can persuade Arthur Meissner to talk to me, for instance, in confidence – then he may be prepared to speak up in court for your client.'

'Samuel Frizis was a friend of mine. We were at law school together. Naturally I should like to see his murderer caught. This puts a different complexion on the matter under discussion. He's a decent man, Stavros Leventis. An idealist. But what kind of a policeman were you, may I ask?'

'A detective. I was a commissar with the Berlin Criminal Police.'

'At the risk of being facetious, all the German police who were in Greece seem to have been criminals. That was certainly my client's experience.'

'There's some truth in that, yes.'

'I'm glad you say so.' He sipped his ouzo and seemed to catch the eye of a woman carrying a briefcase who was standing in the open doorway like a cat, wondering if she should come in or not. She looked worth catching, too, and not just her eye. 'I read a lot of German history, Herr Ganz. I'm fascinated with this whole period, and not just because of this case. Correct me if I'm wrong but it's my information that the Berlin Criminal Police came under the control of the Reich Main Security Office in 1939. That you were in effect under the control of members of the SS. And that you often worked in conjunction with members of the Gestapo. Is that right?' He paused. 'If I sound curious about this it's because I like to know exactly who I'm dealing with. And exactly how they might be of assistance in mounting an effective defence. For example, it's also my information that many members of Kripo were operationally obliged to become members of the SD. In other words, when you were put into uniform, you were only obeying orders. Much like my client.'

'Take a walk, would you?' I asked Garlopis.

'A walk? But I haven't finished my drink. Oh, I see. Yes, of course, sir.' Garlopis stood up awkwardly. 'I'll wait in that café across the street, with Lieutenant Leventis.'

Garlopis went out of the bar looking like a sheepish schoolboy who had been told to play somewhere else. I told myself I was going to have to make it up to him later.

'You're well informed, Dr – ' I shook my head. 'I don't think I'll even try to pronounce your name.'

'I try to be. Where did you see active service? It wasn't Greece, I'll be bound. If you'd been here you'd hardly have come back.'

'France, the Ukraine, Russia. But not Greece, no. I wasn't a Party member, you understand. And I think you're right. Germany behaved abominably in this country. The man Leventis is looking for – the one who committed a murder during the war – he was also in the SD. That's why Leventis thinks I can help.'

'Set a fox to catch a fox, eh?'

'Something like that. If I'm levelling with you now it's so you know that I'll do the same with Arthur Meissner.'

'Well, I appreciate your honesty. And as I said, I'm very keen to help catch the murderer of Samuel Frizis. Although connecting it with a murder that took place during the occupation looks like a much more difficult task. After all, there were so many.'

'True, but there's no doubt in my mind or his that catching this particular fox would take a great deal of the heat off your client. Not to say all of it.'

'Interesting idea.' Dr Papakyriakopoulos nodded at the woman in the doorway, who seemed to have been awaiting his permission, and she came inside the bar.

'What kind of a lawyer was he?' I asked.

'He was my friend. But he wasn't a good lawyer. To be precise, he was the kind of lawyer who gives lawyers a bad name. The rich, cut-corners kind of lawyer who was much more interested in money than in justice. And not above a bit of bribery.'

'The kind of bribery that might go wrong if it didn't work?'

'Enough to get him killed, you mean? I don't know. Perhaps. I suppose it would depend on the size of the bribe.'

'Any German connections?'

'Like me, he didn't speak a word of it. And he lived in Athens all his life.'

'But how could he do that? He was a Jew, wasn't he?'

'Someone hid him, for almost two years. There was a lot of that here in Greece. Jews were never unpopular until more recently, when our governments started to become much more right-wing. This new fellow we've got now, Karamanlis, is a populist who talks about Greece's European destiny, whatever that is. He sees himself as the Greek version of your Chancellor Adenauer.'

The woman who'd come into the bar approached us, and

Dr Papakyriakopoulos got off his stool, kissed her on both cheeks, spoke in Greek with her for a minute or two, and then introduced us.

'Herr Ganz, this is Miss Panatoniou. She's also a lawyer, albeit one who works for a government ministry. Elli, Herr Ganz is an insurance man, from Germany.'

'Pleased to meet you, Herr Ganz.'

She said this in German I think but I hardly noticed because it seemed to my eyes that she reached into me with hers and strolled around the inside of my head for a while picking up things that didn't belong to her and generally handling all there was to find. Not that I minded very much. I'm generally inclined to let curious women behave exactly how they want when they're riffling through the drawers and closets of my mind. Then again, this was probably just my imagination, which always slips into overdrive when a voluptuously attractive woman in her thirties gets near my passenger seat. I shook her hand. And the two spoke some more in Greek before Papakyriakopoulos came back to me in English.

'Well, look, it was good to meet you, Herr Ganz. And I'll certainly speak to my client about what you have proposed. Where are you staying?'

'At the Mega.'

Clearly he wanted Miss Panatoniou all to himself, and I couldn't blame him for that. Every part of her was perfectly defined. Each haunch, each shoulder, each leg, and each breast. She reminded me of a diagram in a butcher's shop window – one of those maps concerning which cut comes from where, and I felt hungry just looking at the poor woman. I finished my drink and quickly went outside before I was tempted to take a bite of her.

Garlopis had gone to fetch the Oldsmobile and, after a brief talk with the lieutenant, during which I agreed that he should look after my passport and he agreed not to arrest me for a while, I hailed a cab back to the hotel. Unlike Berlin taxi drivers, who never want to take you anywhere, Greek taxi drivers were always full of good ideas as to where they might drive you after they'd cut through the knotty problem of delivering you to your stated destination. This one suggested that he should drive me to the Temple of Zeus, where he would wait and then drive me back to the hotel, and maybe come back for me again later on and take me to a nightclub called Sarantidis, on Ithakis Street, where I could be entertained by some lovely ladies for a very special price. Unreasonably, he thought, I declined his kind invitation and went back to the Mega, where I took a much-needed bath and called up the Athenian telephone number on Fischer's business card – 80227 – but it was out of order. At least that's what I think the Greek operator was saying to me. After some time in Greece I'd decided that it wasn't just the Trojan War that had lasted ten years but Homer's telling the story of it, too.

CHAPTER 27

If Captain Alois Brunner was back in Greece this was hardly my concern, in spite of what Lieutenant Leventis had said, albeit rather admirably, too: moral duty was something for philosophers and schoolmasters, not blow-in insurance men like me. All I wanted to do now was get back to Munich with my pockets full of expense receipts and before I managed to find myself with more trouble than I could reasonably handle. To this end I'd decided I urgently needed Dumbo Dietrich to go and find Professor Buchholz in Munich and get his side of what had happened on the *Doris*. Because it seemed obvious now that the loss of the *Doris* and the murder of Siegfried Witzel were intimately connected and probably only Buchholz could shed light on that. If he was still alive. Already I had more than a few doubts on this particular score. So when I went into the office the following morning I sent a telegram to MRE, after which I apologized to poor Garlopis for the peremptory way I'd spoken to him in Brettos.

'That's quite all right, sir,' he said. 'And I don't blame you in the least for that. It's my experience of speaking to the police that any situation can quickly become a whore's fence post, as we say in Greece. This cop could make your life a real roller skate if you're not careful. Your life *and* mine.'

'Let me buy you a drink and I'll feel better about it.'

'Just a quick one, perhaps. It wouldn't do to be drunk before lunch.'

'I might agree if lunch didn't involve Greek food.'

'You don't like Greek food?'

'Most of the time. Lunch is usually a little much like dinner for my taste. But with a drink inside me that doesn't seem to matter so much.'

We went along to the bar at the Mega, not because it was better than any other I'd been in but because I was still keeping an eye out for Georg Fischer and because after lunching out of a bottle I was planning to read the newspaper and then take a nap in my room, like a good salaryman. Garlopis had one and then got up to leave while I was ordering another gimlet.

'I'd best go back,' he explained. 'Just in case head office decides to answer your telegram.'

'Good idea. But I'll wait here.'

'Herr Ganz?' Garlopis smiled politely. 'Forgive me for saying so. You're able to consume cocktails during the day and still do your job?'

'I've always had irregular habits, my friend. Back when I was a detective we used to pull an all-night shift at a crime scene and go for a drink at six o'clock in the morning. Being a cop changes your life forever like that. And not in a good way. More than ten years after I left the Murder Commission my liver still behaves like it's close to a badge and a gun. Besides, this is the only one of my irregular habits that doesn't get me into trouble.'

Garlopis bit his lip at the mention of a gun and then left me in the care of Charles Tanqueray. I waited a while but there was no sign of the man who'd called himself Georg Fischer so I called the barman over and tried some questions, in English.

'The other night. I was in here. Do you remember?'

'Yes, sir. I remember.'

'There was another man at the bar. He spoke pretty good Greek. Do you remember him, too?'

'Yes. He was German, too, I think. Like you. What about him?'

'Ever see him in here before?'

'Maybe.'

'With anyone?'

'I can't remember.'

'Anything you can tell me about him?'

'He learned his Greek in the north, sir. Not here in Athens. Okay, now I remember something else. One time he was in here with some guys and maybe they were speaking French and Arabic. Egyptians maybe. I dunno. One of them had a newspaper – a copy of *Al-Ahram*. It's an Egyptian newspaper. The Egyptian embassy is not far away, opposite the parliament, and some of those guys come in here for a drink.'

'Anything else? Anything at all.'

The barman shook his head and went back to polishing glasses, which he was certainly better at than making cocktails. Having tasted his gimlet I figured mixing paint was more his forte than mixing alcohol. I was just about to finish work at the bar when in she walked, Elli Panatoniou, the probable siren of Dr Papakyriakopoulos.

Nobody had warned me about this woman, or tied me to the mast of my ship, but when I looked at her a second time the parts of my brain usually allocated to thinking seemed to have been affected by some strong aphrodisiac. Normally I'd have called this alcohol, especially as there was still a glass in my hand at the time but I won't entirely discount the scent of her perfume, the glint in her eyes, and the well-stocked baker's tray she had out in front of her. Still carrying her briefcase, she moved toward me like Zeno's arrow in that there were parts of her that seemed quite at rest and others that were perpetually in motion. There are small breasts and there are large breasts – which were almost a joke if the cartoonist in *Playboy* was anything to go by – there are high breasts with nipples that are almost invisible and there are low breasts that could feed a whole maternity ward, there are breasts that need a brassiere and breasts that just beg for a wet T-shirt, there are breasts that make you think of your mother and breasts that make you think of Messalina and Salome and Delilah and the Ursuline nuns of Loudun, there are breasts that look wrong and ungainly and breasts calculated to make a cigarette fall from your mouth, like the breasts that belonged to Miss Panatoniou – perfect breasts that anyone who liked drawing impressive landscapes like the hills of Rome or the Heights of Abraham could have admired for days on end. Just looking at them you felt challenged to go and mount an expedition to conquer their summits, like Mallory and Irvine. Instead,

I climbed politely off my bar stool, told myself to get a grip of what laughingly I called a libido, tore my eyes off the front of her tight white blouse, and took her outstretched hand in mine. She was trying hard to make it seem accidental, her walking into the bar like that, but the fact is she wasn't as surprised to see me in the Mega Bar as I was to find myself there at lunchtime. Then again, I'm a suspicious son of a bitch since they started selling losing lottery tickets. But when I decide to make myself look like an idiot there's very little that can prevent me. Seeing her in front of me and holding her hand in mine made it very hard to use my head at all, except to think about her.

'This is a surprise, Miss . . . ?'

'Panatoniou. But you can call me Elli.'

'Christof Ganz. Elli. Short for Elisabeth? Or are you named after the Norse goddess who defeated Thor in a wrestling match?'

'It's Elisabeth. But why were they fighting?'

'They were Germans. We're like the English. We never need much of a reason to fight. Just a couple of drinks, a few yards of no-man's-land, and some half-baked mythology.'

'We've got plenty of that in Greece. This whole country's rotten with mythology. And most of it was written after 1945.'

She was wearing a tailored two-piece black business suit with piano keyboard lapels and a gathered waist, and a long pencil skirt that fitted her like the black gloves on her hands and she looked and sounded very smart indeed. She was tall and her dark brown hair was as long as Rapunzel's and I was seriously thinking of weaving it into a ladder so that I might climb up and kiss her.

'Are you here to see me or do you just like this bar?'

She gave me and then the bar a withering look of pity and sat down, adjusting herself for comfort a couple of times, which gave me a second to appraise her nicely shaped backside; that was perfect, too.

'My boss is having a meeting with someone upstairs and I was bringing him some business papers he claimed he needed. We both work for the Ministry of Economic Coordination, on Amerikis Street. This hotel has always been popular with journalists and all sorts of people in the government, for all sorts of reasons and not all of them respectable. It's just as convenient as the Grande Bretagne but a lot cheaper.'

'Well, I should fit right in. Expensive things don't interest me. Except when I don't have them, of course.'

'How did you happen to pick this place, anyway?'

'My colleague picked it.'

'He must really dislike you. In case you didn't know, this is the kind of hotel where not a lot of sleeping gets done. It's not a complete flophouse but if a man wants to meet his mistress for a couple of hours and wants her to think well of him, then he brings her here. In other words it's expensive without being too expensive. Also it's where a member of parliament comes when he needs to have a meeting in secret with another member of parliament but he doesn't really want it to be a secret – if you know what I mean – then he arranges a meeting in the bar here. That's why my boss is here. He wants the prime minister to think he's thinking of switching political parties, which of course he's not. This place is like a talking drum.'

'Won't the PM know this is what your boss is up to?'

'Of course. It's my boss's way of sending Karamanlis an important message without sending him a memo and without it being held against him later on. A memo would formalize his dissatisfaction. A meeting in here just hints at it, politely.'

'I'd no idea that Greek politics were so subtle.'

'You've heard that war is the continuation of politics by other means. Of course you have, you're German. Well, politics is just another way of being Greek. Aristotle certainly thought so and he should know. He invented politics. If I were you I'd move to the GB. It's much more comfortable. But don't move there before you've bought me a drink.'

I waved the barman over and she said something to him in Greek; until then she'd been speaking to me in German.

'You speak good Greek. For a German.'

She laughed. 'You're just being kind. For a German.'

'No, really. Your German is all right. Especially your accent. Which is to say you have no accent at all. That's good, by the way. German always sounds better when it's spoken by a nice-looking woman.'

She took that one on the chin and let it go, which was the right thing to do; it had been a while since I'd been equal to the task of speaking to any kind of woman at all, least of all to the task of handing out compliments. My mouth was too small for my wit, as if my tongue had grown too big and ungainly like some slavering Leonberger.

'My father worked for North-German Lloyd,' she said. 'The shipping company. Before the war he was the chief officer on the SS *Bremen*. When it caught fire and sank, in 1941, he came home to Greece. He taught me German because he thought you were going to win the war and rule in Europe.'

'Hey, what happened there? I know I should remember.'

'You may have lost the war but – and this is a first, I think – it looks like you're going to win the peace. Germany is still going to help rule Europe as part of this new EEC. Greece is already desperate to join. We've been trying to be good Europeans since the fall of Constantinople. And mostly succeeding, too, I'm happy to say, otherwise I'd probably be wearing a veil and covering my face.'

'That would be a tragedy.'

'No, but it would be a hardship, for me at least. In Greece, tragedies usually involve someone being murdered. We practically invented the idea of the noble hero brought low by some flaw of character.'

'In Germany we've got plenty of those to go around.'

'This is Greece, Herr Ganz. We're not about to forget any of those.'

'And yet you still want to join our club?'

'Of course. We invented hypocrisy, too, remember? As a matter of fact I'm hoping to be part of the Greek delegation in Brussels when we lobby the Germans and the French for membership next year. My French is good. On account of how my mother is half-French. But you're wrong about my German. I make lots of mistakes.'

'Maybe I can help you there.'

'I didn't know it was possible to insure against those kinds of mistakes.'

'If it was I certainly wouldn't be your man, Elli. I don't sell insurance. I just check the claims. Disappointing people is usually part of my job description. But only when they've disappointed me. There's something about insurance that brings out the worst in people. Some people can just smell dishonesty. I'm one of those, I guess.'

'Papakyriakopoulos said you used to be a cop. In Berlin. Not a German-language teacher.'

'That's right. But I wouldn't mind talking to you, Elli. In German or in French. We might meet from time to time and share a cup of coffee or a drink. In here since it's so public. When you're not too busy, of course. We could have some German conversation.'

'That's one I certainly haven't heard before. Hmm.'

'Does that mean you're thinking about it?'

'You amuse me, Herr Ganz.'

'Next time I'll wear a straw hat and carry a cane if it will help.'

'I bet you would, too. If you thought I'd like that.'

She should have said no, of course. Or at the very least she should have made me work a little harder for the pleasure of her company. She could have asked me what the German was for 'pushy' and I wouldn't have minded in the slightest because she'd have been right. I was being pushy. So I let her off the hook for a moment wondering if she'd hitch up her skirts and wriggle her way back onto it.

'But what about your father? Don't you speak German to him?'

'He's dead, I'm afraid.'

'Sorry.'

'But maybe you're right. We could meet, perhaps. For a little conversation.'

'Those are the best kind.'

'You don't like to talk?'

'It depends.'

'On what?'

'On who I'm talking to. Lately I've gotten out of the habit of saying very much.'

'I find that rather hard to believe.'

'It's true. But with you I could make an·exception.'

'Somehow I don't feel flattered.'

'Haven't you heard? There's nothing like speaking a language with a native to get better at it. You could think of yourself as the horse and me as the emperor Charles V.' Still testing her. The insult was deliberate.

She laughed. 'Didn't he have an unfeasibly large jaw?'

'Yes. In those days you didn't get to be a king unless there was something strange about you. Especially in Germany.'

'That probably explains our own kings. They're Germans, too, originally. From Schleswig-Ḥolstein. And they have the biggest mouths in Greece. But as it happens, you're right. There's not much German conversation to be had here in Greece. For obvious reasons.'

'Lieutenant Leventis speaks quite reasonable German. Almost as well as you. Maybe we could ask him along to our little class.'

'Lieutenant Leventis?' Elli smiled. 'I couldn't meet him without half of Athens getting to hear about it and drawing the wrong conclusion. Besides, his wife might object. Not to mention the fact that he and I hold very different political opinions, so we'd probably spend most of the time arguing. He's rather more to the right than I am. Only don't tell anyone. I try to keep a lid on my politics. Konstantinos Karamanlis is hardly a great friend of the left.'

'There's no film in my camera, Elli. Politics don't interest me. And in Greece they're beyond my understanding. The left most of all.'

'Maybe it could work,' she said, persuading herself some more. 'Why not? I might even get to understand the German people a little better.'

'I know that feeling.'

'You don't think it's possible?'

'I'm not sure. But let me know when you think you've got a handle on us. I'd love to get a few clues as to why we are who we are.'

'My father used to say that only the Austrians are really suited to being Germans; he said that the Germans themselves make excellent Englishmen, even though they all secretly wish they could be Italians. That this was their tragedy. But he liked Germans a lot.'

'He sounds like a great guy.'

'He was.'

The barman brought her something green and cold in a glass and she toasted me pleasantly.

'Here's to the new Europe,' she said. 'And to me speaking better German.'

I toasted her back. 'You really believe in this EEC?'

'Of course. Don't you?'

'I quite liked the old Europe. Before people started talking about a new Europe the last time. And the time before that.'

'It's only by doing away with the idea of nation states that we can put an end to fascism and to war.'

'As someone who's fought in all three, I'll drink to that.'

'Three?'

'The Cold War is all too real, I'm afraid.'

'We've nothing to fear from the Russians. I'm sure of that. They're just like us.'

I let that one go. The Russians were not like anyone, as anyone in Hungary and East Germany would have told you. If Martians ever did make it across the gulf of space to our planet with their inhuman plans for conquest and migration they'd feel quite at home in Soviet Russia.

'But if we meet,' she added, 'for conversation, let's avoid politics. And let's not make it in here.'

'Your boss?'

'What about him?'

'He might see you.'

She stared at me blankly, as if she had no idea what I was talking about. But that could just have been my German.

'In here,' I added. 'With me. Having a conversation.'

'Yes. You're right. That would never do.'

'So. You suggest somewhere. Somewhere that isn't cheap. I have an expense account and no one to take to dinner this weekend except Mr Garlopis. He's MRE's man in Athens. But he's a man. A fat man with an appetite. So it will make a nice change. These days I'm alone so much that I'm surprised when I find someone in the mirror in the morning.'

'If he's the one who booked you into the Mega then I'd say you should have him fired. I bet he's got a cousin in the hotel business.'

'Yes. How did you know?'

'Everyone in Greece has a cousin. That's how this country works. Take my word for it.'

But I didn't know if I would. Seated at the very bar where I'd already been duped by one liar, I wasn't sure I believed what she'd told me but she seemed like a nice girl and nice girls didn't come my way that often. Then again, the truth is never best and seldom kind so what did it really matter why she was there? A lot of lies are just the oil that keeps the world from grinding to a halt. If everyone suddenly started being scrupulously honest there'd be another world war before the end of the month. If Miss Panatoniou wanted me to think our meeting again was purely accidental then that was her affair. Besides, I could hardly see what there was in it for this woman to deceive me. It wasn't like Siegfried Witzel was alive or that she had an insurance claim against MRE I might settle in her favour. I really didn't have any money or any powerful friends. I didn't even have a passport. Nor was I about to persuade myself that she was just one of those younger women who are attracted to much older men because they're looking for a father figure. I was attracted to her, sure, why not? She was very attractive. But the other way around? I didn't buy that. So I searched her briefcase when she went to the ladies' room, like you do and, to my surprise,

I found something more lethal than a few critical reports about the Greek economy. I'd been around guns all my life and about the only thing I didn't like about them was when they were hidden in a woman's bag. Suddenly everyone in town seemed to have a gun except me. This one was a six plus one, a .25-calibre with a tip-up barrel and it was still wrapped in the original greaseproof paper, presumably to protect the lining of her bag from gun oil. They were called mouse guns because they were small and cute. At least that was always the rumour. My own feeling about this was somewhat different. Finding a woman with a Beretta 950 was like discovering that she was the cat and that maybe I was the mouse. I figured there were plenty of moths around to put holes in my clothes without finding one in my guts as well.

When she came back to the bar smelling of soap and yet more perfume I thought about mentioning the Beretta and decided not to bother. Who could blame her if she was carrying a Bismarck? By all accounts Greek men weren't very good at taking no for an answer, so maybe she needed it to defend those magnificent breasts. I told myself everything would be fine between us just as long as I didn't try to put my hands on those, and that her little mouse gun would certainly stop me making a fool of myself, which was probably a good thing. So I ordered another round of drinks and while I was looking at the barman I tried to twist my eyes to the farthest corners of their sockets so that I might at least look down the front of Miss Panatoniou's cleavage, but discreetly, so she wouldn't notice what I was up to, and shoot me simply for being the swine I undoubtedly was. In March of 1957 that was what I called my sex life.

CHAPTER 28

On Monday, March 25, West Germany, France, Belgium, Italy, Luxembourg, and the Netherlands signed the Treaty of Rome, creating the European Economic Community. I suppose it made a welcome change from a peace treaty bringing a war to an end and maybe it would even prevent another one from happening, as Elli Panatoniou had told me it would. But only four years after the end of the Korean War and another briefer conflict more recently concluded in Egypt, I found it impossible to have much faith that the EEC heralded a new era of European peace; wars were easy to begin but, like making love, very hard to stop. The community of economic self-interest seemed almost irrelevant to what real people needed.

More important for me and Garlopis, Philipp Dietrich telephoned the MRE office in Athens, as arranged by Telesilla. While I took the call at Garlopis's desk I watched him out of the corner of my eye flirting with her like an overweight schoolboy. I couldn't hear what was said but the redhead was laughing and, in spite of his earlier denials, I formed the strong impression that they were a lot closer than he wanted me to believe. Not that it was any of my business. For all I cared he could have been flirting with Queen Jocasta.

'I got your telegram,' said Dietrich. 'This Athenian cop, Leventis, sounds like a real pain in the ass. Are you sure you and Garlopis don't need a lawyer?'

'No thanks, I think we're all right for now. If we start throwing lawyers at him he'll probably just toss us in jail and I could be stuck here for months. He'd be justified in doing it, too. Almost. Right now we're both at liberty. At least we are as long as I play detective and help him find the killer.'

'Is that even possible?'

'I don't know. But I can certainly persuade him I'm trying. And that's probably good enough. He's not a bad sort, really. From what I've learned since I came here, the Greeks had a pretty rough time of it during the war. He figures I owe him some personal reparation. Because I'm German, I guess.'

I thought I'd leave Alois Brunner out of our conversation; Nazi war criminals were still a very sensitive subject in Germany for the simple reason that almost everyone had known one. I'd known quite a few myself.

'What the hell happened anyway?'

'Garlopis and I went to an address where we believed the insured party was living, to tell him that we were going to disallow his claim pending further investigation. Witzel carried a gun so, under the circumstances, we were a little concerned for our safety and went in the back door, which is when and where we found his body. He'd been shot dead.'

'Jesus.'

'On our way from the house, the cops turned up and arrested us both on suspicion. We were in the wrong place at the wrong time, that's all. It's an old story and any Bavarian court of law would throw it out in five minutes. But my being German hardly helps the situation here. With the Greek love for cosmic irony they'd be delighted if they could pin this on another German.'

'I'll bet they would. Murderous Germans are all the rage these days. You can't go to a movie theatre without seeing some sneering Nazi torturing a nice girl. Look, do whatever you think is necessary, Christof. Mr Alzheimer is delighted with the way you've handled this so far.'

I didn't doubt that for a minute; a saving of thirty-five thousand deutschmarks would have put a smile on anyone's face, even a sneering Nazi's.

'We're just sorry that this has been more difficult for you than we thought it would be. That it's landed you in trouble with the police.'

'Don't worry about me, boss. I can handle a certain amount of trouble with the police. That's one of the only advantages of being a German. We're used to cops throwing their weight around.'

'All the same, if you change your mind about that lawyer, I'm told by our legal department that you should contact Latsoudis & Arvaniti, in Piraeus. They're a good firm. We've used them before.'

I picked up a pen and wrote the name down, just in case. Then I wrote down Buchholz's name and underlined it, willing

Dietrich to get to the point. I also wrote out the name of Walther Neff, to prompt me, courteously, to ask a little later on, how my sick colleague at MRE was doing.

'I've got a feeling you'll need them anyway on account of what I've found out here in Munich,' added Dietrich. 'I don't think it will help.'

'You spoke to Professor Buchholz?'

'I did.'

'And what did he say?'

'Not much. Nothing I could understand, anyway, on account of the fact that he had a massive stroke before Christmas and it has left him paralyzed down one side of his body. He can hardly speak. He's in Schwabing Hospital right now and is not expected to recover much.'

I drew a small rectangle around Buchholz's name. It was a rectangle that was shaped like a coffin, a toe-pincher like the ones they'd shipped to the Western front in their hundreds before an advance on the enemy trenches, to encourage the men's morale.

'But that's not all,' continued Dietrich. 'I also went to the Glyptothek Museum, where he was assistant director, and they told me they have absolutely no knowledge of any expedition to Greece. None. Nor of any deal done with this museum in Piraeus. Frankly, it's impossible to see how Buchholz could arrange a taxi home, let alone a boat charter for Witzel and the *Doris*. I also spoke to his wife and she showed me his passport. The professor hasn't been out of Germany in over a year. The last Greek stamp on his passport was in June 1951. Either Siegfried Witzel was lying about him or someone has been impersonating Buchholz. He's a goddamned vegetable.'

'So maybe that's why someone picked him off the stall.'

'How do you mean?'

'You remember that break-in at the museum?'

'I remember. Yes.'

'The cops never found out who was responsible. Kids, they thought. But at the time I had my doubts about that.'

'Are you saying these two cases are connected?'

'They were kids who broke into the assistant director's desk and left the cash box alone. Which is a kite that simply doesn't fly. I'm thinking that it was maybe his office stationery someone was after. Business cards, headed notepaper. That and a few small pieces of marble that no one could be bothered to claim for.'

'For what purpose?'

'Perhaps this person wanted to persuade the authorities here in Greece that they were mounting a proper expedition to recover bigger, more valuable historical artefacts. Some official German paperwork and a few bits of bronze and marble might have helped that story stay afloat. And I think your first guess was probably accurate. Either there's been a local invasion of the body snatchers or someone has been impersonating Professor Buchholz. The question is, who? If I can find that out, then maybe the Greek police will let me come home. Look, sir, see what else you can dig up on Siegfried Witzel. War record. Wives. This underwater movie he made. Anything at all.'

'All right.'

'By the way, how's Neff?'

'That's the damnedest thing. He discharged himself from hospital and has since disappeared. The police are looking for him, but so far without result.'

'That is strange.'

'Even stranger than you imagine. His wife reckons a cop from the Praesidium came to visit him at home the day before he suffered his heart attack, only they don't seem to know anything about it.'

I hadn't ever met Walther Neff, but his sudden disappearance made me uneasy, as if somehow it might be connected with what had happened in Athens.

'As a matter of interest, which hospital was he in?'

'The Schwabing. Same as Buchholz.'

'What does *his* wife have to say about it?'

'Not much. She seems as puzzled as the rest of us. Listen, take care of yourself. And let me know if there's anything else you need.'

I started to say something else only there was a click and Dietrich had disappeared. But that wasn't strange at all.

CHAPTER 29

'Did you know Walther Neff well?'

'He came to Greece on a number of occasions, sir,' said Garlopis.

'That doesn't answer my question.'

'I knew him well enough. Better than he was aware of, perhaps.'

'What was your opinion of him?'

Garlopis looked awkward. He opened his desk drawer and closed it again, for no apparent reason. It was the morning after my conversation with Dietrich and I was in the MRE office with Garlopis.

'You can speak freely. I've hardly ever met the man, so I don't care if your opinion is good or bad. I just want to know what it is.'

'I don't think he liked Greeks very much. Or anyone else for that matter. Anyone else who wasn't German.'

'You mean he was still a bit of a Nazi.'

'I think that about covers it, sir. Once or twice he made a casual remark about the Jews and how they'd brought their own misfortunes on themselves. And once he came across an old copy of *Time* magazine that had a picture of David Ben-Gurion on the cover, and his face was a study of loathing. I'd never seen hate that was so visceral. But why do you ask?'

'He's disappeared from the hospital in Munich. Checked himself out and then just walked into the darkness, so to speak. The cops are looking for him. But – well, I don't think they'll find him. I'm afraid this sort of thing happens a lot in Germany.'

'Why's that?'

'Because someone's ghost recognizes someone else from the war. Millions of people died, but people forget that plenty of people survived, too. Thirty thousand people came out of Dachau. Thirty thousand witnesses to mass murder. But there are probably just as many people in Germany right now who are not who they say they are.'

'You mean they're living under a false name? Because of something they did during the war?'

'Exactly. My guess is that Walther Neff had a secret history like so many other of my countrymen. Maybe he was already living under a false name. And someone discovered this and threatened to do something about it. So Neff took off before it could cause him any more problems. These days that's a very common story.'

Was it possible that Neff had even faked his own heart attack after reading the article I'd written on the subject at Alzheimer's request in the company newspaper?

'But I thought Adenauer was pursuing a policy of amnesty and integration,' said Garlopis. 'That many Nazi war criminals had been released. As many as thirty-five thousand people, wasn't it? Why would anyone fear discovery now, after your government has called a halt to denazification?'

'Lots of reasons. The amnesty only applies in Germany. It wouldn't apply if a Nazi came here, for example. And of course some of the left-of-centre newspapers can still make life difficult for old Nazis. Not everyone in Germany agrees with the Old Man's policy. There's that and there are the Israeli Defence Forces, of course. There's no telling what they're capable of. Five years ago the right-wing Herut Party tried to assassinate the Old Man. No, I imagine that sometimes it's just best to adopt another name and disappear. Just like this fellow Alois Brunner that Lieutenant Leventis is after.'

Garlopis was silent for a moment. Then he got up and closed the door to the outside office, where Telesilla was typing letters. 'I don't say that all Germans are bad,' he said. 'Not a bit of it. As you know, my own father was a German after all.'

'What happened to him anyway?'

'He died a few years ago. He was eating breakfast at the time.'

'I suppose you finished it for him.'

Garlopis winced.

'I'm sorry, Achilles, that was uncalled for. I apologize. My only excuse is that I'm a Berliner. Cruelty just comes naturally to us on account of how we were the last pagans in Europe. So go ahead and tell your story. You were going to tell me a story. That's why you closed the door, isn't it?'

'Yes.' Garlopis gathered himself. 'A few years ago – it was the summer of 1954, I think – I accompanied Mr Neff to the Greek island of Corfu to adjust another shipping claim. Corfu is very popular with Italians due to its proximity to the Italian coast. Italians were part of the Axis forces of course but no one in Greece holds that against them now. Unlike you Germans, they were never very enthusiastic in their occupation of Greece. And of course, ultimately, many of them were also victims of the Nazis. In a way, that's been to their moral advantage.

'One evening Mr Neff and I were sitting outside a café in Corfu Old Town and a man at another table kept staring at Neff. Neff tried to ignore it but after a while the man came over and identified himself as an Italian from a village near Bologna – called Marzabotto, I think it was. He proceeded to accuse Neff of being an SS man who had participated in the massacre of almost two thousand civilians in late 1944. Neff denied it, of course. Said he'd never been in the SS. But the man was adamant it was him and started to tell everyone in the café that there was a Nazi war criminal in our midst. Neff got very flustered and angry and left in a bit of a hurry, with me in pursuit. Later on he said he'd never been in Italy and yet by then I already knew this was a lie. For one thing he spoke a bit of Italian. And for another he had even told me how much he loved Bologna. So I knew what the man in the café said had to be true. Another thing was that Neff only ever investigated insurance claims in Greece and France, never in Italy. And once, when it was really hot and he'd taken his shirt off, I saw that he had the letters AB tattooed on the underside of his left upper arm, near his armpit. Later on I learned from a magazine article that this must be his blood group and that all

Waffen-SS men had such a tattoo.' He lit a cigarette and added carefully: 'I imagine that this would help to identify Brunner, if ever Leventis manages to catch up with him.'

'I imagine you're right.' It was almost an uncomfortable moment although not as uncomfortable as the moment when, with the Red Army just a few days away from Königsberg and a German surrender inevitable, I had burned off my own blood group tattoo. Thinking it best to change the subject now, I said, 'That reminds me. I need to speak to Lieutenant Leventis. No offence to your cousin but this afternoon I'm going to move over to the Grande Bretagne Hotel.'

'None taken. And I have to confess the Mega is not what it was. Even my cousin admits this. Much cheaper of course, but I suppose if MRE is paying then why not stay at the Grande Bretagne? I should have thought of that before. But the fact is, Mr Neff always preferred the Mega. That's the main reason why I booked you in there. It was his choice.'

'Did he say why he liked it?'

'The Grande Bretagne has just finished adding four floors, of course. So it's only recently reopened. But according to my cousin, I think Neff had some little fraud going on with the Mega management that enabled him to claim more on expenses than he actually paid. My cousin also had the impression Neff knew some of the other hotel regulars.'

In view of the revelation about Neff's Waffen-SS past I wondered if these other acquaintances of his might have included Alois Brunner, but I still saw no good reason to tell Garlopis about meeting Brunner in the Mega bar. It would only have scared him the way it had scared me. I collected my coat and went to the door.

'Are you going somewhere?'

'I thought I'd walk over to the Megaron Pappoudof and tell Leventis in person that I'm moving hotels. Just to make him feel as if I'm taking him seriously. Policemen like that kind of attention to the umlauts.'

'You are taking him seriously, aren't you, sir?'

'Sure. I want to come out of this in one piece. Any talk about firing squads worries me.'

'I'm delighted to hear it. I'd hate to end up in Haidari among all those awful criminals.'

'I've known a lot of criminals and I can tell you that, with the exception of the ones like Alois Brunner, most are just ordinary people like you and me. They lack imagination, that's all. Crimes are committed when men take an idea that seems like a good idea and then can't think of enough good reasons why it might not be a good idea.'

'All the same, I'd rather avoid the Haidari, if possible. For the sake of my children, you understand. They're at the Lycée Léonin, one of the best schools in Athens. It takes a dim view of parents who don't measure up to the rigorous moral standards set by the monks who run the school. That's the only reason my wife has not yet divorced me. Would you like me to accompany you, sir?'

'No, I want you to stay here and telephone Dr Lyacos at the Archaeological Museum in Piraeus and arrange for us to see him again. I need to speak to him about Professor Buchholz. And see if you can find out from that lawyer, Papakyriakopoulos, if Arthur Meissner has agreed to see me yet. I'll be back in an hour. At least I hope I will.'

'Well done, sir. We'll make a Greek out of you yet. Your pronunciation of his very complicated name was faultless.'

'I'm German, Mr Garlopis. We have some very complex words of our own to practise on. Some German words take so long to say that they have their own damn timetables.'

CHAPTER 30

In his office at the Megaron Pappoudof I told Lieutenant Leventis
I was changing hotels.

'Is that all you came here to tell me, Commissar? That you're
going to the GB? I'm disappointed.'

'I thought you'd like to know in case you wanted to buy
me breakfast one morning. You can probably look out of your
office window and see into my bathroom, if it helps make that
happen.'

'Good idea. But are you sure no one is dead in it?'

'Just my love life, probably. When they find that body you can
arrest me all over again.'

'Why bother? You're still my number-one suspect in the
Witzel case.'

'Clearly you're not very good with numbers. You already told
me the name of your number-one suspect. At best I'm number
three.'

'Who's number two?'

'Garlopis.'

'That's not very loyal of you, Commissar.'

'No, it isn't. But his home is in Greece. Mine's in Germany. And I want to get back there one day. Which is why I'm in here writing my room number on your handkerchief in lipstick.'

'Anything else you want to talk about?'

'Not a damn thing.'

'I told you, Commissar. I'm blind here and I want you to be my dog. So bark a little, will you?'

I lit up a cigarette and blew some smoke at the high ceiling. The fan wasn't moving, which was how I knew it was still officially winter in Athens. Otherwise it seemed quite warm in his office. Leventis leaned back on his chair, looking at me steadily all the time, waiting for me to say something more, and then nodded when I didn't. 'You keep your mouth shut unless you've got something to say. All right. Not many people can do that judiciously. Especially in here. You've a talent for saying not very much, Commissar.'

'I never learned much by listening to myself.'

'No? Then maybe I can tell you something interesting.'

'That'll make a nice change.'

'Don't forget your position here, Ganz.' He wagged his finger at me like I was a naughty schoolboy and grinned. 'You're a little impertinent for a suspect.'

'That's just my manner. It doesn't work with everyone. Only with people, not cops. Look, I said I'd cooperate with you, Leventis, not crown you with wild olive. And we both know I'm a poor choice of suspect. On account of how I turned up at the murder scene *after* the murder. Garlopis, too. It's time you admitted that, copper, or else you're dumber than I thought you were.'

'My name isn't copper, it's Stavros P. Leventis. But you can call me lieutenant. And in here I don't have to admit to a damn thing. I leave that to other people. What's dumb about that?'

'Nothing at all. What does the *P* stand for, anyway?'

'Patroclus. Only keep that quiet.'

'I'll lend it someone else's armour if it will help get me out of this damn country. Tell me what's so interesting, Pat.'

'Last night, the City Police picked up a local burglar by the name of Tsochaztopoulos, only everyone calls him Choc.'

'Now that I can understand.'

'He put his hands up to a whole string of burglaries across the city, but here's where it starts to get interesting.'

'I was hoping it might.'

'He claims he was put up to robbing Frizis's office in Glyfada. Says the job was to take one client file and to cover his tracks so that the lawyer didn't even know he'd been there. Says he was paid to do it by a man he met in a nightclub. The Chez Lapin in Kastella.'

'Sounds like a real hole. Did this man have a name?'

'Just Spiros.'

'That narrows it down nicely. And what was the client's name?'

Leventis grinned patiently. 'Spiros told Choc to look for a client file in the name of Fischer. Georg Fischer. He did the job as asked. Went in and out without a trace. Took the client file back to the club a few hours later, and got paid.'

'So everyone was happy.'

'Now it just so happens that Frizis's diary contains an appointment with a Mr Fischer just a few days before he was murdered.'

'Well, it would if he was a client.'

'Fischer is a German name.'

'That's right.'

'I was hoping you might have a theory on that one.'

'It's the fourth most common German surname there is. That narrows it down.'

'Come on, Ganz. You can do better than that. Whose side are you on here?'

'Whose side? I don't know the names of the teams that are on the pitch here. And even if I did I certainly couldn't pronounce them.'

'You know, I think I must have left my sense of humour in my other uniform.'

'The clean one?'

'I'd hate to kick you on the leg, Ganz. I'd probably get gangrene. What kind of commissar were you, anyway?'

'I wore a shirt and tie, turned up for work every day, carried a warrant disc, and sometimes they let me arrest people. But none of the bosses really gave a shit about me detecting any crimes because they were too busy committing crimes themselves. Nothing serious. Crimes against humanity and that kind of thing. Look, Pat – Lieutenant – I was making a living and trying to stay alive, not preaching the First Crusade. Let me ask you this. Did you show this Choc fellow your photograph of Brunner? The one you showed me?'

'Yes, but he's quite sure it wasn't him who put him up to the job.'

'Hmm.'

'What does that mean?'

'Hegel said it once. It's German for "I'm thinking".'

After a while I shook my head for emphasis, just to let him know I'd finished the thought.

'What do you think you're dealing with here? An insurance claim? Look, I know you know more than you're saying. I can see it written on your face.'

'Now you know why I stopped being a criminal and became a cop instead. All right. Maybe I do know something. But don't get mad when I tell you. I only just figured this out myself. And I'd feel better about telling you what that is if we walked across the street and you let me buy you a drink.'

Leventis picked up his cap and walked toward the office door, buttoning his tunic.

'Two things I can smell from a hundred metres away. My mother's *giouvetsi* lamb stew and a lying cop.'

'I keep telling you. I'm in the insurance business.'

'It's my guess your company hired you because you're an ex-cop and you've got a dirty mind. I'm just doing the same as them. Detection is in your blood, Ganz, as if it was a disease.'

'If you mean it's one that I can't seem to shake off, then you're right. It's like leprosy. I keep winding bandages around my face but nothing seems to work. One day I'm afraid I'm going to lose my nose.'

'That's an occupational hazard for all detectives.'

His secretary handed him his gloves and a little swagger stick and we went downstairs and outside.

Behind the long marble bar at the Grande Bretagne was an old tapestry as big as the fire screen on a theatre stage, depicting the triumph of some ancient Greek who probably wasn't Hector on account of the fact that he was riding in a chariot instead of being dragged behind one. It was a nice quiet bar; the prices were fixed to make sure of that, like heavily armed hoplites. Facing the tapestry were eight tall stools and sitting at the bar was like watching a large projection screen with just one stationary, rather dull picture, a bit like Greek television. They had so many bottles behind the bar I guessed they must have some navy-strength gin and since the barman evidently knew the difference between a fresh lime and the liquid green sugar that came in a bottle I ordered a gimlet and the lieutenant ordered iced raki.

We sipped our drinks politely but I was already ordering another and a packet of butts.

'All excuses sound better after a drink. So now you've had yours, start talking, Commissar.'

'All right. When you showed me Brunner's picture, I took my time about it, right? That was me, racking my brains, trying to remember where I'd seen him before. France, Germany, the Balkans – it's taken me until now to realize I was opening the wrong drawers. I couldn't remember him because he wasn't in my memory. He was at the end of a bar. This bar.'

I only told Leventis this small lie because I didn't want him asking about Fischer at the bar of the Mega Hotel and discovering I'd already asked questions about him myself.

'You mean Brunner was in here? In this hotel?'

'That's right. In this very bar. About a week ago we got to talking, the way two men do when they discover they're both from the same part of the world. He told me his name was Georg Fischer and that he was a tobacco salesman. Gave me a packet of Karelia to try. There's not much more to it than that. I didn't remember him right away because he's almost fifteen years older than that picture you showed me. Less hair. Put on a little weight, perhaps. Gruff voice like he gargles with yesterday's brandy. I mean, you don't connect a wanted Nazi war criminal with a friendly guy you meet in an Athens bar. Well, when you mentioned the name Georg Fischer back in your office I suddenly put two and two together and came up with the man I'd met in this bar.'

'This story you're telling – you spread it on a field of sugar beet, not Lieutenant Stavros P. Leventis.'

'It happens to be true. People look different when they're in uniform. I mean, looking at you anyone would think you know what the hell you're doing. He struck up a conversation because I figure he'd been keeping an eye on me ever since I arrived in Athens. My guess is that he was looking for Siegfried Witzel and that he was hoping I might help him. Unwittingly, of course.'

'I guess that's your own middle name, Commissar.'

'My guess is that he waited for Witzel to show up at MRE's offices around the corner, and then followed me when I followed Witzel to the place where he'd been lying low ever since the *Doris* sank. Went back a bit later and then killed him. He and Witzel probably knew each other from before the war. I'm not sure but I think Witzel was involved in some scheme to look for ancient Greek artefacts that he could sell on the black market. Assuming there is a black market for that kind of thing.'

'Sure there is. It's a thriving one, too. There are lots of museums and private collectors who want a bit of Greek history on the cheap. Not just ours. Roman treasures, too.'

'I'm still working on that. I'm hoping I'll have a little more information after I've spoken to the director of the Archaeological Museum in Piraeus. It looks like there was some agreement between the museum in Piraeus and a museum in Munich to share any discoveries. But that might just have been a cover. Maybe Brunner wanted a share, too. Or maybe it was a revenge thing. I don't know. But if I had to guess some more—'

'You do.'

'Then I'd say that Brunner might have had something to do with the sinking of the boat. I have no idea how. Not yet.'

'Tell me more about Fischer.'

'Good suit. Gold watch, nice lighter, even nicer manners. He looked like he was doing all right for himself. He spoke Greek. Or at least as far as I was able to tell. What I mean to say is that he was reading a Greek newspaper and he seemed to speak to the barman fluently enough. He said he liked it here. And I got the impression he was in Greece a lot.'

'Is that all?'

'Look, I've got lots of faults but protecting Nazi war criminals isn't one of them.'

'Says you.'

'Frequently.'

'And Meissner? Has he agreed to meet you, yet?'

'Right now that's a maybe, too.'

'You've got a lot of maybes, Commissar. Enough to operate a roulette wheel, maybe. Certainly many more than your old bosses in Germany would ever have tolerated. From what I've read of the SS and the Gestapo they didn't much like maybes. They preferred results. We have that in common at least. In case you've forgotten, my own boss is a man called Captain Kokkinos and he's an impatient man. He thinks I should bring you in and sweat you and your fat friend, Garlopis. He's been hitting the walls because I don't.'

'I've seen your walls. And I don't think your decorator will care.'

'Because then I'd have to waste time listening to your lies. So I tell you what I'm going to do, Ganz. From now on, you're gonna tell me every move you make. Anything you do, I want a report. Just like you were a cop again. You can have your secretary type it. If you don't, I'll make sure they bury you in the deepest cell in Haidari. Solitary confinement for as long as it takes to break you. I don't much care about Garlopis. He'll say anything to stay out of prison. But you're another story. You'll be talking to yourself inside a fortnight. Because no one will be listening. Not even me. I'll forget all about you, maybe. This is the home of democracy but we can behave in some very undemocratic ways when we put our minds to it. So you can take your choice. But you need to start confiding in me like I'm your father confessor. Only then can you get absolution. And only then can you go home.'

I nodded, full of compliance and cooperation, like I was the most craven informer ever to be bullied by a policeman. But

I could already see I was going to need the firm of lawyers in Piraeus that Dietrich had recommended and later that day I called them and made an appointment on the same day we were scheduled to see Dr Lyacos again.

CHAPTER 31

Latsoudis & Arvaniti were located on the corner of Themistocles Street, in a modern building overlooking the main port of Piraeus, from where I could easily have taken a ferry to one of the Greek islands. After my conversation with Lieutenant Leventis I was seriously considering it.

Garlopis had at last swapped the Oldsmobile for a smaller Rover P4 and while he parked it I waited in the yellow church on the square and, but for the idea that there were other mugs who tried it already, I might have prayed. When he fetched me, he said the church was built on the ruins of the Temple of Venus, and being a bit of a pagan and generally fond of goddesses, I said it didn't look like much of an improvement.

We went up to the firm's offices and met with two lawyers, neither of whom was called Latsoudis or Arvaniti, who told us in a mixture of Greek and English and the pungent smoke of Turkish cigarettes that we had their sympathy, that one of them would gladly represent us in court, that what had happened was entirely typical of Athens, and that the Attica police were little better than the Greek army, and fascists to boot, for whom torture and the abuse of human rights were second nature, and that Captain Kokkinos fancied himself to be a man with a political future, not to say a potential dictator. It was best, they advised, that we do exactly what we were told, otherwise we should end up like many communist DSE fighters and KKE members and find ourselves sent to the island of Makronisos or, worse, imprisoned in Block 15, where lawyers were not allowed and conditions were nothing short of barbaric, even by Nazi standards. None of this was reassuring to me but as we left, Garlopis said that I should take nothing of what they had said too seriously and that the view of these lawyers was only representative of the kind of people who lived in Piraeus, who had no love for the people of Athens, which came as something of a surprise to me since Piraeus was only five kilometres from the centre of the Greek capital.

'To my mind we would be better off being represented by a local firm,' said Garlopis as we made our way to the Archaeological Museum and our second meeting with Dr Lyacos. 'Such as the one I recommended to poor Mr Witzel.'

'Another cousin, no doubt.'

'No. Although I do have a relation in the legal profession. My wife's uncle Ioannis is a lawyer in Corinth, but I shouldn't wish my worst enemy to be represented by him. Pegasus himself would take flight before retaining a man like Ioannis Papageorgopoulos.'

'There's a brass nameplate I'd hate to have to engrave.'

'Look, I'm sure Mr Dietrich is correct, that Latsoudis & Arvaniti are a perfectly good and highly respectable firm of lawyers. But if it was my money, I'd prefer a firm in Attica. Such as the one in our own office building.'

'Why the hell didn't he recommend them, then?' I asked.

'Because outsiders don't appreciate the antipathy that exists between Piraeus and Athens. No one could who doesn't live here. Yes, Piraeus is on the doorstep of Athens, but it might as well be a hundred kilometres away, such is the loathing between these two cities. A man who lives in Athens would never be represented by a firm in Piraeus, or the other way round. But perhaps you would like me to explain this to you, sir.'

'Not today,' I said.

'Oh, it would take a lot longer than that.'

'I figured as much. It sounds a lot like the hatred between Munich and Berlin. Nobody else gets that either. Nobody else that matters, anyway. Only Germans.'

Things were quiet at the museum again. We were a bit early for our meeting with Dr Lyacos so we walked around for a few minutes looking at the museum's many exhibits. While it crossed my mind that the Nazis had managed to make all classical statuary look just a bit fascist – any one of the outsized bronze figures at the museum in Piraeus might easily have been banged out on Hitler's orders by a stooge like Arno Breker – I wasn't really looking; I was still preoccupied with what Lieutenant Leventis had said and for the first time in months I felt as if I needed an all-risks insurance policy.

Dr Lyacos was wearing a yellow carnation in the lapel of a beige cotton suit, and a yellow bow tie. His previously greyish hair had a lot more yellow in it than before, as if freshly stained with nicotine, which made him look like some hennaed Sufi mystic or perhaps the oldest boy soprano in the church choir. Even the smoke from his cherrywood pipe looked vaguely yellow. All in all there was much too much yellow in the room. It was like staring through a bottle of brilliantine.

'It's good of you to see us again, sir,' I said, and then explained how the real Professor Buchholz could not possibly have met with him in Piraeus, at which point Lyacos stared at me over the top of his half-moon glasses with the look of a dyspeptic judge. Garlopis translated from the Greek.

'Are you calling me a liar?' said Lyacos.

'No, sir. Not at all. What I'm saying is that the man you met was an impostor. That he was impersonating the real Professor Buchholz.'

'Well, who was he then?'

'That's what I'm hoping to find out. I wondered if you could provide me with a physical description of the man you met.'

Lyacos took off his glasses, folded them into a box, and rubbed the end of his pencil-like nose. 'Let's see now. About sixty years old. Large. Overweight. Tall. About as tall as you, perhaps. Silver hair. Large. Trousers too high on his waist – I mean, the man's trousers were virtually on his chest. Spoke good Greek, for a German.' He lit his pipe and considered the matter some more. 'A little self-satisfied, perhaps. Large. I don't know. Maybe not as old as sixty. Fifty, probably.'

I nodded. 'Anything else?'

Lyacos shook his head. 'No, I'm sorry. That's about it, I'm

afraid. But look, there was nothing wrong with his permissions. Those came straight from the ministry. And the signatures were impeccable. They couldn't possibly have been fraudulent. Unless—'

'Yes?'

'Well, it's not unknown for government officials in this country to take a bribe. Not that I'm saying anyone did, mind you. That's up to you to determine. We've got used to the idea of our leaders lying to us and being corrupt; for most Greeks it doesn't matter that they're corrupt. We expect it. Why else would they enter office in the first place? But you surprise me. The man who sat in your chair seemed very polished. And exactly like a man who was a professor. Shall we say he was a gentleman? Yes. An academic sort of fellow, anyway. Well read, I should say. I mean he was quite convincing. Of course, it does explain the mistake he made about the small artefacts found on the wreck site by Herr Witzel. If you remember, I did mention before that these were identified by the professor as late Helladic when they were very definitely much earlier.'

'Thanks for your help,' I said. 'Can I ask you one last thing? Assuming that this man meant to cheat your museum out of its share of any treasures found in the sea, can you tell me if there is much of a market in this kind of thing? I mean is there real money to be made?'

'Oh, yes. And a lot of these antiquities come through Piraeus. Egyptian, Byzantine, Assyrian, Islamic, Greek, you name it. Mostly it ends up in the hands of private collectors in the United States, but also in smaller city museums that are looking to put themselves on the cultural map. The black market trade in antiquities is worth a lot of money and these days it's happening on an industrial scale. A good-condition Roman bust of the second century might be worth up to fifty thousand dollars. I've even heard that Nasser is using ancient Egyptian art to pay for illegal weapons.' He puffed at his pipe. 'Do you think that's what this man is up to?'

'I really don't know. I can't see a better reason.'

'You know my secretary, Kalliopi, she spent as much time with this man as I did. She might be able to add something to what I've told you, Mr Ganz.'

Lyacos picked up the telephone and summoned his secretary to his office. A few minutes later a heavy, grey-haired woman of about fifty entered the room; she was wearing black and generally resembled a poorly erected Bedouin's tent. From a distance she looked pretty good; up close I needed to see a good optician. It wasn't that she was ugly or even plain, only that she'd reached a time in her life when romantic love was a locked door that didn't need a key. I explained my mission and waited. She rubbed the stubble on her face, rolled her eyes a bit, and started talking in Greek, which Garlopis translated simultaneously.

'He was a big man . . . Tall, about one hundred and eighty-five centimetres, overweight, chest about a fifty-six, waist the same as my husband's, which is a ninety-seven . . . Wheezy, bad breath, smoked a lot, walked like a duck . . . Silver hair . . . Brown, globular eyes, with next to no eyelashes . . . Never met your eye, though . . . He had beautiful hands, which were manicured. And he was always tapping the tips of his fingers when he was thinking . . . Jacket pockets full . . . Spoke good Greek . . . Nice watch . . . She saw a poster for a movie at the cinema near where she lives, just off Epirou Street. And there's an American man on that poster that looks exactly like Professor Buchholz. Or at least the man who said he was Professor Buchholz. Not the leading man . . . Merely a character actor . . . Not Orson Welles . . . Only she can't remember the name of the movie.'

I looked at my watch and saw that it was getting near the museum's closing time.

'Maybe we could run the lady home,' I said, 'and then she could point the man out to us. On the poster, I mean. If Dr Lyacos can spare her.'

About half an hour later we pulled up outside the Royal Cinema. The movie playing was *The Mask of Dimitrios*, with Peter Lorre and Zachary Scott. *Evil genius* ran the line on the poster, *plundering for profit and pleasure*. I hadn't seen it. I'd had enough of evil genius to last a lifetime. But Garlopis had seen it, several times.

'This film is very popular in Athens,' he said. 'I think it's always playing somewhere in the city. Probably because it's partly set here, and in Istanbul.'

But it wasn't either of those two actors that Kalliopi now pointed out to us. It was a fat actor, dressed in an overcoat, a spotted silk scarf, and a bowler hat. He was holding a Luger, too. Hers had been a good description, as good as any police artist's. But she was wrong about one thing: The fat man *was* the leading actor in this picture. He was an Englishman called Sydney Greenstreet.

'I believe he plays the part of Mr Peters, sir,' said Garlopis.

And there was one more detail Kalliopi remembered before we waved her goodbye.

'The man had bad teeth,' said Garlopis, translating again. 'From smoking probably. With a single gold tooth, in the front, on the upper jaw.'

'I see.'

'So it would seem we're looking for a German version of Sydney Greenstreet,' Garlopis added, redundantly, because by now I knew exactly who had been so meticulously described, and it wasn't Sydney Greenstreet. Kalliopi had painted a picture of a man I knew myself, the very same man who'd got me the job at MRE, in return for the favour I dealt him back in Munich. Without a question the man she'd described to a T was Max Merten.

CHAPTER 32

Back at the office in Athens, Telesilla was waiting patiently to go home with a large bag of groceries. But first she gave Garlopis his messages and then wrote out the telegram I quickly dictated asking Dietrich to try to contact Max Merten in Munich. The last time I'd seen him he'd told me he was going on vacation and I now assumed he'd meant he was planning to impersonate a German professor of Hellenism in order to mount an expedition to dive in the Aegean Sea for some ancient treasures he could sell on the black market. It was just the sort of thing German lawyers do on their holidays; that or a little quiet embezzlement. If Dumbo Dietrich didn't find Merten, then this would tell me that maybe he was somewhere in Greece, lying low until he was sure that Alois Brunner wasn't looking for him, or possibly trying to find another boat, unaware of the fact that his frogman-friend Witzel was now dead; but that he'd been in Greece I was now absolutely certain.

It worried me that Max Merten could have played me for a fool, although I could hardly see how, or why. But the last thing I needed was for my nice, boring, reasonably paid job to be taken away before I'd even taken delivery of the company car. Just as worrying was the possibility that Criminal Secretary Christian Schramma had been Merten's spanner all along, even when I thought he'd been working a double-cross; that perhaps the murders in Bogenhausen of GVP Party donor General Heinrich Heinkel and his Stasi friend had been ordered by Merten himself. And I'd been the mug who'd insisted the lawyer should keep the money, which was probably what he'd been after from the very beginning. No questions asked and money to help fund a little expedition in Greece, because chartering a boat is expensive, even when it was a boat that had been stolen from Jews.

But I'd already decided on my next course of action, which was to take a drive down to Ermioni, the town on the Peloponnesian coast where Siegfried Witzel had said the lifeboat from the *Doris* had come ashore, and there to ask the local coast guard for more information. I didn't know that I expected to discover anything useful but at least that way I'd be doing something better than sitting around in the office waiting for Arthur Meissner to decide if he would meet with me in Averoff Prison, or for Dumbo Dietrich to answer my latest telegram. Besides, I needed to *look* like I was doing something if only to keep Lieutenant Leventis off my case. I'd met a few high-pressure cops in my time – Heydrich, Nebe, and Mielke to name but three – and while Leventis wasn't a killer like them, in his own way he was effective. Without my passport I couldn't leave Greece and, until it was returned to me, I was the lieutenant's straw man just as surely as if he'd been the Kaiser and I his most slavish subject.

'Mr Papakyriakopoulos telephoned while we were out,' Garlopis said after Telesilla had left for the telegraph office. 'Arthur Meissner has agreed to meet with us on Friday evening, sir.'

'That's something, I suppose. Although I really don't know what I'm going to ask him. Or exactly how I'm going to improve his weekend. Not to mention my own.'

'But I thought you told Lieutenant Leventis that you might be able to persuade him to tell you about Alois Brunner.'

'I had to tell that slippery cop something. He's the type who could find every crime in the Bible and write someone up for it. But I don't see why Meissner would tell me anything new. Leventis isn't offering much of a deal yet. He'll speak up for Meissner if Meissner contributes something useful about Brunner. That wouldn't be enough to convince me to spill my guts. And if he knows nothing, then what? We're back to square one.'

'Yes, I do see the problem, sir. I must say this is all quite worrying.'

I put my hand on the Greek's shoulder and tried to look reassuring. 'Look, I don't think Leventis is that interested in you, my friend. So I wouldn't worry too much. It's me he wants turning the millstone in Gaza.'

'Because you used to be a detective in Berlin.'

'That's right. A German detective to help a Greek detective solve a German murder.'

'Yes, well, in Athens one can understand that kind of Socratic dialogue.'

'For now what matters is that as far as he's concerned, you're just a nobody.'

'It's kind of you to say so, sir. As a matter of fact, I've asked around about this man, Leventis, to see if my first opinion about him – on the likelihood of his taking a bribe – might have been wrong.'

'And?'

'By all accounts he's perceived to be an inflexibly honest man.'

'They're usually the most expensive people to try to corrupt.'

'This is not to say that it's impossible, sir.'

'Yes, but the first time you saw him you said you didn't think he could be bought.'

'Nobody is above being bribed in Greece. Companies, judges, prime ministers, kings – them especially – everyone in Greece has to have his *fakelaki*, his little envelope. It's just a case of working out what might be in it. Even a man like Stavros Leventis would probably not be above five thousand drachmas. At most ten.'

'I might raise a thousand drachmas on expenses. But that's it.'

Garlopis lit a cigarette. 'Is it possible that Mr Dietrich in Munich would authorize this kind of unaccountable expenditure?'

'I doubt it.'

'Not even for a man who has saved them from paying out on the *Doris*? A quarter of a million drachmas.'

'I don't believe they think like that. I was just doing my job.'

'Then we are forced to consider other methods of fund-raising. Perhaps, during the course of your inquiry, you may see the opportunity for a little bit of quiet larceny. In which case you would certainly be advised to take it.'

'You make it sound as if there's five thousand drachmas just lying around in this town. There isn't.'

'You're wrong about that. If I might make a suggestion?'

'Please do.'

'The certified company cheque for twenty-two thousand drachmas payable to Siegfried Witzel.'

'It was on the table at the scene of his murder in Pritaniou. Almost certainly it's now police evidence.'

'Almost certainly it is not.' He took out his wallet and then unfolded the same certified company cheque, which he handed to me with a smile. 'I took the liberty of taking it when we left the murder scene. I suppose you'd like me to tell you why.'

'Go ahead. Meanwhile I'll try to figure out the real reason.'

'For safekeeping, you understand. Just in case one of those uniformed policemen was tempted to steal it.'

'You sly old dog. But how do we—?'

'I have a cousin, sir, who works for the Alpha Bank. I think that for a small commission he might be able to help us out. Of course, we should have to be careful to cash the cheque at a smaller branch outside Athens, most probably somewhere like Heraklion, or Corinth – so that it might seem the cheque was presented for payment before Herr Witzel's unfortunate death. It could also require that you should impersonate Siegfried Witzel. But then that shouldn't be too difficult for a German, with the help of a Greek, that is.'

'You are a man of many parts, Garlopis.'

'Tell that to Mrs Garlopis. Hitherto, it's only the one part that has been of concern to her.'

I clapped him on the shoulder. 'Marriage is hell but loneliness is worse.'

'True.'

'I'm not saying we should bribe that cop. But we ought to have the means to do so at our disposal, just in case it proves necessary. So go ahead and make the arrangements to get the cheque cashed.'

'A wise precaution, sir.'

'Can I see that map of Greece in the drawer?' I asked.

'Which one, sir? We have several.'

'The Peloponnese. I'm taking a day trip to Ermioni. Maybe I can pick up some information on what happened to Witzel and his party when they came ashore after the *Doris* sank. At least that way I can make Leventis believe I'm actually making inquiries. Perhaps you'd be kind enough to tell him that's where I'm going tomorrow.'

'Good idea.'

I hadn't yet told Garlopis that I'd recognized the description given by Kalliopi in front of the cinema, that Max Merten was the Sydney Greenstreet lookalike, and that I knew him. After what Leventis had said about Garlopis I thought it best to keep him in the dark on that one – for the time being anyway. He took the map out and handed it to me. I unfolded it and spread it on the desk.

A cursory glance at the map was explanation enough for the wars of antiquity. Greece was mostly two areas of land – a peninsula on a peninsula – separated by the Gulf of Corinth. Until 1893 and the completion of the Corinth Canal, these two peninsulas had been connected by a piece of land about six kilometres long that resembled nothing quite so much as the union of two sexually reproducing animals – the north mounting the south, or Athens mounting Sparta, depending on how you looked at these things. The rest of Greece was just hundreds of islands, which gave the country one of the longest coastlines in Europe and probably one of the most independent and ungovernable populations in the world. How Nazi Germany had ever thought it might control a country like Greece was a mystery to me and likely to the High Command as well, which was probably why, until the fall of Mussolini, they had ceded control of the Peloponnese to the Italians. The invasion of Greece was, arguably, even greater evidence of Hitler's madness than the invasion of the Soviet Union.

'Ermioni,' I said, trailing my finger along the meandering coastline. 'Looks like a two- or three-hour drive from here.'

'We'd best get an early start,' said Garlopis.

'I've made other plans. No, I think maybe you should stay here and speak to your cousin at the bank.'

'But you'll need someone to translate, sir. Ermioni is only a small port town. They still eat *kokoretsi*. Believe me, you don't ever want to know what that is. They're peasants. I doubt you'll find anyone who speaks English there, let alone German.'

'That's all right,' I said. 'I'll be taking someone who speaks German. Someone Greek. Someone who's a lot better-looking than you.'

'You intrigue me, sir.'

'I don't mean to. And you can park that intrigue somewhere quiet, Garlopis. We'll be back before dark, I expect.'

'This wouldn't be the woman from the Ministry of Economic Coordination, would it? Miss Panatoniou? The very good-looking lady who was at Brettos who, you told me, wishes to improve her German?'

'Yes.'

'I must say, teaching a foreign language never looked like such fun.' Garlopis grinned. 'She's a beauty. You'll forgive me if I say so, sir, but I'm impressed.'

'No need to be.'

'If you don't mind me asking, sir, does she know that you're under open arrest? That Leventis has threatened to throw you in jail unless you help him investigate Witzel's murder?'

'No. She doesn't. She knows I'm investigating the loss of the *Doris*. And I imagine Mr Papakyriakopoulos must have told her that I've asked to see his client, Arthur Meissner, but as of this moment she hasn't mentioned that.'

'So on the face of it, she's going for the sheer pleasure of your company. Interesting.'

'Isn't it? To be perfectly honest I have absolutely no idea why she's agreed to spend the day with me. But I'm planning to have a hell of a lot of fun finding out.'

CHAPTER 33

'It was the left that formed the backbone of the resistance to the German occupation,' said Elli. 'And for this reason it was the left that earned the right to govern Greece after the war. But out of respect for his allies, Stalin ordered the KKE to avoid a confrontation with the Greek government in exile, led by Georgios Papandreou. The British, however, encouraged Papandreou to move against the KKE, and even sent tanks and Indian infantry units to support him against the population of Athens, which had supported the left and the KKE. As relations between the Allies deteriorated, Greece became a kind of British protectorate. The king returned to Athens, and the American CIA set about re-equipping and training the Greek army with the aim of destroying Greek communism, which was itself betrayed by Tito, in Yugoslavia.'

The interior of the Rover P4 was all red leather and walnut veneer, quietly ticking clocks and plush thick carpets, like an exclusive English gentleman's club. Elli Panatoniou looked good seated on the Rover's red leather. She'd have looked good seated on a heap of worn-out car tyres. I tried to keep my nice blue eyes on the twisting road to Ermioni but they kept twisting their way back to her shapely knees, the chiaroscuro edge of her black stocking tops, and the Corinth Canal that was her cleavage. The surreptitious enjoyment of all that makes a good-looking woman good-looking is perhaps the only pleasure remaining to man that is neither illegal nor unhealthy, and it's a wonder we stayed on the road at all. It didn't help that her Shalimar perfume was my favourite because it seemed somehow to encapsulate the delightful difference that existed between men and women; the stuff had the effect of making a woman smell like a woman and making a man want to behave like a rampaging gorilla.

'But for Tito, Stalin would have supported the Greek uprising,' she continued. 'As it was, the civil war that was fought effectively resulted in the destruction of Greek communism in 1949. Since when, the army, with the direct help and interference of the Americans, has been backing a succession of incompetent anti-communist governments. This latest one led by Mr Karamanlis is no exception.'

Of course, I wanted her but I was also dumb enough to wonder if this was a good idea while my liberty was under threat from Lieutenant Leventis. Instead of devoting my energies to Miss Panatoniou and the contents of her brassiere I warned myself I needed to focus all of my attention on getting out of Greece and back to Germany. At the same time I nursed a strong suspicion that Elli must be using me for something other than German conversation but so far I'd failed to see for what. In truth I probably didn't care very much; it's usually been my experience that if a beautiful woman is trying to take advantage of you, then you might as well relax and enjoy it while you can.

'But make no mistake,' she said in her reasonable German. 'This is a country run by the right wing and before very long the army will reveal its true hand. We may look like a democracy but underneath Greece is a very polarized society with a deep divide between the right wing and the left wing. Mark my words, the right will use the excuse of our apparent political anarchy to move against not just the left but Greek democracy as a whole, and we will end up with a military dictatorship.'

Apart from my own suspicions, the main thing wrong with her, given that in every other respect she was perfect, was that she seemed to be a communist. Seemed, because it's one thing talking that communist shit all the time – and she did – and quite another living under a communist government. Most of her political opinions were rubbish like that, the kind that had been rubbish in the 1930s, but were even more so now that it was generally known that the great leader, Stalin, had murdered so many in the name of brotherly love, and most of these were other communists. Whenever she started talking the left-wing janissary talk about how wonderful Russia was I kept my muzzle shut out of respect for what was going on in the Corinth Canal. But a couple of times I couldn't resist teasing her with a glimpse of my own political underwear.

'I thought we weren't going to talk politics.'

'This isn't politics. This is history.'

'There's a difference?'

'Don't you think there is?'

'Not in Germany. Politics is always about history. Marx certainly thought so.'

'True.'

'I'm a Marxist,' I said.

'Somehow I doubt that.'

'Sure I am. Over the years I've learned there's no point in having any money or owning property, on account of how people want to take it and give it away to other people; Marxists, mostly. Or did I miss something?'

'But surely the GDR is better than the Federal Republic,' she said. 'At least they have ideals. You can't surely believe that Adenauer's policy of political amnesty for Nazis was the right one. West Germany is nothing more than a front for American imperialism.'

I could have told her a lot about Russian imperialism but after twenty-five years of the right versus the left in Germany I was tired of the whole damned argument. Instead I tried to move the subject back to her, which was a subject of much greater interest.

'Look here, if the right wing is so powerful in Greece, then how come a lefty like you gets to keep her job in a government ministry?'

'I'm a civil servant, a lawyer, not a politician. And I keep my opinions to myself.'

'I hadn't noticed.'

'One of the nicest things about speaking German with you, Christof, is that I'm able to speak freely. Isn't that sad? I really can't speak freely in my own language. That's one of the reasons I agreed to come with you today. I can relax and be myself.'

'I'm glad to hear it.'

'Anyway, I may be a communist but I'm not a revolutionary. And I strongly believe that this new EEC is probably the best chance Greece now has to avoid a right-wing coup d'état. They simply won't let us join if we're not a parliamentary democracy.'

It was a complicated world, whichever way you turned, and I was almost glad that all I had to worry about was getting home again.

'You know, you remind me of an old girlfriend of mine in Germany. She's called Golden Lizzy and she stands on top of the Victory Column in Berlin. She's got wings, too, and she's meant to inspire us to do better things. At least that's the way I always look at her.'

'Are you partial to angels?'

'Only the female ones.'

'Does Lizzy have any other talents?'

'She's tall.'

'I wish I knew what you thought about things. But you don't say.'

'I'm trying to work out why a country that produced the Parthenon and the Temple of Hephaestus doesn't have much in the way of good modern architecture. Most of the public buildings in this country look like gas stations or high-security prisons. Vitruvius would have swallowed his set square.'

'Money, of course. There's not much money for public building. The civil war left us even worse off than the Nazis. Anything else you're trying to work out?'

'I'm German, so generally I'm working on something profoundly philosophical.'

'And what is it right now?'

'Lately I've been trying to work out why Mickey Mouse wears shorts and why Donald Duck wears a shirt, but no shorts at all. And how is it that Goofy talks and Pluto just barks? It's a mystery to me.'

'You're making fun of me.'

'No. Not at all. And maybe I just prefer to keep my opinions to myself. Anyway, they're usually wrong. Or offensive. Or both wrong and offensive.'

'Try me. I'm really quite broad-minded.'

I wondered about that.

'You asked for it. Well, when a woman says she wishes she knew what some man is thinking it's because she can't understand why he hasn't made a pass at her.'

Elli laughed. 'Is that what I'm thinking?'

'Probably. But I figure you'll tell me what you're thinking on that score soon enough. I'm not about to waste either of my two remaining wishes on trying to work it out on my own.'

'What happened to the third wish?'

'You're here in this car, aren't you?'

Elli looked out the window and smiled, and we were silent for a couple of minutes while I negotiated a winding stretch of high mountain road.

'Aren't you just a bit interested to know if I want you to make a pass at me, or not?'

'Not anymore. You just satisfied my curiosity on that one.'

'And?'

'Now I'd like to get back to Mickey and Donald.'

Elli laughed again. 'You are the most infuriating man I've ever met. Do you know that?'

'Yes. I'm what you lawyers would call incorrigible.'

She put her cool hand on the back of my neck, where it felt good.

'You're also very nice. Much more human than I would ever have thought possible. You're really rather a considerate sort of man, I think.'

'My fatal charm. It never fails. Except when I'm relying on it to get me out of a jam such as my whole life since 1945.'

'What did you do during the war, Christof?'

'Not enough. But here's a useful tip when you're speaking German in Brussels. Unless you're talking to Bertolt Brecht or Albert Einstein never ever ask a German what he did during the war. Not everyone appreciates it when they're told barefaced lies.'

CHAPTER 34

Ermioni was a small port town on the Aegean Sea that resembled every picture postcard of a Greek village I'd ever seen – all blueberry sea and robin's-egg sky, sugar-lump houses and paperwhite caïques. We parked the Rover and stretched our legs for a bit. It felt as if we were at the very edge of the known world, the kind of almost forgotten place where Themistocles, with one eye on the two islands of Hydra and Dokos that occupied the horizon like the grey clouds of an approaching storm, could once have sat on some high colonnaded terrace writing about an improbable victory over the Persians. Walrus-faced fishermen tugged on cigarettes and pipes as big as clay pots while they mended their nets and watched us with ancient eyes that might have witnessed the Greek navy boarding their biremes and triremes to fight mad King Xerxes. Flesh-coloured squid dried in the sun like wet swimming costumes on sagging lines and stray cats dozed on the quayside or wandered between the tables of cafés as if waiting upon the day's customers, who probably weren't going to come. The late-morning air tasted of salt and smelled of

Greek coffee and tobacco, and the otherwise perfect stillness was periodically jangled with the spilling-cutlery sound of a distant bouzouki. It was a long way from Berlin; I couldn't have felt more German if I'd had a black eagle with red legs perched on my shoulder and a snarling Alsatian on a length of piano wire.

We had a drink in one place where we stroked the cats and spoke to a man with a face that was a sunbaked mosaic of cracks and fissures and who informed us that there was no coast guard's office in Ermioni and that we'd best ask at the local harbour-master's office in the main square, where all boat owners tying up in Ermioni were supposed to pay their mooring fees.

The office was a rusticated white building with a blue door and shutters and a Greek flag out front just in case the colour scheme left room for doubt regarding anyone's patriotism. The front door was guarded by a pair of seagulls as big as pterodactyls and probably just as fierce; certainly they showed no fear of a large black Labrador that lay asleep or possibly dead on the porch.

The harbourmaster himself belonged to a species that was different from Ermioni's other archaic humans, having a face with skin that hadn't been supplied by the local leather factory. His name was Athanassios Stratis and he wore a black wool cap with a peak that was only a little less long and hairy than his nose. Explaining that I was from the ship's insurance company in Munich, Elli did all the talking, and after a minute or two Mr Stratis opened an ancient wooden filing cabinet that was as big as a coffin while she explained to me that he remembered the *Doris* and the German who'd owned it very well.

'He's quite sure there was actually a ship that sank near here?'

'Several other people saw them coming ashore in the life raft that's still moored to the quayside where they left it,' said Elli. 'He's been wondering what to do about it. He says he sailed his own boat out to the position given by the German the day after, to make sure that the wreck was not a hazard to local shipping, and found some flotsam – some debris in the water that had not been deliberately thrown overboard and was consistent with there having been some kind of accident. But the water is deep there and he thinks there's zero chance of salvage.'

Mr Stratis found a file in his cabinet and glanced over a handwritten report he'd made of the incident while he rescued a half-smoked cigarette that had got lost behind his ear and lit it again. But his every other look was reserved for Elli; she was that kind of woman – the kind that could cause a traffic accident merely by standing at a bus stop. Every time I looked at her I almost skidded to a halt myself.

'He says there were three men who came ashore in the raft,' continued Elli. 'Two Germans and a Greek. One of the Germans was the boat owner, Mr Witzel. The Greek was the ship's captain, Mr Spiros Reppas. Mr Stratis says the other man didn't give his name and said nothing very much.'

'Ask him if one of the men on the boat – one of the Germans – could have been this man,' I said, and provided a description of the man who'd posed as Professor Buchholz, Max Merten.

After a while Stratis nodded and said that it sounded like it was the same man. Then he and she talked a while and laughed and that was fine, too, because he was only a man after all and it made me think that she'd get more out of him if she made him feel like one. It had certainly worked on me.

'What happened to them after they left this office?'

'One of them, Witzel – he caught the ferry to Piraeus. That's the quickest and least expensive way. The other two took a taxi farther down the coast somewhere. He doesn't know where. But he thinks the driver would probably remember. His name is Christos Kammenos and we'll find him sitting in a black Citroën on the other side of the peninsula, in front of the local chandler's shop.'

I thought for a moment. 'The flotsam,' I said. 'This debris he found floating on the surface of the sea at the place where the *Doris* went down. Anything interesting there?'

'Some papers, that's all,' said Elli. 'He dried them and kept them in case they were important.'

Stratis produced a large waterproof envelope from the drawer.

'If he likes, I'll look after those,' I said.

The harbourmaster handed them over without demur, but to Elli. I asked some more questions but learned nothing new and so we thanked him and went outside; the seagulls had gone but the dog performing the great dead-animal act was still there; as soon as I saw its diaphragm move I found myself stifling a yawn and envying the creature. It was a two- or three-hour drive from Athens. And a two- or three-hour drive back there.

She handed me the envelope. The papers were all in Greek and Elli looked at them and said they were nothing important, just Siegfried Witzel's identity card and some invoices. But being German and therefore punctilious about these things

I asked her to describe the invoices in detail and found she was right – they *were* nothing important, mostly bills for food and drink and scuba tanks full of oxygen, which I supposed was quite important if you happened to be underwater at the time. But one of these wasn't an invoice at all and its importance was immediately obvious, at least to me. It was a waybill for a consignment sent to the *Doris* at the Marina Zea, in Piraeus, by none other than Mr Georg Fischer, and which gave his address as Constitution Square in Athens, and while the waybill didn't actually identify the hotel, I recognized the Mega's telephone number: 36604. Clearly Alois Brunner was more often in the Mega Hotel than I'd been led to believe. The contents of the consignment were very interesting, too: Witzel had taken delivery of a bronze Hellenistic horse's head from about 100 BC which was, I told Elli, the equivalent of bringing owls to Athens.

'That's a real German phrase?' she asked.

'Absolutely.'

'You're making fun of me.'

'No, I'm really not. And the reason I'm saying this is because the specific purpose of Witzel's expedition was to sail to the site of a sunken ship and there to dive for ancient Greek artefacts. Which begs the question why someone had such an artefact sent to the *Doris* on the day *before* he sailed. It seems the wrong way round.' I frowned. 'And here's another thing. Witzel didn't ever mention this horse on his insurance claim with MRE. But it was almost two thousand years old. Yesterday, Dr Lyacos at the Archaeological Museum in Piraeus said that a good Roman bust of the second century might be worth as much as fifty thousand dollars. This horse has to be worth some serious money, too. So why didn't he make a claim for that, I wonder?'

We started to walk up the hill to cross over to the other side of the Ermioni peninsula; the little winding streets were deserted and quiet, which made me quiet while I thought about this latest discovery.

'Unless the whole expedition was only meant to be a cover for something else,' I said after a while.

'Like what?'

'There were some smaller artefacts that Witzel didn't want to claim for, either. And I thought this was because he was trying to prevent me from contacting Professor Buchholz. But now I'm thinking that maybe there was an extra reason. Dr Lyacos told me there's a thriving trade in black market antiquities through the port of Piraeus. Museums in small American cities want them to keep up with their richer neighbours. Apparently there's nothing like a marble bust of Socrates to make people think that Boise, Idaho, is the cultural equal of New York and Washington. Lyacos told me he'd even heard that Colonel Nasser was using ancient Egyptian art to pay for illegal weapons. Now that he's nationalized the canal he's going to have to force people to pay to go through it, I guess. So maybe that's what they were up to. Maybe there were some other antiquities already on the *Doris*. Maybe they were taking those somewhere quiet to exchange them for weapons destined for Nasser. German weapons, I shouldn't wonder. On a remote island, perhaps. Greece has got lots of those.'

On the south side of the peninsula we found Christos the taxi driver, who rubbed a chin that might have doubled as a magnet for iron filings and then said he didn't remember a German travelling with a Greek, at least until I gave him a few drachmas. I didn't blame him for his poor memory; it looked like he'd had a lean morning of it. Pocketing the note he told us that he'd driven two men to Kosta, which was another small port town, about twenty kilometres south of Ermioni.

'Anything interesting or important about Kosta?'

'Nothing much,' came the answer, via Elli. 'But there's a small private airport near there, in Porto Heli.'

'But he didn't drive them there,' I said. 'Or he'd have said so.'

'No,' said Elli, 'he says he dropped them in the centre of town. At a hotel in the main square.'

We got in the back of the Citroën and told him to take us to Kosta. It seemed quicker than finding the place ourselves. Besides, MRE was paying. The Citroën was a Traction Avant, beloved of the Gestapo in Paris, and for a moment or two it was easy enough to imagine myself back there in the summer of 1940; Elli was as beautiful and smelled as good as any French-woman I'd ever seen, or inhaled. I smiled at her a couple of times and she smiled back and once she took my hand and squeezed it; it seemed as if I was making more progress with her than I was with the case.

It took us less than half an hour to find ourselves in another Greek port town that was a little less picturesque than Ermioni. The harbour looked more sheltered than the one we'd just left behind and was perhaps shallower, too, as the sight of a boat that was only half-sunk in the water seemed to confirm. At the main hotel we asked about Professor Buchholz and his Greek friend and learned only that they'd stayed just one night. Where they'd gone after leaving, the proprietor had no idea and it was clear she didn't care to speculate, either, when she heard Elli speaking German to me.

We had Christos drive us back along the meandering coast to Ermioni and there we ate a simple lunch at a little restaurant facing the calm sea on the south quay with more cats for company and enjoyed the pleasant change in the weather almost as much as we enjoyed some Greek food and wine.

'So how is this trip connected with Arthur Meissner?' she asked.

'I was wondering when you'd ask me about that. Tell me something first: what's *your* connection with this whole flea circus?'

'Dimitri Papakyriakopoulos. Meissner's lawyer. I help him out sometimes, doing a bit of legal work to make some extra cash.'

'Is that all you do for him?'

'So far. He's curious, that's all. I'm kind of curious myself.'

'No, I think you're just fine. In spite of the fact that you're a lawyer and a bureaucrat.'

'What I am above all is a single woman, Christof. I need the money. Economic coordination doesn't pay very well in this country. Greeks tend to resist most kinds of coordination. Yes, we gave the world democracy but people tend to forget we also gave the world anarchy.'

'I've always been a bit of an anarchist myself. It was easy enough when we had a ruler like Hitler and authority like the

Nazis. But lately I've been slipping. I'm seriously thinking of hanging up the black flag and getting myself socially stratified. I think I might enjoy it.'

'Anyway, that's not why I came today. I mean, I didn't come to pump you for information about your interest in Arthur Meissner. I just fancied a day off, in a nice car, with a nice man.'

'To be perfectly honest, I don't know that I am interested in Meissner,' I said, ignoring the compliment, at least for the moment. 'But that cop, Leventis, is pressuring me to try to help him solve a case.'

'Samuel Frizis.'

'Yes.'

'Why does he think you can help? Because you were a cop?'

'There's that, yes. And the fact that I'm German. Witzel, my claimant and fellow countryman, got himself murdered and Leventis seems more inclined to make me a suspect instead of a witness. Either I help him or I don't get my passport back.'

'As a lawyer I have to tell you that he has that power.'

'I know. I spoke to another lawyer already.'

'Anyone I know?'

'A firm in Piraeus.'

'Piraeus. That doesn't sound very promising. You'd better let me help you out if you get into any trouble.'

'Sounds better. Thanks. I appreciate it.'

'But where's the connection between Frizis and Witzel?'

'I can't tell you that. Leventis wouldn't like it. But there is one.'

'Fair enough.'

'So why *did* you come today?'

'I told you. I came along for the German. And I don't mean the grammar.'

'I should warn you about my grammar, Elli. Like everything else I have it's a little old and out-of-date. This is your teacher telling you now. So listen. I'm much too old for you, Elli. I drool when I sleep and sleep when I ought to be awake, and my heart feels like it needs a wheelchair to get around.'

'You should let me be the judge of that.'

'I'm serious. I look at my wristwatch and I don't see what time it is, I see the time that was.'

'Or perhaps you just don't like me.'

'I'd probably like you a lot more if I disliked myself a little less.'

'You're better than you think you are. Anyway, whatever happens, we're having a good time, aren't we? I know I am. Nothing else seems to matter right now. Being here today is lovely.'

'I don't disagree about that. The last time I enjoyed myself this much, a witch was baking my sister Gretel in a pie.'

'It's great to be out of the ministry for a while. To be away from Athens. It really does feel a lot like spring. Makes you feel lucky to be alive.'

She was right. It did feel like spring and I did feel lucky to be alive, which was not unusual for me, and this might be why, on the short walk back to where I'd left the Rover, I kissed Elli Panatoniou under an ancient olive tree and maybe it was also why she let me.

It had been a long, cold, lonely winter.

CHAPTER 35

It was almost five p.m. when I got back to the office to check my messages and telephone Lieutenant Leventis after driving Elli to her own office at the ministry on Amerikis Street. It seemed we both had to work late that night.

'Call me,' she'd said. '30931. Extension 134. Maybe we can go and have a drink tomorrow. Or we could go dancing at Kala-bokas, perhaps. That's a club I know. Do you dance?'

'It depends.'

'On what?'

'On who's pulling the strings. The way I see it, when you've got to dance you've got to dance.'

'Next stop Broadway, huh?'

'As soon as I can get out of Greece.'

'Don't be in too much of a hurry. That kiss this afternoon. I liked it. I'd like some more.'

'Good. Extension 134. I'll arrange it.'

Telesilla had gone home but Garlopis was still there. He looked more nervous than was normal even for him.

'Mr Dietrich received your telegram, sir. He is going to telephone again, at five o'clock his time, six ours. So I thought I'd better wait in case you needed any help with the international operator.'

'Kind of you. He telephoned before?'

'Twice. At three and at four. It seemed to be urgent.'

'Good. He must have discovered something important.'

'And did *you* find anything important when you were in Ermioni?'

'Yes, I think so. I've got some evidence that Siegfried Witzel and his friends on the *Doris* weren't looking for sunken treasure any more than they were looking for the lost city of Atlantis. I think they were involved in an illegal weapons deal with Alois Brunner. Neff, too, for all I know. Trading black market Greek and Egyptian sculptures to obtain guns for Colonel Nasser and his Muslim Brotherhood for their war against the Israelis. Frankly it's just the kind of cause that would attract an anti-Semite like Brunner. But from the way things panned out he must have figured he was being double-crossed and decided to wind up the partnership. Permanently.'

'These are troubled times we live in, sir.'

'That's always been the rumour.'

'But surely this is good news. It means you've got something concrete to tell Lieutenant Leventis, doesn't it? Enough to get him off your back, perhaps. Off both our backs.'

'Perhaps.'

Garlopis grinned sheepishly. 'How did you get on with Miss Panatoniou?'

'Yes, that was interesting. We were followed all the way there and back.'

'By who?'

'Two men in a black sedan.'

'They were working for Leventis, perhaps.'

'Perhaps.'

'Did you tell her?'

'God, no. I didn't want to distract her from me. She did an excellent job of paying me a great deal of probably unwarranted attention.'

'You think she was playing you?'

'My strings are still humming. But I have no idea what her game is. At least not while she's using that chest of hers to breathe. It's kind of distracting. She says she does a little extra work for Dimitri Papakyriakopoulos. Meissner's lawyer. It seems he's curious as to why I should want to meet with his client. And because he's curious she is, too. Of course, she says it's more than that. She says she likes me. But.'

'Of course.'

'Right now I'm trying to limit things between us to something platonic; the only trouble is that making love is so much more entertaining.'

Garlopis chuckled. 'You're absolutely right there, sir. Who was it that said a woman is like a tortoise; once she's on her back you can do what you want with her.'

'It doesn't sound much like Zeno.'

'No, perhaps you're right. Anyway, you look like a man who knows what he's doing.'

'That's an easy mistake to make. You see, I've met her kind before. She's a mortar bomb in a tight blouse. A man needs a tin hat and a lorry load of sandbags just to be near a girl like that. The trick is being somewhere else when she goes off.'

'She does have a remarkable figure, sir. Just what the doctor ordered, I'd have thought.'

'Always supposing that one can afford a doctor like that.'

Our discussion of Elli Panatoniou was all the excuse Garlopis needed to find a bottle of Four Roses in the desk drawer and pour us a couple while we waited for Dumbo's call. There are some subjects, like analytic geometry and spiric sections, for which you need a drink and Elli's figure was one of them; she had the most interesting curves since Diocles described a cissoid. After a while I sat down at Telesilla's desk to type out a report on the day's activities for Lieutenant Leventis. I saw no reason not to take his previous threat seriously. I mentioned the name of Spiros Reppas on the assumption he'd already heard it in connection with the house in Pritaniou; and I told Leventis that I'd been followed by two men in a dark sedan – I even gave him the licence plate, just to be insolent. I didn't say anything in my report about kissing Elli Panatoniou, but I figured that if the men following us had been his, they could tell him that themselves. Of course, the report was more or less pointless and mostly demonstrated that I was badly out of practice with a typewriter. But Leventis was right about one thing: it did make me feel like a cop again.

Garlopis read my report and smiled sadly.

'Perhaps next time I could type this for you, sir? In Greek.

There are many mistakes. Perhaps the lieutenant will be more inclined to be sympathetic if your report is in Greek.'

'Next time.'

At last the phone rang. Garlopis answered it, said something in Greek to the operator, and then handed me the receiver.

'Munich,' he said, and pressed his head close to the backside of the earpiece so he could hear. His hair smelled of limes.

'Christof Ganz speaking.'

'About time. I've been trying to get hold of you all day, Ganz. Where the hell have you been?'

Dietrich's voice was testy and irritable, like maybe he'd forgotten how much money I'd saved the company since taking up my employment. I swallowed the rest of my drink; it sounded as if I was going to need it. Garlopis smoothly refilled the glass.

'I've been out of the office, sir.'

'No kidding.'

'Like I said before, the Greek police are proving to be less than helpful. Did you ever try to adjust a claim with a dead body on the floor? It's not so easy doing the paperwork.'

'I get that. It's an awkward situation right enough. Naturally we feel bad having landed you in this situation. But sometimes that's how it is. Adjusting a claim can be a tricky process. A claims man has to expect the unexpected. That's what this business is all about. And sometimes the unexpected is a little more unpredictable than can reasonably be expected, especially when there's a lot of money involved.'

'Did you find Max Merten?'

'No. I didn't.' Dietrich sighed. 'Look here, Ganz, the word

from on high is that you're to drop this whole thing. Right now. I've retained those lawyers in Piraeus on your behalf and told them to deal with the police through the usual channels. We will assist you in any way we can. Bail money, fines, legal fees, none of that is a problem. We'll bring you home, right enough. You've just got to be patient and let the lawyers handle it now. But this whole line of inquiry needs to end. Siegfried Witzel's claim for the *Doris* has been disallowed and that's the end of it as far as MRE is concerned.'

'Is that what Mr Alzheimer says?'

'Mr Alzheimer, me, and God almighty. In that order, see? You're not a cop anymore, you're a goddamned insurance man. It's time you started acting like one.'

'What's the idea?'

'There isn't any idea. There's just orders. From upstairs. You're to drop this inquiry like it was red-hot toilet paper. When you're back home we'll go out somewhere like the Hofbräuhaus and I'll buy you a cheap dinner to celebrate.'

'An invitation like that I can hardly refuse.'

'Good.' Dietrich was oblivious to my sarcasm.

'Sure, boss. Anything you say.' It wasn't what I felt like saying to Dumbo but it sounded a lot better than *Go and fuck yourself*. Working for MRE was still a good job for a man like me, with a car and expenses and what I most craved, which was a quiet life with a little respectability. I was determined to keep the job, in spite of what the big mouth in my square head felt like doing. My father would have been proud of me; he always did want me to go into something respectable like insurance. I picked up my glass and then drained it, a second time. 'Was there anything else, sir?'

'No, that's it, Ganz. Take care now. See you soon.'

I handed Garlopis the receiver and he dropped it on the cradle and shrugged. 'Dale Carnegie he is not.'

'Dumbo's usually all right. For an office man. But it sounds to me like someone's been shaking his pram.'

'Perhaps it was Mr Alzheimer.'

'Could be. In which case maybe someone leaned on Mr Alzheimer.'

'Like who?'

'Frankly I'd rather not know. But I do know that in pride of place in Alzheimer's office is a framed photograph of him looking very cozy with our own dear Konrad Adenauer. If, as Lieutenant Leventis says, Alois Brunner does have good connections in the current German government, then maybe Adenauer asked his old friend Alzheimer to have me lay off the case.'

'If you don't mind me saying so, sir, none of that fits with Brunner being involved in selling arms illegally to the Egyptians. I mean why would the West German government, a NATO member for only a couple of years, risk upsetting its new allies by doing something like that? It doesn't make sense. Unless anti-Semitism is still the policy of the German government.'

'Leventis said he thought maybe Brunner had been working for the German Federal Intelligence Service, the BND. So maybe he still is. Maybe this was an undercover operation. I don't know. The minute you get the peekers involved, then the screen ripples in front of you like a mirage and before you know it

Red Riding Hood turns out to be the wolf.' I lit a cigarette. 'It's beginning to look as though I'll need to bribe that cop after all. Did you speak to your cousin at the Alpha Bank? About cashing that certified cheque?'

'Yes. And he tells me that he can make this happen quite easily. Now all we have to do is bribe someone at the Ministry of Public Order with a much smaller sum to provide you with a fake identity card in the name of Siegfried Witzel.'

'Will this do?'

I handed over the identity card that the Ermioni harbour-master had found floating in the sea at the spot where the *Doris* had gone down. The card was in poor condition but all the pertinent details were more or less legible.

'Oh, this will do very well,' said Garlopis. 'Where did you find it?'

I explained where it had come from.

'The picture is so faded that it actually looks a bit like you.'

'That's hardly a surprise. I'm a bit faded myself. Or more accurately, worn away like the relief on some ancient temple.'

'He suggests cashing the cheque at the bank in Corinth where he has a good friend who owes him a favour. That's less than an hour's drive north of here. It's perfect for us. Nothing ever happens in Corinth. At least not since the earthquake of 1928 and the great fire of 1933.'

'Sounds like a poor choice of place to build a bank.'

Garlopis smiled. 'We could go there the day after you visit Arthur Meissner in Averoff Prison, perhaps. On Saturday. Banks are always quiet on a Saturday.'

'Yes, that should help us focus on what we're doing very nicely. There's nothing like planning a serious crime to give an extra thrill to a prison visit.'

A warm afternoon in Athens and Garlopis was behind the wheel of the Rover, which suited me very well, given the homicidal impatience of other Greek drivers. To drive around Constitution Square was to invite an assault by car horn and amounted to the clearest demonstration of jungle law since Huxley battered Bishop Wilberforce on his pate with a blunt copy of *On the Origin of Species*. No ordinary human could ever have enjoyed seeing Athens from the front seat of a car any more than he could have enjoyed trying to fly off the ski jump at Garmisch. Even Garlopis was a different man behind the wheel of a car – as different as if he'd shared a couple of Greek coffees with Dr Henry Jekyll. We reached Averoff Prison, about three kilometres northeast of the office, in a matter of minutes and a fug of burnt rubber. He could have found the place on Alexandras Avenue in his sleep because it was close to the Apostolis Nikolaidis Stadium, the home ground of Panathinaikos, the Athens football team supported enthusiastically by Garlopis and, he said, the winner of the Greek Cup as recently as 1955. He parked the car and switched off the engine, and at last I was able to let out a breath.

'I was never so glad to see a prison,' I said, looking out of the car window at a grim, castellated grey brick building that was shrouded with palm trees. I lit a Karelia from a packet I'd bought and tried to compose myself.

But Garlopis was looking serious.

'I'm sorry, sir, but I'm afraid I won't be going in there. You see, there's something I need to tell you. You're not the only one with a past. I mean, a past I'd rather not be reminded of.'

'Don't tell me, you were a cop, too.'

'No, but during the war I was a translator for the Occupation Force, just like Arthur Meissner. First for the Italians and then the Germans. So far I've managed to conceal this fact. And for obvious reasons you're the one person with whom I feel I can share this information now. I certainly wouldn't tell anyone Greek. Meissner worked in Thessaloniki while I was based here in Athens but he and I met several times at the Gestapo building in Merlin Street. And I'd much prefer it if we didn't meet again. He might try to blackmail me, to share the blame, if you like. I certainly didn't murder or rob anyone, which is what he's accused of doing by no less a figure than Archimedes Argyropoulos; he's a general and a Greek military hero, so his evidence has been very damaging to Meissner's case. No, all I did was to be part of a pool of translators. I even tried to ameliorate some of the general's orders. Nevertheless, in Greek eyes this makes me a collaborator.'

'Collaborator is just another word for survivor,' I said. 'In a war staying alive is a bit like playing tennis. It looks a lot easier when you've never had to play yourself. Take it from one who can boast a pretty useful backhand.'

'That's kind of you to say. Unfortunately there are plenty of Greeks who would like to see a rat like me disqualified. Permanently.'

'Forget it. I think you're a pretty nice guy – for a rat.'

'You're too kind, sir.'

'I don't mean to be. Tell me, when you were working for the Third Reich did you ever meet this SD Captain Brunner that Lieutenant Leventis has decided to make his life's personal Jean Valjean?'

'On one of the few occasions I met Meissner he was accompanied by some SD officers and perhaps one of them might have been Brunner, but I really don't know for sure. There were so many. And men in uniform all look alike to me. Frankly I'd never even heard the name Brunner until Leventis mentioned him in his office.' Garlopis shook his head. 'What I did know was to stay away from Thessaloniki. You have to understand that things were much harder there because the SD were in charge. There it was all about persecuting the Jews. Here, in Athens, things were easier. Besides, Brunner was a mere captain. Mostly I worked for the military governor, a Luftwaffe general called Wilhelm Speidel who Lieutenant Leventis mentioned to you when we were in his office. This is the real reason I try to encourage people not to stay at the Grande Bretagne Hotel, sir. During the war it was taken over by the German general staff. Speidel's headquarters were in a suite on the top floor. Hitler once stayed at the GB; Himmler, and Göring, too. I actually saw Hermann Göring drinking champagne with Rommel in the hotel bar. I was often in and out of the place to meet with General Speidel and I don't like to go back there in case I'm ever recognized.

'Then, in April 1944, Speidel was transferred back to Germany and I went to stay with a cousin of mine in Rhodes, until I judged it safe to come back to Athens. When Leventis mentioned Speidel and the massacre in Kalavryta, you could have knocked me sideways. Frankly I had no idea he'd ever had a hand in such a thing. I always found him to be very kind, very thoughtful, and a real gentleman. When he left Greece he even gave me a nice fountain pen. His own Pelikan.'

'That's something you learn about life. Sometimes the nicest folk do the most horrible things. Especially in Germany. Along with the Japs we virtually own the monopoly on very kind, very thoughtful mass murderers. People are always surprised that we also like Mozart and small children.'

'I just wanted you to know the truth.'

'It's a tough world for honest men. But don't tell any of them.'

'No, indeed. I shall wait for you here, sir. I shall close my eyes and get some beauty sleep.'

'Try a coma. Then it might actually work.'

Leaving Garlopis to his nap I stepped out of the car and walked toward the gate wondering just how much of what Garlopis had told me was true. Knowing him as I did, I half-suspected that I might have got more information from the Greek insurance man about Alois Brunner than I was ever likely to get out of Arthur Meissner.

The sentry waved me through the gate to the main door, where I rang the bell as if I'd been selling brushes, and waited. After a moment or two, a smaller door opened in the bigger one and I showed the prison guard a letter Leventis had written for me. Then I was taken to a small windowless room where I was searched carefully and ushered through several locked cage doors, to a room with four chairs and a table. There I sat down and waited, nervously. I'd been in enough prison cells in my time to get a sick feeling in my stomach just being there. The only window was about three metres above the floor and on the wall was a cheap picture of the Parthenon. A temple dedicated to the goddess Athena seemed a long way from a squalid room in Averoff Prison. After a while the door opened again to admit a small dark handsome man in his forties and I stood up.

'Herr Meissner?'

When he nodded I offered him a cigarette and when he took one I told him to keep the pack. That's just good manners when you're meeting anyone behind bars. He smelled strongly of prison, which as anyone who's been a convict could tell you is a cloying mixture of cigarettes, fried potatoes, fear, sweat, and only one shower a week.

'You're Christof Ganz?'

'Yes.'

'I'm here because Papakyriakopoulos told me I had nothing to lose by meeting with you,' said Meissner, pocketing the pack for later. 'But I can't see that I've got anything much to gain either. After all, it's not like you're anyone important in this fucking country.'

Meissner spoke German with a slight Berlin accent – his father's, probably, and very like my own.

'That's rather the point, I think. I'm not with the police. And I'm not a member of the legal profession. I'm just a private citizen. I'm only here because Lieutenant Leventis has my balls in his hand and, because I used to be a cop in Berlin, he thinks that you might have something to tell me that you wouldn't tell him. And perhaps since you can tell me in German I guess he believes you can speak in confidence. I don't know. But you could even say I'm an honest broker. Beware of Greeks bearing gifts, and all that shit.'

'So what does he want me to say to the good German?'

'I'll come to that. What he wants me to say first is that he thinks you're small fry.'

'Tell that to the judge.'

'That there are more important fish out there still to be caught.'

'You got that right, Fritz. I've been saying that for months, but no one ever listens. Look, for your information, I was just a translator. A mouth for hire. I never murdered anyone. And I never robbed anyone. And nor did my girlfriend, Eleni. Yes, I took a few bribes. Who didn't? This is Greece. Everyone takes bribes in this fucking country. Some of those bribes I took were to bribe a few Germans, to help people, Jews included. This fellow Moses Natan, who says he bribed me to help his family. Well, I really did try to help him, but the way he talks now you'd think my help came with guarantees. If you were a cop, then you must know what that was like. Sometimes you tried and succeeded, but more often you tried and failed. None of the people I succeeded in helping have turned up to speak on my behalf. Just the ones I failed.

'As for those rape charges. They're nonsense. The cops know that, too. The trouble is that I'm the only one they've ever managed to put on trial in this fucking country for what happened during the occupation. Me. The translator. You might as well charge some of those women who were chambermaids at the Grande Bretagne Hotel when the German High Command was living there. The barmen and the fucking porters, too. But the Greeks want someone to blame. And right now I'm the only scapegoat they can find. So they're throwing the book at me. I'm charged with twelve thousand murders. Did you know that? Me, a man who's never even held a gun. The way they're talking I'm the man who told Hitler to invade Greece. As if the Germans would ever have listened to me. It's a fucking joke. All those Nazi officers – Speidel, Student, Lanz, Felmy – they're the ones who should be on trial here, not me.'

'Oh, I get that. And look, I won't say I'm on your side. But I kind of am because getting you to talk might put me in good odor with Leventis. Helping you helps me. He can't come out and say so to you in person – that would be political suicide for him, not to mention illegal – but he's assured me that if you assist him, he'll speak to Mr Toussis.'

Toussis was the name of the man prosecuting Meissner's case in court.

'Get the charges reduced,' I added. 'Thrown out, maybe.'

'That's all very well, but right now it's possible I might be safer in here than I would be on the outside. Seriously, Ganz. I'm a dead man the minute I leave this place. I've got less chance of going back to my house in Elefsina than I have of becoming the Greek prime minister.'

'Safe conduct on a plane to Germany. I'll even go with you myself. I want out of here as much as you do. How does that sound?'

'It sounds great. But look, here's the biggest obstacle to making all that happen. I don't know that I know anything very important. If I did I would have spilled my guts before now, believe me.'

'Leventis is after someone in particular. One of those big fish. A man called Alois Brunner. He was a captain in the SD. Remember him?'

'Yes. I could hardly forget him. No one could. Brunner was a memorable man, Herr Ganz. Him and Wisliceny and Eichmann. All driven by hatred of the Jews. But unlike Eichmann, Brunner was a real sadist. He liked inflicting pain. A couple of times I was present when Alois Brunner tortured a man at the Villa Mehmet Kapanci – that was the Gestapo headquarters on Vasilissis Olgas Avenue, in Thessaloniki. And clearly he enjoyed it. I didn't want to be there, of course, but Brunner took out his gun and pressed it up against my eyeball and told me I could translate for him or I could bleed on the floor. Those were his exact words. Like I say, you don't forget a man like Brunner. But I haven't seen or heard of him since the summer of 1943, thank God. And I wouldn't have any idea of how to find him.'

'Brunner is back in Greece.'

'He wouldn't dare. I don't believe it. Says who?'

'Says me. I met him here in Athens, although I didn't know it at the time. He's using an assumed name.'

'Jesus. How about that? Now there's someone who really does have a lot to answer for in this country. But for Brunner and Wisliceny, the Jews of Thessaloniki might still be alive. Almost sixty thousand of them died in Auschwitz. It was Brunner's job to get them on the trains out of Salonika. Maybe that's why Brunner feels it's safe to come back. Because there's no one around to identify him.'

'There's you.'

'Sure. And tell Leventis I will identify him if it gets me out of here. No problem. Now all you have to do is find the bastard.'

'So what else can you tell me about Brunner?'

'Let's see now. There was a hotel in Thessaloniki he liked, the Aegaeon. And another one where he took his Greek mistress, the Luxembourg. Her name was Tzeni, I think. Or Tonia. No, Tzeni. I'm not so sure he didn't murder her before he left Greece. A couple of times I accompanied him to Athens and he stayed at the Xenias Melathron, on Jan Smuts. There was a restaurant he liked, too – the Kissos on Amerikis Street. I doubt he'd risk going back to Thessaloniki, but Athens would be different. He wasn't here that often.' Meissner paused. 'How did you know it was him?'

'Because Lieutenant Leventis showed me a photograph and I recognized him as the man who'd been talking to me earlier on in my hotel bar. Calls himself Fischer now, Georg Fischer, and he claims to be a tobacco salesman.'

'You say he spoke to you?'

'That's right. He initiated a conversation when he realized I was German.'

'Was he just making conversation or did he want something? If he did, then make sure you give it to him. That man likes to kill people. And not just Jews.'

'So I hear. At first I figured it was just two Germans a long way from home – that kind of thing. But later on I realized he was looking for someone. He hoped I might lead him to the man. Because unwittingly I did, that someone is now dead.'

'Who?'

'Fellow named Siegfried Witzel.'

'Never heard of him.'

'He worked for a man named Max Merten.'

'Max Merten.' Meissner stood up and lit one of the cigarettes I'd given him. He walked around the room for a moment, nodding quietly to himself.

'That name mean something to you?'

'Oh yes.'

'What can you tell me about Max Merten?'

'Wait a minute. You said this Witzel fellow worked for Merten?'

'Yes.'

'When was that?'

'Now. This year. I think Merten's in Greece, too.'

Meissner grinned. 'Now it's starting to make sense. Why Brunner would dare come back to Greece. Wisliceny is dead – hanged by the Czechs, I think. And Eichmann, well, he's disappeared. In Brazil, if he knows what's good for him. So that leaves Merten and Brunner. It figures.'

'I'm glad you think so.'

'People remember Eichmann, Wisliceny, and Brunner because they were all SD and they think all of the really bad men were in the SS because the SS were specifically tasked with killing the Jews, but the fact is Merten was in charge of the whole shooting match.'

'But he was just an army captain, wasn't he?'

'True. Which would have made it a lot easier for him to stay beneath the radar. But Merten was the chief of military adminis- tration for the whole Salonika—Aegean theatre. The Wehrmacht let him do what the fuck he wanted because they were mostly all in Athens and they didn't give a shit about Thessaloniki. For one thing, there wasn't a really good hotel like the GB. And for another, they preferred to keep their gentlemen's consciences away from the SD myrmidons and what they had planned. But in Thessaloniki if you wanted a truck, a train, a ship, a building, you had to go through Merten. You wanted a hundred Jewish workers to build a road, you had to ask Merten. He was the boss of everything. Even Eichmann had to go through Max Merten. Now there's someone who the Greeks should put on trial. The stories I could tell you about Max Merten. He lived like a king in Thessaloniki. And not just any king. Like Croesus, probably. He had a villa with a swim- ming pool, girls, cars, servants, the best food and wine. He even had his own cinema theatre. And nobody bothered him.' Meissner shook his head bitterly. 'But of course there's only one real story about Max Merten. If you ask me that's probably what your Greek lieutenant is really interested in. Putting Alois Brunner on trial is just a smokescreen. If Max Merten is in Greece, then there can be only one reason. And I daresay Alois Brunner knows that, too.'

CHAPTER 37

I strolled out of the Averoff Prison door and through the main gate with some air under my blue suede Salamanders because prison always affected me that way. Whichever way you walk out of the cement – innocent or guilty – you're always grateful. I was planning on having a hot bath and a drink and a square meal, and maybe an evening on the dance floor with a nice girl and all the other things they take away from you when you're inside. When you've done time, you never again take time for granted. I guess all that nostalgia made me a little preoccupied and unprepared for what happened next. Besides, it was a professional-looking operation, the way the navy-blue Pontiac pulled up with the big doors opening smoothly before the Goodyears had squealed to a stop, and how the two innocent bystanders approaching me from opposite ends of the sidewalk turned out to have neat little pocket automatics almost hidden in their hands and were not quite so innocent as they'd seemed. The next minute I was in the back of the car with four men who looked much fitter than I was and we were heading east on Tsocha, and then southwest on Vasileos Konstantinou. No one said anything, not even me when they frisked me for a Bismarck. It was a different car but I wondered if these were the same guys who'd followed me to Ermioni. I figured that one or more of the usual things were probably about to happen – some threats, a beating, a little physical torture, something worse – and there was no point in protesting too much, not yet; none of them was even listening, anyway. I was just a package to move from A to B, and so far they'd done it very well. It was a story I already knew by heart and I only hoped they could understand German or English when and if it was my turn to speak. I wondered what Garlopis had made of it. Had he even noticed what happened? If he'd seen me being snatched off the street, would he call Leventis? And if he hadn't because he was asleep, how long would he stay napping before he realized I was late coming back to the car? How long would he wait before knocking on the prison door to enquire in his obsequious but somehow endearing way if they'd decided to keep me there overnight? None of that worried me, particularly. What with the Colt .25s pressed against each of my overworked kidneys and the cold expressions on all four faces, I had enough to worry about on my own account.

On Vasileos Konstantinou, the Pontiac stopped in front of an impressive, horseshoe-shaped stadium that resembled a set from *Demetrius and the Gladiators* and the car doors opened again. I was obliged to get out and walk, and with one or two citizens still around I felt able to protest my treatment, a little, even with a small gun discreetly in my side.

'I feel it's only fair to warn you boys I was at the Berlin

Olympics in '36. I managed to get around the stadium and up to my seat in under fifteen minutes. A world record at the time.'

Without reply they walked me to the bottom of the first tier and pointed up to the top one, where high above the track a tiny figure was seated like the only spectator at the matinee.

'Go up there,' said one of the men. 'Now. And best not to keep the lady waiting, eh?'

'I never do if I can help it,' I said, and started to climb.

This wasn't as easy as it looked, since the first marble-clad step was much higher than seemed appropriate; probably this was an easy step to take if you'd been wearing a short tunic or maybe nothing at all, ancient Greek style, but to anyone else it was a bit of a stretch. After that the going was easy; at least it was if you didn't mind climbing up the stadium's forty-four levels. I counted them because it helped to stop me from getting angry at the way I'd been summoned to meet a woman I'd never met before and a woman I didn't find attractive – there was nothing wrong with my eyes; she was much too old for me, which is to say she was about my age. I made a description of her for the police artist inside my head as, ignoring the excellent views of the Acropolis and the Royal Gardens, I completed the rest of the climb: a tall, striking woman with a large mane of dark grey hair gathered in a loose plait at the back of her neck like a Greek caryatid's. She wore a short dark red silk jacket, a mustard-yellow shirt, a long brown skirt, and soft leather boots. Her face was strong and mannish and as brown as a berry. She carried no handbag and wore no jewellery, just a man's watch, and in her hand was a red handkerchief. She looked like a bandit queen.

'What, no friends?' I said.

'No friends.'

'Don't you get lonely, sitting by yourself?'

'I never get lonely – not since I learned what other people are like.'

She spoke fluent German, although I also recognized that this wasn't her first language.

'You're right. It's only when we're young that we need friends and think they're important. When you get to our age you realize friends are just as unreliable as anyone else. For all that, it's been my experience that the people who never get lonely are the loneliest people of all.'

'Come and sit down.' She patted the marble seat next to her as if it might actually be comfortable. 'Impressive, isn't it? This place.'

I sat down. 'I can hardly contain my excitement.'

'It's the Panathenaic Stadium, in case you were wondering,' she said. 'Built in 330 BC, but only faced in marble in the second century AD. The Greeks ran races here and the Romans mounted gladiatorial shows. Then for hundreds of years it was just a quarry, until 1895 when, at the expense of a rich Alexandrian Greek, it was restored to what you see now, so that the first Olympic Games of the modern era might be held here in 1896. That Greek's name was George Averoff.' She smiled a wily, gap-toothed smile. 'I imagine his name is not unfamiliar to you, Herr Ganz.'

'I've heard of him. He seems to have been a very civic-minded sort of man, for a Greek. Although speaking for myself I'd much prefer to have my own name on a park bench or on a cheque made out to cash than on a prison or warship.'

'I'd forgotten about the warship. You're well informed.'

'No, not even a bit. For example, I don't even know who you are or what you want. Just for future reference it's normal practice for the muscle with the gun to introduce the bully who's trying to look tough.'

'It's not important who I am,' she said.

'You underestimate yourself, lady.'

'Better make sure you don't make the same mistake. And in case you hadn't already worked it out, I'm not a lady.'

'It's probably not very polite of me but I can't disagree with you there.'

'If you do it certainly won't matter. That's the great thing about this place. With sixty-six thousand empty seats we can make a scene and no one will even notice. More important than who I am is your conversation with Arthur Meissner at Averoff Prison. I'd like to know all of what he said. Every detail.'

'What's it to you?'

'This will help to answer that question, perhaps,' she said, and pulling up the sleeve of her shirt she revealed a number tattooed on her forearm.

'It helps a little. But I need a little more to work with here. I'm German. Imagination was never my strong suit. I think I'll have to see this picture in full Technicolour.'

'Very well. If you insist. Until 1943 I lived in Thessaloniki. My family were Sephardic Jews originally from Spain, who left there in 1492, after the Alhambra Decree ordering our expulsion. For four hundred and fifty years Jews like me and my family lived and prospered in Thessaloniki, and persecution seemed like a distant memory until July 1942 and the Black Sabbath, when the Germans arrived and rounded up all of the men in the city centre. Ten thousand Jewish men of all ages were drafted for forced labour but first these men were obliged to prove that they were fit for work. This was not done for humanitarian reasons, of course, but so the SS could have some fun. After the long journey from Germany, they were bored and needed amusement. And what could be more amusing than a bit of old-fashioned Jew-baiting. So for the rest of the day, ten thousand Jewish men were made to do hard physical exercise, at gunpoint. Those who refused were beaten half to death or had Alsatian dogs set on them. It wasn't cool like it is now; no, this was midsummer and the temperature was over thirty degrees centigrade. Many of them died, including my own grandfather. We didn't know it then but he was lucky, for much worse was to come, and over the next few months almost sixty thousand Jews were deported to the death camps of Eastern Europe. Along with seventeen members of my family, I was sent to Auschwitz, which is where I learned to speak German. But subsequently I also learned this: that I was the only member of my family who survived and not because I was a doctor – the Nazis had no use for a doctor who was a Jew. No, I survived because of a simple clerical error. You were put to work if your age at the time of your arrival in Auschwitz was between sixteen and forty. At the time I was aged forty-one and so I should have been gassed along with my mother, my grandmother, and my three elder sisters.

But an SS clerk at Auschwitz had incorrectly noted my year of birth as 1912 instead of 1902, and that saved my life. Because of this mistake the camp authorities believed I was under forty and that I should be put to work in Block 24, which was their brothel. I'm alive but it has to be admitted that part of me died in Auschwitz. For example, I never practised medicine again. The things I saw doctors – German doctors – do at Auschwitz convinced me that man was unworthy of modern medicine.'

'Could have been worse. You might have been a lawyer. They say you're never more than six feet from a lawyer.'

'So now I do something different. Now I protect people, my people, in a less prophylactic way.'

'Would it make any difference now if I said I'm sorry?'

'Good God.' The woman next to me laughed and then covered her mouth. 'That's a surprise. I'm sorry but you're the first German I've met since the war who ever said sorry. Everyone else says, "We didn't know about the camps" or "I was only obeying orders" or "Terrible things happened to the Germans, too." But no one ever thinks to apologize. Why is that, do you think?'

'An apology seems hardly adequate under the circumstances. Maybe that's why we don't say it more often.' I reached for my cigarettes and then remembered I'd given them to Arthur Meissner.

'I wish that was true. But I'm not sure it is.'

'Give us time. By the way, is there another reason we're here? Or was it just George Averoff and a classical history lesson?'

'Now I'm very glad you mentioned that. As you will have noticed, the stadium is open at one end, like a giant horseshoe.

Anyone in one of those office buildings to the north might have a fine view of what was happening on the track, or indeed of the two of us sitting here now. Don't you agree?'

'Sure. And having seen Greek television I couldn't blame anyone if they were watching us with greater interest.' I stood up for a moment and stared over the parapet; at the top, the stadium must have been twenty-five metres above ground level. 'It's lucky I've got a head for heights.'

'My only interest in your head is what's in it and if you can keep it on your shoulders. You see I have a man on one of those rooftops. And he's not there for his own entertainment. He's a trained marksman with a high-powered rifle who hates Germans even more than I do, if that were even possible. An American rifle with a telescopic sight, which he says has an effective range of about one thousand yards. I should estimate that it's less than half of that to those rooftops, wouldn't you agree? So by that standard it ought to be an easy shot for him.'

I said nothing but I was suddenly feeling very uncomfortable, like I had a persistent itch on my scalp and all the Drene shampoo in the world wasn't going to fix that. I sat down again, quickly. Now I really did want a cigarette.

'Here's how this works. If I decide that you have been anything less than totally cooperative, then I shall signal to my man and his spotter and – well, you can guess what will happen, can you not? I guarantee that you won't leave this stadium alive, Herr Ganz.'

'How do I know you're telling the truth?'

'You don't. And let's hope you never have to find out. It's one of those fiendishly German questions that used to fascinate us Jews in the camps. Is there water in the showerheads, or is there not? Who knew for sure? The lies you told. The way you used language to obfuscate the truth. "Special treatment" used to mean a lifesaving operation in a Swiss clinic; thanks to Germany it now means a bullet in the back of the head and a shallow grave in Ukraine. But in anticipation of your own question I brought you this small proof that I am indeed telling you the truth.'

She handed me a rifle bullet. It was a .308 Winchester cartridge. And it was just the kind of round a sniper would have used over a distance like the one she'd described. I was trying to keep my head but the prospect of losing half of it meant I was already sweating profusely. I'd seen enough comrades hit by snipers in the trenches to know the fiendish damage a sniper could inflict.

'I know, there's still room for doubt,' she said. 'But that's as much proof as you're going to get right now, short of my giving him the prearranged signal. At which point it really won't matter, will it? This is why I'm wearing reds and browns, as a matter of fact. These are my old clothes. In case some of your blood and brains splash onto me.'

She was smiling but I had the very distinct impression that she was perfectly serious, that she really had chosen clothes and even a colour scheme that might not show a bit of arterial spray. I tried to match her cool manner but it was proving difficult.

'Can I keep this bullet as a souvenir? It will make a nice change from an evil-eye key fob.'

'Sure. Why not? But choose your next joke very carefully, Herr

Ganz, because the next bullet won't be quite as harmless as that one you're holding in your hand.'

'You know, suddenly I'm very glad that I apologized.'

'So am I. It's a good start for you, right enough. If you weren't a German I might actually like you. But since you are . . .'

'I take it you're not from the International Olympic Committee.'

'No. I'm not.'

'And you can't be Greek NIS. I doubt they'd murder me here in Athens. So then: you must be from the Institute. In Tel Aviv.'

'You really are well informed. For an insurance man. Only before this you were a Berlin detective and you worked in Homicide – in the Murder Commission, which is to say you investigated murders instead of committing them, like so many of your colleagues. Many Jews met very grisly ends at the hands of German police battalions, did they not? But clearly Lieutenant Leventis has some faith in you, otherwise he would not have sanctioned you to negotiate a secret deal with Arthur Meissner. I'm reliably informed that he has done this because he has some hope of finding and arresting Alois Brunner. And that's where I come in, because if anyone is going to arrest that bastard Brunner I want it to be me. He's one of several major war criminals we're looking to arrest.'

'Are you sure you mean arrest? I say that as one who has just been informed there is a rifle pointed at my ear.'

'Oh, very much arrest, yes. Have no fear, if he is here in Greece we'll spirit Brunner to Israel for trial. A real trial in front of the whole world, with real lawyers and a real verdict as opposed to the shameful war crimes trials you've conducted in Germany. Because let's face it, Herr Ganz, even the Nazis who were tried and convicted by Germany have had a pretty easy time of it. Why only a couple of months ago, I read an intelligence briefing that said an SS officer called Waldemar Klingelhöfer had been released in December 1956 from Landsberg Prison after serving just eight years of a death sentence imposed for the murder of almost two and half thousand Jews. No, Herr Ganz, the world owes us a proper trial. And why should you give a damn? Alois Brunner was an Austrian. Arguably not even that. His hometown is now in western Hungary, I believe. So then. We Jews want our pound of flesh. Thanks to William Shakespeare, it's what the world expects of us anyway.'

After everything she had said, I didn't have to think too hard about my decision. There were several rooftops from which a sniper aiming at me would have had an easy shot. Perhaps it was my imagination but I fancied I saw the sun reflected from something on one of the more modern rooftops; it might have been a pair of binoculars or a sniper scope. The ruthless bandit queen had sold her story well, like a true intelligence officer, and I was convinced she was telling the truth. I had little doubt now that she was from the Institute for Intelligence and Special Operations in Israel, better known as the Ha'Mossad. I'd had dealings with Ha'Mossad before but only when I was someone else. If she'd known who I really was and some of the people with whom I'd hung around, she'd have dropped that handkerchief in a heartbeat.

'I'll tell you all I know.'

'Not that much. Just what you've learned about Alois Brunner.'

CHAPTER 38

After giving her a lot of extra background detail about Munich RE and the *Doris* that was mostly intended to furnish a super-erogatory demonstration of my cooperation and prevent my getting shot, I said:

'But look here, it's my impression that Meissner is a nobody. He's not even German, just a poor Greek translator with a Kraut name who's been left in the smokehouse by the Greek police in the absence of fish that are worth eating. Although he claims not to have seen Alois Brunner since the war, he did at least know him. And he told me some of Brunner's favourite haunts here in Athens. I'll write them down if you like.' Carefully I put my hand inside my coat, took out a notepad, and started to write. 'One of those places might actually be relevant, given that I saw Brunner a few days ago in the bar at the Mega Hotel, on Constitution Square. Or maybe you already know about that from whoever it is at the Megaron Pappoudof who's been feeding you information about what Lieutenant Leventis is up to.'

'I only know that you saw him. What does Brunner look like these days?'

'Not much different from an old photograph Leventis showed me. Thin, like before, not very tall, mid-forties, a heavy smoker, very deliberate manner, Austrian accent, badly bitten fingernails, gravelly voice, narrow dead eyes as if he'd been staring into a hurricane, a hooked nose, a short grey moustache and a chin beard, like an artist, you know. He was wearing a Shetland sport jacket, whipcord trousers, a plaid-gingham shirt, and a little cravat. A good watch, now I come to think of it; gold, maybe it was a Jaeger. And a gold signet ring on his right hand. He drank Calvert on the rocks and wore an aftershave. I can't remember what brand. Oh, and he was reading a novel. There was a book on the bar. Something by Frank Yerby. Maybe there was a little hat on the stool beside him. I'm not sure.' I shook my head. 'That's about all.'

'And the conversation? Tell me about that, please.'

I tore off the note I'd written and handed it to her.

'I was having a drink and he started up a conversation. Just one German to another. In spite of what you said, we're friendlier than people think, you know. But I never saw him before in my life. He told me his name was Georg Fischer and that he was a tobacco salesman for Karelia cigarettes. Gave me a pack of nails and this business card.' I handed it over. 'Don't bother calling the number, it's out of order. I think he just hands it out for show. To make people like me think he's a regular Fritz. But Leventis believes Brunner is behind two local murders on account of how the modus operandi is the same as an old murder that took place on a train between Salonika and Athens in 1943, when Brunner shot a Jewish banker called Jaco Kapantzi through both eyes.'

I paused for a moment considering the magnitude of what I'd said; talking about that brought back the memory of Siegfried Witzel lying on the floor of the house in Pritaniou, and probably looking not much better than I would look if the bandit queen's marksman opened fire.

'One of these local murders was a boat owner called Siegfried Witzel who'd filed a claim for the loss of a ship. That's where I fit into this whole damn mess. I came down here from Munich to adjust the insurance claim and got rather more than I bargained for. Story of my life, for what it's worth.'

The lady from Ha'Mossad who wasn't a lady nodded. 'That Brunner likes to shoot his victims in their eyes is also my information. At the transit camp of Drancy, in Paris, in 1944, Brunner shot a man called Theo Blum in this same way. Brunner's mother, Ann Kruise, may or may not have worked for an optometrist, in Nádkút. I know, it's not exactly Sophocles. But there may be a psychological explanation for why he kills people in this manner that goes beyond simple sadism. I suspect we'll only know for sure after we have him safely in a cell in Ayalon Prison. Go on, please.'

'Siegfried Witzel and a Munich-based lawyer named Dr Max Merten—'

'He's another person we're interested in.'

'Those two had gone to a lot of trouble to convince the Greek government that they were going to dive in the Aegean for lost art treasures. Museum stuff. The gas mask of Agamemnon for all I know. Until this afternoon I'd started to believe that what they were really after was weapons. That the whole thing was a cover for an illegal arms deal. I was working on the assumption that Brunner was on board to supply stolen Egyptian and Assyrian art treasures in return for guns that could be secretly shipped to Nasser.'

I told her about the Hellenic horse's head that had been delivered to the *Doris*.

'That makes sense, too. Almost certainly Brunner *is* involved with the Egyptian Mukhabarat. Our rivals, so to speak. An agent in Cairo reported Brunner had several meetings with a man named Zakaria Mohieddin, who was until quite recently the director of the Egyptian Intelligence Directorate. But it is our belief that he is secretly working undercover for your own West German intelligence service, the BND, at the behest of a German government minister named Hans Globke, who might even be looking out for him. We'd like to get our hands on that bastard, too. But there's not much chance of it happening. If Adenauer protects his state secretary and security chief as well as he protected his minister of refugees, Theodor Oberländer, then we've little chance of making anything stick to Hans Globke.'

'What is it with you people?'

The bandit queen bristled a little. 'What people do you mean, Herr Ganz?'

'Not Jews. *Spies.* There's not one of you peekers knows how to walk in a straight line. Either way I now think I was wrong about all of that – about an illegal arms deal, I mean. I think it's nothing to do with weapons. Merten and Witzel and perhaps Brunner were diving for something, all right, but it wasn't archaic art treasures to put in a museum in Piraeus. Arthur Meissner told me a story in Averoff. And I'll tell it to you now, if you like. Forgive me if I skip a few details but it's hard to concentrate when a sniper has a bead on you.' I let out a breath and wiped my brow with the cuff of my shirt. I was sweating so much my coat was sticking to me like a butter wrapper. I felt like a man who'd been strapped into the electric chair.

'I should have thought the opposite was true. It's always been my experience that the prospect of being shot focuses the mind as sharply as if one was looking down a telescopic sight. Besides, Herr Ganz, you're perfectly safe as long as I keep a firm grip of this red handkerchief.'

'Well, just don't sneeze. And don't interrupt until I'm finished playing Homer. I wouldn't like your rooftop pal to think you didn't believe me. There are several holes in the rest of this story. You'll have to forgive that on account of how I don't want any extra holes in me.'

'All right. Let's hear it.'

'According to Meissner, Alois Brunner was part of a corrupt syndicate that managed to rob Salonika's Jews of hundreds of millions of dollars in gold and jewels in the spring of 1943. Also involved were Dieter Wisliceny and Adolf Eichmann. But the whole scheme was cooked up by Captain Max Merten, who was in charge of civilian affairs in the region. Merten made a nice friendly deal with the Jewish leaders in Salonika: that he would keep them from being deported in return for all of their hidden valuables. Fearing for their lives, the Jews paid up, only to find that they'd been double-crossed. With the help of Eichmann and Wisliceny, Merten secured the booty, and the treasure was loaded onto the *Epeius*. As soon as it sailed, the SS started to deport the city's sixty thousand Jews.'

'I've heard this story,' said the bandit queen impatiently. 'The ship set sail, struck a mine, and sank off the northern coast of Crete, and all of the gold belonging to the Jews of Thessaloniki went to the bottom of the sea. A message to this effect was received by the Regia Marina – the Italian navy at the Salamis Naval Base, near Piraeus. And by the Kriegsmarine in Heraklion. It was all investigated and verified by the Hellenic navy immediately after the war.'

'For all that that was worth,' I said.

'Maybe. Well?'

'Well, Meissner says different. Back in Salonika, Merten's partners in the SD heard the bad news about the *Epeius* and began to smell a rat. Meissner says he overheard them airing their suspicions at the Villa Mehmet Kapanci; they then attempted to discover the true fate of the *Epeius* and found that yes, the ship had sunk, but not because it had hit a mine. Merten had double-crossed his partners just like he'd double-crossed the city's Jews and had arranged to have the ship scuttled in shallow water in the Messenian Gulf, somewhere off the Peloponnese coast, between the towns of Pylos and Kalamata.

'The captain of the *Epeius* was a Greek named Kyriakos Lazaros; also on board was a German naval officer called Rainer Stückeln who Merten had cut in for a substantial share of the loot. Merten had previously arranged for a second ship, the *Palamedes*, to meet the lifeboat from the *Epeius*, and the *Palamedes* made its way to the western shore of Crete, where Lazaros and Stückeln and the crew transferred to another lifeboat and rowed ashore, for the sake of appearances, to report the loss of the *Epeius*.

'Subsequently Stückeln murdered Lazaros and the first mate, to ensure their silence about the location of the *Epeius*; and then he, too, was killed, in a bombing raid in Crete, but only after he had told Merten exactly where the ship lay. But before the three SD men in Thessaloniki could do anything about it the end of the war intervened. Eichmann, Wisliceny, Brunner, and Merten soon found themselves back in Germany, arrested or on the run. Eichmann and Wisliceny and Brunner were all wanted men after the war; but Max Merten, the lowly army captain, was quickly released and has been living openly in Munich for the last ten years, no doubt waiting for the moment when he judged it was finally safe to come back to Greece and retrieve his pension pot.

'Then, a few months ago, Merten chartered a ship belonging to a German scuba diver called Siegfried Witzel. That ship, the *Doris*, was insured by my company. Lots of ships are. MRE is a very good company. Perhaps the best in Germany. It's my guess Merten and Witzel were planning to sail to the place where the *Epeius* went down to try to recover the gold. It's also my guess that Brunner was tipped off by someone in the BND that Max Merten was planning to return to Greece and decided to try to reestablish their original partnership. But something went wrong, most likely another double-cross. Old habits die hard. The *Doris* sank – I'm not sure why, exactly – and the partnership was dissolved a second time, and with equally lethal effect. Brunner murdered Witzel and may be looking for Merten to murder him, too. I think maybe he just likes killing people. Then again, he's a German.'

I shook my head with uncomfortable vigour, wondering how it looked at the cross point of the sniper's reticle and noticing the bandit queen's perfume now, which was her only concession to femininity. I couldn't identify it beyond the fact that it was paradoxically vanilla and flowery in its base notes, which seemed like the very opposite of her.

'That's it. The whole lousy story. For all I know Merten and Brunner aren't even in Greece anymore. After what I just learned from Meissner, I'm surprised they had the nerve to come back at all.'

'That's not so surprising, perhaps,' said the bandit queen. 'It's been suggested that there are some in this new Greek government who were informers for the Nazis and who were rewarded with businesses and property confiscated from Thessaloniki's Jews. That could be why Merten chose to come back now. Perhaps he's been able to blackmail some of these people.' She shrugged. 'On the other hand, it's not just this government that has failed Salonika's Jews so dismally. In 1946 the Americans arrested Merten, locked him up in Dachau, and offered him for extradition to Greece. Incredibly, the Tsaldaris government said it had no interest in him. So after ten years of living openly in Munich, Max Merten may have decided that he was perfectly safe here after all. And who could blame him? You Germans have managed to draw a very thick line under the war and to start over again. The Old Man's miracle, they call it. The Old Man's whitewash, more like. It makes me sick. There's no justice. Small wonder we're forced to take the law into our own hands.'

She sneered and then looked away, as if she didn't want to get any blood on her jacket after all.

'I certainly didn't vote for him,' I said. 'And please don't give me a dirty look. I'm liable to get a headache. Speaking for myself, I never disliked Jews as much as I disliked a great many of my fellow Germans.'

'I've heard of the unicorn, the griffin, the great auk, the tart with a heart, and little green men from outer space. I've even heard of the good German, but I never thought to see one myself. You never voted for the Nazis and you never liked Hitler. I suppose there was even a Jew you helped to survive the war. You hid him in your lavatory for a couple of days. And of course some of your best friends were Jews. It amazes me how so many of us died.'

'I wouldn't say I did anything to feel proud of, if that's what you mean. But I'll live with that.'

She lifted the fist with the red handkerchief and wiggled it meaningfully. 'You hope.'

'You seem to have an appetite for revenge that makes me glad I'm not on your menu.'

'A menu? Oh, I see what you mean. Yes, we do have one. You know, getting Max Merten might almost be as good as catching up with Alois Brunner.'

'If I meet him again, I'll let you know.'

'Again?'

'I knew him slightly before the war, when he was an ambitious young lawyer in Berlin, and then I met him again a couple of months ago. As a matter of fact it was Merten who helped to get me my job at Munich RE.'

'And they talk about Jews sticking together. You Germans could teach us a thing or two about looking after your own.'

'Believe me, if I see him I'm just liable to kill him myself. I had a nice quiet job in a Munich hospital before I thought to try to improve myself by joining the hazardous world of insurance. The people I was working with at Schwabing were as honest as the day is long. Never had any trouble with any of them.' I bit my lip. 'But the minute I put a tie on again it's like I started having to make compromises with myself. So. Can I go now? It's getting a little chilly up here. But for the waves of hate coming off you I might need a coat. As it is I badly need a change of underwear.'

'Yes, you can go, Herr Ganz. You're an interesting man. No doubt about it. There's a lot more to you than meets the eye. You're staying at the Grande Bretagne, right? Perhaps you have Hermann Göring's bedroom. Or Himmler's. That should make you feel at home. You'll find the car is still waiting. My men will give you a ride.'

'No thanks. I'd prefer to walk if you don't mind. It will give me a chance to clear my head of the idea that it's about to receive an unwelcome visitor.' I stood up, carefully, with one eye on the red handkerchief in her hand. 'Wasn't it Sophocles who said that the end justifies any evil? I read that on a souvenir tea towel. Well, take it from one who knows. It doesn't. It never does.

Germany learned this the hard way. I sincerely hope you don't have to learn the same lesson we did.'

The bandit queen shot me a sarcastic smile. 'Go on. Get out of here. Take care of yourself, okay?'

'I'm German. That's what we're good at.'

CHAPTER 39

I took a cab back to the office but there was no sign of Garlopis, so I found some cigarettes and a bottle in his drawer, typed a two-page report for Lieutenant Leventis on Telesilla's English machine concerning my visit to see Arthur Meissner, and then, on my way back to the hotel, handed it in at the Megaron Pappoudof. Not being arrested and detained in Haidari seemed almost as important as not being plugged between the eyes by some trigger-happy kibbutznik. In my report I'd told the lieutenant nearly all of what I'd already told the bandit queen but since it asked more questions than it answered I didn't think it was going to be enough to get my passport back. I was never much for paperwork, even when I was in the Murder Commission. Anyway, I didn't mention the bandit queen; I wasn't sure that would have helped my cause.

Constitution Square was the usual human menagerie of lottery-ticket salesmen, pretzel vendors, cops, soldiers, pickpockets, beggars, musicians, and office workers hurrying to their bad-tempered buses and then home. Athens's answer to

Alexanderplatz had everything to divert the unwary citizen and I stopped for a short while to watch as a skilled pavement artist sketched out a grotesque picture in chalk that made me think of a picture by George Grosz and served to remind me only of how much I missed the old Berlin with its Biberkopfs and Berbers, its bear and its beer. There's no one quite like George Grosz to make you think you need a stiff drink or, for that matter, that you've already had one. I knew this better than anyone, given my old acquaintance with George Grosz. I hurried into the hotel and found Achilles Garlopis waiting on one of the big sofas under a crystal chandelier. He got up like a beetle struggling to right itself and walked nimbly across the marble floor to greet me.

'Thank God you're all right,' he said, crossing himself in the Greek way. 'When those men picked you up outside Averoff Prison I did my best to follow them in the Rover, but they lost me at the traffic lights. Not that I'd have known what to do if I had caught up with them. They were a tough-looking bunch.'

'That they were.'

'They didn't look like police.'

'No. They weren't police.' I didn't offer any further explanation; the less he knew about the bandit queen the better it would be for him. 'Look, let's just forget it, can we?'

'Surely, sir, surely.'

'No, let's get a drink. I have a craving to shrink my liver. Walking here just now it was all I could do not to drink the contents of my cigarette lighter.'

'Then let me buy you one. On second thoughts, let me buy you two.'

'At these prices? We'll have MRE pay for the damage. It's what they're good at.'

We sat down at the horn of alcoholic plenty that was the GB bar and summoned a waiter, whereupon I pointed at the tapestry of Alexander the Great. A boy on an elephant was holding up a hip flask and a couple of slaves were walking beside the chariot with what looked like a large pitcher full of wine on a stretcher. Another fellow with red hair was sucking on a golden bottle of Korn and trying to pretend it was a trumpet, the way you do after a good night out. Alexander himself was smiling and trying to stay upright and Great in the chariot he was standing in, like he'd already downed a glass or two of something warming.

'I'll have what he's having,' I told the barman.

'I'll have the same,' said Garlopis, and then ordered two large whiskeys on the rocks, which seemed likely to produce the equivalent result.

'Did Meissner tell you anything important? Anything useful? Anything that will satisfy Lieutenant Leventis?'

'No, nothing that will help us. I fear we're going to have to bribe the bastard after all. Either that or I use the money to buy myself a new passport.'

The drinks arrived and almost immediately we ordered two more, as insurance.

'A Greek passport? I wouldn't know how to help you do that, sir. Every Greek is equal to the task of giving or taking a bribe to a public official. Indeed no one would regard such a thing as criminal. But obtaining a false passport is something else, sir.'

'Then we'd better just stick to a bit of honest bribery.'

'So we'll cash the company's certified cheque tomorrow,' said Garlopis. 'We'll drive to the Alpha Bank in Corinth, like we planned.'

'You're sure the banks are open on a Saturday?'

'From nine until twelve, sir. I think you'll enjoy it in Corinth.' He chuckled. 'Especially when we've cashed the cheque and we're on the road back to Athens.'

'What's wrong with bribing Leventis on Sunday?'

'Oh no, sir. That wouldn't do at all. You couldn't bribe someone on a Sunday. Not in Greece. Never on a Sunday. No Greek could tolerate that. And it will have to be done with great skill and diplomacy. Indeed, it's my considered opinion that we should bribe this man not just with money but with appreciation and esteem. We'll have to polish his ego with a soft cloth. "I wouldn't insult you, Lieutenant, by offering you a few hundred, or a thousand," that kind of thing. "For a man like you, Lieutenant, one would feel obliged to offer five thousand." That would not be an insult. Five thousand would be respect. Five thousand would be diplomacy. He will understand this kind of figure.'

'Suppose he wants more.'

'Of course, we *can* pay ten thousand. We should keep this in the toga sleeve, so to speak. Believe me, sir, for any more than ten thousand we could get the minister of justice himself. But like any Greek official, Lieutenant Leventis is wise enough to know his true value. One more thing. If you'll permit me to say so, I think it's best a Greek such as myself handles this matter. Speaking as a translator, it's been my experience that when you're paying a man his *fakelaki* it's best there's no linguistic room for doubt. And no loss of face. One Greek bribing another is commonplace, but somehow a German doing it seems unpatriotic.'

'Sure. I'll buy that.'

'Let us hope we can buy our peace of mind.'

We had a couple more drinks and then I said good night and went upstairs. As I walked back to my room I wondered if Heinrich Himmler really had stayed at the GB or if it was a rumour; Greece had plenty of those. I had a hot bath – I could see the Megaron Pappoudof from the window after all – went to bed, read a book for three minutes before it fell from my hand, closed my eyes, and found myself somewhere blacker than mere darkness, as if death itself had swallowed me whole and I was struggling for breath. That was when Göring walked into the room with a lion cub under one chubby arm and demanded I move to another hotel. He was wearing a sleeveless green leather hunting jacket, a white flannel shirt, white drill trousers, and white tennis shoes. He was insisting that the room was always his whenever he came to Athens and that if I didn't leave he'd have his personal sniper shoot me when I was next taking a bath. Naturally I refused, at which point the telephone started ringing and Göring explained that it was probably the hotel management offering me Himmler's room instead. The Reichsführer-SS was still in Berlin or dead and wouldn't need it. I reached across the bed in the slowly clearing darkness, and answered it and found it was only Garlopis calling to tell me something about the house in Acropolis Old Town, 11 Pritaniou. I sat up, switched on the light, tried to clear my head, told him I was asleep even though I was awake, gulped some air into the tar pits I called my lungs and with it, some more sense into my sleep-confused brain.

'I said, one of my aunts left a message for me earlier on this evening,' repeated Garlopis. 'It's about the house at 11 Pritaniou. In Acropolis Old Town. Remember when we went there and found Herr Witzel's body and Lieutenant Leventis?'

'Maybe I can remember if I try very hard.'

'He said a witness who was cleaning the Glebe Holy Sepulchre Church around the corner had reported seeing two men at the house. That witness was my aunt Aspasia, who lives not very far away from there. She's been cleaning the Holy Sepulchre church for thirty years. I didn't say so at the time because I didn't want to cause her any problems with the cops that might have been occasioned by my being related to her. They might have thought there was something fishy about that.'

'How many goddamn relations have you got, Garlopis? I never knew a man with so many cousins.'

'If you take a minute to think about this, sir, you'll realize that every one of my cousins must have a mother. And every one of those mothers is an aunt to Achilles Garlopis. Aunt Aspasia is the mother of my cousin Poulios, who works at Lefteris Makrinos car hire, on Tziraion Street, the same people from whom we hired the Rover. I have six aunts and uncles on my mother's side and seven on my father's. And for the record I have twenty-eight cousins. This is normal in Greece. But listen, sir, my aunt Aspasia, she left a message that there is someone in the house in Pritaniou again. *Now.* That's why I'm calling you so late. And she is sure it's not the police or the Gendarmerie.'

'How is she sure?'

'Because she doesn't like the police, sir. Not since the civil war. She thinks they're all thieves. And because she doesn't trust them she keeps a careful eye on them, too. She only reported hearing the shots that killed Witzel because she felt she had to. Since then, when the police were at the house in Pritaniou they had a uniformed man guarding the front door. And now there's no one. Also, there's a motorcycle parked in front – a red Triumph with a burst saddle that she thinks might belong to the owner.'

'Is that so?' I sat up, wide awake now, and looked at my watch. 'Can you pick me up outside the hotel?'

'I'll be there in twenty minutes, sir.'

I went into the bathroom, ran my head under a cold shower, drank a glass of water, and dressed hurriedly. I was just on my way out the door when the telephone rang again and I answered it, thinking it was Garlopis to say he'd arrived a bit early. But it wasn't Garlopis. It was Elli Panatoniou and her voice felt like ambrosia in my ear.

'Hey, I thought we'd arranged to go dancing.'

I looked at my watch again. It was still almost midnight. Suddenly I felt very old indeed. 'We did? At this time?'

'This is Athens. Nothing happens in Athens before eleven o'clock. Still, you're right. It wasn't a firm arrangement. But I thought I'd drop by anyway. I just wanted to see you.'

'I'll be down in two minutes.'

'I could come up to your room if you like. But you'll have to call the front desk and tell them.'

I cursed my fortune. It's not every night that a beautiful young Greek woman offers to come up to an old German's hotel bedroom. Suddenly things felt a lot like the two jars that Homer says Zeus kept by his office door, one containing good things and the other bad; he gave a mixture to some men and to others only evil, but to some he gave good that felt like it had been simultaneously snatched away in the course of the same beguiling late-night telephone call. For now I would have to deal with it as best I could, which gave me a new understanding of the concept of the heroic outlook. Suddenly I wanted to stick a javelin between a Trojan's ribs.

'No, I can't do that. As a matter of fact I just got a telephone call from Achilles Garlopis, and I have to go out, but now that you're here maybe you could come along with us. And perhaps we could do something afterwards.'

'Like what?'

'I don't know. Look, I'm coming downstairs. We'll discuss it then.'

I had a pretty good idea of what we could do afterwards – especially as she'd already volunteered to come up to my hotel room – but I thought it best I give her another suggestion, one that didn't sound like I was taking anything for granted.

'A drink,' I said to myself, as I rode the elevator car down to the hotel lobby. 'But it might be best if it's not here. It might look a bit obvious if you were to suggest the bar here. Look, she's bound to know a late-night bar somewhere hereabouts. She'll suggest this hotel if she's comfortable with coming up to your room again. Always supposing she's on the level. Either way Garlopis can drop us off and then we'll see what we'll see. That's nice of you, Gunther. You can be a real gentleman when you think it might get you somewhere. I can call you Gunther, now that we're on our own again, don't you think?'

Elli slipped off the big sofa in the hotel lobby and smiled a smile that was as bright as the chandelier above her head. Her perfume already had me by the knot in my tie and was gently kicking my brain around inside my skull. Sometimes trouble can smell good, especially the expensive kind they keep stoppered up in little jars and bottles and sell to women, or to the men dumb enough to buy it for them. She was wearing black slacks, a clinging black pullover, and red shoes that looked like she really had been serious about dancing after all. The black leather bag she was holding looked big enough to carry a grand piano. Her hair seemed to have grown some and it was even more lustrous than before, as if she'd licked every bit of it clean herself. If I'd been around I could have saved her the trouble. She held me tight for a moment and kissed me fondly on both cheeks, and I came away thinking I was a lucky boy; too lucky probably but I was working on that, slowly. In Greece, it's just standard practice to look a gift horse in the mouth.

'Where are we going?' she asked.

'The owner of that boat we checked out in Ermioni,' I said. 'Siegfried Witzel.'

'I received a telephone call a few minutes ahead of yours. From Achilles Garlopis. It seems there's someone poking around at the house where he got himself murdered. And it isn't the cops. Could be the murderer come back to look for his monogrammed cuff links – a Nazi named Alois Brunner. Or maybe it's another Nazi called Max Merten. Then again, it might just be Witzel's ghost with nothing better to do than haunt the house. I don't know. There's a lot I don't know. I may never know what I don't know. That's a given with a case like this. I could be the dumbest claims adjuster since Woodrow Wilson signed off on the Treaty of Versailles. But I thought I'd go and check it out. Only it might be dangerous, angel. If it is Brunner or Merten, they won't like us turning up and asking questions or threatening them with cops. Could be you should stay in the car.'

At this point most normal girls would have cried off and pleaded an urgent appointment with a bottle of shampoo and a favourite book, but not Elli Panatoniou, who it seemed was made of the same Styx-dipped stuff as Achilles – although not, perhaps, Achilles Garlopis. And I certainly hadn't forgotten the little Beretta in her briefcase she'd been carrying in the bar at the Mega Hotel.

'Okay,' she said simply, as if I'd just proposed nothing more dangerous than a late-night shopping trip or a visit to the local cinema.

Before, I'd been merely doubtful of her motives in befriending me; now I was as suspicious as if she'd been a shy blonde spinster sent to my hotel by Alfred Hitchcock.

CHAPTER 40

If Garlopis was surprised to see Elli Panatoniou coming out of the hotel front door with me he didn't show it. Instead he smiled politely, wished her a good evening, and opened the car door for her while I ducked silently into the Rover's front seat. But I could see he was nervous. Both of us knew that whoever it was at 11 Pritaniou, Greek or German, it probably spelled danger in either language. Near the Acropolis I told him to drive around a bit so that we could scout the area for police cars, but all we saw was an army truck near the entrance to the ancient citadel.

'The Parthenon is guarded at night by a small troop of soldiers,' he explained, 'in case the Persians turn up and try to burn it again.'

'That's the official reason,' added Elli. 'The reality is that Greeks were stealing pieces of the temple and selling it. My own grandfather has a piece on his desk.'

Nearer the Acropolis we saw a few rough sleepers.

'Not so long ago it was the Armenians who fled to Greece,' explained Garlopis. 'Then it was Turkish Greeks. This year, it's the Hungarians and the Coptic Christian refugees who fled from Alexandria when the Israelis invaded the Sinai last October. Who knows who'll come here next?'

'Why the Copts?'

'Whenever there's a problem with Israel the Muslims take it out on the Copts. So they get on a boat – any kind of boat – and come to Greece. And to here in particular, where the tourist pickings are better.'

Elli said something in the backseat about British imperialists and Suez but I couldn't have cared less. The older I got the less I cared about anything. Besides, it was much too late for politics. About twenty-five years too late in my case; but in Athens it was never too late for politics and it wasn't long before Garlopis and Elli were arguing, in Greek.

'Park here,' I told him above Elli's voice. 'And not the Greek way either. Do it neatly. Like you're trying to pass your driving test. So as not to draw any attention to this car.'

Garlopis nodded and pulled up next to a row of small souvenir shops that had finally closed for the night. We were five minutes' walk from the house on Pritaniou but caution dictated a bit of distance. Just because Aunt Aspasia said there were no cops around didn't mean there were no cops around. They might have been watching the house from another address. It's what I'd have done if I'd been the detective working the Witzel case. Garlopis switched off the engine and took out his cigarettes.

'If you don't mind, sir,' he said, 'I'll stay here, in the Rover. The last time we went in that house the police were waiting and we got ourselves arrested. My nerves couldn't take being arrested again. Not to mention Herr Witzel's dead body. I don't like the sight of blood any more than I like having a gun pointed at me.' He picked up one of the towels he kept in the car and mopped his brow with it.

'Coward,' said Elli.

'Perhaps,' said Garlopis. 'But in youth and beauty, wisdom is but rare.'

Elli laughed. '*Coward*,' she said again.

'What the hell made you so hard-bitten?' I asked her.

'Suppose you get into trouble. Suppose you need help. What kind of Achilles is it that stays in the car because he's afraid? No wonder this country is in such a disastrous state if men like this are called Achilles.'

'Leave him alone,' I told her. 'He's all right. And just for the record I don't give a shit about Suez or British imperialists, or anything else for that matter. Look, I think maybe you'd best stay here, too.'

'With him?' Elli's tone was scornful, and she was already getting out of the backseat of the car. 'I don't think so.'

She slammed the Rover's rear door loudly and suddenly I wanted to slap her in the mouth: I was already regretting bringing her along for the ride. Instead I found myself pointing my forefinger at her, as if she'd been an unruly child. It wasn't that she was anything like a child, it was more that I wasn't anything like a boyfriend. I was old enough to be her father and felt guilty about the difference between our ages. Someone should have been pointing at my grey hairs and reminding me of what a chump I was. They'd have been right, too.

'Behave yourself,' I told her. 'Not everyone is cut out for this kind of trouble. But with me it's almost a full-time job, see? Garlopis is a salaryman. An office Fritz. So stop rubbing his nose into his conscience. And if you are coming along, you'd best do as you're told. Got that?'

She took hold of my forefinger, kissed it fondly, and then nodded, but there was still mischief in her eyes; I felt like the floor manager in a casino – the guy that watches the customers to make sure they don't crook the house – only I still couldn't tell how she was doing it and how much she was getting away with.

'Whatever you say, sir.'

'If we're not back in thirty minutes, go home,' I told Garlopis.

He looked bitterly at Elli. 'With pleasure.'

Elli shot him a hard look that was replete with accusation, and I pulled her away before she could utter another reproachful remark. I didn't like her making cracks at Garlopis; that was my job.

We walked up the street. Above us the rock on which the Acropolis was built was so sheer that you couldn't actually see the floodlit Parthenon on top. And I realized I hadn't actually seen it yet. Not close up. If there'd been more time I might have suggested we walk there. As it was I just wanted to close the books on the *Doris* and get the hell out of the city and back to Germany. But I'd begun to see it might actually be a good thing to have Elli along if the address really was under surveillance.

'What have you got against that poor guy anyway?'

'Oh, nothing very much,' she said. 'I suppose he reminds me

of my own elder brother. He could amount to something if it wasn't for his lack of courage.'

'Don't be fooled. I'm a bona fide coward, just like Garlopis.'

Elli grinned. 'Whatever you say, Christof.'

'I mean it. I haven't stayed alive all this time by collecting police medals.'

'So who do you think it will be that we find?' she asked.

'I don't know. But then ignorance is man's natural state. It's not just ex-cops like me who are ill-equipped to separate the true from the false. But no matter how anonymous he or she might be, every murdered man had a family, friends, acquaintances, colleagues, and I'm hoping to run into one of these – someone who can tell me something new so that I know more than I knew before. Detective work is nothing more than uncovering a chain with the murdered man at one end and at the other, his murderer.'

'You make it sound like anyone could do it.'

'Anyone could and those anyones are called policemen. We'll walk past the address a couple of times before we go in. But first we'll act like we're a romantic couple out for a late-night stroll in one of the most romantic cities in the world, just in case anyone's watching.'

Elli threaded her arm through mine and pressed her head against my shoulder. As we reached the Glebe Holy Sepulchre Church on the corner of Pritaniou, we turned the corner and slowed our pace to a crawl. Outside number 11 I stopped and took her in my arms. Behind the shutters on the top floor there was a light on and I could hear the sound of radio music. But the rest of the street looked as if the Persians had just left.

'That's the idea,' I murmured into her ear. 'Give it plenty. The whole Lee Strasberg. Try to act like we don't have eyes for anything except each other.'

'Who's acting? No, really. I've decided. I like you, Christof. I like you a lot. You're not like Greek men. There's a lot more to you than what's floating around on the surface. They're all so shallow. You're – interesting.'

'Of course I am, sugar. I was Scab Professor of Philosophy and Mind at Himmler University from 1945 to 1950. Then president of the Diogenes Society until someone stole my barrel. You should read my book sometime about my work for nuclear disarmament.'

'I'm serious, you idiot.' And then she kissed me like William Wyler was watching us from a hydraulic camera dolly. 'Just don't ask me why. I can't explain it to myself.' She gave me an excited squeeze. 'That's Manos Hatzidakis. Radio EIR. The best music station in Athens. Maybe that's the reason.'

'Must be a Greek in there,' I said, suddenly aware of how much I hated Greek music.

'Or maybe that's all a German could find on the dial.'

In front of the same shabby double-height door was the dark red Triumph Speed Twin with the stuffing coming out of the single saddle, as accurately described by Garlopis's aunt Aspasia. I touched the engine block and discovered that it was still warm. She touched it, too, and said some more crazy stuff about how she was just as warm on me. We walked on a bit, shared a cigarette in another doorway, and then walked back. It seemed quiet enough. I looked at my watch; we'd already been ten minutes.

In another thirty minutes or less Garlopis would leave in the Rover. It was time to close, as the insurance salesmen were fond of saying. The evil eye in the bough of the olive tree was giving it some extra focus in the moonlight and, for a moment, I had a bad feeling about what was going to happen. I suppose that was the point of it. I steered Elli through the wrought-iron gate and onto the flight of stone steps that led up the side of the house. It smelled vaguely of cat piss.

'You stay here, sugar,' I said. 'When I figure it's safe, I'll come and get you.'

'Be careful, Christof,' she said. 'I'm not much of a rescue squad.'

I missed being Bernie sometimes, but it seemed like a small price to pay compared with missing my liberty. I walked to the top of the steps and was about to climb over the wall, as I'd done before, but then I tried the wooden door and discovered it wasn't bolted. In the yard the cat was nowhere to be seen and everything had been cleaned up: the cracked terracotta pots and the rusted motorcycle were gone and even the fossilized grapes had been taken off the vine. There were no lights in the basement but on the upper floor the back bedroom was brightly lit – enough to illuminate the whole yard – and the window was open with a net curtain billowing gently out like a ghost that couldn't quite make up its mind whether to haunt the place. I walked down the steps to the French windows, pushed them open, and stepped into the squalid room where Witzel had met his death.

On the floor was a kit bag full of some very dirty laundry and a copy of *Gynaika* magazine with a picture of Marilyn Monroe on the front cover. A British Webley .38 revolver lay on the table next to a pair of old binoculars, some stale bread, and a plate of tzatziki. There were also some keys, and one of these had a little brass ship's wheel, around the edge of which was engraved the name Δώρης. It was the same type of fob that I'd seen on Witzel's key chain when I'd met him for the first time in the office on Stadiou and my new knowledge of the Greek alphabet was just about enough for me to have a vague idea that the name in Greek was 'Doris'.

I picked up the clunky gun and broke open the top to check if it was loaded, and found it chambered with the same anaemic .38-calibre rounds that had almost cost the British the last war – I could never figure out why they made a Great War showstopper like the Webley .45 into a .38 – but the smaller revolver could still do plenty of damage. I didn't take the gun along on my passage through the house because now that I was an insurance man I thought I should avoid as many risks as possible and all the actuarial tables prove that when you carry a gun people get shot, even the people holding them. So I emptied the six rounds into my hand and pocketed them, just in case.

I headed upstairs, tiptoeing toward the source of the Greek music and what looked like a seaman's peacoat that had been left lying across the banister. I don't know what I thought I was going to do but I didn't think shouting hello to the house was an intelligent option; I suppose I wanted to assess the risk, as Dumbo would have said, which meant finding out exactly who I was dealing with before announcing my uninvited presence.

When I got to the top of the stairs I saw the bedroom door was half-open. A Greek wearing a vest was lying on a single bed; he had his back to the door and didn't see me. He was a strong-looking man maybe in his forties, with a sea serpent tattooed on his bare shoulder. I knew he was Greek because he was reading a Greek newspaper and because he was even smellier than his laundry. He was wearing a blue seaman's cap; what with the novelty key fob downstairs and perhaps because he was smoking the same kind of revolting menthol cigarette that Witzel had smoked, I thought I was probably looking at the captain of the *Doris.*

'I'm guessing your name is Spiros Reppas,' I said.

'Who the fuck are you, *malaka?*'

He tossed the newspaper aside and jumped off the mattress, but the cigarette stayed on his lip. He had black eyebrows and a bushy grey moustache that resembled the horns on an old water buffalo. There was a largish scar on his face that almost made me regret I hadn't brought along the gun. He had small piggy eyes that were full of what was in a bottle beside the bed. The man was drunk and more dangerous than I had supposed.

'Take it easy, friend. My name is Ganz. I'm a claims adjuster from the company in Munich that insured the *Doris.* If you've come here looking for Siegfried Witzel, then I'm afraid I've got some bad news for you. Your boss is dead.'

'Dead, huh? How'd that happen?'

'He was shot, in this house. Someone murdered him.'

'You did it, maybe?'

'Not me. Maybe you haven't noticed but I'm not holding a gun on you. No, there's a cop says it was Alois Brunner shot your friend. Although you might know him better as Georg Fischer. Like I say, I'm just a claims adjuster.'

'Is that what you call it?'

'That's what everyone calls it. You've heard of insurance, haven't you? It's when you pay money in case something bad happens and if it does they give you a lot more money back. I don't know, but most people seem to understand how that works.'

'Maybe you'll pay me to stop something bad happening to you now.'

'That's a different kind of insurance. That's called extortion. Look, just cool your blood a minute, I'm not here to steal anything. Just to talk. Maybe I can help you.'

'You've said enough already, Fritz.'

Speaking German had been a mistake, not because he didn't understand it – he did – but because he must have thought that my being German meant I was there to kill him. It was a reasonable assumption, given the record of my countrymen in Athens; everyone knew that most Germans were ruthless and not to be trusted. But it was much too late to fetch the two native Greek speakers I'd left outside the house to try to reassure him in his own language that I was on the level and meant him no harm. I knew it was a mistake because his hand dipped into his trouser pocket and when it came out again it was holding a pearl-handled switchblade. A nice one. I decided to buy one myself if I ever got out of the house alive. He hadn't yet pressed the button to release the blade so there was still a second or two available for common sense to prevail.

'You really don't like insurance, do you?'

'Could be. But most of all I don't like you. I'll probably think of a good reason why after you're bleeding to death on the floor.'

'Look, friend, there's no need to be as stupid as you look. I can see you haven't yet understood the principle of risk. You'd be surprised at how many idiots are injured getting out of a bath – although that obviously wouldn't ever happen to you – or just walking across a bedroom floor. But I promise you that's exactly what's going to happen unless you put away the toothpick.'

'Say your prayers, *malaka*, because you're the one who's going to get injured.'

CHAPTER 41

Spiros Reppas thumbed the button on the pearl handle of the switchblade and it sounded as harmless as a camera shutter, but when he came slashing and jabbing at me with the point, I guessed he didn't want me to say cheese so I turned and ran down two flights of stairs three at a time with the idea of reaching the Webley on the table by the French windows. Of course, he couldn't know the gun was empty but I wanted it because even an empty Webley will get you further than no Webley at all.

I heard his feet close behind me and, realizing I wasn't going to make it to the Webley in time, I grabbed the navy peacoat off the banister to help me try to defend myself. When we reached the bottom of the stair, I spun around and using the coat, I smothered his first and second lunge with the knife. He took a step back, feinting with the blade, which he clearly knew how to use, drunk or sober, while I twisted the coat around my left forearm and prepared to parry a third thrust. Neither of us spoke. When two men have an honest difference of opinion it's best to let them settle it with a more old-fashioned sort of dialectic than pure reason. The third time he came snarling at me like a rabid dog he went for my throat and I raised my thickly wrapped forearm to prevent his switchblade from slicing through my jugular. The navy peacoat absorbed most of the blade's sharp length but it wasn't thick enough to stop the tip of the knife from stabbing my arm. I yelled with pain, twisted my arm and the knife to one side, and then lashed at him with my right. It was a good punch, a big Schmeling uppercut that ought to have broken his jaw except that he ducked under it, clawed the coat away with the knife, and came at me again. There was fear and murder in his red-rimmed eyes and maybe just a hint of uncertainty now about the outcome; I expect I looked much the same way myself. Fortunately the knife came within reach now, a few inches from my nose, and high enough for me to clap my two hands hard on opposite sides of his arm simultaneously – one on the back of his hand and the other on the inside of his forearm – a fortunate bit of training I remembered from the Berlin police academy in the days when it seemed every punk on the streets thought he was Mackie Messer. I got lucky. Luckier than I deserved, given the injury to my own forearm. My right hand stopped his wrist from moving and my left smacked hard on the back of his big hairy paw, forcing the Greek's fingers to open suddenly so that the knife flew out of his fist and clattered onto the floor. It was his turn to yell with pain; I might even have broken his right wrist but he stayed on his feet and even barged past me to grab the Webley off the table with his left.

Instinctively I took a step back and raised my hands long

enough to discover blood was dripping down my left arm from where he'd managed to stick me. I knew I was going to need some stitches in a hospital, which would certainly spoil the rest of my evening and reduce my chances of sleeping with Elli. And that irritated me. But I let him think he had the upper hand for a minute in the hope of learning something more before I showed him the error of his ways and punched him very hard on the nose – the nose was probably best, there's nowhere that can end things quite as abruptly as a good punch on the nose, especially when you're least expecting it.

'So where is Professor Buchholz?' I asked.

Reppas thumbed back the hammer of the Webley as if he really meant to shoot me. I knew that all six rounds were safely in my pocket but even when you know a gun is empty it still makes you feel uncomfortable to have one pointed at you by someone who wants to murder you. You ask yourself if you really did empty every chamber, or if someone else might have reloaded the weapon while you were out of the room. Crazy stuff like that.

'Or shall we say Max Merten? What about him? My guess is that you and he have been lying low somewhere since the *Doris* went down. But where? Somewhere near Ermioni? Kosta, perhaps? Does he even know that his partner is dead? And that there won't be any insurance money now.'

'I hope you're insured, *malaka*,' said the Greek.

'Siegfried Witzel came back to Athens to claim on the insurance for the *Doris*, didn't he? Leaving the pair of you safely down there. And he said he'd call you when he'd completed the paperwork. But when he didn't, you got impatient or curious or even worried and so you decided to come and look for him. Is that how it was? Look, I didn't shoot him. But the cops want the man who did on account of how he also killed a lot of Jews during the war.'

The next second Reppas pulled the trigger – I heard another harmless camera-shutter sound – and at that point I felt the hammer come down on my own shortening temper.

'I take that very personally,' I said.

Even while he was glancing dumbly at the Webley and realizing what had happened, I stepped forward and smashed his nose with the heel of my hand, which saves a lot of unnecessary wear and tear on the knuckles. The blow carried him across the table and through the open French window. He lay still for a moment in an untidy heap of bloody nose and broken glass and I cursed Bernhard Gunther's stupidity for giving the man a fair chance in the first place.

You should have put the Bismarck to his thick head and saved yourself the bother. The old tried-and-tested ways are the best. You do it to the other guy before he does it to you. When are you going to realize that there's nothing to be gained in trying to be decent in a situation like this? The war should have taught you that much, anyway. Malaka *is right. This has cost you a good suit. Not only that but now you're going to have to wait around until he's stopped bleeding to get some answers.*

I shook some life back into my stunned hand, took off my jacket, and checked the wound on my left forearm – which, while it wasn't quite as bad as it felt, was still going to need a few stitches – and then collected the gun and the knife off the floor. I pocketed the knife and slid the lozenge-shaped barrel of the Webley under the waistband of my trousers. If there had been a clean towel to hand I might have wrapped it around my arm. Outside Reppas was groaning a little too loudly for comfort so I picked up a foot and started to drag him back into the house, just in case his neighbours were the sort of Greeks to complain about noise. What with the Persians burning the Acropolis and raping the priestesses in the temple they ought to have been used to it. Probably they thought it was just the sound of Reppas smashing some dinner plates at the end of a jolly evening, the way Greeks do when they're having a good time. It makes you wonder what might happen if they ever got upset about something. As I pulled, his boat shoe came off, which meant I dropped his leg for a moment. So I picked it up again and, in spite of his horribly stinking sock, folded his foot under my arm and finished bringing him back into the house. I closed the French windows, switched on the light, took a close look at the strawberry jam mess I'd made of the captain's face, and then his right wrist, which wasn't broken after all. Concluding he no longer posed much of a threat, I searched his trouser pockets and, finding nothing, went to fetch his peacoat. I found his wallet, stepped out of the front door, and walked around to the side of the house, to speak to Elli.

She threw away the cigarette she'd been smoking, stood up, and took my arm gently. 'You're hurt,' she said.

'It's really just a scratch.' Even as I said it, I doubted that it was true.

'Must have been some cat. What happened in there?'

'Not a cat. A shark with pearly white teeth bit me, dear. It's my suit that's ruined, not me. You didn't hear anything?'

'No.'

'Good.'

'So who is it in the house? The Nazi?'

'No such luck. It's Spiros Reppas. The captain of the *Doris*.'

'You didn't kill him, did you? Only, there's quite a lot of blood on your hands.'

She was a cool one, all right. The way she spoke made me think that it wouldn't have bothered her very much if I had killed him.

'He won't be sniffing any roses soon, but otherwise he's fine. Just a headache and a broken nose.'

'Thank God for that. In my experience the Greek police take a pretty dim view of murder.'

'Look, go and fetch Garlopis, will you, angel?'

'All right. But I don't like it here. This is hardly my idea of a night out. We could have been having a lot of fun if you weren't an ex-cop.'

'I'm sorry about that. But we can't leave. Not quite yet. I need to ask our seafaring friend some questions first. Up until now we were just exchanging blows. He's been pacified so tell Garlopis the danger is over but that I need those clean towels he keeps on the car seats. I have to use one of them on my arm and the other on the captain's face. And be nice. For a coward Garlopis is actually quite a decent fellow when you get to know him. I should know. Like I already told you, I'm often a coward myself.'

'I sincerely doubt that.'

'It's true. The only reason I went in there was because I was afraid of what might happen if I didn't. Believe me, sometimes bravery is just the very small space that exists between two kinds of fear: his and mine. Now go and get him like a good girl. And the towels. Don't forget to bring those towels.'

CHAPTER 42

I threw one of the clean towels at Spiros Reppas, who was now seated quietly on the battered sofa, and waited for him to wipe his ruined face; his nose looked like a butcher's elbow and his eyes were full of whatever protein-filled plasma fills them when you rearrange a man's face for the worse. Aqueous humour, I suppose, but nobody was laughing. With my left forearm wrapped in another towel, I was seated at the table and had the Webley right in front of me hoping it might underline my questions and lack of patience with the way things had gone up until now; but the gun was still unloaded because I'd shot people before who tried to murder me and I didn't want any more blood spilled. A broken nose and a cut on a forearm were enough splash for one evening.

Elli and Garlopis were hovering in the doorway beside the stairs, uncertain and uncomfortable witnesses to an interrogation they'd rather have avoided. They probably wondered if I was capable of hurting Reppas again. I was wondering the same thing. In the bedroom upstairs the radio was playing another jolly Greek tune and Elli was quietly humming along with it until I shot her a narrow-eyed, irritated look that was supposed to make her desist. She was nervous, I guess, and trying to hide it. The sight of guns and knives and quite a bit of blood will do that to some women. On the other hand, maybe she just didn't see that this was hardly the time or the place to have a song in your heart.

'Why don't you go upstairs and turn that damn radio off?' I said. 'It's irritating me.'

'Don't you like Greek music?' she asked.

'Not particularly. And while you're up there, have a peek around and see what you can find.'

'What am I looking for?'

'You'll know it if you see it.'

'There speaks the great detective.'

'Whatever gave you that idea?'

'I had the strange idea that Leventis believes you are.'

'Everyone looks like a great detective to a cop like him. Even an old Kraut like me.'

'You're not so old, for an old guy.'

She went upstairs. She moved like a black panther – rare, beautiful, and still steeped in unfathomable mystery – and after a while the radio went quiet, which left some room for my brain to untangle itself.

I tossed the injured man's wallet to Garlopis. I'd already looked through it, but everything inside was printed in Greek.

'See what this can tell us,' I growled at him, still irritated but now more with myself, mostly for being irritated at Elli. Then again, someone trying to shoot you will do that sometimes. I lit a couple of cigarettes, because a cigarette is the perfect panacea for injured forearms and broken noses, a heal-all nostrum that requires no medical training and always works like magic. I tucked one between the captain's bloodstained lips and smoked in silence for a moment, remembering something Bernhard Weiss had told me when he was still the boss of the Murder Commission at Berlin's Alex:

'Make the silence work for you,' he'd said. 'Just look at the way Hitler makes a speech. Never in a hurry. Waits for the audience to settle, and the expectation to mount. "When will he speak?" "What will he say?" It's the same with a suspect. Have a cigarette, check your fingernails, stare at the ceiling, like you've got all the time in the world. Your suspect will be telling himself that he's the one who's supposed to have nothing better to do, not you. Chances are your man will say something even if it's to tell you to go and screw yourself.'

After a minute or two Reppas wiped his nose again, inspected the amount of blood on the towel, removed the cigarette from his mouth, and spat a scarlet gob to one side. Cigarette and psychology were evidently working well.

'So what happens now, *malaka*?'

'That's up to you, Captain.'

'Says the man with the gun.'

'Look, friend, it's your gun, not mine. And if you hadn't pulled the trigger on me you might still be breathing straight.'

'It doesn't work unless you pull the trigger.'

'That was your second stupid mistake. The first was leaving it lying around where someone could come along and unload it.'

He looked at the gun, then at me. 'So if it's not loaded then why am I sitting here and listening to you? What's to stop me throwing you out of here right now?'

'Me. That's what. Look, your nose is already broken. Be a shame if I had to break your arm as well.'

'Maybe I'll risk it.'

'If you do I'd advise you to take out lots of insurance first. You're still drunk and already in quite a bit of pain. That gives me all the edge I need.'

Reppas nodded. 'So what else do you advise?'

'Only that you give me a short history lesson. Recent history. There's no need to relive the glory that was Greece. Just everything that happened since Max Merten showed up in Attica. You see, there's this cop called Lieutenant Leventis at the Megaron Pappoudof on Constitution Square, here in Athens. He's the one who found your boss dead in this house, probably murdered by Alois Brunner, also known as Georg Fischer. A tenacious sort, he's been very anxious to speak to anyone regarding Brunner's present whereabouts. So anxious that he's been strong-arming me to do some of his investigative work for him. Working a murder case is a little outside my current terms of employment but what could I do? The lieutenant can be a very persuasive fellow. He's holding my passport as collateral. I guess he concluded that since Siegfried Witzel was a fellow German and a client of my company in Munich, I could help him clear up this whole damn mess. I imagine this might be your job now. Then he can ask *you* all the awkward pain-in-the-ass questions he's been asking me. So one possibility is for me to call him up and have him come here to arrest you. Because let's face it, you know more than I do what this is all about. I'm just a claims adjuster from Germany who wishes he'd stayed home.

'All of that is on one side of the actuarial balance sheet. Maybe you're a talker and perhaps you can gab your way out of trouble. I won't argue about it. I'll leave that to you and Lieutenant Leventis. He likes to talk, and to argue. For hours. But on the other side is that I have a small claim of my own against Max Merten. But for him I wouldn't be in this mess. So I was thinking I might be persuaded to let you walk out of this house without involving cops. I might even return your wallet and pretend you'd never been here. You could take off on that motorcycle and disappear for a few weeks, while I go and visit Max Merten. Only you'd have to tell me where I can find him. And then, when all this is over, you can come back here and pick up the pieces of your life.'

I shifted some of the shards of glass under my feet as if to make a metaphorical point.

'If I might interrupt you, sir.' Garlopis was holding up an identity card. 'According to his ID this man – Spiros Reppas – he lives on Spetses. That's a small island just a few kilometres south of Kosta, which is where the taxi from Ermioni went after the *Doris* sank. Mpotasi Street, number 22.'

Garlopis continued to search the wallet.

'That fits. Anything else?'

'Just some money. A ferry ticket. A driving licence. A business card that describes a scuba diving business, also on Spetses.'

'Spetses. Is that where Max Merten is hiding, Captain?'

'Maybe,' said Reppas. 'Maybe not. Maybe you just want to kill him, too.'

'From what I've heard concerning what he did to the Jews of Salonika, he needs killing, badly. Only that's not up to me. I'm an insurance man, not an assassin. Frankly I'd much prefer to make a gift of Merten to the Greek people. Lieutenant Leventis tells me that he would dearly like to arrest Alois Brunner and put him on trial for war crimes. But I'm guessing that Leventis will probably settle for getting Max Merten in his place. The way I see it, if I can deliver Merten to him on a plate then it will be a big feather in his cap; he'll give me my passport back and I can go home again. Simple as that.'

'You'd do that? For me?' Reppas grinned a sarcastic sort of grin that almost made me want to break his nose again.

'No, not for you. But for the people of Greece, yes, I would. Only you'd better hurry up and spill your guts before my friend over there finds any more useful information in your wallet. Now that I have an address your own currency is shrinking faster than a wad of wet drachmas, Spiros.'

'All right, all right. But first just tell me exactly what happened to Siegfried Witzel. Please. He was my friend for twenty years. A good friend, too. For a German.'

'Exactly, I don't know. Like I said, I'm just the fellow from the insurance company. We came to this house to make Witzel an interim payment, pending final settlement, and found him dead on this floor. He'd been shot through both eyes. There was a cop here, too. Since when that cop's been inclined to pretend that we had something to do with it, as a means of catching the real culprit. Plugging his victims through the eyes is the signature of Alois Brunner, the Nazi war criminal. I think Brunner used me to lead him to this house because he was after Witzel. That's as much as we know about what happened here.'

'What happened to the body?'

'The body?'

'Is Siegfried buried yet? Cremated, or what?'

'I have no idea.'

Reppas nodded sombrely. 'That's a pity. He was a good friend to me.'

'So far this is me patiently answering your questions, Captain Reppas. What's more I've a cut on my arm that's in urgent need of repair. Not only that but it's telling me to see if I can't straighten your nose with my fist if you don't tell me what I want to know, and soon.'

The room was silent. Reppas gave no clue as to his thoughts. Then, just as I was about to make a fist and tap him with it, he said: 'All right. I'll tell you everything.'

'Make sure you do. And by the way I already know the real purpose of your expedition wasn't to dive for an ancient Greek treasure but for a modern Jewish one. And I might as well tell you that it's not just the Greek police who would love to meet you, my friend. There are some Israelis in town who are interested in this story, too. You wouldn't want to meet them. Not because they're Jews. But because they're not as patient as me. Can't blame them for that, I guess. History has taught them that if it is going to repeat itself, this time they're going to be the ones with the guns and the hard faces and the bloody-minded will to come out on top.'

CHAPTER 43

Elli came back downstairs and shook her head.

'Nothing,' she said. 'There's plenty of that lying around. I used to wonder what it might be like in one of these little houses next to the Acropolis. Well, now I know. This place is a mess.'

Reppas dragged hard on the cigarette and exhaled slowly through his twisted nostrils. In their mangled state, it looked as if the ruins of his nose were still smoldering after a small explosion in the centre of his face. I handed him another cigarette and he lit it with the butt and then looked for an ashtray; it was a fastidiousness that bordered on the absurd, given the state of the carpet. Garlopis fetched one from somewhere and presented it to him as gravely as if he'd been a butler offering his master a silver salver. Elli took a cigarette too, and let him light her.

'No one said you could stop talking,' I told Reppas.

'Sometimes my German is not so good,' he said. 'The boss spoke Greek to me when he was sober and German when he was drunk. Which was quite a lot of the time. When I realized you were German, I thought you were working for Brunner.

That's why I pulled the knife on you. With a man like that it doesn't pay to take any chances. I'm sorry. This was my late sister's house. Nobody lives here or even knows about this place. At least, that's what I thought. So when you just appeared in the bedroom like that I thought you were here to kill me. Next time, knock on the door or bring a parrot to speak some Greek for you. Otherwise one day you're going to end up dead.'

'Maybe I would have done if Witzel hadn't already met his maker here. And if his murderer wasn't still at large. And if the cops who were supposed to be keeping an eye on this place hadn't vanished. All of that tends to make an insurance man a little cautious.'

'Sure, I can understand that. I've been a bit cautious myself since the ship sank: lying low at my house in Spetses. Merten was flat against Siegfried coming back to Athens to make the claim until we were quite sure it was safe. They argued about it when we were still in the dinghy. He said Brunner would surely be looking for us. It was Brunner who sank the *Doris*, see? Some sort of delayed-action incendiary device. But the boss wouldn't hear of not coming back here to make the claim as soon as possible; he said the ship was his whole world and unless the insurance company paid up he stood to lose everything, not just some gold he never had in the first place. The *Doris* wasn't just his livelihood, it was also his home, see? So he figured it was worth the risk. Besides, the boss could always look after himself. And we figured it was safe him coming here, given that no one knew about this house. I inherited it from my sister a few months ago. She lived in Thessaloniki and, well, you can see I haven't got around to doing very much with it.'

'Now I can refuse the insurance claim with a clear conscience. But back up a bit. I said I knew that the real purpose of the expedition was to find some sunken Jewish gold, but I want the full story. Take it from the beginning. The whole alpha to omega. How did Max Merten know your boss in the first place?'

'From before the war. In Berlin. Siegfried Witzel started out as a lawyer and then changed to studying zoology. Don't ask me how that works. During the war he was a member of a combat diving unit in the German navy called the Division Brandenburg. But he'd already trained with the Italian Decima Flottiglia MAS, who were the leaders in underwater warfare. That's where he got this passion for scuba work and that's how I got to know him; I'm part Italian myself. In the last months of the war he bought himself the *Doris*. I think Merten had something to do with that. And then almost as soon as he could he came back down to Greece and the two of us went into business together making underwater films. One of them even won an award at the Cannes Film Festival. That went to the bottom of the sea, as well as all our cameras.

'Anyway, a few weeks ago Merten shows up with another German. A fellow named Schramma. Christian Schramma. Except that there wasn't anything very Christian about him. He was a thug, from Munich, and I think Merten brought him along for security.'

'I was wondering if he'd make an appearance in this story.'

'Only a brief one. He's dead, by the way. Brunner shot him.

But before Brunner turned up to spoil the show, Merten and the boss seemed to have it all worked out; we were going to sail to some shallow waters off the Peloponnesian coast, dive to the wreck of the *Epeius*, and bring up part of the Jewish gold under the cover of an expedition to find ancient Greek artefacts. You know about that, right?'

I nodded. 'As much as I need to know, for now.'

'Not all of the gold, you understand. Just as much as we could get in a week or two – perhaps a couple of hundred bars – using just one diver: the boss. Everything looked perfect. We had the proper permissions from museums and ministries, which Merten, passing himself off as some important German professor of archaeology, had previously arranged. I have to admit he was very thorough. We were all set to sail when this fellow calling himself Georg Fischer shows up. He came aboard the ship while we were still moored at the marina in Piraeus, cool as you like, and it was obvious he and Merten knew each other, and that Merten was afraid of him. It soon became clear that Merten and Fischer had once been partners and that Fischer – it was only when we got to Spetses that I found out his real name was Alois Brunner – had been double-crossed by Max Merten during the war. Along with some other SS officers they'd stolen the gold from the Jews together. Now Brunner told Merten that he wanted his share and that he'd decided to come along on the expedition with us, just to keep an eye on things, but that he'd also decided to give himself an insurance policy by lodging a letter with a local lawyer explaining what Merten was really up to. If something happened to him and he didn't return to

Athens within thirty days, the letter would be sent to the Greek authorities. Merten agreed; well, he didn't have much choice. Brunner said he'd even provide us with a genuine artefact to help with our cover story – just in case the coast guard showed up and started asking questions – because, conveniently for us, he was in the business of exporting art treasures. So we took delivery of a packing case with a Greek horse's head inside, and that's probably how we ended up taking the incendiary on board.

'As soon as Brunner left the boat the boss asked me to follow him and I tailed him back to his hotel, the Xenon, in Piraeus. Later on, I went back there again and, for a few drachmas, the hotel operator showed me all the telephone calls Brunner had made from his room. By ringing them, one after the other, I managed to find the name of Brunner's lawyer in Glyfada, Dr Samuel Frizis. The boss knew this local burglar called Tsochaztopoulos and we met up with him at the Chez Lapin club in Kastella. The boss gave him fifteen hundred drachmas to break into the lawyer's office and steal Brunner's letter, only he was supposed to do it without the lawyer ever finding out. Simple as that. Just find the file for a client named Fischer and steal what was in it. I waited outside the office while Choc went inside. Took him no time at all. Said it was the easiest fifteen hundred he'd made in a long while.

'I brought the letter back to the ship and we waited for Brunner to join us, as previously arranged. The plan was that by the time the lawyer discovered the letter was missing from his office Brunner would be at sea with us and we'd just chuck him over the side with the horse's head tied to his feet. But something went wrong. I think Brunner had some thugs of his own and one of them saw me following him to his hotel. Anyway, the bastard smelled a rat and before joining us on board he asked his lawyer to check to see if he still had the letter. And when the lawyer couldn't find it, Brunner must have figured he was going to be double-crossed by Merten a second time, because he came aboard secretly the night before we were to sail. Schramma disturbed him and the two exchanged gunshots. Schramma was killed and Brunner hightailed it off the ship and onto the quayside in Piraeus. Not long after that we set sail, and so it ended up being Christian Schramma's weighted body we dropped over the side.'

'That's the first bit of good news I've heard in a while.'

'You knew him?'

'Yes. And well enough to say he got what was coming to him. He murdered two people in Munich and got away with it, thanks to Max Merten. And I have to say, to me as well. I made a mistake there. I thought I was protecting Merten. I thought Merten was innocent. But he wasn't. He never was.'

'Merten's a crafty one, and no mistake. After we set sail we decided that since Brunner hadn't any clue as to the area we'd planned to dive in – and don't ask me where that is, honestly, I don't know. Merten kept the exact longitude and latitude to himself for fear that we would double-cross him and now I realize why – we could lie low in Spetses for a while, just in case Brunner had blown the whistle on us. Then, when we judged things were safe, we'd go and look for the gold as planned. None of us had a clue that before he'd shot Christian Schramma and left the ship Brunner had activated some sort of delayed-action incendiary device in the packing case beside the horse's head. Probably that was the real purpose of his coming aboard in the night. Anyway, it was a couple of hours before the thing went off. By which time we were far out to sea. We'd just finished sending Schramma to the bottom when we discovered we were on fire. We tried to get it under control but it was impossible; the boss reckoned the incendiary was made of phosphorus and there was no putting it out.

'We started to sink and so we had to abandon ship. We grabbed a few things, came ashore in the dinghy, and Merten and I took a taxi and then a ferry to Spetses, while the boss caught the ferry to Piraeus. Said he would make contact with us as soon as he could, and for several days the telegrams kept coming. But when the boss stopped sending them I decided to come up to Athens on my motorcycle and find out what had happened to him. And here I am.'

'So Merten is alone at your house in Spetses?'

'Not entirely alone. There's a local woman who comes in every other day to cook and clean.'

'Is he armed?'

'Yes. He has Schramma's own Walther pistol.'

'I shall want the door key.'

'In my coat pocket you'll find another key with an address label on it.' He pointed at the coat lying on the floor at my feet and I nodded.

'Get it.'

He picked up the coat, found the key, and handed it over.

'Is your house on the telephone?' I asked.

Reppas paused, and waved his fingers in the air. 'I have to think of the way to say some of these things in German. Merten only ever speaks Greek to me. Speaking German like this, it's tiring, you know. The only telephone in Spetses is at the hotel. But it's not working right now. This is island life in Greece. Lots of things don't work like they're supposed to. They've only just discovered the wheel on Spetses. Priests cross themselves when they walk past a bar with a jukebox. Or see a woman wearing a bathing costume.'

'I'm kind of religious about that myself. How did you get the telegrams from Witzel?'

'I had to go to Kosta on the ferry and collect them from the post office in the town.'

'How long will Merten stay put down there? Before he figures out that you're not coming back. Which you're not. Not for several weeks, if you've got any sense.'

'I have a nephew in Thessaloniki. I shall stay with him.' He tried to look thoughtful, but it came off as something grotesque, like a gargoyle trying to solve a crossword puzzle. 'But Merten? I don't know for sure. I do know he's scared. Every time he heard the door open he thought it was Brunner and grabbed Schramma's Walther. My guess is that he'll be staying put for a while. Originally, I was going to travel back the day after tomorrow, even if I didn't find the boss here.'

'Where were you planning to look for him?'

'I was going to check out some of our old haunts in Piraeus. Bars and brothels mostly. The boss liked a drink and a girl, usually in that order. So maybe you have several days to go down to Spetses yourself, right? And do whatever it is you say you're going to do. Cops or killing, it makes no difference to me now. But for Merten, my friend would still be alive and we'd still be in the scuba business.'

Reppas finished his second cigarette and stubbed it out. All his previous belligerence was now gone. He dabbed his nose and inspected the towel for another red mark, like a woman checking her lipstick.

'Are you really intending to let me walk out of here?'

'Sure. Why not? You're a fish I'm throwing back, Spiros. It's Merten I want to make a lot of trouble for, not you. He's the real criminal here. You can even take your gun with you.' I picked up the barrel and handed over the empty Webley and a handful of bullets. 'You might even need it. For all I know Brunner might still be in Athens. He strikes me as the kind of fellow who isn't easily scared off. It could be that he thinks he owes you a bullet in lieu of a share of the gold. If I were you I'd keep away from some of your old haunts in Piraeus. He's already murdered that lawyer whose office you burgled in Glyfada – Dr Frizis.'

Reppas put the Webley and the ammunition in his coat pocket. 'Thanks for the advice,' he said.

'Tell me, why did your boss go along with Merten's scheme in the first place? He was a marine biologist, an important film-maker who'd won a prize at the Cannes Festival. He didn't strike me as a Nazi. Surely he'd left that world behind.'

'Clearly you don't know much about filmmaking.' Spiros Reppas shrugged. 'Making any kind of film is expensive but underwater films, more so. And it doesn't pay that well. It's not like they were queuing around the block to see our little movie, right? Who goes to see a film like *The Philosopher's Seal*, about Mediterranean monk seals?'

'I must admit I missed it myself.'

'He sold it to a few television companies and that was it. He was in debt. And he needed to raise money to make our next documentary – a film about the lost city of Atlantis. You don't have to be a Nazi to be greedy for money. There was that. And then there was all of that Jewish gold lying in only fifteen fathoms of water just waiting for someone to come and salvage it. Millions and millions of dollars' worth of gold melted down and recast as gold bars by a foundry Max Merten had specially built in Katerini, sometime in the spring of 1943. According to Merten, all of the bars on the *Epeius* carried a specially faked date and stamp from the Weigunner foundry at Essen.'

'How does that help?'

'The significance of this smelt is that it's dated 1939, which predates both the invasion of Greece and the murder of Europe's Jews. It looks like prewar Reichsbank gold bullion. All of which makes it much easier to move on the world's bullion markets. Well, who can resist a story like that? Not me, and not Siegfried Witzel. But maybe there was one more thing, I don't know. I think there was maybe something about the way the *Doris* had come into Witzel's possession that Merten knew about and which he was prepared to exploit.'

'There was,' I said. 'Like the gold, the ship was originally con-fiscated from the Jews of Salonika, and Merten sold it to Witzel, in 1943, for a knockdown price. He changed the name of the ship to make sure this remained secret.'

'Yes,' said Reppas, 'that would explain a lot. It was always stick and carrot with Merten; sometimes he was leading the boss on with estimates of how much gold was down there – each time more than the last – and sometimes he was threatening to tell the police about how the boss had acquired the ship in the first place.'

'One more question: Did Max Merten discover exactly how Brunner found out about your expedition? After all, it was fourteen years since Merten double-crossed Brunner and arranged for the *Epeius* to be scuttled. And twelve since the end of the war. Max Merten has been living openly as a lawyer in Munich all this time. The Americans offered to extradite him to Greece in 1945 but the Greek government said he wasn't wanted in connection with any war crimes. He's been a model citizen in Munich, a man with friends in the West German government. By contrast, Alois Brunner is a hunted war criminal living under a false name. The Greeks want him, as do the Israelis, and so I imagine do the French. How did he find out that Merten had come back to Greece?'

Spiros Reppas frowned. 'Like I said, sometimes my German is not so good. I understand German when someone speaks to me and I can see their lips moving. Overheard is not so easy for me. Also the longer compound words are difficult. But I think maybe I heard Merten tell Witzel that someone close to Adenauer must have told Brunner that he, Merten, was coming to Greece. And that Brunner wouldn't be the first old Nazi to go to work for the new German government.'

Reppas took a superhuman drag on the cigarette and threw up his hands in defeat.

'That's it, mister. Every damn thing I know. I've no idea what's to become of me now.' He sighed. 'I've lost my best friend and I've lost my livelihood. Can I ask you a question?'

'Fire away.'

'Diving can be dangerous. The boss always said that if anything ever happened to me while he was diving the *Doris* would be mine. I don't suppose there's any chance you'll reconsider your decision on the insurance money. That you could make out a cheque to me instead of him. I'd be more than happy to accept a reduced figure. Ten cents on the dollar, perhaps. After all the ship was old and probably not worth half of what the boss said it was.'

'Sorry, no. My employers are kind of funny about paying out in cases involving arson. They don't do it, as a rule. But if you can find a last will and testament naming you as my client's sole heir, you could always take them on in the courts. I wouldn't give much for your chances, mind. Even in Germany there's probably some small print that discriminates against the kind of people who go after millions in stolen Jewish gold.' I took out my wallet and handed him some money. I decided I could probably afford it out of the twenty thousand I was going to have when we cashed the certified cheque on the way to Spetses in the morning. 'But to show you there are no hard feelings, here's fifty. Get yourself a new nose.'

CHAPTER 44

The next morning we cashed the certified cheque at the Alpha Bank in Corinth, with me pretending to be Siegfried Witzel, as planned. While we were still in the bank there was a small earth tremor, which did little to make me feel better about what I was doing, although that might as easily have been the ten stitches in my left forearm – now in a black sling, as if I was in mourning – and the painkillers I was taking. But even for a self-confessed coward like Achilles Garlopis it seemed that the Venetian blinds swaying gently on the bank's windows were nothing to be concerned about.

'In Corinth these things happen all the time,' he said, crossing himself just to be on the safe side. 'Which is to say, when the gods are angry with us. I often think that earth tremors are why we believe in the gods in the first place.'

'I'm sure I can't think of a better reason.'

'Oh, I can.' He nodded at the window, through which we could see the Rover and Elli sitting inside it, and smiled a mischievous smile. 'At least I can when I look at Miss Panatoniou.'

She was outside because I thought it best for her legal career that she should stay away from the larceny being carried out inside the Alpha Bank. Not that she seemed to care very much about that. For a lawyer she wasn't averse to taking risks. More than seemed at all judicious.

'Maybe you should become a priest,' I said. 'A sermon like that beats anything the Lutherans have to offer.'

'It's strange, but she really seems to like you, sir. Women are odd creatures, aren't they? I mean, there's no accounting for a woman like this. And when she's around it's like the sun is out. The way she looks at you – it's like she's shining upon you.'

'A man can get burned if he stays in the sun for too long.'

'I don't think she's the type to burn you. Just dazzle you a bit. Always supposing such a thing is even possible.'

'Actually, I'm not sure it is anymore.'

When the tremor finally stopped the money was paid over without so much as a raised eyebrow. We hung around in Corinth afterward only long enough to meet the Alpha Bank clerk less formally in a nearby bar and to pay him the five per cent handling fee that had been agreed upon with the cousin of Garlopis. The clerk was not much more than a boy with a face as cold as a marble statue. Corinth itself was equally dull and featureless, a bleak, low-lying city on the sea, with little to recommend it except the eponymous canal, which cut straight across the isthmus like the scar on my forearm. It was hard to imagine the apostle Paul bothering to send a long letter to the Corinthians except to question why they were living there and not somewhere else more interesting like Athens or Rome.

More usefully, Corinth was halfway to Kosta, where there was a regular foot ferry to Spetses. Since I couldn't turn the heavy steering wheel of the Rover without my arm hurting, it was Elli who was driving the car. We took Garlopis to a bus stop so that he could travel safely back to Athens. I felt bad about involving Elli in the business with Max Merten, but not as bad as Garlopis felt about exposing himself to something he considered much more dangerous than the simple movement of the earth.

'I know this man,' I told Garlopis in a last attempt to persuade him to come with us to Kosta while we waited for the bus to arrive. 'Max Merten. And take it from me, I can handle him. Rough or smooth. Last time I saw him he was fat and the only danger I was in was that his liver might explode. He's a pen pusher, not a dangerous sadist like Brunner. And I've dealt with hundreds of men like him.'

'I know you think that, sir. But there are ten reminders stitched into your arm to suggest you might just be wrong. Besides, you heard what Spiros Reppas said. Merten has a gun and he's nervous. Which makes it all the more perplexing to me that you should have returned that Webley to Reppas. A gun might have been useful insurance against all kinds of otherwise uninsurable risks.'

'I can see why you believe that but take it from me, it's not. Two guns don't make a right. Just a lot of noise. A gun's a lot more risk. More risk requires a bigger premium. And I can't afford it. My soul – always supposing I have one – can't handle the payments anymore. Does that make sense?'

'I think so. But you don't strike me as a man who has much on his conscience, sir.'

'Don't be fooled. You might not see him, but even without his top hat the Jiminy Cricket who follows me around is six feet tall.'

When the blue-and-white bus finally hove into sight like a piece of outsized, metallic chinoiserie, I offered Garlopis the envelope containing the twenty thousand drachmas I'd received at the Alpha Bank.

'Keep this in the office safe and put a stop on buying that cop – for the time being, anyway,' I told him. 'If I can pull this off with Merten, we may save ourselves some money.'

But of course I didn't believe this, not completely. In spite of everything I'd told Garlopis I knew there was considerable danger involved in confronting Max Merten on the island of Spetses. I certainly didn't expect Merten to quietly give himself up, not for a moment. He was going to need some friendly persuasion. Fortunately I had a plan and knew just what to say and, given half a chance, I was going to say it – if necessary, with force. A lot of it.

Garlopis shook his head. 'If you don't mind, sir, I'd prefer you looked after it. Twenty thousand drachmas is a lot of money for a person of my moral calibre. The fact is, you're not the only man with a loudly spoken conscience. Mine has taught me that I can resist almost anything except real temptation. Especially when it comes in the form of a lot of banknotes in an envelope.'

'All the same, I still think you should take it with you. This wad of cash is not quite thick enough to stop a bullet.' I looked at Elli expectantly, in the hope that I might finally have scared her, but she still seemed quite unperturbed by the prospect of the two of us going up against a potentially desperate man. 'I'd hate to think it wouldn't find a good home if something did happen to me.'

'All right. I'll take it. But please be careful. I'm looking forward enormously to corrupting that cop. No, really, sir. There's nothing that's quite as much fun as discovering the price of a truly honest man.'

After the bus had left, we got back in the Rover. Elli checked her face in the rearview mirror although I could have saved her the trouble; her face looked perfect. I'd seen the faces of women before and hers was the kind to launch a whole fleet of passenger ferries in the general direction of Troy. She was wearing a short-sleeve white blouse, an under-the-bosom belt that had its work cut out, a full pink skirt with deep pleats and, underneath it, multiple layers of sheer fabric, not to mention the invisible and impertinent scouts for my very active imagination. The fawn suede driving gloves added a nice touch to the whole ensemble. She looked elegantly in control of the car and of herself, like a woman who'd meant to enter a beauty contest and ended up competing in the Mille Miglia. Humming lightly, she steered us quickly along the meanderingly scenic Greek coast and was proving to be an excellent chauffeur; with her eyes on the road and her feet on the pedals I had all the time in the world to admire her shapely calves, and sometimes her knees. Her elbows weren't so bad either and I was becoming very fond of the line of her jaw, not to mention her body's sublime,

S-shaped curves. She looked like one of the Sirens, and possibly sounded like one, too.

But my admiration for Elli was accompanied by the growing suspicion that she was using me to help her exact some sort of personal revenge against the Nazis; that perhaps she was intent on murdering Alois Brunner, or Max Merten – that maybe her mother or her father had been killed during the occupation. It was the only explanation for why she was with me that made any real sense. In which case I was going to have to be very careful because I wanted Max Merten alive and for a purpose I'd only just learned to appreciate myself; nothing is more compelling to a man nearing the end of his useful days than the sudden realization that he has the chance to do one good thing.

There's no sacrifice that's too great for an opportunity to do something like that.

CHAPTER 45

'Are you sure you know what you're doing?' she said. 'I mean, I wouldn't like anything to happen to you.'

'Not you as well. I already told Garlopis, I can handle Max Merten.'

'Actually I was talking about your plans to bribe that policeman. Or try to. If he doesn't take the *fakelaki* it would be all the excuse he needed to put you in prison.'

'He's already got more than enough of an excuse to do just that.'

'I really do wonder if you know what you're getting into, that's all.'

'I know what I'm getting out of. This damn country, I hope.'

'That's not very flattering, Christof. To me or my country.'

'You're right. I'm sorry, sugar. Look, I just want my lousy passport back. When I can see my picture in that little green book again, maybe I'll feel a bit more comfortable about staying on for a while.'

Her eyes stayed on the meandering road ahead; I was glad

about that; it meant she couldn't look straight through me. I glanced out of the passenger window at the sumptuously appointed view; with its bright blue sky, sapphire sea, and majestic coastline, it looked like the set for some inspiring Cecil B. DeMille epic. On a road like that, and with a driver like Elli, it was easy to think of Muses and Graces and of returning home after a long journey. Munich wasn't exactly Ithaca but it would do.

'Did you take a day off work?' I asked, changing the subject quickly.

'It's a Saturday.'

'Yes, but you said you work on a Saturday.'

'We have a different attitude to work than you Germans.'

'So I noticed.'

'Greeks don't believe that God will like us better because we work hard, or because we deny ourselves pleasure. We prefer to believe that God wants us to go to the beach and admire the view. That contemplation of all the Unmoved Mover's works is the highest form of moral activity there is. It's the only way of understanding him.'

'That doesn't sound much like Marx.'

Elli smiled. 'It's Aristotle. Actually he has a lot more in common with Marx than just an impossibly large beard.'

'I'm sure he does, but please don't tell me what. I'm too busy right now, admiring the view.'

Elli glanced at me and saw that I was looking at her.

'The view's the other way, isn't it?'

'I've seen it. But you. You're always worth looking at.

Garlopis was right. Looking at you is enough to make a man believe in God.'

'He said that?'

'Even if I can't quite bring myself to believe in you, my lovely. Snow White is supposed to wait for her handsome young prince, not fall for the grizzled huntsman with an axe to grind.'

'I see we're back on the age-old debate about my age and you being old.'

'I can see what's in it for me. That's obvious to any mirror on the wall, not only a magic one. I'm trying to figure out what's in it for you, that's all.'

'You think I might have an ulterior motive for choosing to spend time with you? Is that it?'

'Women usually do.'

'Perhaps you underestimate yourself, Christof.'

'I just don't want to disappoint you the way I usually disappoint myself.'

'A woman falls for a man and maybe he falls for her. There's aesthetics and chemistry and biology and a lot of other technical stuff. Then there's what he says and how she responds to it. And let's not forget the metaphysics of it, too: the things we can't know – the time and place, and the men I've known before, and the women you've known before. I don't have a secret agenda here. I don't have a wicked stepmother or even seven friends who are dwarves. I like you. Maybe it's just as simple as that.'

'Maybe.'

'You know what your real problem is? You want to try to understand something that goes beyond understanding.'

'That's the German in me, I guess.'

'Then we'll have to make a Greek out of you. I think you could use some cheering up. Sometimes you're just a little bit too contemplative. Like you have something else on your mind.'

'There usually is. The gun in your bag, perhaps – that might give anyone pause for a whole series of thoughts.'

'You think I'm planning to shoot you? It's an idea at that.'

'One that's already crossed my mind.'

'Why on earth would I shoot you?'

'You know, I still can't think of a good reason. But I was hoping I might find one before you got around to actually doing it.'

'Let me know when you come up with one. It will be interesting to hear it. Who knows? Maybe it will seem like such a good reason that it will inspire me to shoot you for real. I could certainly use a little target practice.' She shook her head. 'Your head is a mess, do you know that? With all that suspicion it's a wonder you can think straight. I'm guessing, of course, but I think you must have had some very interesting girlfriends before me. Maybe some of them were the type to go and shoot a man.'

'Then you should feel sorry for me. Besides, I'm a victim of my own upbringing. The fact of the matter is that I come from a broken home. All Germans do, you know. My home's been broken so many times it looks like the Parthenon.'

Elli was quiet for a while, during which time she bit her lip a lot as if she was trying to prevent herself from telling me something important and I let her alone in the hope that, eventually, she would; but when she did speak again it was to tell me something much more personal than I might have expected, and that brought a tear to her eye.

'You really want to know why I carry a gun?'

'Sure. But I'll settle for your explanation.'

'My father gave it to me.'

'Beats a bottle of perfume and a doll, I suppose.'

'He gave it to me because last year, not long before he died – on the Ochi Day, which is the national anniversary of General Metaxas telling Mussolini to go and screw himself – a man tried to rape me, in Athens. He was a much younger man than you – a *mutamassir*, which is to say an Egyptianized Syrian who'd been living in Alexandria before being expelled from the country by Nasser. I made the mistake of trying to help him find a job with the Red Cross. He made me do things – horrible things – and he would certainly have raped me if he hadn't been interrupted by George Papakyriakopoulos.'

'Meissner's lawyer.'

'That's right. George has been a pretty good friend to me ever since.'

'Glad to hear it.'

'There's a lot of rape these days in Greece and I carry a gun to make sure it doesn't happen again or, if it does, that I'm able to take my immediate revenge. But I also carry it in case I ever run into the bastard who almost raped me.'

'You didn't report it to the police?'

'This is Greece. Reporting a rape, or an attempted rape, is almost as bad as the actual act. Not that I've ever seen him again. He disappeared, I'm glad to say. But if I ever do see him again I intend to kill him and to hell with the consequences. In the meantime I like older men like you because I think your sex drive isn't nearly as strong as that of younger men like him, which means you're more likely to take no for an answer. Especially if I have a gun in my hand. Does that make sense? I hope so. There. Now you know my dirty secret.'

CHAPTER 46

I might have laughed at the way she'd ended her story with a joke at my expense – if it was a joke. Instead I uttered an audible, sympathetic sort of sigh and handed her my handkerchief. 'I'm sorry, Elli.' I nodded firmly. 'Makes perfect sense now that you've explained it. The men in this country being what they are.'

'I don't know that they're much different anywhere else.' She threw the handkerchief back at me almost as if I'd insulted her.

Of course, I didn't quite believe what she'd told me. It wasn't that I doubted Elli so much as I doubted my own capacity for trusting anyone. Which is to say that I'd believed other women before. Of course, these days honesty is a joke, thanks to politicians, and men just lie because they have to in order to stay alive. But long before Hitler and Goebbels and Stalin and Mao, all women were liars and all women lie unless they're your own dear mother when they always tell you or your father the unvarnished truth even though you and he really don't want to hear it. No one could mind the gentle nurse with a heart of gold who lies out of kindness to your best friend because she can't bring herself to tell him that the shell took away both his legs and that he's never going to walk again. But the rest of them lie like Cretan Jesuits with a college degree in amphibology, and about everything, too, including why they're an hour late showing up to a restaurant, their weight, their delight at the present you just bought them, and the pleasure you gave them as a lover. There's nothing they won't lie about if they think you'll swallow it and if it advantages them in some way. But mostly women lie and they don't even know when they're doing it, or if they do, then you had surely left them with the clear and unequivocal impression that you didn't ever want to know the truth, which means it's your fault, of course; or else they simply believe they have a God-given right to lie since being a woman gives them that right whereas you are just a poor dumb fool called a man.

So there was the fact that women are just natural liars and the fact that I was German and, given everything we'd done to the Greeks in 1943, it was hard for me to imagine there were Greeks like Elli Panatoniou who were prepared to put all of that history behind them. Which is to say I didn't think it was healthy to believe her because I was going up against Max Merten and I was worried I might find a small hole in my back just because I was German like him. Knowing what I did about how Germans had behaved in Greece I could hardly have blamed her for wanting a bit of revenge. But because I had to be absolutely sure of Elli, I needed to furnish her with a motive that might make the woman reveal her true hand, if she had one, which meant telling her a dirty little secret of my own, and this had me shaking like a dice box.

'Since you showed me yours then perhaps I should show you mine,' I said. 'Only I have to warn you, sugar, mine's a lot dirtier than yours.'

'Should I park now or wait to drive us off the road with shock and horror?'

'It is kind of horrible, Elli.'

'So don't tell me. This is a dress I'm wearing, not a surplice.'

'Believe me, I like it a lot. Especially with you in it.'

'I wonder about that.'

'Do you ever wonder what I did during the war?'

'I'm not naïve. You're a German. I didn't think you were running an orphanage or working for Walt Disney. Just don't tell me you used to have a small moustache.'

'Look, I was never a Nazi but, for a while, I was a detective in the security service of the SS. I honestly didn't have much choice about it. Luckily I wasn't stationed here in Greece. But my war is not something I feel proud of. Which is why Christof Ganz isn't my real name. Things were difficult for me after the war. Changing my name was a quick way to a fresh start. Or at least that's what I hoped. I still have a lot of sleepless nights because of the war. And once or twice a bit more than just a sleepless night.'

'Meaning what, exactly?'

'There's an old Hungarian song called "Gloomy Sunday" that was banned by the Nazis. Goebbels thought it was bad for morale. So did the Hungarians. It was even banned by the BBC because it's been blamed for more suicides than any other song in history. But the fact is that despite Goebbels forbidding it, I used to like that song. Lots of men in uniform liked that song. You might say the song performed a useful service because some of those men aren't around anymore, if you know what I mean. But I almost wasn't around myself.'

'All right. You feel bad about it. Maybe you even feel guilty. I get that. Lots of people feel guilty about what happened during the war. Even a few Greeks. What of it? Why are you telling me and not your psychiatrist?'

'Let me finish my own horrible story. Then you can judge me. I joined the Berlin police not long after the Great War. The first war, that is. There was nothing great about it except perhaps the extraordinary numbers of men who fought and died. Millions. For four years I woke up every morning with the smell of death in my nostrils. Do you have any idea what that's like? Let me tell you, the amazing thing is not that so many of your comrades die, but the fact that you get used to it. Death becomes something routine. Every man who came out of the trenches was like that. Some were finished forever as human beings, their nerves shot to pieces. Others were angry and wanted to blame someone for what had happened – communists, fascists, Jews, the French, anyone. Me, I wasn't angry, but I needed to do something useful with my life. In spite of everything I'd seen in the trenches, I still believed in law and order and, yes, justice. What kind of a cop doesn't believe in that? So when people were murdered, we tried to do something about it, you know, like investigate the crime and then arrest the man who did it. That was the contract we made with the people who employed us. We protected them and when I did that, being a detective felt like something decent and good. For a long time I had a sense of pride in myself and life felt like it meant something. Well, most of the time. I had a few low spots along the way: 1928 wasn't such a good year.

'But then the Nazis came along and made nonsense out of all that, which was bad for me and bad for detectives everywhere in Germany. Because of that, it's been a long, long time since I had a chance to feel like I was on the side of anything clean and good. Too long, really. Most of the time I feel bad about myself. I don't expect you to know what that's like but I'm asking you to understand that this might be my last chance to do something about it. The fact is, I agree with Lieutenant Leventis. I want to help put a real criminal in the dock, instead of some damn Greek who was unlucky enough to speak fluent German and steal some office stationery. And I want to do it not for Leventis, not for the people of Greece, no, not even so I can get my passport back and go home; I've just realized I want to get Max Merten so that I can feel like I've done something good again. Perhaps for the last time I can feel like a real cop again. Redemption is a pretty grand idea for a Fritz like me, but that's what I'm after. So if you are after your own personal reckoning with Max Merten, I'd like to know now so I can be sure I don't get between you and your ladies' pocket pistol.'

Elli pulled up at the side of the mountain road and switched off the Rover's V8 engine. She kept a hold of the wheel for a while almost as if she didn't risk letting it go in case she hit me. Then she peeled off her gloves, reached for her handbag, took out her cigarettes, and lit one; after a couple of puffs she left it on her lip, fumbled around in her handbag some more, and this time when the hand came out again it was pointing the Beretta at me.

'So we can't all be good girls,' she said.

'You're joking.'

She thumbed back the hammer. 'Does it look like I'm joking?'

'Take it easy with that thing,' I said. 'At this range you could hardly miss.'

'Then you'd better bear that in mind. Get out of the car.'

I reached for the door; it was lucky for her she'd asked me nicely. I stood there dumbly for a minute with my hands in the air while she stepped out of the Rover on her side. Sometimes it feels bad to be proved right. The sea was at Elli's back; at least it was if you'd climbed down a series of jagged rocks. You could hear the waves and smell the salt in the air and the sun on my face felt like a small atom bomb; if it hadn't been for the little gun in her hand I'd have said it was an excellent place for a picnic.

'I have to hand it to you, sugar. You picked a nice spot. It's kind of romantic here.'

'Do I have your attention?'

'Undivided.'

'Good.'

'So what happens now?'

'Just this,' she said, and hurled the gun into the sea before coming around the car. 'Do you still think I'm planning to shoot you?'

I put down my hands and breathed a sigh of relief; people who think a shot from a ladies' gun won't necessarily kill you are almost right; but a little Beretta will fire six or seven in very quick succession and, close up, six or seven will kill you just as effectively as a single bullet from a 9-mill Luger.'

'Not unless you're an expert climber and a hell of a swimmer.'

Elli shook her head, then took my face in her hands and planted a big kiss on my mouth.

'Well, that's more like it,' I said, and was about to kiss her some more but she stopped me and said:

'No, listen. Until I met you I'd never even heard of Max Merten, okay? But if he's anything like you, he's so deaf I doubt he'll even hear you knock on his door. Like I told you already, that Beretta was for my own personal protection on account of how a lot of men don't listen when a woman tells them something important such as "No, I don't want to sleep with you," or "I carry a gun because I was nearly raped and I intend to make sure it doesn't happen again." Just like you, Merten probably won't be listening when you tell him to give himself up to the police, or try to arrest him. Although how you propose to do that I'm really not sure. But I'm certainly looking forward to seeing you try.'

'Me too. Especially now you've got rid of our only weapon. I was counting on you backing me up with your little pistol if we found ourselves in a tight spot.'

Elli frowned. 'I thought you said you were afraid I was going to shoot you.'

'Not really,' I lied. 'Like you said, why would you want to shoot me? No, I just wanted to see if you still had it with you.'

She managed to contain her momentary irritation with me and the loss of her Beretta. She had my sympathy, too; I always liked the little ladies' pistol and often a lot more than the ladies who carried one.

'So, Christof Ganz, what's your real name? And please don't tell me it's Martin Bormann.'

'Bernie. Bernie Gunther.'

'Sure about that?'

'Pretty sure.'

'I really don't know what you're going to say next. I think that you just might be the most unpredictable man I've ever met. *Bernie*. And, on occasion, quite the most infuriating, too. Maybe that's why I find you attractive. But, on reflection, I should have shot you when I had the chance. *Bernie*.'

'You know, a lot of people have said that, and somehow I'm still here.'

'They must have liked your sense of humour as much as I do. But I shall miss having that little gun.'

'I'll buy you another, for Christmas.'

CHAPTER 47

We parked the Rover in Kosta and then travelled by water taxi
to Spetses, a journey that took all of ten minutes. I wanted to
leave Max Merten with the impression that we were escaping the
island by the skin of our teeth, so I paid the boatman approximately five times the going rate on the understanding that
he would be waiting on the quayside before six the following
morning for the return trip to the mainland. It was a beautiful
island and I was sorry not to stay longer, especially with Elli, who
told me she'd been to the island several times before because,
in summer, it was a popular bathing resort much frequented
by Athenians, which was also why there was a first-class hotel
on the island, the Poseidonian, with a hundred beds and a good
restaurant, which had recently opened again after being closed
for the winter. We checked in, and while I kept a low profile by
staying in the room – I hardly wanted to run into Max Merten
on the street – Elli went out to buy a little flashlight and to
reconnoitre the address Spiros Reppas had given us.

'I walked past the house several times in case anyone was

watching, the way you told me,' said Elli, while, later on, we ate a dinner that might have been described as typically Greek except that it was good. 'It's a small fisherman's cottage with two floors, and more or less typical of the houses on the island. A little dilapidated. The curtains were drawn and no one went in and no one came out, but there was wood smoke coming out of the chimney and there was a light burning in one of the bedrooms. By the way, I'm certain it's someone German in there.'

'How did you work that out?'

'Because there was a washing line in the little front garden, and one of the shirts still drying on it had a German label, from somewhere called C&A.'

'That was smart of you.'

'Don't worry, I didn't actually go in the garden, I just leaned over the front wall and took a quick look. It was quite a large shirt, too. You said Merten is fat? The collar on the shirt was a size forty-five. And not well-washed either; there was still grime on the inside of the collar, like he'd forgotten to take a bar of soap and a stiff brush to it, the way you're supposed to. My guess is that it's a man who's living alone because there's also a burned saucepan left out on the kitchen step. A man like you, probably. And then there's the fact that a woman would have remembered to take in the washing. A woman like me, perhaps.'

'You're very observant. And you saw all this in the dark?'

'There's a small bar opposite, which was closing up, but all the lights were on.'

'Anyone suspicious hanging around?'

'Only me.'

'Were you seen near the cottage?'

'No. I got a couple of comments on the seafront, but any girl expects that in Greece.'

'You're not any girl. Not in my eyes. If Paris was here now he'd sling you across his shoulder and leg it for the ships.'

'You need to get out more.'

'Take the compliment. Please. Was there anyone suspicious in the town? Anyone like me?'

'You mean any Germans? No.' She sipped at a glass of white wine and then frowned, but not because of the taste; it was a good Mosel we were drinking. 'I wish I knew what you're going to do. I expect you want me to stay here in the hotel safely out of the way. Well, try and get it through your square German head, I'm not going to do that. Not now that I've come all this way. I'm in this until the end.'

'I didn't see it happening any other way.'

'Besides, it's the only way I can be sure of killing you both with my spare gun. Brunner, too, if he should decide to put in an appearance while we're there.'

'Another present from your father, no doubt.'

'I was never one for playing with dolls.'

'Just make sure you shoot to kill, sugar. Brunner's not the type you can only wound.'

'Of course. There's no other way with a rat like that. But just for the record, *schnucki*, I shall regret having to shoot you. *Schnucki*. Did I say that right?'

'Sure. By the way, your German is much improved.'

'I've a good teacher. Shame I'll have to end the lessons, and so abruptly, too. What does it mean anyway? *Schnucki.*'

'It doesn't mean anything very much except that you don't want to shoot me, *schnucki*. It's generally held to be a term of affection.'

We went to bed and after a few hours we got up early, very early, which is to say at the kind of uncivilized hour the Gestapo – and you don't get more uncivilized than them – used to favour when they decided to make an arrest, because experience had demonstrated that people put up less resistance to the police when they're still fast asleep.

Leaving the Poseidonian Hotel we walked through the necropolis-like white town and along a narrow street and then up a steep hill to the address Elli had already reconnoitred. The front of the grey cottage belonging to Reppas was covered with a lot of bright blue tiles and on top of the twin gate pedestals were a couple of crouching stone lions painted yellow; it looked like a cut-price Ishtar Gate. There were no lights and the shirt with the German label was still hanging motionless on the line where Max Merten had left it, as described by Elli. Behind the gatepost was a cardboard box containing several empty schnapps bottles, which led me to suppose that Merten hadn't been entirely wasting his time on the island.

As soon as I opened the front door with the key Spiros Reppas had given me and I moved the flashlight around a bit I knew for sure Merten was living there. The place was pungent with the smell of the same distinctive Egyptian-style Fina cigarettes Merten had been smoking back in Munich. There was a copy of an old German magazine called *Capital* on the floor by the sofa and a half-empty bottle of Schladerer on the coffee table. There was a hat and an overcoat with Munich labels lying on the sofa, but no gun in the pocket. On the wall was a picture of King Paul, and a framed Imray chart of Greece and its islands. There was plenty of light through the window – enough to conduct a search of the place – and I whispered to Elli to look around for the Walther automatic that Spiros Reppas had mentioned back in Athens; then I headed for the carpeted stairs. Every step was furnished with a pile of books, as if the cottage belonged to a keen reader who didn't own any shelves; most of the books were cheap paperbacks, crime novels and thrillers by English and American writers for whom choosing a red wine with fish was probably the kind of clue that would reveal the socially maladroit murderer's identity to the very clever detective. I wondered if any of them had advice on how to approach a sleeping man with a gun. I placed my foot on the first step and tested it for sound with my weight. The wooden step stayed silent so I tried another; and then another, until I was at the top of the stairs with my heart in my mouth. I turned and looked down and saw Elli standing there looking up at me; she shook her head as if to say *No gun,* and I nodded back and prepared to open one of the bedroom doors in the knowledge that Merten probably had the gun on the bedside table; that was certainly where I would have left mine if Alois Brunner had been looking for me. And you didn't have to be much of a shot with a Walther to hit someone coming through your bedroom door. A three-legged cat could have made a shot like that.

The master bedroom was empty, but had recently been occupied by Spiros Reppas; there was a picture of him and Witzel on the bedside table and, on the wall, a small icon and a photograph of the *Doris*. The bathroom door was open, which left only one other room; that door was closed but, on the other side, I could hear a man snoring as loudly as an angry rhinoceros. So far everything was much as I'd imagined in my mind's eye. I told myself the Webley would only have slowed me down: with the gun in one hand and the flashlight in the other, I'd have needed a third hand to grab hold of Merten's Walther before he could use it. Taking a sleeping man alive when you also take a gun has its pitfalls and I hoped he'd had enough schnapps from his bottle to slow him down even more than deep sleep.

I turned the loose doorknob and pushed firmly on through the deafening sound of the creaking hinge and my own heavy breathing, until I could see Merten's body lying on its side in the bed. How he didn't wake up I didn't know. Possibly the racket caused by his own snoring was louder than any commotion I could have made. A Panzer tank would have made less noise. At this point I might have hit him on the head with something hard to stun him while I searched for the gun but I wanted to avoid this if I could, if only because transporting a man with a head injury back to Athens might prove to be difficult. I pointed the beam from the flashlight at the bedside table, where there was a light without a shade, a copy of a novel by Ian Fleming, a pair of spectacles, a glass of something stronger than water, and, ominously, an open box of 9-millimetre ammunition.

Still looking for the gun I bent carefully over Merten's head;

his loud snoring smelled strongly of cigarettes and schnapps, while his rotund body was sour with the smell of sweat. From the way his hand was under the pillow I concluded that it was probably holding the Walther, which also meant that unless he was very nervous indeed, or just foolhardy, the safety catch had to be on. The safety on a Walther was usually stiff and might give me another vital second if we had to wrestle for it. I considered rolling him out of bed unceremoniously, and then rejected the idea, thinking he might still be holding the gun when he hit the floor on the other side of the bed. I was considering my next option when the naked man stirred, let out a loud grunt, and turned onto his other side, and I caught a glimpse of something black under the pillow. As the snoring resumed I reached for the object quickly, and came up with a leather-bound New Testament, as if he'd been reading it before or after reading the copy of *Casino Royale*. I wondered if perhaps there was a useful text in there for the spiritual guidance of someone who had helped to engineer the deaths of sixty thousand Jews after robbing them blind. My father, an enthusiastic Nazi but all his life a churchgoing man, could probably have told me what it was.

I stepped back from the bed and glanced quickly around the malodorous room and this time I spotted the Walther on a table by the window, next to another bottle of Schladerer and a packet of Finas. With some relief I fetched the gun, checked the safety, and dropped it into my jacket pocket. Sweeping the table with the flashlight I also found Merten's passport and some ferry tickets as far as Istanbul, and from there, a first-class ticket aboard the Orient Express to Germany. From the dates on the tickets, Merten would have been back home in Munich in just a few days. I pocketed these, too, thinking I might use them myself if things got desperate. Feeling a little more relaxed, I switched on the overhead light, helped myself to a drink and a cigarette, sat down in the room's only armchair and while I waited for the sleeping man to stir under the glare of the bare bulb, I glanced over his passport; Merten was only forty-six but looked ten years older. Not much of a testament to a complete lack of conscience, I thought. After a minute he groaned a bit, sat up, yawned, belched, rubbed his bloodshot eyes, and frowned at me blearily. He looked like a crapulous Buddha.

'Gunther,' he said, scratching his pendulous breasts and large belly. 'What the hell are you doing here?'

CHAPTER 48

'I'm the man Munich RE sent down to Athens to investigate Siegfried Witzel's insurance claim for the *Doris*.'

'I see. Well, no, I don't actually. You're not a marine-insurance man. You don't know one end of a ship from another. Why you, Bernie?'

'Neff, the regular marine-claims adjuster, went sick, and Alois Alzheimer asked me to step into his boat shoes. Although frankly I could wish I hadn't.'

Merten coughed for several seconds, tapped his chest, and then pointed at the packet of Finas. 'Cigarettes,' he said, trying to catch his breath.

I tossed them onto the bed, followed by a book of matches.

Merten lit one and smoked it gratefully. 'I would say it's good to see you again, but then again maybe it isn't. At this hour I get the feeling you're here to do more than adjust an insurance claim. Come now, Bernie. You have to admit it looks very odd.'

'Look, Max, there's not much time so you'd better listen

carefully. Meanwhile I strongly suggest that you get dressed because we have to leave the island as soon as possible.'

'Leave? You're joking.'

'I wish I was.'

'You'll forgive me if I ask, why? Why would I want to leave?' He exhaled a cloud of smoke and waved his hand at the barely finished room. 'I'm on holiday and in spite of any evidence to the contrary I'm enjoying myself here.'

'It's your neck. Well, to cut a long story short, since arriving in Greece I've learned what you and your friends were up to. Spiros Reppas told me about the Jewish gold from Salonika, including the fact that since the *Doris* went down off the Peloponnesian coast he and you had been lying low here, on this island.'

'Now why would Spiros say something as fanciful as that?'

'Because his boss, Siegfried Witzel, is dead and I guess Spiros felt he had nothing much to lose in telling me. Someone put a bullet through each of Witzel's eyes.'

'Oh.'

'For a while a local cop thought I did it – me being a fellow German and all. Cops like things to be tidy that way – one German murders another German. They were almost right; however, it was your old pal Alois Brunner who shot Witzel, but only after torturing him for several hours. You won't believe what a man's feet smell like after they've been held to the fire, like Cortés did to that poor Aztec king, Cuauhtémoc. It's amazing how cruel a man can be when there's a lot of gold involved.'

I was laying it on a bit to try to scare Merten.

'I was on my way to see Spiros again – we were planning to come here last night, as a matter of fact; I'd agreed to help you out for old time's sake, but luckily for me, I saw Brunner and a couple of his thugs arriving at the house near the Acropolis and so I made a hasty withdrawal before they saw me. Of course, that wasn't so lucky for Spiros and I expect Brunner's not far behind now.'

'I see. When was this?'

'Three or four hours ago.'

Merten glanced at his wristwatch and nodded thoughtfully. Then he got up slowly, fetched his trousers off the floor, and put them on. He nodded at my sling. 'It seems as if you've been in the wars yourself, Bernie. What's wrong with your arm?'

'A three-headed dog bit me on my way here. But it's nothing compared to what Brunner will do to us both, probably. That lawyer whose office in Glyfada you had burgled – Samuel Frizis – Brunner murdered him, too. Look, Max, I'm sure I don't have to remind you just how dangerous Brunner can be. The man's a killer and a sadist. So we need to get a move on.'

Merten remained cool, however, and continued to move at a snail's pace. 'He does have a most violent temper.'

'I can't say that I blame him where you're concerned. Spiros told me the whole story. I'm here for old times' sake, to get you safely off this island. After that I figure your best chance of staying alive is to seek the protection of the Athens police. Luckily for you I have a good contact there, a Lieutenant Leventis. He's the cop I told you about, the one who fancied me for Siegfried Witzel's murder. Those handcuffs will still fit me if he can't find anyone else for it, however, it's Brunner he wants for those two murders, if he can get him. I think it would be a real bonus for Leventis if he were to arrive here on Spetses and catch Brunner red-handed, so to speak. The red being your blood, Max. That kind of forensic evidence is a lot easier to stand up in court than some old war crimes. Finding witnesses to what Brunner did to some Jews in Salonika fourteen years ago wouldn't be so easy. Of course, we'll have to find a better reason for you seeking the protection of the Greek police than the fact that Alois Brunner is trying to kill you. That would draw attention to what you've been doing here.'

'What kind of reason? I don't understand. Even supposing I wanted protection from Brunner – and I'm not saying I do – how could I get protection without telling this cop exactly why he's trying to kill me?'

'It occurred to me that you might offer to be a witness yourself, on behalf of Arthur Meissner, the translator who's currently on trial in Athens for all the things Brunner and Eichmann probably did. You can tell Leventis that you were so moved by the plight of your old colleague Meissner that you came to Athens to give evidence on his behalf, but that you were also concerned that doing so might expose you to some danger from Greeks who don't like Germans, and there are certainly plenty of those.'

'Is everything all right?' said Elli.

'Who's that?' asked Merten.

'A friend. The girl who drove me here. My left arm isn't equal to much driving now.'

I went to the top of the stair and found her looking up at me anxiously.

'Yes, everything's fine. We'll be down in just a few moments.'

CHAPTER 49

Back in the bedroom Merten was shaking his head.

'Walk into a Greek court of my own free will?' he said. 'I don't know. Lawyers hate going into court, you should know that. Suppose they find some pretext to arrest me? Never can tell with the Greeks. Look at the way they screwed Socrates.'

'Why would they? You're not wanted by the Greek police for anything that happened in 1943. I already checked. You're in the clear. It's those bastards Brunner and Eichmann they want, not you. And what better proof of your innocence than making yourself a volunteer witness in Meissner's defence?'

'Yes, I do see that.' Merten extinguished his cigarette in an ashtray and lit another. 'By the way, whatever rubbish Spiros Reppas might have told you, Bernie, I had nothing to do with what happened to those Jews. Just for the record, it was all Brunner's idea. To trick them into giving up their wealth. By the time I heard about that gold, it was already too late for those people. They were on the trains to Auschwitz and Treblinka.' He sighed. 'Brunner – I never met a man who was so set on getting Jews deported.'

'Like I said, it was a long time ago. And none of my business.'

'I just wanted you to know, since you're trying to help me. For which I am very grateful.' He took a puff of his cigarette and shrugged. 'Why *are* you helping me? I'm still not a hundred per cent clear about that either.'

'You helped me, didn't you? Got me the job with MRE. Now that I'm down here it would seem ungrateful not to help you, Max.'

'Well, when you put it like that. I always did like you, Bernie.' Merten nodded; he put on an undershirt, glanced around the room, and frowned. 'Now where did I leave that clean shirt?'

'It's outside. On the washing line.' I looked at my watch as if Brunner really was on our tail. I'd almost managed to convince myself that he really had captured Spiros Reppas and was squeezing him for information back at the house beside the Acropolis. My plan was to drive Merten back to Athens and, once there, to persuade Lieutenant Leventis that while Max Merten wasn't Alois Brunner he was the next best thing; betraying Merten seemed to be my best option for getting my passport back and, along the way, delivering up a criminal to well-deserved justice. It was the right thing to do and yet – and yet there was something about this deception that left a sour taste in my mouth. 'You need to hurry, Max. The sooner we're off this island, the better. There's a boat waiting for us on the quayside, to take us to Kosta, where I have a car.'

'Yes, of course.' Merten sat down to put on his stinky socks and then his shoes. 'You say we have a three- or four-hour start on Brunner? Since he got hold of Spiros?'

'That's right.'

'That might be a lot less if Spiros talks right away. Think about it. Why would he stay silent if Brunner puts his feet to the fire, like that poor Aztec, Cuauhtémoc.'

'While poor Spiros might easily say where you've been hiding, Max, he can hardly tell him what Brunner probably wants to know most of all, which is the true location of the *Epeius*, and the gold. Spiros told me that only you knew where it was – that you kept the location a secret even from him and Witzel – but I can't imagine a man like Brunner will believe that story, not for a minute. Which, like I say, and unfortunately for Spiros, ought to slow Brunner down just long enough for us to put some distance between him and us.'

'Yes, that makes sense. Bad enough to be tortured, but to be tortured for something you don't actually know. Jesus.' Merten pulled a face. 'It doesn't bear thinking of, does it?'

'Then don't think about it. That should be easy for you, Max. You don't strike me as a man much troubled by conscience. But there's no time for any more delay. I'd hate it if my theory about Spiros proved to be wrong. Being here now I'm in as much danger as you are. And so is the friend I have who's waiting downstairs. She's going to drive us straight to Athens. Her name is Elli.'

'Short for Elisabeth, no doubt. I can't wait to meet her.'

'So finish dressing and come downstairs.'

'You know, I really appreciate you helping me like this. You were always a good man in a tight spot. Especially now that you have my gun, not to mention my tickets home. If you need a ticket home, Bernie, you only have to ask. I've more than enough money to buy you a ticket, too. In gratitude for saving my neck. Again.'

'That would be the money you and Schramma stole from General Heinkel in Munich, wouldn't it? Money you needed to fund this expedition.'

'That money was given to the general by the communists, with the intention of compromising West German politics. Money that was probably stolen from the proletariat they purport to represent. So I'm not much troubled about the origins of that money. Anyway, what do you care?'

'What I care about was the way you let me talk you into keeping it, Max. The way I was supposed to be the stooge meant to take the blame. Did you plan that, too?'

'Don't be so melodramatic, Bernie. Of course not. And I certainly didn't ask Schramma to kill the general and the other Fritz who was with him. That was his own stupid idea. You know if only we'd met again sooner I could have cut you in on this instead of Christian Schramma. I never did feel comfortable with that man. There's something about Bavarians I realize I just don't like, especially now I live there. I sometimes wonder if any of us will ever get back to Berlin.'

'Not while the Russians are drinking our beer.'

'But look, let's forget all that unpleasantness. Munich and its complacent, middle-class Catholic values are a long way away. You and I, Bernie – we're both Berliners, you and I, and that makes all the difference, doesn't it? We're old comrades, *Bolle* boys, right? So we should be straight with each other. So why don't we just forget all this nonsense about Arthur Meissner and this Lieutenant Leventis and let's talk about the real reason you came here to help me. Let's talk about that, shall we?'

Merten was wagging his finger at me with a grin on his face that made me want to slap it onto the floor.

'You want a share, don't you? Of the gold. Of course you do. And why not? Have you any idea how much is down there, in just fifteen fathoms of water? Hundreds of millions of dollars' worth. Spiros and Witzel couldn't have told you how much, because even they had no conception of even half of what's there. Not in their wildest dreams. There's enough gold to keep us in tax-free, mink-lined luxury for the rest of our lives. Think of it. More gold than Cortés and his conquistadors could even dream of. Free of income tax, Bernie, free of any tax. And it's ours. All we have to do is go and get it. After which we can go and live on an island in the Caribbean. Buy one, perhaps. One each. Or go our separate ways, as you prefer.'

Merten took a drag on his cigarette and then used it to light another. 'All right, it's a deal,' he said, not waiting for my answer; his assumption that I was as greedy as Witzel or Schramma bothered me. But it bothered me more that I even paused to consider what he'd said. 'So I'll cut you in for twenty-five per cent. That's fair, given that all of the expenses have been mine. Also I have partners in Bonn I need to pay off. Politicians I owe favours to. But look here, instead of driving to Athens, we should head north, to Alexandroúpoli, and cross over into Turkey. Then, one day, in the not-so-distant future, when Alois Brunner has given up looking for me, we can come back down here, charter a ship, and make another attempt to retrieve the gold. I can assure you it's quite safe where it is. Safer than in any Greek bank. After all these years another few months won't make any difference.'

I shook my head but I can't say I wasn't tempted. Becoming very rich has its attractions for someone with nothing in the bank, not even a bank account. 'No thanks, Max.'

'What do you mean, no thanks? Are you mad? Don't you want to be as rich as the Count of Monte Cristo? Richer.'

'Not really. Not while I still have a conscience. That money is covered with the blood of sixty thousand dead Jews. My mind would be on them every time I bought myself another Caribbean island.'

'Think about what you're saying for a moment, Bernie. Are you seriously suggesting we just leave the gold there for the fishes to enjoy?'

'So maybe you should tell someone about it. Maybe even hand it over to the Greek government so they could return it to the Jews. Besides, all your partners have an unfortunate habit of finding themselves double-crossed, or dead. I'd rather take my chances with the Greek police than go on a sea voyage with you. Frankly I wouldn't trust you on a rowing boat in the Tiergarten. Lieutenant Leventis has my passport in his desk drawer. That's all I need now. You can come back here and go diving for gold another time, and with someone else. Me, I just want to go home. Thanks to you I have a nice respectable job, a salary. I even have a company car. That and a good night's sleep are worth all the sunken treasure there is.'

'For old times' sake I'll make it thirty per cent.'

'Look, forget about the gold for now and let's get going.'

'Do you honestly think that those Jews would ever see a penny of that money if we just handed it over to the Greek government, or ours?' Merten uttered a scornful laugh. 'No, of course not. The governments and the banks are the biggest robbers on the damn planet. They steal from people every day, only they call it taxation. Or interest on a mortgage. Or a fine imposed by a court. This new EEC they've made is just another way of robbing us all with yet more taxation and fines in the name of peace and prosperity. And those Jews, how the hell do you think they got all that gold in the first place? From lending money. By robbing us. By being bankers in their turn.'

'I'm afraid all that sounds very cynical, Max. But I guess I'm not surprised. You're a lawyer, after all.'

'You're not an educated man, Bernie. Are you? I mean you got your *Abitur*, but you never went to university. If you had, then you'd know it's intellectually respectable to be cynical. It's the only way you can see the lies for what they are. Unless you're cynical about things you might as well give up on life. You think I'm cynical? I'm an amateur by comparison with what governments do. These respectable men – our leaders – are the same leaders, the same men who just made a war in which fifty million people died. It's never the cynical men who start wars but the virtuous, principled ones. Adenauer, Karamanlis, Eisenhower, and Eden, the leaders of the free world, but it's the same old lie called democracy.'

'There was nothing virtuous about Hitler.'

'Yes, but it was Neville Chamberlain who declared war on Germany, wasn't it? Kind of makes my point.'

'Nice idea, Max. But still, thanks but no thanks.'

'I've misjudged you, Bernie. After everything that's happened to you is it possible you still believe in good? That you think there's some morality in this lousy world? Experience should have taught you by now that good simply doesn't exist, old friend. Not for you, not for anyone, but I have to say especially not for you. People are generally wasting their time if they think they can overcome evil. It's nonsense. In this world there is nearly always only evil and degrees of evil. Any good that exists results only when an organism such as a human being like you or me acts in his own self-interest out of biological necessity. That's how things prosper and survive. By looking out for number one. That's certainly been true for you.'

'I don't believe that,' I said, now feeling a sense of disquiet at a vague suspicion I had that there was something in what he'd said. Wasn't I selling him to the Greeks out of my own self-interest? 'I can't ever believe that.'

'Pity. You know, your conscience won't bring any of those dead Jews back, Bernie. Most of those poor devils from Salonika don't have any families to whom one could return the money, even if one wanted to. Brunner and Eichmann and others like them made absolutely sure of that. They're all gone; any of the ones who survived have good reason to lie low themselves, out of shame. The only Jews who survived were the ones who did something crummy to bring that situation about. And it's not like you or I killed those people. They're just numbers now. Statistics in a history book. Emaciated faces on an old black-and-white newsreel. Poor Jew stories in *Life* magazine.

What happened happened but it's over now. No sense crying about it.'

Max Merten smiled a decayed smile, which served to remind me of just how rotten his soul was. Among all Merten's rotten teeth his single gold incisor resembled a tiny nugget found in the dirt on some grizzled Klondike prospector's pan and, in his brutally cynical mouth, gold couldn't have seemed less precious.

CHAPTER 50

Thanks to Elli, life seemed as if it was a bit more worthwhile, especially now I'd eliminated my earlier suspicion that she was pursuing her own secret agenda. Even after the incident with the Beretta she continued to show every sign that she was a little stuck on me and I now realized, like a very stupid dog, that I liked her, too, although not as much perhaps. In truth I still couldn't understand why she was attracted to me but I'd stopped worrying about it. Looking a gift horse in the mouth never looked so pointless. She made me feel good again, the way you felt when you'd tanked up on schnapps, like you felt when a beggar blessed you for giving him money or when you were in church and you thought there was just a smidgen of a chance that God was actually there. With her around there was a bit more room for optimism. This wasn't to say that I saw a real future with her but I could at least see a future for myself. For the first time in a long time it felt like I had a friend; maybe a bit more than just a friend. And to think I'd almost chased her off with my paranoid suspicions. Even as I caught her eye she smiled back at me, as if wondering why I was smiling so warmly at her. I was never much of a smiler.

'What?' she said.

'No, it's nothing.'

'You're laughing at me.'

'No. Really. I'm not.' But for the benefit of the large German in the backseat of the Rover I added a moderating lie: 'I'm just pleased to have got off that island before Brunner could catch up with us.'

'Oh, him,' she said, as if that name was of no account and, for the first time since speaking to the bandit queen, I wondered where Brunner was. Still hiding out in Athens, perhaps. Or back in West Germany. Or possibly in Egypt, working for Nasser, at the behest of Germany's intelligence service. But wherever he was I judged him still a threat.

'Yes, him. That's why we're in a hurry, sugar.'

'I hope I never see that man again,' admitted Merten. 'I once saw Brunner shoot a man on a train because he asked him for a drink of water.'

'This would be the train from Salonika to Athens. In 1943.'

'Yes. How did you know?'

'And the victim was a banker called Jaco Kapantzi. Brunner shot him through the eyes. Same as poor Siegfried Witzel and that Greek lawyer you fingered. I told you. For that murder alone Brunner is a wanted man in Greece.'

Elli shivered. 'He scares me.'

'He scares me, too, sugar.'

She held out her hand and to reassure her that everything would turn out all right, I took it and squeezed it affectionately.

As soon as I'd done it – done it in front of Merten, that is – I realized I'd made a mistake.

We were on the road north, back to Athens, and making good time; I estimated we'd be back in the capital city before lunchtime, but before we arrived I planned to make a telephone call when we stopped for gas – to the Megaron Pappoudof, to warn Lieutenant Leventis that I was bringing in Max Merten. For the German's sake I didn't want him arrested, at least not right away; I wanted to make it clear to Leventis that Merten was handing himself in as a witness in the trial of Arthur Meissner; that would be something in his favour when the Greeks charged him with war crimes.

'This is a nice car, Christof,' said Merten.

'It's a rental,' I said. 'And by the way, Elli knows my real name. She even knows I was in the SS.'

'That was brave of you. Telling her.'

'Not really.'

'British, isn't it? The car, I mean.'

'Yes. A Rover.'

'How romantic. Their cars have names and our cars have numbers. It's good. But not as good as a Mercedes-Benz. Nothing is as good as a Mercedes-Benz.' He sighed. 'Sometimes I wonder how we ever lost the war. I mean we make the best cars, the best washing machines, the best radios. The British might have won the war but there's no doubt that they're already losing the peace. In ten years from now they'll be eating our dust and you won't be able to find a British car anywhere in Greece. With this new EEC, Germany can be what it was always meant to be:

the undisputed master of Europe. You have to hand it to the Old Man. He's done what Hitler could never have done. In fifty years Britain and France will be asking our permission to go to the bathroom. We'll make the French pay, too. A franc just to take a piss.'

'You're more of a Nazi than I thought,' I said.

'That's not Nazism. That's just capitalism.'

'What's the difference?'

'If you genuinely believe that, then you're more of a lefty than I thought.'

'Temperamentally, perhaps. But not at the ballot box.'

'Poor Bernie. As if voting ever changed anything.' Merten lit another cigarette. 'So, Elli. May I call you Elli?'

'Yes.'

'Short for Elisabeth?'

'Yes.'

'How did you meet Bernie Gunther?'

'I picked him up in a bar,' she said. 'In Athens.'

'Which one?'

'The Mega Hotel bar. I went there to have a meeting with someone else. And saw him looking miserable, so I decided to cheer him up.'

'I'd say you succeeded.'

'So would I.'

'And where did you learn German, Elli?' asked Merten.

'From my father. He worked for North-German Lloyd. The shipping company. Before the war he was the chief officer on the SS *Bremen*.'

'You speak it very well.'

'I'm getting better since I met Bernie.'

'Yes, there's a lot you can learn from Bernie. I don't know what kind of a teacher he is, but he's a good man in a tight spot. It's thanks to him that I came through the war with nothing very much on my conscience.'

For the sake of a peaceful drive back to Athens I let that one go. But did he really believe that?

'Wait,' said Merten. 'Didn't the *Bremen* catch fire?'

'Yes,' said Elli. 'It sank. In 1941.'

'I was stationed in Bremen in 1941 and I seem to remember there was some talk of negligence on the part of the captain.'

'I don't remember that,' she said, bristling a little. 'But my father wasn't the captain. He was the chief officer, like I said.'

'What was his name?'

'Panatoniou. Agamemnon Panatoniou. Why?'

'I'm just curious.' Merten puffed his cigarette and, irritably, Elli wound down her window. 'That's one of the things I love about Greece,' he said. 'I mean here I am, being driven by Agamemnon's daughter. And the woman who came to clean at the house in Spetses – her name was Electra. Like something out of Homer, isn't it, Bernie?'

'Yes.'

'You shouldn't smoke so much, Herr Merten,' said Elli. 'It's not good for you.'

'You're right. But in Greece who would notice?'

'I notice,' she said. 'Because it's not good for me.'

'When you've lived through what Bernie and I lived through,

a small health hazard like a cigarette seems hardly worth worrying about. But you're right. I should cut down. For the sake of my family.'

That was the first time I'd heard Merten mention a family. Under other circumstances I might have asked him about them. But I didn't want to think about them; not now.

We stopped for gas in a small village called Sofiko, where I went into a bar and made the telephone call to leave a message for Lieutenant Leventis at police headquarters. A little to my surprise he was working on a Sunday.

'I thought you'd be in church,' I said.

'Whatever gave you that idea? No, I usually come in on a Sunday and catch up with some paperwork. What have you got for me, Commissar?'

I told him about Max Merten and the gold and its history, and how I was bringing him in so that he could be a volunteer witness in the defence of Arthur Meissner, and that I thought that this should count in his favour if Leventis decided to arrest him.

'He's not Brunner,' said Leventis. 'I wanted Alois Brunner. He's why I started this whole investigation. I told you before, Commissar. Jaco Kapantzi, the man he killed on the train, was a friend to my father. Plus he killed Witzel and he killed Samuel Frizis. Arresting Merten doesn't help my clear-up rate.'

'He's not Brunner, and he's not Eichmann, but perhaps, if you were a Jew in Salonika, Max Merten is the next best thing. He was Wehrmacht, not SS, but by all accounts they could do nothing without his say-so. Eichmann, Brunner, Wisliceny – they all had to go through him. That's what you wanted, isn't it?

Someone who was in charge of things who you can put on trial. A real Nazi war criminal and certainly someone who's a lot better than a mere translator.'

'Yes. I suppose you're right.'

'Only if I bring him you're to give him every chance. In other words, you're to give him the benefit of legal advice.'

'What? A German is telling me about a man's legal rights in Greece?'

'I'm talking about the rules of natural justice, that's all. I don't know, you Greeks probably invented them. What I mean is, this will be in the newspapers and it won't just be Max Merten you're putting on trial, it'll be Greece, too. Greece then. And Greece now. Believe me, I know what I'm talking about. Just look at the exemplary way the Allies handled those trials in Germany. Even the Russians looked like they were being fair. Besides, according to his own account, Max Merten witnessed Jaco Kapantzi's death on the train from Salonika. That means you have a useful witness if ever you do catch up with Alois Brunner.'

'True. All right. I agree. He'll get a lawyer and all his rights.'

'One more thing. All of this. Me playing Judas, and bringing this man in.'

'I get it. You want your thirty pieces of silver.'

'Just my passport. This gets me off the hook, right? Me *and* Garlopis.'

'If he's who you say he is, sure, Commissar. No problem. You bring him in and you can have your life back. If you can call it that now that you're an insurance man and no longer a detective, like me.'

Not so as you'd notice was what I felt like saying. But I'd been smart before with cops and they usually didn't like it. Cops never like it when people are smarter than them. It reminds them of how dumb they are. I'd been a dumb cop myself on several occasions when a case wasn't coming together and I didn't like it then either.

I left the bar, went back to the car, and paid for the gas. Merten wasn't there.

'Where is our friend?' I asked Elli.

She pointed across the deserted village square, festooned with Greek flags and filled with the smell of frying potatoes. In the distance I saw Merten sitting on a bench next to a bus stop with his valise on the dry ground beside him.

'What's he doing there?'

'I imagine he's waiting for a bus.'

'Did you two have words?'

'Not exactly. But I don't like him, Bernie.'

'Are you sure you didn't just tell him where to get off?'

'No, nothing of the sort. He just took his bag out of the trunk, said something in German that I didn't understand, and walked off without a word.'

'Did he now? What did he say?'

'One word. *Hündin*, I think. What does it mean, anyway?'

'Never mind.'

'I think he's changed his mind about coming back to Athens with us.'

'I think you're right. It looks like I am going to have to persuade him.'

'How?'

'I can be very persuasive when I want to be. Give me five minutes and then drive over to fetch us.'

I sat in the car for a moment, checked that Merten's Walther was loaded, tucked it into my sling where it couldn't be seen, and then went to have a quiet word with him. He didn't yet know it but he was about to exchange his future for mine.

CHAPTER 51

'Surely you're not leaving us, Max?'

Merten looked momentarily apologetic. 'Yes, I'm sorry about that. But I was afraid you'd think me very foolish and cowardly if I told you exactly why I was running out on you like this.'

'Try me.'

'It's what Goethe says, that's all: precaution is better than cure. When you mentioned Jaco Kapantzi's murder in the car back there I realized that under Greek law I might easily be charged as an accessory before and after the fact. Because I was there, on the train, as you now know. And I did nothing to prevent Alo Brunner from shooting that poor devil. Not that there was anything I could have done, of course. He'd have killed me, too, if I'd interfered. When Alo's blood is up, he's a fucking Fury. By the time I knew he was going to do it, he'd done it, if you see what I mean. Yes, he always was a bit crazy that way. Quick with a gun, or to hand out a beating. So I've decided to take my chances and go it alone. Don't think I'm not grateful to you for coming to fetch me off that island, Bernie.

I am. There's no telling what might happen if Alo ever does find me. The first time he showed up on the boat in Piraeus I thought he was going to shoot me then, only his appetite for a share of the gold held him back. But I don't much like the idea of walking into a Greek police station with my pants down. Think about it. Just for a minute, if you will. If the Greek state prosecutor is prepared to charge a damned interpreter with war crimes, then what chance is there for a German army captain to whom that interpreter sometimes reported? What's to stop Meissner from saying he was only obeying my orders? You see, Bernie, I remember Arthur Meissner very well. It was me who got him his houses in Athens and in Salonika. He's guilty only of being a bit greedy. A bit of larceny. That's not exactly a crime against humanity. Find me a Greek who hasn't got his fucking hand in the till, then and now. But somehow I can't see my evidence playing well in court. I can easily imagine myself in the dock instead of Meissner and I'm already thinking your cop's idea of protection might amount to the same kind as once practised by the Gestapo. A night in the cells that turns into something altogether more permanent. By the way, have you seen Greek prisons? They're almost as bad as the fucking hotels. The Grande Bretagne excepted, but then that's virtually the Adlon. No, it was a nice idea, Bernie, but I'm afraid it simply wouldn't work. They'd make jam out of me.'

'All right, Max. It's your funeral.'

'Don't worry about me, I can look after myself. I speak pretty good Greek. And I've more than enough money to get home to Ithaca. We'll see each other back in Munich, perhaps. I'll buy you a dinner at the Hofbräuhaus and we'll have a good laugh about this one day.'

'Maybe.'

'Sure we will. If you're good I'll even let you stroke the golden fleece.'

'Just out of interest, why did you call Elli a bitch?'

'For the simple reason that she is a bitch. At least as far as I'm concerned. You're too blind with love to see it. Haven't you noticed the way she looks at me? It's very different from the way she looks at you, my friend. Very different. She despises me.'

'What did you expect? It's not like you planned to build a Greek orphanage with that gold. You and Brunner stole it for yourselves. And bitch or not, you should be glad she came, Max. Without her I'm not sure my arm would have permitted me to drive down here to save your neck.'

'What a romantic fool you are, Bernie. They may have different faces, but all women are the same. I thought you'd understand that by now. For your sake, I hope she's worth it.'

Ignoring him, I took the ticket for the Orient Express out of my pocket, still hoping that I could get him back in the car with friendly persuasion – that my giving him his ticket might convince him that I was on the level.

'I suppose you'll be wanting this back.'

'Keep it. You use it. Now that I've thought about it some more, Istanbul might not be such a good idea for me. Italy probably suits me better. I can get a ferry to Brindisi from Corinth and then a train to Bari, where I know another good scuba diver. Fellow from the Decima Flottiglia MAS, who trained Siegfried

Witzel as a matter of fact. Of course, he's Italian, not German. But nobody's perfect.'

I believed very little of this; it was clear that Merten didn't trust me. I could see that in his eyes. And now that I looked at them more closely I could see that they resembled two old snails on the glass of a very green aquarium. Slow and slimy and inhuman. Not that I blamed him for not trusting me; anyone who'd double-crossed as many friends as Max Merten must have had a good nose for when he was about to be double-crossed himself. And if he was telling me he was bound for Brindisi and Bari then it was probably more likely he was going to try for the Orient Express after all. For a moment we stood there watching as Elli drove the car slowly toward us, smiling sheepishly at each other like two old friends now struck dumb by the uncomfortable realization that they weren't friends at all, not anymore and probably never had been.

Which meant there was no longer any reason not to pull the gun out of my sling and shove the business end up against the fat covering his ribs. Merten regarded the gun as if it had been ink on his shirt.

'Is that my gun? It certainly looks like it.'

'Get in the car,' I said. Ignoring the pain in my arm, I opened the rear door of the Rover, shoved Merten onto the backseat, threw his valise after him, and jumped in alongside them both. As soon as the car door was closed, Elli hit the accelerator. The Rover twisted a little on the gravel before gaining grip and then speed. Merten sat up, sighed loudly, and stared at the gun and then at me with something like pity, as if I was a tiresome schoolboy.

'I was wondering when you'd reveal your true hand, Bernie,' he said. 'And there it is. Holding a Bismarck on me. It's very disappointing.'

'That's good, coming from you,' I said. 'I wonder if your left hand even knows what the right is doing sometimes.'

'Well, then, we have something in common, you and I. Double-crossers both. What's the plan? Deliver me up to the Greek police and get your passport back?'

'Something like that.'

'Jesus Christ, you're selling yourself a bit short, aren't you? Just listen to yourself. A passport. If you'd thrown in with me you'd have been as rich as Croesus. Still could be, if you'd only listen to sense.'

'Your wealth comes at the kind of price I can't afford to pay.'

'"Thus conscience does make cowards of us all."'

'You excepted, it would seem, Max.'

Merten snorted with contempt. 'When did you start working for the war crimes office? Anyone would think you were a Jew yourself the way you keep mentioning them. Don't be so gloomy, Bernie. For a German you're very mixed up about all this. What do you care about the Greeks, or the Jews? Let them look after themselves. Me, I'm looking out for number one. Which reminds me, would you mind not pointing that thing at me. Greek roads aren't the best. If your lady friend hits a pothole, you might shoot me, accidentally.'

'And if I did, you'd probably deserve it.'

'What would happen to your passport then?'

Merten took out his foul Egyptian cigarettes and lit one, before adopting a very serious expression.

'Listen to me carefully, Bernie,' he said gravely. 'This foolishness can only end badly for us both. I can assure you that whatever moral high ground you think you're standing on here is nothing but quicksand. I'm warning you, as an old friend. The way you once warned me, back in '39. Let me go right now or you'll regret it. And very much sooner than you think.'

'You seem to forget that I'm holding the gun, Max.'

'And *you're* forgetting where you are. In the electric chair. With my hand on the switch. I can burn you to a stinking crisp in less than a minute, my friend.'

'I don't know what you think you've got on me, Max, but you're bluffing. Those Jews from Salonika deserve some justice and I'm going to make sure that they get it.'

'Justice? Don't make me laugh. Do you honestly think that the lives of sixty thousand Jews can be paid for so easily? Really, Bernie, you amaze me. Not just a romantic but an idealist, too. You're full of surprises today. There's no human justice that could ever be enough for what happened to those poor devils. And certainly none that could be got from my own humble person. So what you're proposing is absurd. Besides, I had absolutely nothing to do with their deaths. I was just a paper pusher. A bureaucrat.'

'But you were prepared to profit from it.'

'I certainly didn't hear the dead objecting to what I did. And they've certainly not troubled my conscience since. I told you. I can't afford to have one. No, it's Eichmann and Brunner who deserve to be on trial. Not me. I was just a humble army captain. Not even a footnote in history.'

'Perhaps. But you'll have to do for now.'

'What a prig you are. What a prig and what a fool.' Merten puffed his cigarette coolly, as if he didn't have a care in the world. 'Be sensible. Last chance. Let me go, Bernie. You'll regret it if you don't.'

'Just shut up and smoke your cigarette.'

'I tell you what I'm going to do,' he said calmly. 'I'm going to smoke this cigarette to the end. And then, when it's finished, if you haven't stopped this car and let me go on my own merry way, you'll be finished, too. You have my word on that.'

CHAPTER 52

Max Merten threw his cigarette out the car window and then wound it up again. He was smiling like a chess grand master who was about to make a winning move; like his witless opponent, I still couldn't see what this might be. But instead of saying anything, he stayed silent and closed his eyes for a long time and I supposed he must be asleep; when he opened them again we were only a few miles southwest of Athens.

'Almost there,' said Elli.

'Thanks for driving all this way,' I said. 'I couldn't have done it without you.'

'Sweet of you,' she said. 'I'm glad to be of help.'

'Well, isn't that nice?' said Merten. 'You know there are some men who find other people's romances touching. Not me. When I see this kind of thing I wonder if the two parties involved really know the truth about each other. Speaking as a lawyer, I can tell you that truth has been the ruin of many a good romance. No relationship and certainly no marriage can take too much of that. Mine couldn't.'

'Whatever you think you know,' said Elli, 'I don't want to hear it.'

'Let me tell you something about this sweet man seated behind you, Elisabeth,' he said softly.

'Don't bother treating me like a jury. I'm a lawyer myself and I know all a lawyer's tricks.'

'Oh, it's no bother.'

'As far as I can see, Mr Merten, you have only one advantage over me and it's that you never had to endure a car journey with Max Merten.'

'I know the real Bernie Gunther. That's one advantage.'

'The number of times I've heard people say they know the real me and what they actually knew was just the me they imagined I was. The longer I live the more I realize that no one knows anyone. So do yourself a favour and save your very unpleasant breath.'

'But you do like him, don't you?'

'Are you looking for an answer or an explanation?'

'An answer.'

'Yes. I like him.'

'Why?'

'Now you want an explanation. And I'm not obliged to give you one. Not obliged and certainly not inclined.'

'I've known this man for almost twenty years, Elisabeth. A man whose reputation around police headquarters in Berlin went before him during the thirties. For a lot of younger and impressionable men like myself Bernie Gunther wasn't just a successful detective, he was also something of a local hero.'

'I distinctly remember telling you I wasn't interested in anything you had to say.'

'You heard the lady, Max. Why don't you give it a rest?'

'Famously Bernie caught Gormann the strangler, a man who murdered many aspiring young film actresses. When were those Kuhlo murders – 1929? I'm not sure about that. But I think it was probably 1931 when Bernie joined the Nazi Party and became the Party's liaison officer in the Criminal Police, because it was definitely the following year when he helped to form the National Socialist Civil Service Society of the Berlin Police. Which means he was a die-hard Nazi even before Hitler came to power.'

'You know I was never a Nazi. Not even in my worst nightmare.'

'Oh, come on, Bernie. Don't be so bashful. Let me tell you, Elisabeth, this man was one of the first in the police department who had the courage to declare his hand, politically. And because he did, many others followed. Me included, although to be quite frank I only did it to advance my career; unlike Bernie I really wasn't much interested in politics and certainly not in persecuting Jews and communists. I'm not sure what he thinks about Jews but I'm quite sure Bernie hates the communists. Then, in the autumn of 1938, your friend here caught the eye of Heinrich Himmler's number two, Reinhard Heydrich. Heydrich was a slippery sort –'

'Almost as slippery as you, Max. You could spread this stuff on a field and it would grow two crops a year.'

'– the very embodiment of fascist evil and the architect of many atrocities, which is why later on they called *him* the Butcher of Prague. To be fair to Bernie I expect Heydrich saw someone he could use, the way he used many others. But it was Heydrich who promoted Bernie to the rank of commissar and until Heydrich's death, Bernie was his number one trouble-shooter; the joke around headquarters was that when Bernie saw trouble he usually shot it.'

As Merten laughed at his own joke I lifted my injured arm, grabbed him by the tie and twisted it, the way he was twisting the truth, but not enough to silence him.

'I'm beginning to see why Alo Brunner is so keen to kill you, Max. With a mouth like yours it's a wonder how you managed to stay alive for this long.'

Still talking quickly, Merten retreated along the leather seat, pressing himself into the corner.

'For example, in November 1938 it was rumoured he murdered a doctor by the name of Lanz Kindermann, because he was homosexual. The Nazis never liked homos all that much and Bernie was certainly no exception. But by then he was exceptional in one respect and that was in the amount of licence he seemed to enjoy from his pale-faced master, Heydrich, and so his crime went unpunished, as most real crimes did by then. The following year – a few months before war broke out – Bernie was even invited to Obersalzberg, to stay at Hitler's country house, the Berghof. It was Hitler's fiftieth birthday and a singular honour for anyone to be invited, let me tell you. Not many people could say as much unless they were very highly thought of. No one ever asked me there for the weekend.' Merten chuckled. 'Isn't that right, Bernie? You *were* the leader's houseguest, weren't you? Tell her.'

For a brief moment I considered trying to explain the real reason I'd been at the Berghof – to investigate a murder – but almost immediately I could see the futility of doing so. There was no way my being there could ever have been satisfactorily explained. So I did what any man would do when confronted with another's man barefaced lie. I laughed it off and lied straight back.

'Of course I wasn't there. It's absurd even to suggest such a thing. I have to hand it to you, Max. You must be quite a good trial lawyer. Next thing you'll be trying to persuade her that Hitler was my long-lost uncle.'

Elli laughed. 'Don't give him any ideas.'

'The story is actually just getting started. A couple of years later, in 1941, when Germany invaded the Soviet Union, many of Berlin's senior policemen were drafted into the SD, which was the intelligence agency of the SS, and that's how Bernie here came to be an SD captain in uniform, just like Alo Brunner. Tell me, old man, which part of *that* isn't true?'

'Shut up, Max. Shut up. I swear I'm going to crack you one with this gun if I have to listen to any more of this.'

I caught Elli's eye in her rearview mirror; what I saw didn't worry me that much. She was shaking her head as if she didn't believe him.

'I can see exactly what he's up to,' she said. 'He's a rat and like any rat he'll squeak when he's cornered.'

'Some rats need extermination,' I said, and pressed the muzzle of the Walther up against Merten's cheek.

'Go ahead and shoot,' said Merten. 'Do it. Put a bullet in my head. That's what you're good at, old man. You've had plenty of practice, after all. Better dead than doing life in a Greek jail.'

'I'm not going to shoot you, Max. But people can lose gold teeth for this kind of thing.'

'You mean for telling the truth? Surely this nice Greek girl deserves to know just what kind of man you really are.'

'Your version hasn't got much to do with truth, Max.'

'It's a long time since I was scared by a fairy story,' said Elli. 'Especially one told by some fat old Nazi.'

'Hey, less with the old,' said Merten. 'I may be putting on the pounds but I'm more than a decade younger than your friend here. Maybe you can convince her that you were a good German, Bernie, but I know better. Have you still got that SS tattoo under your arm or did you burn it off? What did you tell her it was? An old war wound?' Merten laughed.

'Light me a cigarette will you, Bernie?' she said.

I put a cigarette in my mouth, fired it up, and guided it between her lips.

'Thanks.'

A minute later we took a bend in the road a little too quickly, which had Merten sprawled onto my lap for a moment. I pushed him away roughly.

'There might be capital punishment in Greece, Bernie. But the Greeks don't much care for killing people. Unlike Germans. Germans like you, that is. Because this is where the story starts to become really unpleasant, Elli. I'm afraid I can't help that.'

'I wish you would shoot him, Bernie. It's what he deserves,

not just for stealing that gold but for being such a bore. I'm tired of listening to his voice. We should shoot him and throw his body in a ditch.'

'Then Bernie's your man, Elisabeth. Perhaps you already know something about the mass murders that took place in Russia and the Ukraine during the summer of 1941. Bernie had volunteered to join another senior policeman, his old Berlin friend Arthur Nebe, as part of a police battalion attached to what was called an SS *Einsatzgruppe*. This is not an easy thing to translate, my dear Elisabeth. It means the group was tasked with just one special action. Can you imagine what that was? Yes. That's right. I can see you've guessed it. There was only one sentence that those SS men were obliged to carry out: the sentence of death. In short, Einsatz Group B was a mobile death squad operating behind Army Group Centre, and tasked with the extermination of Jews and other undesirables such as communists, Gypsies, the disabled, mental retards, hostages, and generally speaking anyone they didn't much like, in order to terrorize the local population. They operated in and around Minsk, and were very successful. Nebe and Gunther here were good at mass murder and managed to fill enough mass graves to render that part of Ukraine Jew-free in double-quick time.'

'I didn't murder anyone in Minsk. But you have my word, Max, that I really don't mind killing you.'

'Why then you wouldn't get your precious passport back. Not that it's worth much since it's in a false name. Ask yourself why that should be the case, Elisabeth. How it is that I'm here with a passport in my real name, and Bernie has a passport in a false name? Anyone might conclude that he has more to hide than me. It might just have something to do with the fact that between July and November 1941, Group B managed to kill almost fifty thousand men, women, and children. *Fifty thousand.* Try to imagine what kind of men they were who could do such a thing, Elli. I've often tried myself and again and again I find myself without an answer. It's inexplicable.' Merten smiled. 'What's the matter, Bernie? Is the truth too much for you? I think it's getting to be too much for poor Elli.

'After the horrors of Minsk, Arthur Nebe and Bernie returned to Berlin and were both decorated for a job well done. Didn't Martin Bormann give you the Coburg Badge, Germany's highest civilian order, for services to Hitler? That must have been a proud moment. Bernie was even a guest at Heydrich's country house in Prague, a few weeks before his assassination. Again, quite an honour. Meanwhile Nebe and Bernie resumed their more routine duties with the Criminal Police, and even worked for Interpol, this in spite of the fact that they had just helped to perpetrate the crime of the millennium. The arrogance of it simply beggars belief, does it not?'

'The only thing that beggars belief,' she said, 'is your arrogance.'

'I, on the other hand,' he persisted, 'a humble army captain and no one's idea of an entertaining Nazi houseguest, was sent here, to Greece. Please note the fact that I was never in the SS or in the SD or the Gestapo. Nor did I receive any medals or promotions. This much is easily verified. Even Bernie will admit that much, surely. It's true I stole some gold from SS men who'd already stolen it from Salonika's Jews. But that's the limit of my felony. I never killed anyone. The only time I ever saw anyone get shot was when Alo Brunner killed that poor man on the train from Salonika. Meanwhile, Bernie went on to do special work for Heydrich and the minister of propaganda, Josef Goebbels himself, no less; he was even sent to Croatia with some sort of carte blanche from the minister in his pocket. You would think he'd had enough killing but not a bit of it; in Croatia he assisted the fascist Uštase in murdering many thousands of Serbs and Gypsies, to say nothing of Yugoslavia's Jews.'

'You're good, Max. Smearing me in the hope that some of this mud sticks.'

'It's exactly what any unscrupulous lawyer would do,' said Elli. 'If he was really desperate.'

'You know I really do think she loves you, Bernie. Or at least she thinks she does. Look, Elisabeth, I can see that it might be hard to accept all of what I've just told you about a man you're fond of. I can't say I blame you. Believe me, after the war many German wives had the same problem. Could my dear Mozart-loving husband Fritz really have murdered women and children? Tell me you didn't shoot any children, dear husband mine. Please, tell me you had nothing to do with that.'

'Didn't you hear me, you lying *malaka*?' she said loudly. 'I don't believe a word of it.'

'But you can certainly believe this, Elisabeth dear: Bernie also has a wife. Perhaps he's already told you about her? She lives in Berlin. You didn't know? No, I thought not. In which case you're in for an even bigger surprise. You might say it's a coincidence and maybe a convenient one at that – since he should have no trouble remembering your name. I expect it was hard enough remembering his own, or at least the one written on his passport. You see his wife's name is Elisabeth, just like yours.'

CHAPTER 53

Elli had stopped the car and switched off the engine. We were in a western suburb of Athens and surrounded by a strange landscape of fuel tanks and gasometers. In the distance we could just see the range of mountains that guarded the peninsula of Attica like the giant walls of a more ancient Troy. A beggar came to the window of the Rover and Elli shook her head angrily, which sent him away. She gripped the steering wheel firmly and stared straight ahead of her as if she'd been planning to crash into one of the storage tanks so that we could all die in the explosion like the final scene of *White Heat*. She probably found my silence even more deafening. I know I did. Merten stayed silent, too. He'd done his worst and this was all that was required; it was obvious to everyone in the car that anything else said by him would have been redundant, not to mention the fact that it would have earned him a punch in the mouth. It was also obvious that Elli was upset. There was anger in her eyes and her voice sounded hoarse, like she was getting a cold. Suddenly I was feeling pretty cold myself.

'Is it true?' she asked, after a while. '*Do* you have a wife in Berlin?'

'Yes, but we're estranged.'

Even before I'd finished this short sentence Elli had got out of the car. She collected her bag off the passenger seat, slammed the door behind her, leaned back on the wing, and lit a cigarette angrily. I followed her outside.

'She left me more than a year ago while I was living in France, and went home to Berlin. Unlike her, I can't ever go back there. At least not while the communists are in charge. The Stasi is every bit as bad as the Gestapo. Worse, probably. Anyway, the last conversation I had with my wife she told me she wanted a divorce. And for all I know she's already got one. Given the fact that the city is surrounded by the GDR, communication is difficult, to say the least, so we haven't spoken in a long while. A letter I had last year turned out to be a put-up job by the communists trying to lure me back to Berlin.'

'And is her name Elisabeth? Like that Nazi bastard said it was?'

'Yes.'

She stared down at the ground for almost a minute while I stumbled, badly, through the rest of my explanation: since my wife and I hadn't seen each other in months I'd ceased to think of myself as married and so, I imagined, had she; we'd known each other as friends for more than twenty years; we'd married for the sake of convenience as much as anything else since we both needed to escape from Berlin at around the same time; this wasn't very long ago – 1954 – which ought to have provided a useful snapshot of just how inconvenient the convenience of our marriage had become when, finally, she lit out for Germany and home. It wasn't much of an explanation, but it was the only one I had.

'When were you thinking of telling me?' she asked. 'If at all?'

'I should have mentioned it before,' I admitted.

'Yes, you should. You could have mentioned it last night, for instance. Before we checked into a double room at the Poseidonian Hotel. But you didn't. You were oddly silent about your wife back then.'

'You're right. But in my own defence, yesterday I still half-believed you were going to shoot me with your little Beretta. I'd only just started to believe in you and me so it didn't seem to be that important. It felt like a small thing. At least while I was trying to put that rat Merten in the bag. As if I couldn't concentrate wholly on you, the way you deserved, until Max Merten was properly out of the picture. But I would certainly have told you eventually. When we were both back in Athens. Made a better job of it, too, with dinner and chocolates and flowers. I could still do that, you know.'

'Flowers wouldn't have helped this.'

When she said nothing more, I felt obliged to add an explanation about everything else Merten had told her.

'As for the rest of what he said, there was less than ten per cent truth in any of it. I was a detective at police headquarters in Berlin and I did work for the Nazis but only under considerable duress, and while I did meet some of those people he talked about I never murdered anyone, Elli.'

'Damn that man,' she said angrily. 'Damn him for finding

the weak spot. And not yours. This is my weak spot. That's the irony. He was looking for yours and he found mine. Look, I'm sorry but I don't like married men. Especially when they're married to someone else. Maybe I should have mentioned *that* last night. A few years ago I had an affair with a married man, someone in the ministry, and I swore then I would never get involved with a married man again. That's not your fault. But it's just how it is, do you see?'

'I told you; we're separated. And we're getting a divorce.'

'That one's as old as the *Odyssey*,' she said. 'You should read it sometime. In the end Odysseus goes back to his wife. I have to say that this is what happened to me.'

'That isn't going to happen with me.'

'Like everything else, I've only got your word for it.'

'And my word won't do, I guess.'

'If you didn't happen to be a man it would probably do just fine.'

'So where does this leave us?' I asked.

'I'm not sure where it leaves you, Bernie, or whatever your real name is, but I already know the way out of this particular labyrinth. Me, I'm going home. On my own. Leaving you and your fat friend to sort things out between you.'

'You're reading this all wrong, sugar. I was fixing to stay on in Greece a while, just to be with you. With the hope of making that stick.'

'That's going to take a box of tools you neither own nor know how to use.'

'Tell me where to get them and I'll try to make this work.'

'I'm standing on higher ground than you, Bernie. I already see what you can't. I was brought up Greek Roman Catholic and we believe in dead wives, not in divorced ones. Which reminds me. I'm pretty sure you told me your wife died eight years ago, in Munich.'

'Kirsten. That's right.' I thought it best not to mention that I'd had a wife before Kirsten. I figured there were only so many ex-wives, dead or living, that poor Elli could take.

'That explains but doesn't excuse it. Not in my book. When you changed your name, maybe you forgot that women don't change quite as easily as that. In fact, most of them don't change at all. Most of us want the same things: a nice handbag and a husband we can trust, but we'll generally settle for one or the other.'

'I'm sorry you feel that way.'

'You don't know the half of how I feel. Honestly, it's not even your fault. I'm that kind of woman and you're just that kind of guy. A survivor. I guess maybe the war did that to you. Perhaps you had standards once, and lived up to them, too. I don't know but I have standards, too. My only regret about all this is that I threw away my father's Beretta. Probably just as well. If I had it now I might even shoot you. Maybe I wouldn't kill you. What you've done to me isn't so bad in the great scheme of things that you need killing. I can't answer for the rest of humanity. But you'd always have a little hole to remember me by.'

'I suspect I'll have one anyway. I'm not likely to forget you, Elli.'

'I think you'd best try,' she said, and walked quickly away.

I watched her go. I felt a pang of regret seeing her go. There was a real possibility that it might have worked between us. Then again, we might just have been friends and it wasn't like I had many of those. You can never tell how these things will play themselves out. But if I'm honest I have to admit I also felt a degree of relief that she had walked out on me. The age difference was only one thing. There was something else, too, and again it wasn't her fault: the fact was I didn't have the patience for any woman, not anymore, and not just her. I'd probably been on my own for too long and I guess I preferred it that way.

I kept on watching Elli for a while thinking she might look back, but of course she didn't and I didn't really expect her to. I watched her until I couldn't see her anymore and then turned to look at Max Merten still seated in the back of the Rover. I pulled the Bismarck from under my waistband and waved him out and when he stayed put I opened the door and, ignoring the pain in my arm, hauled him out by the scruff of the neck.

'Move.'

'You're not going to shoot me?'

His eye was nervously on the ditch behind him and the gun in my hand as well it might have been. I had killed people – he'd been right about that much, at least, although arguably most of them had needed killing. But it had been a while since I had shot anyone and although it would have paid him back for his lawyer's smart mouth, I knew it wouldn't have solved anything very much. It never does. It certainly wouldn't have brought Elli running back.

'No, I'm not going to shoot you,' I said. 'I want you to drive. Drive the car, Max.'

'Sure. Whatever you say, Bernie. Just say where to.'

He slipped behind the steering wheel and I got into the front passenger seat.

'Police headquarters. Constitution Square. Next to the Grande Bretagne Hotel.'

'Right away.' He checked my expression nervously and then said, 'She'll be back. Just as soon as she's calmed down a bit.'

'Not this one.'

'It's not their fault. They're irrational creatures in need of protection from themselves – all of them ruled by their ovaries. Take my word for it, Bernie. She'll get over it. Maybe not today. Maybe not tomorrow. But soon. Look, women are sensitive beings. Like children. They feel things more than us men. Especially Greek women. They're very excitable. All they need is firm guidance and direction. You see a woman like that and you can understand Aristophanes. I tell you, she'll think better of whatever it was she said to you and then come crawling back. They always do.'

'I don't think so and neither do you.'

'Maybe you should have listened to me.'

'I think that's where the problem lies, Max. Look where listening to you has brought us today.'

'I did warn you. Look, you might still have had her if you hadn't wanted me as well. You could have let me go and held on to that lovely girl without any difficulty. But you were greedy.'

'Don't talk to me about greed, Max. Better not say that again. And don't even think of apologizing, because then I really will do something I'll regret.'

Max ground the car into gear and we set off. On the way we

passed Elli walking along the street, and when we drove by her it was like she was wearing blinkers and we weren't even there. She paid us less regard than if we'd been just another couple of racehorses coming up on the outside in a big steeplechase. I think that was the moment I knew I was right about her: she wasn't coming back, not ever, and I let out a sigh they could have heard on Mount Olympus. Merten heard it, too, and must have concluded he needed to say something – anything – to take my mind off her.

'However did you catch Gormann anyway?' asked Merten. 'I always meant to ask.'

I suppose he was asking in order to avoid having me smack him in the mouth with the pistol. It was certainly what I felt like doing, and if ever a man needed to lose teeth, it was Max Merten. But since the gift horse had already bolted, I saw little point in fixing his rotten dentistry. So I answered him as calmly as I was able, which was a very useful way of controlling my own violent temper.

'There was nothing to it. My whole reputation around the Alex wasn't built on anything very substantial. The key to being a good detective is to find time to do nothing, which runs counter to the whole idea of being German. Teutonic efficiency seems to cry out for someone to be busy. That's the problem with Germany – we worship industry – but avoiding work, or at least what other people perceived to be work, was the only way I had time to think. I would close the door, clear away the reports, take the phone off the hook with orders that under no circumstances was I to be disturbed. Only that way did I ever find the time to think. You're wasting your time if you don't find time to waste. Letting your mind wander above the clouds like Caspar David Friedrich is what makes a detective any good. That's what I mean by doing nothing. Doing nothing is usually the best thing to do, at least until you have worked out something better to do. Just like now. My first instinct when she got out of the car and stalked off like Achilles in a sulk was to put a bullet in your face, Max. Only I am not going to do that. In fact, I am going to do nothing to you I wasn't going to do before she left.'

Merten breathed a sigh of relief.

'Now that she's left there's no reason for us to stop being friends,' he said. 'You were trying to do the right thing in her eyes. I understand that. But those beautiful eyes have gone. And nothing much is going to be served by handing me over to the Greek cops.'

'Just for the record, we were never friends.'

'Sure we were, Bernie. Hey, what was the name of that brandy bar you took me to once, near the Alex? The one near that weird hotel with the word "Hotel" upside down? You know – that bar with the picture of the lion over the electric piano.'

'The Grüne Quelle.'

'That's right. Do you remember the sign on the wall? "Roar like a lion roars when you need another shot." I could use a glass of that stuff now, couldn't you, Bernie?'

I didn't answer but I remembered the bar, all right, and the taste of the brandy. I could even hear the tunes on the pianola, too: 'I Kiss Your Hand, Madame', followed by the Glorious Prussia March and everyone in the bar full of cheap brandy and singing along at the top of their voices. I even found myself recalling the taste of the giant fifty-pfennig steamed sausages they served. I missed it all and more than I cared to admit; I certainly wasn't about to start reminiscing about the old days with a man who'd just scared off my girlfriend. It was important not to forget, but sometimes it was even better not to remember, to permit the new to overwrite the old.

Merten was still full of talk about old Berlin but because I knew why he was doing it I'd almost stopped listening.

'And surely you remember that little restaurant near the courts? Hessel's, was it? You'd been giving evidence in a murder case – the Spittelmarket Murders. It was there you gave me the best advice I ever had. About not joining the SS.'

'You should have taken it.'

'But I did take it. I told you, I was just an army captain.'

'Perhaps you didn't join the SS, Max. And maybe you didn't kill anyone, like you said. But what you did was as bad as anything any of those others did: Eichmann, Brunner, the whole rotten crew. You lied to all those people in Salonika. You took all their money and all their hopes and then you sent them to their deaths. That's a terrible thing to have done.'

'Nonsense. Look, the war is history. No one gives a damn about Hitler in Europe. That's the whole point of this new EEC. So we can all forget about the horrors of the war and become good Europeans instead. Life is one enormous horror, Bernie, and periodically society proclaims its natural fascination with evil and then feels obliged to destroy itself. For the last time, there is no soul, there is no creator, there is merely this poor thing of flesh and blood called man, which, for whatever reason, other men feel compelled to gas and to burn. It's been happening for centuries. Take my word for it: no one is going to remember the Jews of Salonika in a few years' time. Hardly anyone remembers them now.'

'You're wrong about that, too, Max. It was another German, Heinrich Schliemann, who proved that the Trojan War was a real event in history. Homer was writing about it five hundred years after it probably happened. And we're still talking about it today. It's the same with the Second World War. This stuff isn't going away in a hurry. We Germans are stuck with it, like the Greeks and the Trojans were. Whether we like it or not.'

'So what happens now?'

'You're going to drive us into the centre of Athens. To police HQ And there you're going to volunteer yourself as a witness in the ongoing trial of Arthur Meissner. After that it's up to the Greeks what happens.'

'Look, you're still not thinking straight. Maybe she has gone, but there are plenty more fish in the sea. Think of the gold on that sunken ship. Think how many girls like her you could have with a proper share of that treasure.'

'Maybe you weren't listening but there is no proper share of money obtained like that, Max. And I just lost the only treasure I was ever likely to have. That's the nature of real treasure. You just don't know how precious it is until you lose it. So, drive.' I brushed his earlobe with the sights on the gun. 'And please, Max, not another word until we get to police headquarters. If you can keep your mouth shut until then, you stand an even chance of staying alive for the rest of the day.'

CHAPTER 54

Crossing the palatial lobby of the Grande Bretagne Hotel I saw her, seated underneath an enormous gilt mirror, with her back to the wall and facing the main entrance. It was the best place to sit if you wanted to see everyone who was coming in or going out and you were professional about this kind of thing and, given that profession, very serious about staying alive, which I had no doubt she was. On this occasion she was wearing a brown two-piece business suit with square chocolate patent buttons and a little brown beret.

I thought about ignoring her and then decided against it. I thought it unlikely that she was alone and although I couldn't see him I felt sure one of her more muscular men would have shepherded me to the empty seat beside her. So halfway across the marble floor I checked my walk and went back toward her. She stood and smiled pleasantly as if she'd been an ordinary housewife, there for a more prosaic purpose than revenge and murder, and extended a gloved hand for me to shake, which I did if only to show I was unafraid.

'Where is he?' I asked.

'Who?'

'Your sniper, of course. Behind the potted palm, I suppose. Or hidden among all of those liquor bottles in the bar. Just be careful he doesn't put the wrong kind of optic to his eye. He's liable to see things very differently.'

The bandit queen smiled. She was smaller than I remembered and better looking, but not so you'd have wanted to do something about that. Her brown eyes were on me and then on someone I didn't see, someone over my shoulder who stayed out of sight for the moment. I glanced around but didn't make him; the lobby was full of largish men in cheap suits attending an air-conditioning convention in one of the hotel's many conference rooms, and her armed guard could have been any one of them. Now that I was about to renew my acquaintance with the bandit queen I wouldn't have minded a little extra air myself; just looking at her gave me a tight feeling in my chest, like someone was going to put a bullet in one of my lungs.

'Good idea,' she said. 'Alexander's Bar, I mean.' She glanced at the steel Rolex on her bony wrist. 'And not too early, perhaps. So. Let me buy you a drink, Herr Ganz.'

'Sure. Why not? Poison's more discreet in a place like this.'

'If we wanted to do that you'd be dead already. Trust me on that. We'd have added a secret ingredient to your toothpaste. Radium, probably. That's standard procedure in these circumstances. Radium adds a whole extra dimension to the idea of tooth decay. They say that victims have the cleanest teeth in the morgue.'

'Maybe I should switch brands. Nivea doesn't seem to shift

tobacco stains very well. But you know, I don't scare so easily in this place. For one thing I've started to carry a gun.'

'You've nothing to fear from me, I can assure you.'

'I'm pleased to hear it.'

I followed her into the bar to a table in the quietest corner with a reserved sign and a waiter who was already hovering there, as if he'd been briefed to wait on us with extra vigilance. For all I knew he worked for the Ha'Mossad, too, but I couldn't have said if he looked Jewish. As a copper who never once took a race education class under the Nazis, I wasn't much good at identifying Jews. It has to be said that some people do look Jewish but neither the bandit queen nor the waiter did. We sat down and ordered a pair of large whiskeys. She found a packet of Tareytons in a tapestry handbag, lit one, and smoked it with what sounded like a sigh of relief, her first sign of weakness.

'I'm trying to cut down so I make myself wait until I have a drink in my hand before I can light one.'

'That's not the way to cut down.'

'What would you recommend?'

'You could try having a drink only when you're celebrating murdering another old Nazi.'

'To be honest we don't do that anymore. We used to, of course. Grawitz, Giesler. Geschke. Back in the day we were very active all over Europe.'

'Did they only give you the Gs? You're making me nervous again. My name is Ganz, remember?'

'These days we're keen to show ourselves in a better light, as a democratic country with fair trials and proper legal procedure.

That's why we wanted Brunner, with a B. To give him a fair trial in front of the whole world before we hanged him.'

'I like your idea of justice, lady. It doesn't suffer from any nit-picking jurisdictional doubt. Trial first. Then the hanging. And to hell with any reasonable doubt.'

'We can't afford doubt. Not when we are surrounded by our enemies. Syria. Jordan. Egypt. Eventually we will have to defend ourselves, most likely against all three at once. This makes for a certain conviction in everything we do.'

'I noticed that about you the last time we sat down together. Tell me something. Did you really have a guy with a rifle on the rooftop? Aiming at my head?'

'We never make idle threats.'

'Nothing wrong with a little idleness. Especially in the threat department. Too many people are in a hurry to hurt other people. That's the way I look at it. I figure we could all use a little more humanity.'

'I hope that works for you. But it didn't work for us Jews.'

The waiter came back with the drinks and she took hers like it was nothing stronger than an infusion of tea. I sipped mine more carefully; the demon drink was best handled with care when you were drinking with a genuine demon, albeit one who was currently behaving herself very well.

'By the way, have you a name now? Or is that still not important?'

'Rahel Eskenazi.'

'Is that true?'

'Mostly.'

'But I'm right in thinking you are from the Ha'Mossad.'

'We prefer to call it the Institute. Or just Glilot. It's more discreet.'

'As an insurance man I can certainly see the sense of that. Why take risks if you don't have to?'

The bandit queen looked up at the ceiling and nodded. 'I always liked this hotel,' she said quietly. 'The German insurance business must be good if they can afford to put you up here. In what was Göring's favourite hotel. He knew a thing or two about luxury.'

'It doesn't spoil it for you? Knowing that?'

'Knowing what happened to Göring, no, not at all. In fact, it makes me like the place all the more. It reminds me of how quickly a moral order can be restored. More or less. I like to think of Göring in his suite upstairs quite unaware that in the next room Nemesis awaits her chance to enact retribution against those like him who succumb to hubris. Yes, that's what I think.' She smiled wryly. 'I also think a man like you is wasted in the world of insurance.'

'I get paid sufficient to drive a car, eat sausage, and drink enough beer to be drunk once a week, not necessarily in that order. In Germany we call that making a living.'

'There are not many insurance men who carry a gun.'

'They might sell a few more policies if they did.'

'A living, perhaps. But not a life. Not for you, Christof.'

I shrugged and let that one go. I figured if she was driving at something she'd pull up and let me take a peek at what was on the front seat, eventually.

'I hear you have your passport back,' she said. 'And that you're leaving Athens today.'

'That's right. I was on my way out to visit the Acropolis when I saw you. All these weeks I've been here and I still haven't been up to take a look at the thing. I hear it's seen better days but that it's worth a look.'

'You can see it another time. It will still be there in a thousand years.'

'Yes, but I'm not so sure I will.'

'I also hear that Max Merten has been arrested by the Greek police.'

'Not arrested. Not quite yet. But his passport has been taken away. And they've got him in a safe house in Glyfada. They'll arrest him only after he starts to give evidence in Arthur Meissner's trial. That's the deal I made for him. Makes him look a bit better.'

'In Greece? I doubt that. But it makes you feel a bit better, and that's important, too, right?'

'Also right.' I shrugged. 'I'm only sorry I couldn't deliver up Alois Brunner for you.'

'We'll get him one day.'

'I hope so.'

'Do you mean that?'

'Sure. A man like Brunner gives all Germans a bad name. And who better than Germans to help find him? I can't say I agree with Adenauer's policy on this matter very much. I think it will come back to haunt us. That's one of the reasons I persuaded Merten to give himself up to the Greeks.'

'We'd have hanged him for sure.'

'That's the other reason.'

CHAPTER 55

'It won't stick, you know,' said the bandit queen. 'The charges against Max Merten. Not in a Greek court. Not for long, anyway.'

'I don't see why. There must be plenty of witnesses still alive. People from Salonika, victims of genocide, men and women who came back from the camps, who'll testify against him. Surely the Nazis didn't kill all of them.'

'You're so naïve. This has nothing to do with justice or genocide or crimes against humanity. There's too much going on behind the scenes you don't know about. Sure, the Greeks will go through the motions of giving Merten a proper trial in open court. And the public will lap it up like cream. Toussis, the state prosecutor, will sound like Ajax when he narrates this country's misfortune. The judge may even hand down a prison sentence. But Merten has too many friends in the government to serve any real jail time.'

'Which government are you talking about?'

'Good question. So then ask yourself why the Greeks have never before tried to extradite anyone from Germany for war crimes committed in this country.'

'All right, I'll play. Why?'

'Until recently it was quite simple: the Greek government wanted the German government to pay reparations for its war crimes. They proposed an amnesty on all war crimes committed in Greece in return for half a billion dollars. An important part of those reparations was that gold stolen from the Jews of Salonika. But the government in Bonn refused. Called it blackmail. Which it was. And which is why Arthur Meissner was put on trial, as a very small and unimportant example of what might follow if Germany continued to drag its feet on this issue. After all, Greece is a NATO member state and it would be embarrassing if Greece started applying for the extradition of German nationals on the soil of other NATO members, as well they might.'

'Max Merten is hardly small,' I objected. 'He's the real deal, I tell you. A genuine war criminal. Maybe he didn't summarily execute any hostages. But he extorted hundreds of millions of dollars in gold from your people and then abandoned them to their fate.'

'Oh, certainly. I didn't tell you before but it's always been our belief that the vast majority of this gold was actually sent to Germany aboard a special SS train in 1943 and currently remains on deposit in a Swiss bank; that the West German government is well aware of this fact; and that only a tiny per centage of the total amount was ever put on a boat privately owned by the likes of Merten and Brunner for their own nefarious use.

'In spite of what you may have been told by Merten and Meissner, there is no vast hoard in a sunken ship off the Pelopon-nesian coast. Indeed, it's my own suspicion that all the time he has been here in Greece Max Merten has been the secret agent of the West German government, witting or unwitting. That this whole scheme was cooked up by someone in the German intelligence service – most probably Hans Globke – to persuade the Greek government that Germany doesn't have *any* of the gold looted from Greece back in '43. I think you have been played, my friend. Played by your bosses in Munich, who were themselves doing the bidding of others in the West German government. My prediction is that Max Merten will be back home in Munich within the year, where he will find himself very well compensated for his trouble.'

'I don't believe that. Look, what you say doesn't make any sense, Rahel, if that is your real name. Frankly, what you're suggesting – it's much too far-fetched. Merten financed this expedition by the commission of another crime in Munich. Why would he have to do that if the West German government was backing him?'

'You're talking about General Heinrich Heinkel, aren't you? An old Nazi who was once of interest to us in the Institute. It so happens that your German BND wanted the Stasi man bankrolling General Heinkel removed, permanently. And having removed him, they decided that the money could be used to bankroll Merten instead. Christian Schramma worked, occasionally, for the BND. As an ex-policeman surely you understand that's how these things operate. One covert operation is often wrapped into another for the sake of convenience. And state intelligence agencies usually employ a lot of criminals, like Schramma, at a lower level for the sake of deniability, so that they can carry out undercover work without revealing their true hands.'

'Is that how you got the job with Ha'Mossad?'

The bandit queen smiled patiently. More patiently than previous acquaintance might have led me to expect. 'Formerly I was a colonel in Amman. Our military intelligence section. I'm telling you this because I want you to take me seriously since I have a favour to ask of you, Christof. If that's your real name.'

'You haven't finished telling me why I'm being naïve about Max Merten. Why would Merten go along with a scheme like the one you're suggesting? Why would he risk going to prison for the rest of his life?'

'He may be in on the conspiracy, or not. I'm still unsure of how far his complicity in the scheme goes. But there's certainly no risk of him spending the rest of his life behind bars. If you were a real insurance man you'd price that risk at next to zero. And my explanation would once have been simple enough for anyone to understand. But nothing about this whole affair is simple anymore. Not since the Treaty of Rome was signed.'

'You'll have to explain how the EEC is the least bit relevant, Rahel.'

'Would it surprise you to learn that the person who signed the Treaty of Rome with Konrad Adenauer was Professor Walter Hallstein?'

'That name rings a bell. I seem to remember Schramma mentioning him back in Munich.'

'Hallstein was a member of several Nazi organizations and, after the war, a close business associate of Max Merten. Walter Hallstein will be the first president of the commission of the European Economic Community.'

'I still don't see how this is relevant.'

Rahel Eskenazi smiled. 'I told you this was complicated. Sometimes I'm not even sure I understand it all myself. And I haven't even started. You see, Greece has already applied to join the new EEC. However, my German sources tell me that Adenauer and Hallstein will certainly veto Greece's application unless Max Merten is released. Meanwhile my Greek sources tell me that Greece will defy them and put Merten on trial regardless, but that following his conviction and sentence he will be sent back to Germany before serving any time. In return for his freedom and a general amnesty for other Germans, Adenauer and Hallstein will not only approve and fast-track the Greek application for membership in the EEC, but they will also approve a two-hundred-million-dollar loan to Greece by the German central bank. A loan Greece does not expect to have to repay. Although I'm not so sure the Germans think that. It's their belief that membership in the EEC will be more than enough compensation. You've no idea how financially advantageous this new economic community can be to all who are in the club. But especially Germany. No one stands to benefit as much as your country. Or to suffer as badly as Greece if Germany turns its back on her. What, for instance, do you think would happen to all that valuable tobacco that Greece exports to Germany?'

The bandit queen finished her whiskey and snapped her fingers for two more like one who was used to being obeyed. A former military colonel, she'd said. I didn't doubt it. She finished one cigarette, lit another, and leaned back in her armchair. Her arms were almost the same colour as the mahogany woodwork and probably just as strong. Easy enough to imagine her fighting Arabs, I thought.

'You may think you've done a good deed by handing Merten over to the Greek authorities,' she said, 'but I'm afraid it's our considered opinion that he always planned to be caught.'

'But what about Brunner? You're forgetting he killed three people in pursuit of that gold.'

'I doubt anyone in the BND expected Brunner to put in an appearance down here. That was where the plan went badly wrong, as plans often do. As for the gold itself, I seriously doubt there was ever more than a million dollars' worth of gold on that boat. A half share of a million dollars is not chump change. Certainly enough to interest a rat like Alois Brunner. But it's nothing like the hundreds of millions of dollars' worth that was sent back to Germany in 1943. It was one thing to steal from the Jews but tell me, honestly, as a man who used to be a detective with Kripo, do you think the likes of Eichmann, Brunner, and Merten would ever have had the courage to steal from the SS? Those who did and were caught risked being sent to the camps themselves. Isn't that so?'

'Now you come to mention it, that does sound a little unlikely.'

'Take my word for it, this whole thing was a put-up job designed to mislead the Greek government into thinking the West Germans don't have a single ounce of that gold, that it really is lying on the bottom of the Aegean Sea in some secret location that only Max Merten knows about. And that there's no point in asking the Germans for the gold back because they know nothing of its whereabouts. Neat, wouldn't you say?'

'If it's true.'

'I don't suppose we'll ever be able to prove any of this. But we might hurt a few of the principal players. Adenauer's state secretary Hans Globke, for example. Yes, we might make some trouble for him. It was Globke who promulgated the Nuremberg Laws, and who was the most capable and efficient official of the Nazi Ministry of the Interior. His participation in the so-called Reich Citizenship Law is a similarly irrefutable fact. Think of that for a minute, Christof. One of Hitler's leading Jew murderers has a hand on the helm of the West German state. He is without doubt the prolonged arm of the chancellor and his most intimate confidant. But worse, this means that when Adenauer takes a holiday, Globke becomes the de facto federal chancellor of Germany and the nearest thing to Martin Bormann that there exists today. Which brings me to the question I wanted to ask you. Are you going back to Munich now?'

'Yes.'

'Then my question is this: when you get back to Germany, when you're ready, will you help us get Hans Globke?'

'What do you mean by "get"? Don't you mean murder? There's a strong rumour your people ran down and killed Globke's Nazi boss Wilhelm Stuckart in 1953.'

'I mean get by any means necessary.'

'I don't know why you think I can help get a man like that, and in that way.'

'I'm asking because I sense in you the need to do something to atone for your country's sins. For your own, perhaps. I don't know but I think that's why you helped Lieutenant Leventis to get Max Merten, isn't it? Because you have a conscience about what happened here?'

The next round of drinks arrived and the bandit queen snatched one of the glasses off the tray and started drinking it before the other was even on the table. But she waited until the waiter was gone before she continued speaking:

'I know that's an emotive word, "atonement". In Judaism this means the process of causing a transgression against God to be forgiven or pardoned. So perhaps it's blasphemous of me to take it upon myself to offer you that chance, Christof. But that's exactly what I'm doing. A chance to do something good with what's left of your life. Israelis and Jews – there are plenty of them I can get to work for the Institute. None with the experience I need. What I really need are a few *Germans* who aren't Jews. Germans with a conscience. Germans like you who are in respectable jobs, and who have some background in intelligence. That's you, isn't it? You're not quite as innocent about these things as you like to pretend.'

I nodded. 'It's a long time since I felt innocent about anything.'

'Then take it from one who knows all about collective guilt. I'm a Jew. We've been paying for the death of Jesus Christ for two thousand years. Well, I certainly don't believe we could or should even try to atone for that particular fairy story. But I do believe that an individual can help to atone for something that happened not much more than a decade ago. An individual like you, perhaps. Someone who could help to influence the future of his own country and the new moral order for the better.'

'Those are grand words for a small man like me.'

'Make them yours, Christof.'

'You really think Max Merten will walk free?'

'Not today. But before the end of the year, yes, I'm more or less certain of it.'

I thought for a moment. It's not unusual for intelligent people to end up working in intelligence; some of them are very intelligent indeed; but I was struck by the bandit queen's great perception – by the way she seemed to see straight through the hard carapace to the part of me that was a man with a vestigial conscience. It was almost as if somehow this Israeli spy chief had, like some Hebrew prophet, managed to spy into the very depths of my soul. I answered her carefully before shaking her hand again.

'I'm not sure how I can help you get Hans Globke. But I think I can help you get someone else.'

I caught a taxi up the Acropolis, to see the Parthenon up close and touch it as I might have touched a valuable holy icon. After all the tea towel prints and plaster model copies of the temple I'd seen I hadn't expected the real thing to be as impressive as it turned out to be. Had it been as refined a piece of architecture to those poor ghosts the ancient Athenians as it was to us living mortals now? I couldn't see how not – how it wouldn't always have been viewed as one of the premier works of man and no less of an achievement now because it was substantially ruined, perhaps *more* of an achievement, for did this not remind every man of his own temporal fragility? There's nothing like a Greek ruin to make you feel like reading one of those old books by Plato or Aristotle.

Built as the temple of Athena, it became a Christian church in the fifth century AD and, for a while, in spite of its amorphous, pagan origins, it was even an important destination for Christian pilgrims. I wondered if they'd really cared all that much what God was called. Or what the hymns were, silent now, once sung by those high priestesses of Athena. Surely what mattered to them more was this perfect celebration of the immortals. It was certainly what mattered to me. I was hearing voices all right.

Following the Ottoman conquest, this anonymous stone glory was a mosque for more than two hundred years, until 1687, when it was heavily fortified and turned into a gunpowder magazine with the result that the Venetians turned up and bombarded it with cannon, and the Parthenon was partly destroyed, perhaps the first sign of where science would one day lead us. But somehow it had survived all that. And since 1832 the Doric ruins had been the most important cultural site in Greece, which was why I was there now, I supposed, with an hour to kill before Garlopis took me to the airport, and feeling unexpectedly moved, like one of those Christian pilgrims, perhaps. There were plenty of tourists around, most of them Americans and Japanese from the real world of salaried salesmen and menu-making housewives, but I expect I was one of the few who were there who saw the front façade of the Parthenon and felt homesick for my real home, which was in Berlin. With neoclassical buildings such as the Brandenburg Gate, the New Guardhouse memorial, and the National Gallery, Berlin had more Greek revivals than the cult of Dionysus and knew more than one thing about destruction, too. By the time the Red Army had finished its own brutal pagan handiwork, the old island of Berlin and its Parthenon copies looked much more like the original than anyone except Stalin would ever have wished.

Walking quietly around and through this petrified forest of columns and the epic affirmation of what man was capable of, I could also reflect on perhaps the other major lesson of the place, which, at least for me, was that anything and everything could change, even something as great as the Parthenon.

And if that, then why not Bernie Gunther?

It seemed that when things from the past looked to every cynical eye as if they'd been irreparably destroyed they might yet have a future. A different future but, perhaps, a no less important one. Like Gunther, parts of the Parthenon still looked hopelessly beyond repair; the causeway leading up to the façade was a builder's yard of fallen pediments, damaged metopes, and broken columns; perhaps the Parthenon would take as long to preserve and repair as it had ever taken to build. Longer, perhaps, since preservation always moves at a slower, more reverent pace than construction. But I decided you could either complain about the cultural vandalism of the Turks and the Venetians, hope that someone else better qualified would one day get around to fixing the place up a bit or, perhaps, you could find a crane, pick up some of the marble stones, and erect some scaffolding yourself.

My own hymns to love were probably forever silent now, but what of it? I was too old for all that malarkey anyway. Elli couldn't have known it but in a way she'd spared me. Probably we'd spared each other.

And to mark where I had been and to testify to what I still had in me to accomplish, I needed only that place in the new moral order offered by the bandit queen, where a drifting ghost like me could feel like something real again and breathe the dream of true atonement.

AUTHOR'S NOTE

DR MAX MERTEN was arrested in an Athens court during Arthur Meissner's trial for war crimes and property pillage in the spring of 1943. Queen Frederica of Greece (herself a German) questioned Merten's prosecution, asking if 'this is the way Mr District Attorney understands the development of German and Greek relations.' When he was held in Averoff Prison on remand, the West German government strenuously protested his arrest. Two years later, on February 11, 1959, Merten went to trial accused of murder, property pillage, gold coins expropriation, and other war crimes against Jews. The president of the court, one Colonel Kokoretsas, excluded the attorneys for the Jewish community of Salonika from presenting evidence in court; only individual Jewish plaintiffs were allowed to testify, thus diminishing the true scale of the crime against Greece's Jews. Merten pleaded not guilty to all of the charges and his defence was paid for by the federal government of Germany. On March 5, 1959, Max Merten was convicted of war crimes and sentenced to twenty-five years in prison. After serving just eight months Merten was freed by Prime Minister Konstantinos Karamanlis in a general amnesty on November 5, 1959. In March 1960, an 'economic agreement' was signed between Greece and Germany stipulating the sum of just 115 million marks (about $26 million) to be paid as reparations. A laughable amount of money, given all that Greece had suffered. Germany also agreed to provide separate sums as 'loans' to Greece. Max Merten returned to Germany, where he received substantial damages for the period he'd spent in jail. He provided written evidence during the Eichmann trial in 1960 although he did not attend, and he died in 1971 or 1976. He never returned to Greece.

After serving with the SS, ALOIS BRUNNER probably worked for German intelligence before travelling to Egypt in 1954, where he was an arms dealer. Later, he moved to Syria and may have worked for the Syrian intelligence services of Hafez al-Assad. The exact nature of his work is unknown. In 1954, he was condemned to death in absentia in France for war crimes committed at Drancy. In a 1985 interview with a German magazine called *Bunte*, in Damascus, Brunner was unrepentant about his work for the Nazis. The Israelis tried twice to kill him, and failed. As a result of a letter bomb in 1961, he lost an eye and the fingers on his left hand. He died in 2001 or 2010, depending on which source you believe. At the time of his death, he was the most wanted Nazi war criminal in the world. He was buried in Damascus.

DR HANS GLOBKE gave evidence both for the prosecution and the defence at the Nuremberg Trials. He left office in 1963, following attempts by the federal government to influence the Eichmann trial; material that exonerated Globke was fed direct to the Eichmann prosecutors by the BND. Globke died in 1973 but not before he was honoured by Konrad Adenauer with the Order of the Grand Cross of the Order of Merit of the Federal Republic of Germany. He remained an active adviser to Adenauer and the Christian Democratic Union right up to his death.

All of my information about MUNICH RE comes from the company's own website which, to its enormous credit, makes no secret about the company's wartime history. It states that Munich RE's chairman in 1933, Kurt Schmitt, was appointed Reich Minister of Economics and, on the strength of his convictions, Alois Alzheimer joined the Nazi Party, the only other member of MRE's board to do so. MRE did indeed insure the barracks and 'operations' at Auschwitz, Buchenwald, Dachau, Ravensbrück, and Sachsenhausen. After the war, Schmitt and Alzheimer were taken into custody by the US military. Neither faced charges, although other board members were given prison sentences. Alois Alzheimer became chairman of MRE in 1950 and directed the company until 1968. If only all German companies were as open about their pasts as MRE! As far as I am aware, the chairman of Munich MRE was no relation to the more famous Alois Alzheimer who gave his name to a type of presenile dementia.

In 1960, *Der Spiegel* published excerpts from Merten's deposition to the German authorities, which claimed that various members of the Greek government and their relations were informers during the Nazi occupation and had been rewarded with businesses confiscated from Jews in Thessaloniki. Some of these same figures successfully sued *Der Spiegel* in 1963.

Following a coup in 1967, GREECE was ruled by the military – the so-called Regime of the Colonels – for a period of seven years. Thousands of communists were imprisoned or exiled to remote Greek islands. Many were tortured. After the restoration of democracy in 1975, Greece applied to join the EEC and successfully acceded in 1981. The country joined the Euro in 2001, having faked the figures required to qualify for entry; since then, the country has buckled under the weight of debts the European Central Bank seems unwilling to forgive.

The GOLD of Thessaloniki's Jews has never been recovered. In 1945 vast quantities of Nazi gold were moved from the Reichsbank in Berlin to Switzerland for 'safekeeping'. In a book called *Nazi Gold* (1984), by authors Ian Sayer and Douglas Botting, it was estimated that this gold would be worth approximately ten billion dollars on today's market. Of course, anyone who has seen the movie *Kelly's Heroes* (1970) knows that the gold was stolen by Clint Eastwood and Telly Savalas.

In 2003 KONRAD ADENAUER was voted the greatest German of all time by viewers of German television station ZDF.